THE

DOMINIONS

ASH & EMBERS

For D,

*Thank you for being the man to show me the kind of love
that inspires novels.*

*& to the ones who have lost themselves in the Darkness and
clawed their way back into the light.*

And for all the ones still fighting their way through it.

PERSEIS MILITARY STRUCTURE

	basic officer	specialty warrior
 SKY	KAPPI	SOTURI

	basic officer	specialty warrior
 LAND	FENRI	AMAROK

	basic officer	specialty warrior
 SEA	CETO	PONTOS

PRELUDE

Mikkal pulled his sword from the chest of a dying Eligos; dark, black blood dripping from the blade. The enormous beast was sprawled on its side, its onyx eyes empty and lifeless. The red flecks inside the pools of midnight black slowly faded, and the smallest hint of color resting in its pale, skeletal shaped face drained. Its unnaturally long limbs went limp at its sides.

Mikkal's chest rose and fell rapidly as he gulped down death-filled air. The stench of the creature's blood singed his nose, and his eyes watered.

Even after all these centuries, Mikkal never became used to the burning reek of the creatures, as if they had been forged by a fire burning deep within the pits of the Hells.

Sweat trickled down his back as he glanced at the beast once more. Screams and cries rang out across the battlefield around him.

The Eligos looked like so many of the other Shadow-blades. Its face brandished a sinister sneer, and the fangs jutting from its mouth had been molded for a singular purpose—shredding skin and snapping bones. Its thin, pale fin-

7

gers, tipped with jagged stygian nails, stretched as long as a man's forearm. Mikkal had been killed by hands like that before, on more than one occasion, and not once had it been an enjoyable experience.

Dying in war rarely ever was.

He wiped the thick, oily blood off his sword and picked his way across the field, carefully avoiding the littering of bodies that covered the rocky ground.

Bloodied warriors were scattered amidst beasts, friend and foe alike. None of the figures stirred. Many of the lifeless forms were human, many were not; and the blood saturating the rugged stone ground was a blend of colors. Red. Black. Blue.

A smog of shadowed sounds strangled the air, but he could not discern the sobs of agony from the groans of pain. It did not sound like the cries of triumph.

He looked over at the setting sun, pressing deep into the horizon, readying to dip into the blood-soaked sea.

It would not be long now.

As he waded through the ocean of the fallen, he passed slain soldiers, slaughtered firebirds, and butchered wolves. Their red and blue blood trailed behind where their crumpled forms lay. They had fought, blood pouring from their bodies, until the last breath. From the blue and red wakes of blood lapping in the waves beyond the coast, he knew the hippocas and their warriors had done the same.

It would not be long before the blood-soaked firebirds rose once again, their bodies renewed from the ashes beneath them. But Mikkal knew there were many warriors and wolves lying beside him, many soldiers of the sea beyond, who would not be lucky enough to experience the same fate. To experience another life—a better world.

The Adversary's soldiers had done their work well.

Mikkal and his warriors had fought against the Shadowblades and their dragons, but the dragons and the dark soldiers had fought back. And they had fought mightily.

He stumbled up the hillside to the colossal rock perched above the battlefield, overlooking the ruin and waste. Plunged inside the stone stood seven erected staffs, each possessing its own unique features. One was crafted of gold, adorned with an all-seeing eye plated in diamonds. Another was made of deep, cobalt glass, with a carved goat fixed atop the head. The third looked like cracked magma, with deep red burning between the fissures in the onyx stone. Beside it stood a staff made of the earth, with a globe of glowing green light pouring from the iron shaft and a serpent coiled around the hilt. Two more were erected on the far side of the stone, one hooked and crafted from a pale blue rock, the other molded from a deep, burned copper. The final staff stood tall in the center, wrapped in a bright, radiating violet with flames that flickered atop spiked tips.

As Mikkal dragged his gaze from one scepter to the next, he could see the one commonality that bound all the staffs to one another—an engraved crown etched into the top of the hilt. One crown for each of the Six Princes of Shadows, *The Wraiths of War and Ruin*, and a final, larger crown for the King of Darkness.

Mikkal's eyes lifted from the rock, and in the distance, he saw the end was near.

As the Lords of Light and Darkness battled, the skies shook and the veils between realms were torn apart. As the war between the gods was waged, they ripped through time and space until the world shattered, and the victor made the world anew.

BOOK

ONE

ASH & EMBERS

3,500 Years Later

"WE SHALL NOT BE AFRAID OF THE TERROR BY NIGHT, NOR OF THE ARROW THAT FLIES BY DAY, NOR OF THE PESTILENCE THAT WALKS IN DARKNESS, NOR OF THE DESTRUCTION THAT LAYS WASTE AT NOONDAY. A THOUSAND MAY FALL AT OUR SIDE, AND TEN THOUSAND AT OUR RIGHT HAND; BUT THE WRAITHS OF WAR AND RUIN SHALL NOT COME NEAR US. THE PRINCES AND THEIR SHADOWS SHALL NOT DESTROY US."

—AN EXCERPT FROM THE LOST EPISTLES OF THE WARRIOR

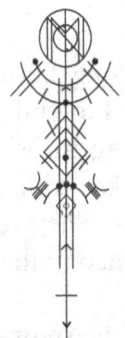

PROLOGUE

Time doesn't heal grief—it teaches those suffering how to wear it. And the ones who linger too long in the Darkness, they become dangerous.

They know how to make the Hells feel like home.

That was the place Asha Akselsen Raynor found herself as she watched the sun break over the horizon, warming the waves beneath it—in unyielding and unremitting Darkness. And as she stood atop the edge of the eastern crest of the Iron Mountains, battling against the shadows raging war inside her soul, Asha understood three things with unwavering certainty:

One—the devouring night lurking deep inside her heart had never left; it simply went dormant, biding its time before it was ready to unleash itself once again.

Two—the sand in the mortal hourglass was quickly reaching its end, and she was no longer sure if the magic pulsing through her veins was enough to change the outcome.

And three—Asha Akselsen Raynor knew she was going to die.

Raging flames had long burned deep inside her and, over time, she had learned to embrace them, becoming fire itself, scorching everything in her path. She was made of burning embers and sparks, with splintered thorns and ice running through her veins. She greeted the Hells as if they were old friends and laughed in the face of Death.

A branch snapped in the snow-dusted wood line behind her. The summer sun had melted much of the white powder, but a lingering layer of flakes remained on the highest peaks.

Her head whipped around, and she scanned the trees, searching through the shadows for any unwelcome beasts.

She had been waiting for her end for a long time now and welcomed it with open arms. She no longer feared Death, and she supposed that was what made her so dangerous—because the most threatening warrior isn't always the strongest, or the most conniving—it's the one who has nothing left to lose.

And Asha had lost herself many years ago, in the shattered parts of her soul that were now scattered across the earth. She tried many times to pick them up, to fit them all back together like pieces of a sad, broken puzzle. But each time she found herself close to completing the picture, the darkest parts of the world would crawl out of their holes and once again rip her life to shreds. And, through the years, the number of pieces grew, and grew, until they became too great to count. She was full of wounds, riddled with scars, and her mind overflowed with memories darker than night.

But she was still standing. Somehow, in some way, she still managed to put one foot in front of the other. She was no longer sure if she considered it a blessing or a curse.

The creature had been with her a moment before, she was sure of it, but there wasn't any sign of the beast now. She could feel it moving between the trees; her nose was full of its reeking smell.

An echoing screech rang in the distance. He would be here in moments; she only needed to endure a little longer.

Asha crept slowly towards the summit's edge, the snow's crunch near silent beneath her feet. Another twig snapped, and her head whipped towards the sound of the splintered crack.

The beast's eyes were caliginous and glassy, and the faintest of red specks glowed deep within the dark pools.

She had seen those eyes before, long ago, when they belonged to another. Lifetimes ago.

The creature took a step towards her, still partly obscured by the forest's shadows. Her heart thumped wildly against her chest.

She took another step back, keeping her eyes locked on the distorted, skeletal-shaped face sneering from the shaded tree line. Loose rocks kicked over the edge behind her, tumbling to the earth hundreds of feet below.

A stream of white flashed across the contrasting blue of the sky above. The dark, fanged creature crouched down, digging its hind legs into the dirt-streaked snow beneath it. It growled, and the thunderous snarl sounded guttural and otherworldly, as if it came from a Darkness not of this world, but of another. Once the grumble escaped its throat, the beast leapt from its hiding spot within the darkness.

As the creature hurdled itself towards her, Asha took a final step back, throwing herself from the mountaintop and into the frigid air beyond.

The ground came up to meet her, much quicker than she believed it would. And as she neared the end of her free fall, the stream of white flashed once again, coming up beneath her, and she landed on the back of her firebird.

The blunt impact against Uriel's feathers punched the air from her lungs, knocking the sense from her head. A pained, gasping moan slid from her lips, and she struggled to replace the breath that had been stolen in the collision.

As Uriel swiftly carried her away, Asha glanced back at the creature peering down from the mountain's edge. And when she looked into the red-flecked eyes of the monster atop the hill, she felt the devouring night inside her heart slowly begin to resurface, as if the dark creature had beckoned it, and her shadowed soul had no choice but to answer the call. As Uriel swiftly carried her away, Asha glanced back at the creature peering down from the mountain's edge. And when she looked into the red-flecked eyes of the monster atop the hill, she felt the devouring night inside her heart slowly begin to resurface, as if it the dark creature had beckoned it, and her shadowed soul had no choice but to answer the call.

CHAPTER ONE

Thirty-nine.

That was how many days had passed since Asha had last spoken. The words that left her tongue were foreign and felt bitter, slick with oil; so, she had stopped speaking—complete, unfaltering silence.

A silence that mirrored the Darkness enveloping her mind, the Darkness pumping through her veins. A silence that echoed the claws that ripped through the shadows inside her head.

But her silence was not empty. It was full of answers.

It was meaningful. Strong. Deep.

It was a silence that held so much weight she could write novels about it. It was elegant, noble, endless.

No one had ever told her how loss would make her a liar. That eventually everything that came out of her mouth would be like the black ash of a smoky exhale. But the most harrowing part was that she seemed to be the only one able to see the cloudy tendrils. Everyone else treated the rotten things falling from her lips as if they were sugar, spun and soft. They refused to look at the ugly side of her words when it was far less painful to search for something pretty inside someone's head.

But pretty gardens and wishful dreams had not grown in Asha's mind for quite some time. Enveloping Darkness was the only thing that lurked there, prowling in the lightless corners. So, as she trudged through the thick shadows, she chose to tightly grasp the comfort of silence.

She found no point in explaining how the ocean inside her head was so deep and dark, a thousand versions of her had already drowned inside it. She saw no need to explain that her mind was an abyssal sea, filled with the buried remnants of her nightmares.

Or were they her memories?

The two blended together so well, she could no longer tell them apart. And even if she could, a part of her did not want to know which terrible version of the truths inside her head she had truly lived.

She held shipwrecks in her ocean-filled heart, with torn-down sails and sea-swept decks. They were beautifully shattered, but they sat marooned between the fierce tides of her heartbeats, caught in the anchors that she hid in every breath.

And in the midst of the sea-fearing battle raging inside her, her soul had gone into hiding. And, over time, she became so adept at hiding the fact that her soul was missing, no one had noticed the blank space standing in place of where she once existed.

And those who peacefully watched from the outside, mistaking her silence as weakness, did not realize when Darkness stays silent and still for too long, a baleful hurricane swells on the other side, ready to rattle the earth.

So, as she waded in the lightless space, Asha reminded herself that the air always stills before the onset of a storm.

Steadying herself on the sloped clock tower roof, Asha nocked an arrow into place, the lightly brushed sound holding enough promise against the bow's strings to unnerve Anubis, the God of Death, himself.

She took in a deep, calming breath as she drew her arm back, the bow unwavering in her calloused hands. A light breeze caressed her cheek, a sweet whisper in the dawn's silence.

She locked her sights on her target a hundred yards away, the iron arrow swallowing the sun's rising beams. She exhaled, and just as she reached the silent pause between breaths, that moment in between heartbeats, she released.

Asha slung the quiver over her shoulder and turned towards the clock tower's stairs, the arrow still soaring through the sky. She did not wait to see where it landed—she already knew.

The tower boomed as she descended. Five long blares rang through the morning air as she dropped step after step. On the final ring of the clock, Asha's arrow struck dead center.

As she scurried down the winding, alabaster walkways, her feet silent against the stones, a chilled breeze wafted over the Base. The morning air was cooler than usual for late summer, and a shiver ran down her back. She pulled her deep brown Kappi jacket tighter to her chest. The coat was weather-beaten and torn, tattered from years of fighting and flying, frayed by blades and sharp weapons, and hastily stitched back together after the fighting had ceased.

Two shadowed figures sauntered along the open colonnade across the courtyard, heading in the opposing direction from where Asha had come. She slowed her pace, ensuring she would not cross paths with the other early-rising warriors, and straightened her posture in an attempt to conceal the quiver hung across her back. A small smile twitched on her lips as she reached behind to adjust the pack, running her hand along the worn leather.

It felt safe, familiar, broken in from years of hard use. She'd had the quiver a long time. It had followed her through Kappi training in her home city of Valhol, across the eastern coast of Perseis, and all the way down to the Kingdom's military Base of Sveaborg.

Asha scoffed as she rounded the final turn, heading towards her Base room, and a widespread picture stared down at her from above.

A large mosaic was fastened against the exterior wall of the Barracks, its familiar image conjuring powerful feelings of bitterness within Asha's heart.

Hundreds of tiny, gold-plated tiles were fixed beside one another to form a glittering portrait that sparkled in the dawning sunlight. The ceramic squares, stretching across the building's alabaster stones, created the lavish image of a majestic lion with a pair of polished wings spread out behind it.

The Sacred Seal of Perseis.

Asha had known the image her entire life, never able to escape the Kingdom's overreaching hand.

It was how she had ended up at Sveaborg—Perseis's military Base for the Kingdom's Specialty Team training.

After a long series of hardships and ill-fated events, Asha knew her arrival to the Base ultimately resulted from the reformed edicts of the Perseisian King.

King Balthasar redesigned Perseis's military structure at

the beginning of his reign—a strategic move intended to better prepare his army for conquering the six rival Kingdoms of Darnella.

For the past two thousand years, the seven Kingdoms had battled for control of Darnella's two Continents, a great, never-ending war between monarchs who aimed to become the Sovran—the absolute ruler of the realm.

The Great War began only a few centuries after The First War—the final culmination of the continuous battles waged between the two Preeminent Gods that shattered the worlds and thrust the realm of Darnella into a new vestige of time and space.

Light and order were brought back into the realm, and peace was formed in a world that before had only known of chaos and destruction.

But, as it so often does, the peace did not last, and Darkness slithered its way back into the hearts and minds of the Continent's citizens.

It had been an adjustment for the soldiers when the King's military realignment took effect.

Some citizens, and soldiers alike, said he was mad. The Great King of Perseis, obsessed with conquest and absolute power, had no regard for the devastating results of his edicts.

The members of his court claimed he was a visionary, a redeemer, fighting to keep order in the Kingdom and waging war for his subjects to maintain their freedom from the tyrannical Kings and Queens south of the Strait—the foreign monarchs rumored to rule with callous, iron fists.

Asha let out a heavy sigh. Her gaze fell to the bottom of the mosaic, landing on the inscribed words carved beneath the tiles.

Bend the Knee or Die – King Balthasar's first and most infamous decree.

Asha held back the desire to find a chisel and forever expunge the appalling edict from the wall.

The Brand seared on her wrist began to prickle beneath her jacket.

She clenched her hands into tight fists, turning away from the art piece to head down the enclosed hallway to her room. But just before she entered the Barracks, the six words beneath the King's edict caught her eye: Perseis: The Gilded Kingdom of Dreams.

Asha spat on the ground before the golden lion and quickly disappeared into the hall.

Even from an early age, Asha had seen through the Perseisian King's charade of diplomatic smiles and wish-filled promises, because any ruler willing to continue the sacrifice and enslavement of his own people should never be trusted.

So, over the centuries, as thousands of power-wielding children in Perseis were forced to bond with magic-releasing creatures, the once bright soul of Perseis dwindled, and its citizens began to drown in their own misery.

It was never talked about, but Asha knew the cruel, avaricious King had committed a crime far worse than the requisite bonding of the Kingdom's children.

He broke the spirit of a once radiant and hopeful people. And, as Asha knew far too well, the body could always heal, but the mind would forever hold on to its scars.

Long before, she had been a dreamer. A true dreamer. Filled with hope and longing for a better life—a better world. Until the years started to pass and the price of dreams had grown so high, she could no longer pay.

Her own imprisonment had been wrapped up like a shiny gift. Packed in a sparkling box that held vows of magic and promises of honor and distinction.

But just the same as the other innocent Perseisian children gifted with magic, Asha had never been given a choice in her future. She had been forced to bond, bound to serve a wicked crown with the power in her veins and the breath in her lungs. And, similarly to the other soldiers, the cage she had been put in was plated in polished lies, the same ones she had been spoon-fed her entire life, continuously assured that what she ate was something good.

But a golden cage was still a cage.

And what infuriated her the most was that she seemed to be the only warrior who noticed what they had done.

Back in her room, Asha dressed for the day, avoiding the long mirror fixed against the wall. She hadn't looked in a mirror for ages. Not really. Not since the first ribbon of dark, black ink etched itself onto the skin of her shoulder, curling upward towards her neck. The Markings scattered on her skin were born from pain and loss. They were intended to serve as a reminder of death—permanently displayed pieces of the bearer's broken soul. The Markings were a result of the magic pulsing through her veins.

When Ianoda—the God of Life, the Gifter of Magic and the Breaker of Chains—unsealed magic and allowed it to reenter the mortal realm, he also ensured the wielders graced with power would forever bear reminders for any misuse of the gifts they carried. Because everything had a price, Asha had learned, and nothing was free, not even the magic that burned through her body since the day she was born. And, at some point, everyone was forced to decide what they were willing to pay—to sacrifice—to keep it. Even if it came at a cost to others.

Asha's tattoos looked like spirals of mist and smoke,

billows of whipping wind all twirling around one another like floating ribbons.

The first coil of smoky lines appeared many years ago, when the first crack was severed deep inside her soul and the lurking Darkness found a crevice to seep inside. Over the years, each breaking of her soul carved another misty ribbon somewhere on her body, adding to the scars and wounds already covering it.

So, Asha avoided mirrors. She avoided the reminders of her broken soul and the haunting memories that accompanied the ink. She had seen some warriors display their Markings like trophies, proud of the horrors they had overcome. But Asha hid her tattoos underneath long sleeves and high necklines—shame and pain the only feelings the ink conjured.

Most other warriors did not earn their first Markings until they were stationed at one of the Kingdom's war camps. Almost all the soldiers were lucky enough to make it through basic training without severed pieces of their souls.

But luck was a friend Asha had never been blessed to become acquainted with.

She earned her first Mark shortly after she set foot in her hometown of Valhol's basic training camp for the Kappi cadets, the soldiers who had bonded with phoenixes.

The Valhollian Fort was located on the northern coast of the Iron City and proudly trained a quarter of the Kappi cadets in the Kingdom of Perseis. Its southern neighboring city, Elysia—home to the greatest steel crafters on the Northern Continent—was charged to train the rest.

A cool morning breeze fluttered through the open window in Asha's room, pulling her from her memories. She quickly shrugged on her riding leathers, knowing most of Sveaborg's Base was still asleep, before heading for the Aviary, eager to sneak off for one more morning of freedom before she was locked inside the Base's impenetrable walls.

That's how the last fourteen years had felt, locked inside the confines of Fort Valhol for years of Kappi training—like she was a prisoner trapped inside a cage, more than a soldier training for war. Leadership had tried to dress it up, to make the bars shine and hide the emptiness harbored within, but Asha saw the gilded cage for what it was. Because she knew cages are not always made of bars and stone walls; they are just as often carved from fear, forced thoughts, and dictated choices.

They gave her two weeks between Kappi graduation and the start of Soturi tryouts, half of which she used to leisurely travel down from Valhol, before she was required to report to Sveaborg to continue her military training. Only six more months, she told herself, then her training would be complete, and she could start the real work.

Asha arrived at Sveaborg the evening before. After checking in with the front gate, she was guided through a labyrinth of white stone colonnades until she reached the room that would be her home for the next twenty-four weeks. It was simple, but spacious. A large bed, dressed in an onyx covering, golden trim, and white pillows, sat in the corner. A small wooden side table rested beside the bed, and a large glass window, stretching from floor to ceiling, covered the remainder of the far wall. In the opposing corner, a deep mahogany wardrobe, large enough to store all her uniforms, stood tall against the cream walls. A small desk was shoved beside it. An ornate fixture hung from the ceiling, filled with bright luminos to give light to the room. She softly smiled at the permission of lesser magic on the Base. Too many nights had come and gone in Valhol where Asha found herself living in the dark, the only lights approved to use were the faintly burning candles she hoarded in her room, courtesy of Valhol's refusal to allow any magic on the Fort's premises, luminos included.

Valhol was unlike any other city on the Continents. There were no tall buildings, no towers or high rooftops for Asha to climb. Such constructions blocked out the presence of Ianoda from the city's heart, or so the priests of old used to say. By Valhollian decree, buildings were prohibited from exceeding three stories in height, the top of the city's main Temple, and so the city's citizens were forced to make do with a stunted skyline. And while law and statutes had halted any vertical progression, winding twin rivers strangled the city horizontally, as well, leaving a stretch of habitable land in the middle for the original citizens to settle that was quickly overgrown.

And, as a consequence of those old superstitions and enactments, Valhol, rather than rising towards the skies, plunged deep into the Continent's underground. A network of passageways and residences, unimaginable in number, was woven underneath the rocky terrain and stretched westward, into the base of the Iron Mountains. The structure gave the Valhollian city an unprecedented advantage in attacks, for the spies that were sent to survey the Iron City repeatedly underestimated its population tenfold. But perhaps even more crucial than possessing a strategic combat position was the new wisdom that had been opened to the Valhollians while residing deep within the Continent's core, an insight that even the priests of old could not have imagined.

Centuries ago, Valhol had discovered—whether through the whispering of creatures lurking deep inside the network of iron tunnels, or by pure luck—how to conjure the Advent of the Odyssey within the Iron City.

Every year, on the eve of the Vernal Equinox, chosen

specifically for the day's balance of light and darkness—a tribute to Ianoda's demand that all nature be in balance—Valhol celebrated its Day of Benefaction.

The day was celebrated as an offering to the Odyssey's phoenixes, where the city presented the children who had reached their eighth year or older and allowed the Bonding to take place. Most of the children were not chosen, left unbonded to be offered again the next year, while a small handful of less fortunate ones were plucked from the Presentation Platform and swept away by sharp claws, never to be seen again. The stolen children were more than likely burned to ash by phoenix fire. Everyone blamed the child's parents, saying both the gods and the Odyssey must have been displeased with their offering. Asha thought the whole ceremony—as well as the parents who sacrificially offered up their children—was insane, and she only hoped that Helia, the Goddess of Fire, had ensured the children's deaths were swift. Only a hundred or so children each year were lucky enough to be deemed worthy to channel a phoenix's power and keep it.

No one had ever quite figured out how the phoenixes chose which child they bonded to—many Valhollians speculated the Odyssey gave orders and approval, while others argued that the phoenixes inherently knew which children could harness the magic pulsing through their veins the best. The one thing the Valhollians all inarguably agreed on was that the honor of bonding was rare, and a phoenix only bonded a rider once in its limitless lifetimes.

Asha still remembered her Day of Benefaction fourteen years ago—two weeks after her eighth birthday. Standing in the center of the small city square, atop a long wooden platform constructed specifically for the day, she and the other Valhollian children, all adorned in purity white, were presented to the Odyssey as an offering—sacrifice—for the continuation of unsealed magic for the Kingdom and Valhol. The sun's rays broke through the clouds high above as Asha's turn arrived, and just as she had been instructed, she took a step forward, breaking apart from the line of children to her left and right.

She stood tall, her back straight and chin held high—unquestionably fearless, even for one so young.

The phoenixes, all perched atop the erected viewing ledge, halted. Silence fell amidst the crowd; even the wind froze in place.

A moment passed. Then another. Asha held her breath.

Then, like a whispering sigh, a caress of wind brushed against her cheek, and the venture of phoenixes gathered atop the ledge parted to each side. Uriel strutted through the opening, his otherworldly eyes locking with Asha's. He towered over the other firebirds, swallowing them with his size, even with his snow-white feathers tucked in neatly against his body. Asha took another step forward, her arms stretched out with the palms facing up, and inclined her head. After a moment, she flicked her eyes up, catching Uriel still staring down at her, and a triumphant grin spread over her face. Even then, she could feel the quiet burning of her magic deep within her bones, itching to be released. The firebird continued studying Asha, her head still tilted downward, before he leapt from the viewing ledge and flew down to the Presentation Platform, landing mere feet in front of where she stood. Gasps rang throughout the crowd. Asha did not move. Uriel let out a loud screech, piercing through the tense air. Asha straightened her body, lifting her eyes to gaze at the firebird, towering more than two stories high. As their eyes locked, the Bond snapped into place. A silence-shattering, agonizing scream broke from Asha's lips as the burning magic in her veins was finally set free.

The dawning sun continued its slow rise in the sky over the Base's pristine, pure-white buildings as Asha weaved through the winding corridors that connected her room to the Aviary.

She knew from the first moment she saw the phoenixes' resting grounds that it would be her favorite place on the Base. The rustling of wings, the rainbow of feathers painting the open field; it was the natural picture of peace. Surrounding a large, infinite pool, filled by water rushing in from the sea below, was a vast expanse of open space that housed a blend of every imaginable landscape. From rock-dusted cliffs and lush green tree lines to magma-filled crevices and snow-lined fields, all sides of the grounds mingled together in the center, where a clean strip of grass held a shelter next to the infinity pool for the firebirds to rest. The grounds were designed with the venture's needs in mind.

Each phoenix was unique in its own respect—its appearance having been reformed after death to incorporate the elements of whatever place it had last risen. Some of the firebirds were dressed in feathers of deep ocean-blue, with a small set of shimmering scales and shells hidden beneath their wings. Others wore layers of molten red quills, with lava rock underbellies, harder to pierce than Elysian steel. A handful of forest-green phoenixes were mixed into the bunch as well, with flower-filled moss coating the top of their earth-brown wings.

Only one in the venture donned pure snow-white feathers, tipped with shards of sculpted ice.

Uriel.

A huge smile spread across Asha's face as she approached the massive beast, his colossal tail swaying as she neared. She lifted her hand to stroke his face, and he nuzzled into her side in reply. She let out a small chuckle as she fastened on a saddle and climbed onto his back, settling into place before grabbing the reins.

She supposed that was one thing she had to thank the Dominions for—her firebird.

From her Kappi training in Valhol, Asha had unquestionably learned that the magic thrumming through her veins—the very reason she had been permitted to bond with Uriel—was not singularly granted by the God of Life. Like all magic wielders of Darnella, Asha's power had ultimately been approved by the Dominions—the divine administrators of Ianoda's Authority.

Throughout her studies and from endless hours spent poring through old scrolls, Asha had also discovered that the Dominions possessed a past almost as tumultuous as her own Kingdom's.

Intent on maintaining a balance of power amidst the encroaching presence of the Lord of Darkness, Ianoda separated his Authority into three divine factions: the Thrones, the Virtues, and the Dominions, issuing each branch divine control over a distinct discipline of magic.

The Thrones, appointed for their strength and protection, controlled all magic related to the physical realm.

The Virtues, based upon fairness and truth, controlled the power of justice, as well as its closely related companion of Mind Magic.

Last were the Dominions, the most loyal administrators of Ianoda's will. These divine servants were granted the authority to bestow all magic associated with the elemental and Spirit Magic.

As time passed, the war between the Lords of Light and Darkness continued, and the structure of Ianoda's arrangement slowly began to falter.

No one truly knew what happened to the Authorities; most of the tales passed down were all speculative rumors shared at late-night fires.

But the residents of Darnella did know that the Thrones and the Virtues were no longer present. Some claimed the two Authorities had died off long ago, slaughtered by the evil servants of the Lord of Darkness in The First War; others argued they had gone into hiding, fearful of whatever Dark magic the other side possessed.

A small group believed they had been killed off by their own brothers in an internal war—a war that was waged before The First War, when the Authorities themselves fought one another, each faction intent on claiming the favor of the gods and securing their seat of honor amongst the servants.

No one knew the truth of what had happened amongst the divine, but what they did understand was that in the arduous times surrounding The Annihilation, the Virtues and Thrones had been wiped out from the realm. Killed off and thrust into another world—another vestige of time and space.

And now the only remaining faction of the Authorities was the Dominions, and the very finite traces of Magic left over from the two missing Authorities.

Asha inclined her head towards the two guards stationed at the Aviary outpost, and they nodded in acknowledgment, permitting her to take to the skies with her firebird. It was the last day she would be allowed to freely soar through the skies until the six months of Soturi training were completed.

She didn't need to say a word before Uriel crouched down and thrust himself into the air, his wings flapping as he

CAMERON L. JIMENEZ

lifted off the ground and shot into the clouds above.

Freedom—that was what it felt like. With the wind in her hair and the skies surrounding her in every direction, Asha was free in the sky.

For too many years, she lived a life that others had chosen for her; a captive to thoughts that were not her own. But over the last eighteen months, she fought her way to a place of freedom—to a place centered in truth and honesty, absent of any lurking Darkness. She fought to hold on to the freedom she experienced every time she let loose in the clouds. And Asha intended to guard the newfound liberty planted deep in her soul with a ferocity the world had never seen.

They flew for miles and miles, over open waters and bustling towns. It was an adventure on the wind, and it shivered down her spine with delight. She let the breeze kiss her face as Uriel guided them through the air, not a word spoken—they had never needed them.

His unending strength was one of her favorite qualities about him. She had never discovered why Uriel never seemed to tire, why his flight endurance was so much greater than the other phoenixes she had encountered, but she treasured it, grateful for his ability to travel to far lands and glide through the skies for hours on end. Her other favorite quality was his steadfast loyalty. He had proven it to her time and time again, and this occasion was no different as the bonded pair circled high above Sveaborg, searching for an opening in the Base where she would be able to slip out, undetected, when the time came.

As the pair soared over the Base, Asha took in the stone buildings spread out among the rocky mountains shooting up from the center of the islands. Everything on the Base looked so clean—pure—as if bloodshed and death did not lurk around every corner.

Intermingled within the mountains were lakes and trees, with more fields and structures built for various instruction.

The four islands were connected by long, stone bridges, suspended high above the ocean waters of the Gulf of Ahti. Towering, whitewashed walls encircled each of the masses of land that made up the Base.

The Main Island, settled farthest to the East, was the largest and housed the Academic Building, a monstrous and magnificently crafted structure separated into three connecting wings. The exterior was surrounded by columns and high windows that overlooked the Gulf. The building curled around a large, well-manicured courtyard, with dozens of pathways stretching southward from the center. Several of the paths connected to the Barracks and other training facilities through a tangle of open colonnades.

On the furthest side, nestled on the strip of land hanging off the east side of the Main Island and pressing up against a towering mountain that jetted straight into the skies, was a group of dark, granite stones, stretching so high they looked like walls. Uriel did not fly close enough for Asha to make out the fortified barriers, but even from high above, she could sense the eerie feeling radiating from the rocks.

On the northern side of the Main Island, large cliffs towered above the rest of the land masses and appeared to plunge straight up from the waters below.

Uriel flew the perimeter of each island, and Asha scoured every inch of the fortress walls.

After they made their rounds, she turned the reins and guided Uriel westward, across the Gulf, towards the Perseis coast. The pair soared high above the small fishing town of Reyka, and Asha took in every inch of the village below. A small smile curled on her lips as Uriel took one last lap in the skies, curving a little further out of the main ports of the village center. She gave him a small pat on his back, and he returned to the Base.

After hours in the open sky, Asha dropped Uriel off at the Aviary before making her way to the dining hall, positioned just north of the Barracks, for dinner. She sat alone, quickly scarfing down her food, and then headed back to her room, knowing she needed to rest before the Soturi Initiation Day the next morning.

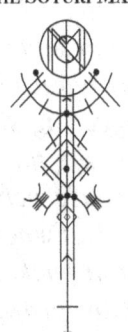

CHAPTER TWO

A pair of silver flecked eyes, buried beneath strands of matted auburn hair, stared up at Asha, all light having left the irises. A wet trickle began to drip down the side of her hand. An overwhelming stench surrounded her, strangling her nostrils. It reeked of rot and decay, suffocating her breath. The songs of birds above went silent, the grass around her lost its lush color, as if life had been completely drained from it. The nearby flowers went limp. And a pervasive feeling of cruelty—evil—lingered around the open field. Asha glanced down to find a spattering of deep crimson staining her fingers—blood. Nina's blood.

A low, menacing snarl escaped from behind her, and the growl came deep from within the beast's throat—it sounded otherworldly. Asha's gaze whipped to the tree line, darting back and forth. That was when she saw it, buried back in the shadows. A colossal creature prowled through the trees on all fours, its black scaly skin moving with predatorial poise.

With each step the beast took, its long, jagged claws raked through the ground. But what sent shivers of ice down Asha's spine was not the creature's bared teeth, exposing long, sharp fangs, nor was it the staggering size the beast stretched to when it stood upright—it was the glaring red-flecked eyes that peered through the space between them, straight into the depths of Asha's soul. And when she locked her burning sapphire stare onto them, a wicked smirk stretched across the creature's face, and a low growl rumbled in its throat.

Tears slid from her eyes, and Asha's heart raced, threatening to rip itself from her chest. This was it. This was the end.

But the creature did not advance, the sinister grin still plastered on its face. And then, in a blink, as if the beast had turned to dust before her eyes, it disappeared in the wind.

Asha looked down at the woman she held in her arms, her hand still on the dagger she had thrust into her chest. A sob escaped her lips, and her heart cracked. The sound rang so loudly in her ears, she was certain if anyone else had been present, they surely would have heard it.

The skin on her arm began to burn beneath her jacket. Another splintered wail escaped Asha's mouth, and she gasped, trying to fill her lungs with air that was not there. She looked back down, into the dark, silver flecked eyes that had brought so much light into her life—so much love—but all that she could see now was darkness.

Asha jolted awake, gasping for air. Sweat stuck to every part of her shaking body, and her head started to spin, nausea churning in her stomach.

It was a dream.

It was a dream.

It was a dream.

She forced herself to focus on her breathing. She attempted to slow her racing heart as she repeated the words over and over in her head. Darkness surrounded her, save for the faint moonlight leaking in from the open window. It took her eyes a moment to adjust to the shadows before she remembered where she was.

Sveaborg.

Asha's jagged breath slowly returned to normal. A sharp breeze crawled in through the cracked opening beside her bed and brushed over her sweat-slicked skin, chilling her bones like splintering ice. She shivered in response. Asha gulped down another deep breath before reaching over to shut the large glass window that stretched from the wooden floor up to the vaulted ceiling.

As she sat back on her bed, the rich, leather-bound journal lying on the bedside table caught her eye. It was still open to the page she fell asleep reading. She picked up the book and stared down at the moonlit scribbles filling the page. The ink was smudged in a few spots, swirling in chaotic directions, as if the author couldn't get his thoughts out onto the paper fast enough. That was what Asha missed about him most—his mind. How, in time, he was always able to create the most complete and beautiful picture from the frantic ideas racing in his head. But time was not his friend. The journal showed that—it served as a reminder of all the turbulent thoughts he would never have the chance to bring together, of the clock that had run out of time.

Eighteen months—that was how much time had passed since the foot soldiers came to tell her Mathieson was dead; how much time had gone by since they had dropped her brother's belongings on her doorstep like a pile of trash. That was how long the writhing knot inside her stomach had refused to unwind.

She knew she should have burned the journals. She knew at some point she would answer to Anubis for holding onto them, for not sending them out on the boat with the rest of Mathieson's possessions to watch as engulfing flames turned them to ash during his water burial. But she couldn't bring herself to part with them, not yet, at least.

Because the scribbled journal entries were all Asha had left of her brother, and she promised herself the first time she read them that she would not stop until she found an answer to every last one of them—for Math.

That was why she had chosen to come to Sveaborg.

After completing her Kappi training back home in Valhol and graduating at the top of her year, she realized she needed to make it through Soturi training to find the answers. And to exact retribution—because she had a long list of names and one of them here was written at the top in blood-red ink.

The military base was enormous compared to the basic training Fort Asha had left in the north. The size of it shocked her when she arrived. She supposed the vast amount of space was needed since the Base housed the Specialty Team training grounds for all three branches of the Kingdom's military.

Three delineated groups—the Soturi warriors, selected from the Kappi soldiers; the Amarok, chosen from the Fenri soldiers; and the Pontos, picked from the Ceto soldiers—all shoved together between inescapable walls.

After King Balthasar's decree had gone into effect to

reorder the Kingdom's military, the southwestern city of Takama, due to its advantageous position along the Smaragdus coast, was ordered to build a Fortress to train Perseis's Ceto cadets; and Lorca, the stronghold nestled high on the western side of the Iron Mountains, built the Citadel—an extensive training camp for the Fenri cadets and their wolves. That left the two eastern cities of Valhol and Elysia to train the Kappi soldiers, and both cities proudly claimed to produce the fiercest and most brutal warriors, surpassing the rest of Perseis's military branches in strength, bloodlust, and discipline. And Asha, hailing from Valhol, had learned from the best.

It still shocked her that all three groups would agree to train at the same Base, knowing how much separation and friction had been instilled between the branches during basic training.

The one positive Asha figured was that she and the other Soturi cadets would only have to work with the Amarok and Pontos trainees on rare occasions. Learning land navigation with the Amarok's wolves and how to fare at sea with the Pontos' hippocas were not something she looked forward to—and working with the bonded soldiers sounded even less appealing. She figured Uriel felt the same.

She knew the impression she and the other Kappi soldiers gave off, the air of superiority they wielded that made them seem impervious to other people's feelings. She didn't care. Considering everyone else's feelings when you're at war is what gets you killed.

Mathieson cared more for other people than anyone else she'd ever known—and look how that ended up for him. Asha shoved the thought from her mind before it could take root.

So, for the last eighteen months, that was who she had

allowed herself to become—cutthroat, cold, numb. Brutality became her best friend as she clawed her way to the top of her Kappi training class. She finished first in every event during the Inferno—the final, culminating test of her fourteen-year Kappi training, designed to force the cadets to their physical and emotional limits. Seven days of cold, wet, and brutally difficult operational scenarios with little or no sleep. It was never a choice for her to place anywhere but first. Ever since the first time she read Math's journal entries, Asha knew becoming a Soturi was the only way she would be able to find the answers. Knew it was the only way she would be able to get to the bottom of the ceaseless questions that ran through her mind. She knew following in Math's footsteps was the only way she would be able to figure out what really happened to him in Aaru. To find out the truth.

So, Asha had left nothing to chance. It was not enough to simply finish in the top fifteen percent of Valhol's sixty Kappi cadets; no, Asha Raynor made sure she surpassed every single one of her classmates and left the instructors with no option but to put her name on the list of officers recommended for Soturi tryouts—even if she was the first woman of Valhol to accept the offer.

Later that morning, Asha dressed in her Valhollian fighting leathers, throwing on a matching long-sleeve brown shirt to cover her tattoos and the iron bands fixed around her forearms just below the elbow. The Kingdom required the iron bands to be anchored in place as soon as the Bonding occurred, preventing magic from being accessed until after the child completed their military training and learned how to properly channel the power, but even the bands did not stop the magic from continuing to course through her veins.

Asha had tried many times to remove the shackles, but they were engraved with locking runes, impossible to unfasten without spells or the Skeleton Key.

She didn't know why she had even bothered trying to remove them—it wouldn't have made any difference.

Because the iron bands were not the only thing forced onto her body as soon as the Bonding occurred.

Even with her sleeve pulled down low, she could still see the Brand as it peeked out from beneath her shirt.

Inside the scarred flesh sat a branded *E*.

Einvala.

Written in the Old Language of the Founders, the idiom translated to "chosen by the gods."

The Council had claimed it was to celebrate the honor of Ianoda's chosen warriors and to distinguish magic wielders from the others. But Asha saw it for what it truly was—a branded shackle.

A shackle imbued with High Magic—a magic that forcefully kept the Perseisian soldiers loyal to the Crown, even after their iron bands had been removed.

It sickened Asha to look at it. To be reminded of how the Council had convinced generation after generation that their bondage was a privilege—a beautiful honor granted to them by the Seven High Gods.

But Asha knew it was anything but that. Because if her service to the Crown—and the magic flowing through her veins—was truly an honor, then she would have been able to choose it for herself. And her wrist would not have been branded with High Magic that forced her to remain loyal, rendering her wholly incapable of defying Leadership.

Asha took a deep breath, pushing the rage from her mind. She fastened a belt around her waist and tucked two daggers into the band—one iron, one Elysian steel—before jetting out of her bedroom door. The Base was buzzing with anticipation and fear as Asha made her way down to the central courtyard.

Initiation Day.

A line had already begun forming beneath the columns lining the south side of the exorbitantly open space, large enough to hold two hundred soldiers aligned in formation.

Asha joined the back of the line winding its way up to a daunting Soturi warrior holding a quill and scroll. A quick peek at the singular chevron on his jacket indicated his rank of sergeant.

Asha glanced around the rest of the space, realizing the check-in for the Amarok and Pontos soldiers must have been located elsewhere on the Base, as only Soturi and Kappi were in attendance. As she surveyed the Kappi officers in line and the Soturi warriors collecting in the courtyard, her gaze landed on a warrior—lieutenant, she noted, a single golden bar donned on each side of his jacket. He looked young to have already achieved such a high rank, likely only a few years older than Asha herself, *likely close to the age Math would've been*, she thought.

His movements were made of lethal grace as he strode across the grounds towards the sergeant registering those in line, stopping to give orders to several warrior groups along the way. His towering build was enhanced by the dangerous allure of his eyes. She had never seen such fatal and destructive beauty, surely honed over time to be used as a weapon in itself. He stopped a few yards from the registration spot, his arms, wrapped in coiled muscles, were crossed in front of him, and his stare was locked on the line of gathered officers—monitoring.

Asha neared the front of the line, her eyes fixed on the Kappi officer in front of her. As he gave his name to the sergeant, another warrior frantically rushed into the courtyard, calling over the menacing lieutenant.

"Lieutenant Eros?" the warrior bellowed, waving at him with papers in hand.

Asha's body went rigid.

Her head snapped up, meeting the fierce face staring back at her.

Anselem Eros. Revered warrior of the Elysian Soturi.

His piercing emerald eyes glared at her, absorbing every detail as they poured out an unnerving amount of disapproval. His gorgeous, angular features were spread over flawless, honey-brown skin. A piece of leather secured the top half of his long, dark hair, and the remaining pieces flowed down to the middle of his back, with tiny braids intertwined amidst the loose strands. A neat, close-trimmed beard surrounded a grin that masked lethal for charming. Beautiful, yes. But in a way a sword can be if it's safely tucked behind glass.

His dark-brown uniform fit snugly against his sculpted body, and the sleeves were cut high on his shoulders. The exposed portion of his left arm was covered in a myriad of dark ink that wrapped around his muscles and branched out in erratic lines of electric lightning. His right forearm bore the sacred Soturi Mark, and an array of additional tattoos wove their way up above the Mark. A single, onyx cuff was fixed on his wrist, covering the branded *E* burned into his skin.

He strode over to the warrior's side, keeping his gaze locked on Asha's face, as if he was trying to place where he had seen it before.

"Name?" the sergeant barked. But Asha did not turn to look at the sergeant with the scroll. No, she continued staring back into those gorgeous green eyes, and as she did, she knew she wanted to be the one to kill him.

Forty days.

It had been forty days since Asha had last spoken. And as she opened her mouth to respond, she looked the lieutenant dead in the eyes as the words fell from her lips.

"My name is Asha Akselsen Raynor."

A singeing silence burned through the air. She watched the gleaming eyes of the lieutenant darken as her name hit his ears. Her lips curled back in response.

"Raynor?" the sergeant repeated, softer this time than his previous words. His glance slowly slid to the lieutenant before coming back to look at Asha. She cut her eyes at him and grimaced. She nodded once, swift and concise.

As the sergeant scribbled her name onto the paper before him, she lifted her gaze once more to the lieutenant, rage simmering in her veins. If it wasn't for the sacred rule prohibiting her from killing another warrior on Base, the dagger hidden in her waistband would have already found a new home in his throat.

Eros raised his eyebrows, as if he could read the thoughts running through her mind. Then he smirked, daring her to try.

Asha's eyes narrowed, the Darkness inside her rising to the surface, and she pressed her fists against her sides to keep from reaching for the knife. Her knuckles turned white.

Eros finished speaking to the warrior who summoned him and swiftly turned away, his face schooled into a neutral and seemingly unfazed expression.

Fumes simmered inside Asha as she made her way into formation amongst the other officers. The lingering gazes from the warriors lining the court's edges burrowed into her, and she watched as they whispered to one another, nodding in her direction.

The final officer registered with the sergeant and filed in formation in the back.

Thirty-six.

Thirty-six Kappi officers for this year's Initiation Rite. She knew the nine from Valhol, liked some of them even, but she had no intention of getting to know the rest of the officers standing between her and one of the twenty spots open for this year's Soturi training. At least not today.

She glanced around the group once more.

No other women.

"Good morning, officers," a voice called from the front of the courtyard. The hushed whispers fell silent as the Base commander's words carried through the space.

Major Coatl Bardick.

His snow-white hair had been cut short, showing no allegiance to his Valhollian roots. His pale face was clean-shaven, and his deep-brown uniform looked pristine and flawlessly tailored. An image of wisdom and discipline. No signs of the blood-lusting warrior of his past days.

Standing before the crowd, he looked the picturesque embodiment of the Council of Satraps.

Even behind the polished smile and political charm, Asha could see the unsatiated hunger for power looming in his dark eyes. She scanned his arms. The lack of a crowned lion branded onto his wrist confirmed her assumptions—the Major may look the part of the Council, but he had not yet slithered his way into their exclusive ranks.

But Asha would bet a lot of gold that the Major likely answered to one directly—no one received the honorable position of Base Director without someone championing for them at the Council's table.

The Council of Satraps had been established centuries ago, when the Kingdom of Perseis had grown too large for a single leading Headship.

The Satraps were the six appointed governors who presided over the designated provinces of Perseis. The seventh member of the Council was none other than the Gilded King himself.

The Council had been modeled after the Holy Council of the Seven High Gods—and the rulers had done an appallingly good job at instituting their counterfeit assembly to such a degree that even now, centuries later, the Perseisian citizens still took their word as holy law.

Staring up at the Major, Asha wondered if pretending oneself to be a god was a newly founded concept, or if the Kings of Old had pursued the same idea. She leaned towards the latter.

"I would like to welcome you to this year's Soturi Initiation Rite," the Major greeted.

His beady eyes shifted among the cadets, no sign of light inside the dark pools. A silver pin resting on his collar glinted against the overhead sun.

"As you look around," the Major continued, "you will find a collective of Soturi warriors assembled. They have been assigned to help facilitate today's events."

Asha could feel a gaze digging holes into the side of her face. She refused to turn, but from the corner of her eye, she could see the dark marks of electric ink sprawling up his arm.

Her dagger burned a hole in her waistband.

"First and foremost, I need to inform you of a change in this year's program. Instead of the customary twenty candidates selected to attend training, this year we will only be taking sixteen."

Hushed whispers broke out among those gathered, officers and warriors alike.

Four less spots.

"Due to an increase in manpower needs across Perseis," he continued, whispers still floating through the wind, "Sveaborg is having to send both resources and instructors to other parts of the Continent. The decrease in available staff has caused us to consider a variety of changes."

Asha wondered what was happening in the war across the Strait to require such an increase in warriors. Usually, Perseis's aerial support was first pulled from the Kappi. So, if they were drawing from the Soturi, then that either meant they were losing too many soldiers, or their enemies had developed an aerial unit...

"The Amarok and Pontos sections will also be decreasing to sixteen candidates per group."

The lurking shadow of twisted electricity moved from the corner of her view, and she instinctively slid her hand inside her jacket, palming the dagger at her waist.

"Aside from the change in numbers, the structure of this training course will proceed as usual," the Major continued, "following this meeting, you will divide yourselves into four lines at the front of the courtyard, where Soturi instructors will inspect and reinforce your iron bands. Afterward, all thirty-six of you will participate in the most acclaimed event of the Soturi Initiation Rite—the Crucible. Tomorrow morning, the officers who have survived the Crucible will participate in the second event of Initiation, the Minos Maze. This year, we plan to offer the winner of the Maze a prize." The Major's eyes twinkled with a spot of amusement. "Tomorrow evening, The Rite will conclude with the selection of the top sixteen candidates chosen for this year's Soturi Training Academy, followed by your Division assignments. Those of you who do not make the cut will return to your respective Forts to receive your Kappi orders."

An unnerving silence filled the air around Asha.

Tightened iron bands. The Crucible. The Minos Maze.

She forcefully pushed back her fear before it swallowed her whole.

She knew more than most of the other cadets before starting her Kappi training. Mathieson had told her everything she needed to be prepared. But the Soturi tryouts? Asha never had the chance to ask him before he left for Aaru. And now she never would.

Major Bardick's voice broke through the piercing silence once again, "Now, please line up."

The group of officers started shuffling together, branching out into four separate lines. The Soturi warriors surrounding the courtyard began to disperse, some making their way towards the officers, while others disappeared down the corridors. Asha fell in place behind a tall, unfamiliar Elysian Kappi. As two more Kappi filed in behind her, she attempted to gaze past the man standing in front of her, but she was too short to see around him without leaning. She heard the clinking of keys against metal, and a shiver ran down her spine. She forced herself to stand straight, staring into the back of the officer in front of her.

As the clinking of metal rang through the air, Asha's mind went blank. She couldn't think straight. Was she sixth in her line? Or seventh? She tried to do the math as her line inched forward, step after step. *If there were thirty-six of-*

ficers and we needed four lines... A bead of sweat dripped down her back. She was still trying to clear her mind when the Elysian Kappi in front of her stepped over to the side, his iron bands resecured.

Piercing emerald eyes glared down at her.

No.

"Seven," he stated, a wicked grin stretching over his angular face. His voice was deep and gravelly, laced with intoxicating venom.

No. No. No.

Asha's hands started to shake at her side. She willed them to cease as she removed her jacket. She pushed the sleeves of her shirt up to her elbows, thankful her misty tattoos had not yet marked her forearms.

The lieutenant's calloused hands were surprisingly gentle as he grabbed the band on her right arm, inserting the ivory key into the lock. The warmth of his fingers melted through her icy veins, heating the skin beneath. He twisted the key, and she waited for the tightening click. It never came. He removed the key and proceeded to do the same to her left arm. Holding the band and twisting the jagged, carved bone inside the lock. The left side made no reinforcing sounds either, and she dared to look up at his face. His expression was set in an uninterested mask of neutrality. Eros pulled out the replica Skeleton Key, a duplicated copy that could only re-lock the bands, and dropped her arm. The key was pale white, with a skull carved into the head, and the smooth material looked as if it were truly made of bone.

The warmth of his fingers left a dull coldness behind on her skin. He looked past Asha to the next officer in line. "Eight," he called, and she stepped to the side.

What in the Seven Hells...

CHAPTER THREE

Staring down at the panic-stricken group of officers assembled before him, Anselem Eros was *pissed.*

As his nails dug deeper into the palms of his clenched fists, he forced his face to maintain the detached and disinterested expression he had perfectly mastered over the years. He tried to focus on Major Bardick, standing before the large replica of the Crucible's obstacle course, as he explained the sequence to the participants, but Anselem found that his eyes kept returning to the silver blonde Kappi standing in the second row.

Her hair was pulled out of her face and twisted into a long, cascading braid that flowed down her back. She carried herself with a confidence that skirted the edge of arrogance, but her movements were made of such fatal elegance he knew it was not unfounded. Even under her Valhollian fighting leathers, Anselem could see the toned muscles and generous curves of her figure. Her words had been filled with the sweetest venom, and she kept her face permanently fixed in a beautiful death stare.

But *those eyes*. Anselem had never seen such captivating eyes. They shimmered like pools of sapphire when the sun's rays brushed her face, but, even in the brief moment she had glanced up at him, he saw a Darkness prowling deep within the cerulean blue. A Darkness that spoke of heartbreak and suffering—an agony he knew he had caused.

What the Hells is she doing here? Anselem thought, his skin warming as rage continued to pulse through his veins.

"The Crucible," Major Bardick explained, interrupting Anselem before he dove into deep speculation, "consists of eight events. The course will begin here," Bardick pointed to the open field beside the Administration Building, "on Sveaborg's Main Island, and will conclude at the North Island, at the Pontos' training grounds." Anselem's gaze followed along as the Major's hand glided to the northeast corner of the map.

"The Crucible will take place over eight collective miles and will commence with The Devil's Rope." The long scar on Anselem's thigh burned beneath his uniform as he recalled the first event, a one-hundred-yard crawl through a pit covered in barbed wire.

"The second obstacle will be Thunderbolt, followed by the Rock Climb."

Anselem could see the fear waft over the participants. He could almost hear the clicking of the Thunderbolt's wires as thousands of volts crackled through them. The second obstacle had always been a rite of passage for participants and a favorite amongst spectators who enjoyed watching the carnage. Anselem was thankful his body had been designed to harbor electricity, or else he never would have made it through the Thunderbolt's dangling cables.

"Following the Rock Climb will be Walk the Plank." A thirty-foot plunge into freezing ocean water, the obstacle had been designed to test the participants' fear of heights and cold all in one. Walk the Plank never failed to claim at least one participant each year. Anselem figured this year would be no different.

"Once in the water, you will complete the Sunken Anchor, ending over at the North Island." The mile-long swim through the sea's choppy waves and swirling winds always seemed to be the easiest of the events, but Anselem had not forgotten the gallons of swallowed ocean water he had heaved up on the North Island's shore.

"After you reach the shore, the Gated Ladder will greet you." Major Bardick pointed to the sixth obstacle, and a wave of pride washed over Anselem as he recalled his own Gated Ladder—he was the fastest member of his year to complete the event, jumping the metal bar between the vertical rungs with unnatural ease until he reached the top.

"Once you reach the summit, you will arrive at the Swaying Vines." Another event Anselem had excelled in as he'd swung himself between the hanging ropes, suspended fifty feet in the air.

"Finally, the last event will be the Log Jump." Anselem knew seeing the zig-zag logs, which spun in varying directions, intimidated some of the participants, but he also knew the greater threat lay in the waters beneath. No one who had ever fallen into the sea serpent infested lake had ever made it out alive.

"The first sixteen candidates to complete the Crucible will be selected for this year's Soturi Training Academy. The first event of the Initiation Rite will begin in one hour. Are there any questions?"

Only fear-charged silence responded.

Heading out to the field, Asha's stomach rolled, bile rising in her throat. She knew, to the blurred faces she walked past, that she looked the perfect picture of composure, her face poised, breathing even, but internally, she was screaming. That had always been her biggest secret—she was scared. All. The. Time.

She remembered the day she told Math a few years back, when he came home from Soturi training for a few days during the midway break.

His thundering laugh filled her ears. "You have no fear," he said as she jumped across the gap between the rooftops. Mathieson leapt after her, landing by her side. It had been so long—too long—since she had seen that bright smile. Gods, she had missed him.

They continued to dance their way across Valhol's skyline, leaping from rooftop to rooftop, scaling up and down the sides of the buildings. So much time had passed since they had let loose above the city together—free in the air, adrenaline rushing through their veins, pushing each other and testing the limits of one another's training. They ran and climbed and scrambled across so many structures until they at last came to the Valhollian Temple of Freyja. Unmoved from the center of the city, Freyja's Temple had long since burned to ash. Abandoned and half in ruins, the ring-shaped marble columns still standing stretched more than four stories high. The sanctuary had been built for Freyja, the Goddess of War and Seider Magic, but after the Valhollians declared she had abandoned them in The Great War, the goddess, along with her Temple, had been deserted, and it was left to decay and ruin. Many other Temples had been erected in Valhol throughout the years, still standing and maintained, but not one of the Valhollian citizens ever came to redeem and rebuild Freyja's Temple. And no one dared enter for fear of the rejected goddess's wrath.

Asha and Mathieson slowed their bounding run to catch their breath. She sat down on one of the nearby roofs, overlooking the ruins. Mathieson followed, taking a seat beside her.

She was quiet for a long while before she interrupted their comfortable silence. "It's not true, you know."

"What's not true?"

She paused before looking over to meet his assuasive eyes. "I'm not fearless like you think. I'm scared. All the time."

He looked at her for a long while. His ash-blonde hair, shaved high on each side, was pulled back into a braid at the top, but several of the pieces had managed to escape from the knot and were sticking to his face with sweat and grime. His kind, sapphire eyes, the ones that mirrored her own, studied her face as he found his words.

"That's good," he replied. Her brow wrinkled at his words.

"You have to have fear in order to have any courage." A soft smile formed on her mouth. "Brave is not the one who feels no fear, but the one who triumphs over it." Her smile grew wider as her brother spoke the words their father had repeated all their lives.

"And we must build barriers of courage to hold back the flood of fear," she finished, and Math's smile mirrored her own.

"I'm proud of you, Ash." Tears threatened to line her eyes as she offered him another smile. Genuine and rare, one

she did not often let others see.

"On the other side of every fear you face is freedom. Never forget that. So, the next time you find yourself face-to-face with something that scares you, look it dead in the eye and say, 'I will not be afraid of the terrors held by the night, nor the horrors that walk in the darkness. I am a master of my fear. I have power beyond measure. I am unbreakable.'"

Asha chuckled, her smile reaching her eyes. "Yeah? You say that whole thing every time?" She laughed again, and her brother grinned in response.

"It's gotten me this far," he shrugged. And then he jumped up from his place and peered off in the distance. Glancing back down at his sister with a wide grin, he said, "I'll race you to the docks." She looked up at him for only a split moment before she sprang to her feet and began running across the rooftops.

"Cheater!" he called from behind, and a wild laugh escaped both of their mouths.

Asha's eyes were brighter than they had been in years.

As she reached the open field beside the Academic Building, Asha pulled herself from the memory. She scanned the space stretched out before her, trailing her gaze over the rolling grass and the edge of the cliffside in the looming distance. Her eyes halted as they came to the pit before her, only a hundred yards away from where the candidates were lining up.

A whip of frozen air cooled the sweat beading on her brow. She sucked in a deep breath and closed her eyes, willing her nerves to settle. She took several more long, drawn-out breaths, and her racing heart began to slow. She settled into the space of her mind where there was only lethal stillness. Only room for revenge, bloodlust, and cunning. And

she whispered to herself, *I am a master of my fear. I have power beyond measure. I am unbreakable.*
And she waited for the carnage to begin.

A kind voice broke through the silence. "Raynor, right?" Asha opened her eyes and glanced up at the man standing to her left. He looked so young, but there was a feel of regal dominion he held in his elegant face. His golden-blonde hair complemented his lightly sun-kissed skin and fell just above his bright, tawny eyes. His boyish features were handsome, friendly even, and she could see the lean muscles hidden beneath his dark brown jacket. He stood tall, shoulders squared in a non-threatening type of way. He had a quiet confidence about him, and she wondered how many cunning ideas the boyish grin plastered on his face had hidden throughout his years.

She made a point to look him up and down, once, like a predator assessing her prey, before she turned and faced forward, ignoring his question.

"Greystone," he offered, "Jeremiah Greystone." Asha simply looked down at the hand he offered, blinked once, and then turned her gaze back upon the open field before them.

"Ah, so it's true, Valhol's Greatest Marksman really doesn't speak." Asha cut him a look that would have sent lesser men running. "Markswoman?" he tried, his tone light. She cut another glance his way, but he only laughed, the sound bright and free, and it was foreign to her ears.

"I think I'm going to like getting to know you, you seem like you're fun. In a frightening, not-sure-if-you-might-kill-me type of way, but fun." His voice was genuine and kind, and he let out another chuckle. His words were spoken with such sincerity that it took everything in her to maintain her composure. To hide the wave of shock and gratitude swelling inside her at the mere idea of someone, even some random stranger in a field, speaking in a way that suggested they believed she would make it. That they truly thought she would become the first to be selected as a Soturi.

"Alright, candidates," Major Bardick's voice amplified through the yard.

"Good luck," Jeremiah whispered and threw her a wink. Her only acknowledgement was a curt nod in his direction, eliciting a wide grin from the stranger before he turned his attention to the Major.

"I hope you are all ready to begin." A grin stretched across Bardick's face as he dragged his gaze down the line of officers.

Flashes of color whipped over their heads, filling the sky. Various hues of blue, red, and green firebirds were scattered throughout the clouds, flying into various positions along the course to assess. At the far end of the field, a singular onyx phoenix, darker than midnight shadows, hovered above the pit. Several of the officers gasped, and every candidate in attendance took in its ethereal beauty, the pure black feathers as rare as the snow-white ones that adorned Uriel.

Asha only stared, not at the magnificent beast suspended in the air, but at the rider sitting atop.

Eros.

Her eyes turned dark.

The Major pressed the bone white horn to his lips and blew one long blare.

And all the Kappi ran towards the impending carnage.

Asha had never been thankful for her build. Her height,

her short stature, always put her at a disadvantage in training. But right now? Crawling through skin-ripping metal wire? She thanked the gods of old for her size.

She barely fit underneath the barbed wire as she crawled her way through the muddied pit. Inch by inch, yard by yard, she crawled, and the further down the line she made it, the closer the skin-shredding wires pressed in on her. Ten yards were left between her and the grassy field beyond The Devil's Rope. She was in the lead, thanks to her size and ability to quickly move through the first three quarters of the pit, but the others were not far behind. She'd had to slow herself down the past fifteen yards, making more contemplative movements to ensure the metal didn't catch and rip through her skin as it pressed in closer. Pull after pull, she dug her fingers into the muddied earth beneath, her feet burrowing into the ground behind her as she propelled herself forward. She reached the last few yards, and she knew she would not make it through unscathed. The wires pressed too closely to one another. She took a deep breath as she pulled herself the last few yards, metal slicing and cutting through her sleeves and into her forearms. She hoisted herself up, out of the pit, and onto the grassy land above. Blood began to pool, and she swore, clasping her right hand over her forearm. The cut was deep, jagged. She ripped a piece from the bottom of her shirt and quickly wrapped it around the cut before she took off in a sprint, heading to the Thunderbolt.

The mud caked onto her body began to dry, turning gritty, as she neared the crackling volts.

She scanned the obstacle, looking for any way through that would not send thousands of volts of electricity through her body. The rustling of grass and thundering of footsteps behind her had her eyes darting back and forth between the hanging wires. She stepped to the side, watching as the Kappi who closely trailed her heels whipped past. He dodged the first few lines of wires, slipping in between the small openings, but as he crossed the halfway line, Asha knew his broad shoulders wouldn't make it. She seized her chance and sprinted after him.

Just as she was gaining ground, carefully twisting her body between the lines of electricity, that was when his scream ripped through her ears. She snapped her head up, watching as the officer, caught between two wires, locked up, the electricity pulsing through his veins, refusing to release him from its grasp. He screamed and screamed. Until there was no life left in him, no voice left to carry across the wind. And as she approached the Kappi, his body fell to the ground, skin singed off from where the wires had wrapped around him.

She avoided touching him, fearful of any other wires possibly still attached, and seized the gap his fried body had opened for her to slip through.

She pressed through the rest of the frame, a wire grazing against her thigh as she threw herself the last two feet. A scream escaped her lips as the jolt of electricity blasted through her leg.

But the pain was gone as quickly as it had come, and she thrust herself into the air and ran for the Wall.

Asha made it to the bottom of the mountainside and glared up at the rock surface. Three stories of gaps and grooves for her to navigate. She gulped down air, taking a moment to glance back and assess where the rest of the candidates were. Three officers were sprinting behind, no further than a half mile away. She took one more gulp of air and forced herself to begin the ascent.

All the time she spent scaling buildings and rooftops in Valhol had prepared her well for the climb. She quickly made her way up the rocks, her footing only slipping once as she hung high up the wall. She dug her nails so deeply into the rock that most of them were cracked and bleeding.

She rushed to the cliff's edge and peered over, down to the murky depths below. Her heart raced faster, and a heat broke out across her body. She took a steadying breath, and her hands began to shake. A figure flashed past her, and she watched as the candidate hurled himself over the ledge to the frigid waters below. Asha took no time to contemplate, and she threw herself off the edge after him, praying his crash into the waves would help break her impact.

As she fell, down, down, down towards the ocean below, she braced for the cold that would rip through her body; and as she neared the water, she drew in one last deep breath before the icy sea swallowed her. The impact was hard when she hit the surface, and the ripping current thrashed and pulled as she fought her way back up. She had to keep moving. The water was cold. So, so cold. Salt poured into the open gash on her arm, stinging as it hit.

As Asha swam, she heard crash after crash of the candidates behind her hitting the water. She didn't let herself look back.

The raging sea pounded into her from every direction as she fought her way across the water, gulping down mouthfuls of seawater as she went. The North Island looked so far away. And as Asha battled, swimming stroke after stroke, the shore never seemed to grow any closer.

Two other candidates passed her along the way, but she did not relent. Her muscles burned, her skin went numb from the icy water, but she did not stop, she did not give in to the fatigue threatening her body and her mind.

And after what felt like hours, or possibly even days, Asha finally made it to the shore, gasping and heaving up seawater onto the sand.

She looked to her left, and twenty yards from the shore, nestled against the towering rock wall, stood The Gated Ladder.

A pile of metal rods was placed next to the obstacle.

She looked skyward, towards the vertical rungs climbing their way to the top of the cliff, looming five stories above. Asha quickly scanned the ground. Lurking just behind a large boulder leaning against the wall was a bush of hibiscus, covered in honeydew. She swiftly grabbed a handful of the plant and brushed it against her palms. Her hands quickly became sticky, and she grabbed the metal rod resting beside the ladder. Her hands welded themselves onto the metal, no chance of slipping off.

Then she began to climb. Rung after rung, she hoisted herself into the sky, pulling herself higher with each jump. Her shoulders and back began to cramp, her muscles burned beneath her dripping shirt. She could hear the clacking of metal against the rungs beneath her, and the sound propelled her faster up the ladder until she threw herself onto the rocky ground above. Her breathing heavy, she let out a long sigh before picking herself up off the ground, her body heavy and strained. She glanced over to the Swaying Vines and saw the two candidates who had passed her on the swim, hanging from the ropes. She wasn't sure where the third officer who had jumped into the water before her was; she didn't care.

She threw her body back into a sprint, surveying the hanging ropes for the quickest path through as she approached. She grabbed onto the two closest vines and swung herself towards the outer edge. As she crept her way along, she gained ground on the two officers in front of her. Just as she was about to pass the Kappi closest to her, his hand reached for the next rope in succession and slipped.

Asha went rigid as his eyes flared wide, then his body tumbled to the earth. She couldn't move, couldn't breathe, as she watched the screaming officer fall fifty feet to his death. She wasn't sure how long she hung there, frozen in the air, before her arms began to cramp and she forced herself to remove her eyes from the lifeless Kappi below. Three more swings and she safely fell onto the grassy edge of an open field. The other officer who had passed her in the ocean was still navigating his way through the last few ropes, seemingly more careful after watching the man next to him plunge to the ground.

Asha did not wait before she sprinted across the grass to the final obstacle. Only fifty logs separated her from victory. As she approached the edge of the Lake, eerie threats beckoned from the waters below.

She jumped onto the first log, making sure her feet hit the center so she could balance herself. Her movements were steady, flawless.

She made it several logs in when she heard heavy breaths from behind. She chanced a look over her shoulder as a menacing officer jumped onto the first log. His eyes were dark, almost feral, and he looked up to meet her gaze.

"You're dead," he growled, his voice darker than night.

Then he pounced, jumping between the spinning logs, each step bringing him closer and closer to where Asha stood. She whipped her body back around and hurled herself forward, moving with the feline grace she had honed so well over the years. Step after step, the Lake's edge came closer.

Four logs away.

Three.

Two.

Just as she was about to jump to meet the final log, Asha felt a hand snatch the back of her collar and throw her from the spinning wood.

Her stomach launched into her throat. The world shifted. A streak of darkness flashed across the sky, and then she plunged into the murky water below.

A rush of splintered ice ripped through her body. She was dragged further and further into the depths of the Lake, and her eyes were met with nothing but endless dark, as if the currents had decided to swallow all the light from above. She thrashed and pulled, using every ounce of strength to claw her way out of the cold, inky blackness. The waters around her shoved and twisted, pushing her in every direction. She kicked and kicked, praying her movements would guide her back to the unseen surface. And as she fought and clobbered against the rippling waves, she heard it. Felt it. A roaring silence that spread over the whipping waters.

And Asha knew she was not alone in the dark, murky depths.

Anselem, saddled atop Kapheria, hovered above the Lake, scanning the still, inky waters. He had seen her fall— no, *shoved*—he had seen her shoved in. A howling gust of wind bit through the air around him. He did not move from the skies as he waited, watching. Several candidates crawled their way across the logs as the moments passed.

The water below sat still, unwavering. A flash of white feathers ripped across the sky, and a moment, later a wrath-filled screech rang through the air.

Anselem did not take his eyes off the black waters below.

She could feel it circling her in the darkness. Taunting her. Waiting until the right moment to pounce. To rip and shred and devour.

So, she let the snake circle. And she waited in the deafening silence. She knew how the game went. She had played it many times.

And while she waited, she found it to be peaceful in the dark. Comfortable. She had spent many days inside her own room of Darkness, and this place felt familiar. Secure.

Because the Darkness she'd known before had become a safe place over time. A place she could go on the days she'd refused to see the sun; on the days when she mended the broken pieces of her soul back together into a shield that blocked out all the light.

Yes, Asha knew Darkness well. But she knew the dim light inside of her still had a story left to tell. It still had one more fight to finish.

So, as the serpent neared, readying to strike, Asha ripped the iron dagger from her waistband and shoved it through its clamping jaws.

Too long.

It had been too long since she went under. Anselem watched the minutes pass as candidate after candidate jumped their way over the logs. Nine officers had run past the spot where she had crashed into the water, swept under by the sinister beings who ruled the tides below. She would be out of air soon, if she wasn't already. The ink on his right arm, just above his Soturi brand, began to burn. He looked up, locking his gaze with the snow-white firebird across the sky, and he swore the phoenix narrowed his eyes. And before he broke his stare, a crash ripped from the waters below. Frozen in the sky, Anselem observed as wet, ash-blonde hair crashed through the Lake's surface.

As soon as her head broke out from the water, Asha filled her burning lungs with air. Gasping and gulping down as many breaths as she could, she managed to grab onto the nearest log before exhaustion took hold. She was tired. So, so tired.

She knew she needed to pull herself up one last time. Needed to only jump a couple more logs and make it to the nearby land, and then she could rest. But all she wanted to do was close her eyes.

Her body ached, her head felt heavy, and a piercing pain throbbed in her forearm. She glanced down to find another long gash set beside the cut she had received earlier in the course, courtesy of the sharp, whipping tail of the Sea Serpent.

She wasn't sure how long she stayed there, wading in the water, clinging to the wooden log.

It could have been minutes. Hours. Days.

She didn't care.

She just needed a moment to rest. Just needed to close her eyes…

"Come on, get up."

Asha's head spun. She felt strong hands tugging up under her arms.

"Get up, let's go."

She cracked open her eyes, and the beaming sunlight burned. Her head was *pounding*.

"Hurry up, we have to move, the others are not far behind."

She could still feel the cold water lapping up around her, and she forced her eyes open all the way and looked up at the voice above.

Damp golden blonde hair fell just above his kind, tired eyes. And his sun-kissed skin looked paler than before. She couldn't remember his name.

Couldn't even remember her own.

"Raynor, move!"

Raynor. That was it. That was her name.

She felt his hands clamp around her forearms as he yanked her onto the log. She let out a piercing cry as pain singed its way up her arm. But before she had time to register, he was hauling her to her feet and holding her steady as they stood.

"Can you make it?"

Asha shook the dizziness from her mind, forcing her eyes to focus.

She nodded once.

"Okay, let's go. The rest of them are catching up."

She didn't turn around, didn't take the time to see how far away the rest of the candidates were, before she leapt to the next log, her companion right behind.

Then, as one, they both jumped from the final long and threw themselves onto the grassy field beyond.

Asha had never loved the feel of grass beneath her feet more than she did in the moment her heels landed on the open field.

All they had left was to run.

The exhaustion threatened to swallow her again, and her feet felt like boulders beneath her legs. But she forced herself to pick them up, one after another, step after step.

And in the quarter mile of the Crucible's final stretch, the Kappi who pulled her from the Lake's trenches never left her side.

Anselem watched from the finish line as Asha and a tall, golden-haired kid crossed over the designated endpoint. She was still gasping for air, but she was alive.

Several more candidates trickled in shortly after, all equally as drained.

He stood to the side of the collecting group of officers and watched as the scene unfolded.

He watched as Asha collected herself, as she shoved back the exhaustion and fatigue. He noticed how she let burning, spine-chilling rage rip through her veins and how she leaned in and whispered something to the golden blonde officer standing beside her. He followed the officer's tawny eyes as they flitted across the field, and he saw how the Kappi leaned in closely to whisper a hushed response. A confirmatory nod was the only sign of her acknowledgement.

And Anselem watched as Asha prowled over to the domineering officer leaning against a nearby pine.

The Kappi's dark eyes were wild—savage—as she approached, and disgust was plastered across his harsh face.

The full group of officers gathered went silent as they witnessed the developing situation.

Asha reached into her waistband, grabbing whatever was hidden beneath her jacket.

The Kappi standing against the tree reached towards his

own belt, but he was too slow, and Asha chucked the hidden object at his feet before he had time to pull a weapon.

The officer went rigid, wrath filling his onyx eyes.

Asha's voice carried through the square, laced with pure, unrestrained venom.

"You're going to have to try a little harder than that if you want to kill me, Moros."

She looked him up and down once, as if assessing an unworthy opponent, before she turned away, heading back across the field.

"Bitch," he spat back, his voice low and threatening.

She stopped her steps and turned to look over her shoulder at him. Then she smiled, a grin so wicked, Anselem knew it would send most men running. "Next time you want a godsflaming souvenir, go get it yourself." Then she turned back around and sauntered across the grass.

Anselem, along with every Kappi soldier and every Soturi warrior who was gathered in the field, turned to see what Asha had left resting at Moros's feet.

Lying in front of the Kappi's boots was the severed tail of the Lake's Sea Serpent.

A life debt. Asha owed the Greystone kid a life debt. She remembered his name once the pounding in her head had finally subsided. Once the world stopped spinning and the ringing in her ears had calmed.

She didn't know how many made it through the Crucible. She didn't care.

Her body ached. Her muscles throbbed. Her throat burned.

She barely heard the Major mumbling about the next day's reporting instructions, barely remembered the first half of her walk back to the Main Island.

Everything felt so heavy. Her feet, her head, her eyelids.

All she wanted to do was lie down. Rest.

She sat against a nearby rock, taking a moment before she forced her feet to continue carrying her to her room.

A cool, gentle breeze caressed her cheek. She heard a fluttering of wings a moment before the snow-white feathers landed on the grass beside her.

She offered a soft smile, the greatest response she could muster.

Uriel gently nuzzled into her side. She pulled her wrapped arm up to his face and brushed her hand against his face. He let out a huffed breath in her palm.

He opened his eyes, lined with a single tear, and stared down at her arm.

"I'm okay," she said to him. He only huffed again in response. She smiled gently.

"Fine." She unwrapped her arm, wincing at the pain shooting through her. The gash was bad. And the inky water from the Lake had made it worse.

Asha didn't want to know what other vile creatures were lurking in the waters to have caused the Lake to turn such a deathly color, but she knew that whatever was in it was likely to cause infection.

Uriel bent down and leaned his face towards her arm. The single tear from his eye fell straight onto the gash in her forearm.

The relief was instant. Asha let out a sigh as she watched the firebird's tears heal her wound.

A small wave of magic rippled through her body, easing the aches and mending her wounds. The cut from the barbed wire healed quickly, leaving no trace of the ripped skin. But even with Uriel's tears, the wound beside it, the one she had received from the thrashing tail of the Lake's serpent, left behind a deep, silver scar that almost seemed to glow.

"Thank you," she breathed, as she softly rubbed the top of his head.

He curled up beside her, and they stayed like that for a long while, content to detach from the world around them until the sun began to set on the horizon and she ushered him back to the Aviary. She shuffled her way back to her room, exhaustion still creeping into her newly mended body, and when she crossed through the door, her head barely hit the pillow before she let the darkness of sleep claim her.

CHAPTER FOUR

Bardick's voice grated down Anselem's spine as the Major snidely welcomed the officers gathered on the field. "Good morning, candidates. I'm glad to see everyone's bright and shining faces this morning." A jeering smile was fastened on his face.

Anselem scanned the crowd. The officers all looked war-torn and ragged, as if the night had provided no rest.

"This morning, you will participate in the final portion of the Soturi Initiation Rite."

Anselem threw another glance across the throng of officers collected—only thirty had survived the Crucible.

The Major continued his commentary, "The late Soturi, Daedalus Minos, designed the Maze nearly two hundred years ago, and the event has been implemented as a portion of our Initiation Rite ever since." The Major motioned to the large stone labyrinth behind him, winding its way down the entirety of the small sliver of land jutting out from the Main

Island.

"The goal of the event is simple: Be the first to make it through the winding corridors and pull the Golden Lever.

"Momentarily, each of you will be placed inside the Maze. Once everyone has been positioned inside the walls, the bells will chime, and the clock will begin. Every quarter hour, another set of bells will chime. You will have one hour to navigate your way through the Maze and pull the Golden Lever in the center. Whomever pulls the lever first will be declared the winner of the trial and will be worthy of the prize that accompanies it. The winner will then be immediately transported out of the Maze. Those of you who do not make it to the center will remain in the Maze until you find an exit, or the time runs out." A wicked grin stretched across the Major's face as he uttered the final sentence.

Anselem wondered if the officers understood his vile grin was courtesy of the twisted pleasure he experienced in knowing no exits existed. Daedalus had designed the labyrinth to ensure it was impossible to find a way out once inside. The only hope a participant had of surviving was to either find the lever and be transported out or hold on long enough for the clock to stop as they uncovered various ways to escape the monsters prowling inside.

Anselem chose the latter of the options during his own Initiation Rite. Inside the labyrinth of endless twists and turns, passageways and corridors spiraling in every direction, it was too easy to get lost. Too difficult to find his way through.

The Maze had been birthed from chaos and confusion, and over time, mystery and challenge had seeded their ways into the walls as well. Every step a candidate took could lead to a new discovery or send them down a path towards impending death. Anselem attempted to navigate the labyrinth when the bells first chimed, but disorientation quickly set in, and turn after turn began to blur together, until he gave up any semblance of hope for finding the center. Instead, he focused on surviving the ripping claws and the severing teeth of the beasts lurking within.

His only saving grace was luck. He had managed to last the entire hour without running into the Minotaur—the immortal beast rumored to belong to the Maze, forever imprisoned by the labyrinth's walls. The creature was subjected to a life of confinement, forced to hunt down the soldiers to feed its insatiable hunger for human flesh. He was not sure he would have made it out alive if he had encountered the beast.

Asha glanced behind the Major, towards the stone walls towering above him, stretching more than thirty feet into the air. The granite rocks, bare and non-scalable, looked like an inescapable prison. She gazed up at the overcast sky and saw the impending storm looming over the Gulf of Ahti, stalking its way towards the Base. A single drop of rain fell against her cheek.

One hour. She just needed to survive one hour in the complex labyrinth of tunnels and chambers.

"Captain Oran, will you please come to the front?" A short gentleman, donning a light gray uniform of the Amarok warriors, walked to the Major's side. Bardick nodded towards the captain.

Oran turned to the crowd and sent a glowing shield of gold light towards the warriors in attendance. The warm light wrapped around each of the instructors standing in the field. The candidates were left exposed. Asha's stomach dropped.

A second gentleman, wearing the pale blue robes of the Rapha—the Perseisian healers stationed in the East Wing of the Administration building, who worked with tonics, powders, and elixirs—ambled to the other side of Major Bardick. A metallic taste filled Asha's mouth as the Rapha pulled a vial from his pocket.

A vicious grin spread over the Major's face. "Good luck," he chimed, and the healer pulled the top from the vial and released the powder over the group of candidates.

Asha tried to hold her breath, to wait for the wind to drag the particles away, but an unseen magic wrapped the substance in the air around the officers until they had no choice but to inhale the pale blue dust.

Her insides felt like they had been replaced by some kind of dark hole, and nausea crept from her abdomen to her head. A shiver ripped through her body as her memory began to fade away, and then the whole world went black.

Asha's head was throbbing. Her vision was blurred, and she staggered side-to-side as she rose to her feet, attempting to shake off the sleeping powder. The world was spinning, and a steady rain began to fall from the open sky above as she took in her surroundings. Towering granite rocks closed around three sides, and a long, ominous passage stretched before her.

She was completely alone.

Her palms went clammy, and her heart thudded against her ribs. The bells chimed, and the time began to tick. Sweat dripped down Asha's spine, and she shivered.

The surrounding air was musty, filled with mist, and it held a strange, eerie essence that belonged to another world.

The path looming before her looked entirely featureless, with blank walks and properly elusive landmarks. She heard no other candidates, only the scraping of large claws against the stone floor and the distant groans of beasts she prayed she would not encounter.

She reached for her waistband and let out a relieved sigh. They had not taken her blades. She tried to steady her jagged breath, tried to ease her racing heart and mind.

She kept her eyes on the corridor before her as she whispered, *"I am a master of my fear. I have power beyond measure. I am unbreakable."*

She swore a malicious spirit, lingering in the shadows ahead, laughed in response.

Against every instinct, Asha stepped forward and headed deeper into the Maze.

The decaying air provided the perfect abode for the lurking beasts who worshiped the darkness rather than the light. She came to the first intersection, and to her right rose another dead end. In each of the corners, tucked inside the dense shadows, gossamer webs shimmered like meshed steel dipped in silver. Hundreds of tiny, beady eyes, blazing with hunger, were scattered throughout the strings. Asha quickly turned to the left, leaving behind the spiraling webs, and headed down the passage.

The overcast sky made the dim corridors appear even darker, and the misty air weakened her ability to see too far ahead. But she could hear every scrape, every groan, and every step of the beasts stalking her from the shadows. She could see the glowing eyes through the mist that disappeared as she approached. Hungry predators assessing their prey, with the hope of dining on flesh and blood. She did not stop her steps as sweat continued to run down her back. As she wound her way through the stone halls, she heard occasional growls from far-off distances, followed by human screams. She did not stop to think about what was unfolding within the other open halls.

She came to another long, stretching corridor, careful to look in every direction for any impending threats, and as she made it halfway down the stretch, she barely saw the pitfall trap in front of her before she almost fell in. She peered down into the hole, the drop nearly fifteen feet below, and saw the metal spikes jutting out from the ground. Even through the mist, she could see the impaled candidate who had fallen to his death. The blood drained from her face.

She gathered herself and studied the ground around the trap, assessing what the mechanical trigger looked like and how to avoid setting off any others.

She took a moment to gauge the distance across the gap in the stone floor. It was only a couple of feet wide. Asha took a few steps backward, and with a running start, she leapt over the trap and continued through the Maze.

She wound her way through more corridors and passages, working her way through dead ends and wrong directions, and with each nerve-wracking step, Asha slowly crawled closer to the center of the Maze. She wiggled her way around a few weight-triggered traps and scarcely managed to avoid a pool of quicksand that she almost tumbled into after jumping over one of the mechanical triggers.

The second set of bells chimed.

Forty-five more minutes.

She continued her slow-paced walk, and the smoky mist grew so thick, the next step in front of her was nearly imperceptible. As she turned another corner, she heard the mechanical *click* of the platform beneath her.

Her heart sank.

Before she had time to move, the swinging poles collapsed in on her, one at her head, the other at her shins. She barely had time to process the oscillating metal spikes before she reacted, ducking the top part of her body to avoid the barbed pole plunging into her throat. The pole at her shin collided with her left leg, and the spike tore straight through the flesh. A blood-curdling scream escaped her lips as razor-sharp pain ripped through her calf. She felt the warm rush of blood as it poured down her leg. She couldn't breathe. Sharp needles blossomed from the wound and expanded up her leg.

Her ears rang, and then the world went quiet.

She closed her eyes and focused on breathing. She couldn't pass out; there were too many prowling beasts waiting to pick her off and finish the job the undulating poles hadn't managed to accomplish.

She took another breath and opened her eyes. She looked down and saw the dark blood still pouring out. She needed to put pressure on it. Now.

She ripped off the bottom part of her shirt and stuffed it into her mouth. She took one more deep breath through her nose, sent a prayer up to the gods of old, and ripped her leg from the spike. Another guttural scream escaped from her throat, scantly muffled by the fabric stuffed in her mouth. She paused for only a moment before removing the shirt from her mouth and tying it around the wound. As she pulled it tight, a few tears escaped from her eyes. She quickly wiped them away, clearing the blur of her vision, and pulled her leathers back over the makeshift wrap. She looked ahead, still unable to see past the misty haze, and began a slow shuffle, stifling the raw sobs that collected in her throat.

She could hardly put any pressure on the limb, and every step sent searing pain through her body. She limped her way around the next turn, and the mist subsided. She hobbled only a few more steps before she halted, seeing a large, shadowy figure lurking in the middle of the corridor.

She turned her body to head back, unsure of how well she would fare in a fight in her current state, when a bewitching voice drifted towards her.

"For permission to pass, I only ask for you to answer my questions."

The beast took a step forward, out of the shadows and into the dim light. The first thing Asha noticed was the creature's beautiful face. Its head bore a resemblance to that of a stunning woman, with alluring gold eyes, fair skin, and onyx hair. Its arms were replaced with lavish ebony wings that flowed down into the haunches of a black lion. Its voice was enchanting, but Asha caught the promise of treachery and mercilessness hidden within the tone.

A spidery smile stretched across the creature's lips.

Asha did not speak but instead shook her head and moved towards the opposing direction, her leg throbbing beneath her leathers.

The creature called after her again, stopping her retreat.

"I will even include a prize along with permission to pass," it crooned. It gestured with its head to the shadow-covered corner. Through the darkness, Asha could faintly make out a shining gold bow tucked into the sphinx's alcove. The bow hailed from the tales of old, the same ones she had read countless times as a child. The silver string, the golden limbs, and the three gold-tipped arrows resting beneath it looked as if they had been plucked directly out of the pages of the Book of Legends itself.

Windrunner—The Messenger of Mourning.

"How many questions?" Asha asked, still eyeing the bow she knew was essential for surviving the remaining time.

"Three questions. One to pass, one for the treasure you seek, and one to satisfy my own pleasure." Another black-hearted smile appeared on its ruby lips.

Asha contemplated her choices. She knew it was stupid to make deals with devils, but she also knew she needed the bow to survive the remainder of her time in the imprisoning Hells of the Maze. Plus, she realized, the path behind the monster was the only way towards the center.

When she first awoke, Asha had decided to simply survive, bide her time until the clock ran out, but with each passing moment, more blood continued seeping from her calf, and she was not sure her body would be able to hold out until the final chimes.

"I accept."

The sphinx's eyes darkened with delight. Asha limped closer to the beast and slid her hand underneath her jacket, palming the iron dagger hidden in her waistband.

The creature's voice sang as it asked the first question: "What is always old, sometimes new; never sad, occasionally blue; never empty, sometimes full; never pushes, always pulls?"

Asha contemplated the answer for a moment. Then another. She remembered hearing a similar riddle from her mother when she was younger. She pulled the story from her mind, trying to recall the answer within the tale. She remembered her mother telling her and Math a spooky story about a wolf in the Iron Mountains, lurking through forests and hiding in the mountainside caves until it grew big and strong. She remembered her mother telling them the tale to keep them from wandering out into the surrounding forests of Valhol at night, because she and her brother had wanted to go out during the full—

"The moon," Asha replied.

The beast only pursed its lips, a pressed frown appearing on its charming face. The sphinx wasted no time before diving into the next question.

"There are two sisters; one gives birth to the other, who in turn gives birth to the first. Who are they?"

Sweat beaded on Asha's brow. She searched through her mind, ran through her experiences and knowledge—anything that would help. The creature's frown upturned into a wickedly delighted grin as it watched Asha struggle to find the answer.

The third set of chimes sounded in the distance, echoing off the towering stone walls.

Thirty minutes remained. Asha's leg throbbed as she readjusted her weight, trying to keep as much pressure off the injury as possible. She returned her focus to the riddle.

She tried to recall the other tales her mother had shared with her as a child, fables she'd been read from the Book of Legends. She even combed her mind for any stories she had heard during her training in Valhol, circled around late-night fires under the cover of the stars. Images of the Valhollian Fort flashed in her head. She recalled memories of her pious classmates and how, on the nights when the group would gather to swap stories and share ale, the devout soldiers would bow their heads and send prayers up to Nyx, the Goddess of the Night, whenever the sun set over the horizon and darkness encircled the group. As the prayers she had heard so many evenings ran through her mind, she was reminded of Nyx's sister, Hemera, the Goddess of Day, and the many prayers she'd heard in the early hours of the morning, when the sun would rise, and dawn would break. A wide smile broke across Asha's face. *Night turns to day, and day into night; two sisters, forever the deliverers of one another.*

"Night and Day."

A flash of rage and disappointment flared across the sphinx's face as it realized there was only one question remaining before it lost its bargain. But the creature's rage only lasted for a fractional moment before it was replaced with a nefarious grin, knowing deep down Asha would never be able to guess the answer to the final riddle.

"I am felt but never seen, I'm not a whisper but I can scream. In my presence, they will never dream. What am I?"

Asha was screwed. Absolutely and unequivocally screwed. She had no inkling, not even a sliver of a hint, as to what the answer could be. She racked her brain for any possible reply but came up empty. Her hand grasped the dagger in her waistband tighter, as she already knew she would not be walking away without a fight.

"Don't worry, child. It's not as dark a fate as it seems." A spidery smile crawled on the creature's face.

That was when it hit her, like a tidal wave—smacking into Asha like the weight of a thousand oceans. The sphinx did not even recognize its mistake, and Asha nearly laughed at her own inability to see the answer right away, for it was a force she had known for a long time. A fate of her own that had been sealed for many moons, she was merely waiting to meet it.

The beast laughed and took a step forward, closing the space between them.

"Death."

The creature halted its forward steps, embers of rage burning in its eyes, and Asha knew she had won.

A proud smile broke across her face, but quickly turned to a wincing grimace as she hobbled over to the golden bow. When her hands touched the limbs, a force trembled through her, as if the weapon had come alive once again from an eternal sleep.

"I suppose I will be on my way with this," she said, picking up the arrows alongside the bow. The creature's glare burned holes into Asha's face, but she did not stop moving.

"You cannot run from destiny. You will be ours."

She did not look back at the creature as she slung the bow onto her back and continued her hobbling limp down the rest of the corridor, slowly inching her way closer to the center.

Anselem had been standing in the downpour for half an hour, and two bodies had already been dragged out from the Maze. One impaled by shiny metal spikes, the other looking as if his blood had been completely sucked dry, his skin paler than the snowcapped tops of the Iron Mountains.

Anselem glanced over at the Major. He was standing across the field with a sly look upon his face as he amusingly observed the bodies being lifted onto the transport boards. His neatly polished appearance seemed less maintained, and in the falling rain, his dripping snow-white hair fell sloppily in front of his eyes; or perhaps his distasteful guise was simply a result of the unsavory enjoyment he displayed as dead soldiers were hauled away after a gruesome end.

The Major's gaze flicked up and met Anselem's. It took every ounce of training Anselem had ever experienced to keep his face fixed in the neutral expression he always wore. Unrelenting rage charged through his body. As their eyes met, Major Bardick took a step forward, slithering his way across the field. With each pace bringing Bardick closer, Anselem pushed the fiery temper raging inside him down until it lurked so deep, only a few smoky embers were able to reach the surface.

"Major," he nodded.

"How are you faring, *lieutenant*?" The slippery smile smeared on his face made Anselem want to rip it off, right along with the disdainful tone attached to his words.

"Fine," he answered. Anselem had purposefully refrained from attaching a rank to the response; he believed no title was fit for the Major other than the Snake—the personal Vice of the Satrap of Sveaborg province.

The Vices were the ruthless enforcers of the Satrap's authority—personally selected by each Headship.

The Satraps hardly ever deigned to mingle with the soldiers and citizens of the Kingdom, and due to their lack of desire to be deeply embedded in the issues of their provinces, the Council had created positions of power that allowed the Headships to pass along their rule to the Leadership members who fell beneath them—the Vices.

Anselem had only seen Satrap Astaroth, the governing Headship of Sveaborg, once in his time at the Base.

The seven Vices, one belonging to each Satrap, had all earned various ill-famed monikers.

Bardick—the notorious Vice of Sveaborg province—was called the Snake.

Soren Thane, the Vice of Valhol, had received the title of the Spear, and Aloysius Rook, the Elysian Vice, claimed the Skull.

Anselem did not know the given names of the other region's Vices, but he had learned of their titles long ago.

The Vice of Takama earned the renowned label of the Sparrow—the lone female of the enforcers.

Lorca housed one of Leadership's most prized enforcers—the Star; and the Midlands, the region composed of the smaller villages in the heart of Perseis, was watched over by the Scythe.

The final province of Brienza—headed by King Balthasar's enforcer—was handled by the Shifter.

The Vices were hand-selected by their commanding Satrap from all branches, and the Headships had ensured their appointments consisted solely of the rarest gifted warriors— those who possessed the scarcest forms of magic. Those with powers granted not by the Dominions, but by the Virtues and the Thrones.

Bardick's eyes narrowed the slightest bit, clearly picking up on the lack of attributed rank. Anselem reminded himself of his purpose, of the role he had to play, and forced a smile to his mouth, coerced his tone into wielding an air of respect, "And you, sir?"

The darkness in Bardick's eyes abated.

"Very well. It looks like it will be a successful academy."

Anselem nodded, not trusting his voice. His emerald eyes dipped down to the silver pin fastened on the Major's collar.

A dark, looming eye was etched onto the small metal— the pin of the Vices. The Infinite Eyes of the Council.

Bardick turned his serpentine eyes towards Anselem. "I would like for you to keep a close eye on the Raynor girl. We don't need any more incidents like a few years ago."

The rage inside him blazed brighter, threatening to combust. Anselem remained even-faced, no sign of the exploding thundering within, and nodded once more at the Major's words.

Another serpentine smile crossed the Snake's mouth. "You always have been such a devoted warrior."

And with those departing words, the Major turned and headed back across the field. As he slithered off, Anselem genuinely considered shoving his knife through the Snake's neck.

❖ ❖ ❖

Winding along the corridors, her limp growing greater with each painful step, Asha dodged trap after trap, working her way further into the Maze.

That was when she heard it—the unnerving silence that poured over the shadow-veiled critters belonging to the Maze. She quickly moved into a nearby fissure, pressing herself up into a corner crevice as quietly as she could. A moment later, the creature turned down her corridor, a loud, huffing exhale of breath escaping its nostrils.

From a distance, she could only see the silhouette of the beast, but from its prowling stalk, she knew exactly what it was.

It skulked down the passageway, each step bringing the predator closer to where Asha hid.

Thirty feet away.

Twenty.

Ten.

Asha held her breath, but her heart thundered so loudly in her chest, she wondered how the beast could not hear it.

It paused just before the crack within the stones, the small space in which Asha had shoved herself, but it did not turn towards where she was hidden. The creature instead took in a deep inhale, breathing in the rancid air of the murky, mist-filled stones, and stared towards the end of the corridor.

The beast's frame towered nearly ten feet high, and in the dim light of the Maze, Asha was able to catch a shadowed glimpse of the monster. A sinewy male form shaped the lower half of the creature's figure, but fixed atop the body was the head of a feral bull with blood red eyes that hungered for flesh. Asha willed her body to remain still, but a steady drip of warm blood continued to leak from her calf. The beast took another long whiff of the stifling air.

Asha closed her eyes and slid her hand over her mouth to quiet her breath. She heard near-silent steps against the stone, and when she opened her eyes once again, the Minotaur had disappeared down the corridor.

Asha sat motionless for several moments, unsure how far away the beast had traveled, until the fourth set of bells chimed.

Slowly, she peered out from the crevice. The corridor was clear in both directions. She slid out from the fissure and began her limping walk once again. Her head turned light, and her vision was beginning to blur. The dribbling of blood from her leg started to slow, and she knew she was losing too much blood.

Turn after turn, she forced herself to keep moving, but each step became harder and seemed more impossible than the last. Bile rose in her throat, and nausea rolled in her stomach, but she continued pressing on towards the center.

She had to be getting close. The Minotaur did not lurk in the outer parts of the Maze, but she was unsure if her body would hold on long enough to make it to the lever.

And she didn't know what she would do if she finally made it to the lever but discovered she had not been the first to arrive. She pushed the thought from her mind and continued pressing on, each step more gut-wrenching than the last.

She turned what felt like the hundredth corner, and she saw him.

Jeremiah.

He turned the corner at the opposite end of the corridor a moment after she rounded her own. There was no more than fifty yards between them, but neither of them spoke, fearful of attracting any nearby predators. Asha nodded towards him as he met her gaze, but as Jeremiah took a step forward, his eyes splayed wide.

Within a fraction of a second, his feet were swept out from under him. Asha had no time to warn him; the scream only escaped from her lips after the net whipped him into the air above.

She watched as he dangled from the netting fifteen feet in the air, twisting and thrashing as he attempted to free himself. Asha rushed over to him, limping with each step as piercing shards shot up her leg.

"Do you have a knife?" she called up to him.

"No, I lost it earlier when I nearly fell into a spiked pit."

Shit.

The air around them went still, and the unnerving silence once again drifted over the hidden critters in the shadows. A shiver ran down Asha's spine.

She knew she only had moments to spare before the beast emerged.

"Listen to me," she whispered to Jeremiah, "I am going to toss my knife up to you. You need to cut your way through the netting and climb down. I will hold it off as long as I can, but you need to be quick."

"Hold what off?" Jeremiah's eyes went wide with confusion and fear.

She did not take the time to respond as she unfastened the sheathed Elysian dagger from her waistband and tossed it into the air. She pulled the bow from her back and nocked a golden arrow into the string. She could hear the severing blade as Jeremiah cut string after string of the thick ropes. She kept her eyes focused down the corridor.

Then the beast emerged from the swirling shadows at the end of the passageway. Asha heard the momentary pause of Jeremiah's blade, followed by a snapping of threads as the sawing picked back up. The pace was more hurried than before, filled with a frightful urgency.

The beast let out a savage bellow and took a step towards them. Asha raised her bow, the arrow aimed at the creature's throat.

She knew the gold would not kill the beast, but she hoped the arrow would maim it long enough to buy them some time. And if it came down to it, she still had the iron dagger fastened on her belt. She knew she wouldn't survive a fight with the creature, but she would certainly go down swinging—and she'd be damned if she didn't take the beast back to the Hells with her.

The Minotaur watched Asha as she raised the arrow, rage flashing in its dead eyes. It let out a single, shattering roar, and then it charged.

She heard the crash of flesh against stone behind her, but her eyes did not move from the beast as it surged closer. She sent the first arrow soaring for its throat, but the otherworldly creature had preternatural speed, and it dodged to the side, the arrow lodging into its shoulder. The beast's only indication of pain was a lurid grunt, but it continued barreling towards the warriors. Before the first arrow struck, Asha already had the second nocked in place. She felt Jeremiah now beside her, heard his labored breathing alongside her own. She took a deep breath as the beast plowed closer. But she waited. She had one shot.

Fifteen yards away.

Ten.

And when the Minotaur crossed the imaginary line Asha had drawn in her head, so close she could almost reach out and touch it, she let her arrow fly.

Straight into the left eye of the Maze's beast.

It fell before their feet, but Asha wasted no time as she grabbed Jeremiah's arm and hurled the two of them down the final corridor.

The world was spinning, but she fought against the darkness that crept into her vision. She could feel Jeremiah's arm underneath her arm, half-dragging her down the stone passage.

They turned the last corner, flying through the opening, and there it was—the Golden Lever.

Asha let out a sob of relief as she beheld the center's promise of escape.

She took one limping step forward, Jeremiah right by her side to steady her, and then she halted. She could feel Jeremiah's eyes on her, trying to read her face, before he followed her gaze across the center's opening.

At the opposite side, standing in the second opening to the Maze's center, was Moros.

Asha nocked the last golden arrow into her bow. Her hands were shaking. She had lost too much blood. But she knew from this distance, with her leg, she would never out-run him.

The world spun as she raised the bow. She could see Moros's eyes darken as he took off running. He was only twenty yards away from the lever.

She aimed in, her eyes blurring.

Ten yards.

She aimed for the center of his chest, giving herself the largest space for error as the world tilted, and released. The arrow sang through the air, and when it impacted, she watched Moros fall to the ground, a wail breaking from his mouth as he clutched his shoulder.

She had hit, but barely.

"Go!" Jeremiah yelled to her.

She didn't wait for Moros to get up as she ran, half-limping, towards the lever. It felt like burning splinters were racing up her leg and ripping through her entire body.

Step after step, the darkness threatened to close in, but she pushed forward, refusing to stop.

From the corner of her darkening eyes, she saw Moros crawling to his feet. She pushed herself faster.

Only ten more yards.

Five.

The darkness crashed around her, and she leapt onto the center platform, grasping the Golden Lever as she fell. She pulled it down, and then her body felt as if it were propelled through space and time.

Lying on the ground, she looked up and saw she was back on the field outside the Maze. Soturi instructors and Rapha rushed towards her. The downpour of rain falling against Asha's face quickly began to abate, and moments after she landed in the grassy field, the final chimes of the bells sounded.

And then the darkness claimed her.

Shit. Shit. *Shit.*

Anselem stood in the infirmary next to Asha's bed as the Rapha worked to heal the gaping wound on her leg. The wing was divided into dozens of individual rooms, each holding a single bed, covered in cream sheets. The walls and ceiling were clean, free of any decorative adornments, save for the three luminos hung inside the room. A larger light was fixed in the center of the high wooden ceiling, enclosed inside gold-plated rods. The two others sat on each side of the blanched oak door that led into the lengthy, white stone hallway. The only marks of color that smeared the room were the pale, dusty-blue curtains hung on each side of the corner window. The blue hue was the same as the robes worn by the Rapha. Anselem glanced again at the bed, staring down at the unconscious warrior lying upon it. Her skin was so pale; he knew she had lost too much blood.

What the Hells happened in there? he thought.

Anselem had seen the golden bow clenched in her hand as she flickered from inside the Maze and into the open field. With the iron bands still attached to her arms, he knew the flickering had been on account of pulling the Golden Lever and not by her own magic. The gift of flickering, the ability to jump through small spaces of time, was an ability gifted to very few magic wielders, and among the limited number of those who had been granted the skill, the gift could not be used without greatly draining the wielder's well of power. Anselem had only ever met one warrior with the gift.

His brow furrowed as questions began swimming through his mind. She had won, that much he'd been able to gather, but what happened while she was inside? And where were the arrows that he assumed accompanied the bow she'd dragged out with her?

He needed answers.

The Rapha glanced over at Anselem, and her soft voice filled the room, "She will not be up for several hours while the sedative wears off. I will send for you if anything changes, Lieutenant." Anselem glanced at the clock and turned back to the healer. He nodded once and then marched through the door, heading back to the fields outside of The Minos Maze.

As he approached the gathered group of people, Anselem scanned the crowd for the tall, golden blonde officer. He found the Kappi standing off to the side of the group, his tawny eyes looking dead and defeated.

"You," he said, pointing towards the officer. The Kappi looked up at him and straightened a bit, but no light entered his eyes. "Come with me." Anselem turned around and did not wait to make sure the soldier followed. He crossed the field, heading towards the base of the mountain overlooking the Maze. He turned around to face the trailing officer.

"What is your name?"

"Jeremiah Greystone," he replied, his voice sounding as dead as his eyes looked. Anselem looked at the officer, his lightly sun-kissed skin was cut and bruised, his fighting leathers looked disheveled and ripped. Anselem knew the officer had just escaped the Hells.

He softened his tone as he asked, "What happened?"

Jeremiah's eyes lifted, and his brow crinkled. "What do you mean?"

"I know something happened in there, something... unusual." Anselem hated the word. Hated that he had to play the stupid games and politics. Horrid. Despicable. Heinous. All words better fit to describe the outrageous event Leadership had sent the candidates through.

"I think she killed it," Jeremiah replied.

There is no way in the Seven Hells...

"Killed what?" Anselem asked, knowing plenty of vile beasts lurked within the stone walls.

Jeremiah reached behind his back and pulled out a golden arrow. It matched the bow Asha had been clutching when she flickered out.

"This was the only one I could grab as we ran past it," his voice grew quiet, just barely above a whisper, "I think she killed the Maze Beast." Jeremiah handed Anselem a gold-tipped arrow covered in dark, black blood.

"Can you make sure that gets to her? ...Lieutenant." He tacked the rank onto the end of his sentence, as if it were an afterthought, and he realized he was speaking to a commanding officer.

Anselem only nodded, tucking the arrow behind his back to secure it in place. He attached it to the spot where one of his two war-ravaged swords was ordinarily strapped. It was not looked upon kindly for him to don the twin blades when he was on Base as an instructor, and Anselem appeased Leadership by occasionally honoring the suggestion.

He said nothing else and simply motioned his hand over to the group on the field, an invitation for Jeremiah to go and join the others.

Jeremiah recognized the dismissal and nodded once before turning to head towards the candidates.

He walked merely three steps before he turned back, worry flooding in his eyes, and asked, "Will she be okay?"

Anselem nodded. "The healers say she got out just in time. A minute longer and even phoenix tears would not have been able to heal her."

Jeremiah nodded his head, more to himself than to Anselem, and looked back to the lieutenant, offering a small smile. "Good," he said. And before he turned back to continue his exit, he added, "She saved my life in there. And I may not know her well, but I truly don't think there is a single candidate here who deserves the chance to become a Soturi more than her." He didn't wait for a response before he turned and walked back to the grassy field below.

Anselem stared after him as a lump rose in his throat. He forced it down as he marched back towards the East Wing.

A constant, dull ache throbbed in Asha's head as she clawed her way out of the suffocating darkness. She waited a moment before opening her eyes, trying to take in where she was and recall what had happened before she revealed her consciousness. Flashes of stone passageways raced through her mind. *Had it all been a terrible dream?* A shooting pain splintered up her leg. *Nope, not a dream.*

She slowly opened her eyes. The dim luminos in the room were almost too bright as the dull pain in her head began to slightly sharpen while her sight adjusted to the light. Her vision was blurred as she forced herself from the groggy darkness and tried to focus.

She first looked over at the window and could see that the sky outside had gone dark, the moonlight the only source of illumination.

How long had she been out? Asha pulled her gaze from the window and scanned the rest of the room until she reached the corner and went stiff. Sitting within the shadows, staring at her with unnatural stillness, was Eros. His striking features looked dulled, tired, as if he had sat there motionless for many hours. A flare of rage began to boil inside her, but it was quickly extinguished by the exhaustion still looming over her. She watched as he studied her for a moment, then he leaned forward in the chair.

"Eight hours," he said. Her brow furrowed.

"I'm assuming you were wondering how long you've been in here—it's been eight hours."

Had he been sitting there for eight hours? She did not reply. Her gaze drifted down to her leg, wrapped in white bandages.

"They were able to heal it. Fully." She could still feel the shadow of pain ripping through her calf. Eros rose to his feet and took a step towards her bed. She whipped her eyes over to him, pinning him in place with a glare. His eyes slightly widened, and a flicker of mischief danced across the seas of green.

"I just came to personally congratulate you." A smirk pulled at the corners of his lips. "This year's winner of The Minos Maze. How impressive."

Asha's eyes narrowed at his mocking tone. She reached for the dagger in her waist belt, but her hands were met with air.

A low, deriding laugh escaped from Eros. He nodded his head towards the metal hook beside the door. "Looking for those?" Asha followed his gaze and saw her leather belt, daggers sheathed in the front, hanging beside the door. She dragged her glare back to his face. He flashed another captivating smile. "Like I said, I am here to congratulate you. It seemed that Leadership believed I would be the best person to deliver the details of your prize."

He did not continue. He was going to make her ask him. Make her speak to him. She'd rather cut out her own tongue. Several moments passed, but all she did was glare at him.

"Are you naturally this much of a pain in the ass, or do you have to try?" She left her face expressionless, but the corner of her mouth threatened to curve up as a small spark of amusement winked through her. He let out an aggravated sigh.

"Your prize for winning the trial is a day of one-on-one training with me each week."

Her emotionless expression faltered, and she knew he could read every feeling that crossed her face.

"No." Her voice sounded so far away from herself. She could not—*would not*—be alone with him. She barely had enough restraint lying on the bed, only half recovered, to keep herself from jumping up to grab the dagger hanging on the wall and thrust it through his neck. Eros must have read every thought racing through her mind as he gruffly cleared his throat and responded, "You *will* be attending. I am expected to help train the winner, and that is what I will do."

She scoffed. "You do have a reputation to uphold after all. I'm sure you wouldn't want to ruin your highly held prestige with our Leadership." She rolled her eyes but caught the flash of irritation that flashed across Eros's ever-composed face.

He took another step closer to her bed and peered down into her eyes. His voice dropped low, into one matching the lethal, frightening warrior she knew him to be, and he snarled, "A little piece of advice—if I were you, I would take every godsflaming chance I could to become better. To learn as much as I could to survive, because one day soon, you're going to need it."

Eros walked out of the room without another word.

Exhaustion began to sweep over Asha, but before she succumbed to the lurking sleep, she glanced over to the corner chair where Eros had been sitting. Placed on the wooden seat was a golden bow and arrow, glinting against the moonlight. A phantom throb shot through her calf, and a splinter of pain blasted up her leg.

She let the endless dark swallow her again.

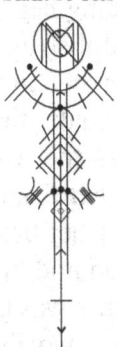

CHAPTER FIVE

The following morning, Major Bardick, standing before the twenty-seven surviving candidates in the main courtyard, read the names of the nine fallen officers. One Valhollian Kappi, Chilion Immer, was among the deceased. Asha shifted on her feet, the phantom pain from the night before was nowhere to be found.

"May their souls be absolved in Judgement," Bardick murmured. Asha knew the Major meant the Final Judgment of Anubis. She recognized most Perseisians feared the God of Death more than any other, and she assumed Bardick was among the masses by his intercession.

The fear was rooted in a desire for Anubis's approval. Most Perseisians worried about the god's punishment in the Afterlife. But Asha had danced with Anubis far too many times to be afraid of his wrath. Her soul was already gone, slaughtered on a doorstep in Valhol many months ago. She knew a place had already been set aside for her in the Underworld, she was just biding her time until Anubis came to collect her body. But, as foolish as it was to hope, part of her still prayed that whenever her time at last ran out, Ianoda might intercede on her behalf; that at Final Judgment, he would erase the dark scars the Angel of Death had carved deep inside her soul, save her from the Seven Hells, and she might once again get to see her brother.

"And may they live on and burn well," the Major concluded. The entire group that was gathered in the yard, Kappi and Soturi alike, raised two fingers to their brows and echoed the expression in unison.

Without missing a beat, Bardick's voice chimed back in, "It is now my privilege to announce the top sixteen candidates of this year's Initiation Rite. Please step to the front as your name is called."

Half hidden by shadows, Eros leaned against one of the pillars behind Bardick, his muscled arms crossed over his chest.

The first name announced was Moros.

Shocker, she thought, hiding the roll of her eyes. She didn't see any signs of a wound from where her arrow had lodged through his shoulder the day before. A soft smile formed on her lips as she recalled the memory.

Major Bardick continued to list off nine more officers—she only recognized two of the names as hailing from Valhol.

As name after name was read from the list, Asha's heart pounded more rapidly in her chest. A bead of sweat slivered down her spine, but she left her face schooled in an expression of calm composure.

The Major looked down once again at the list of names he held in his hands. He raised his eyes back up to the crowd and took in a deep breath.

"Asha Raynor," Bardick bellowed.

Her body went momentarily still. Her heart paused.

She couldn't believe it. She was not positive she had heard him correctly.

Her heart swelled slightly in her chest as she stepped forward to join the selected officers standing on the elevated platform, no limp present.

She always knew, even with the loathing feeling in her bones, even with every odd stacked against her, Asha knew she would find a path through what before was only wilderness. She knew she could be equally brave and careful, propelled forward by not only her own longing to reach her destination, but also the desire to leave a viable way for the other women who would follow. The first woman to be selected for Soturi training.

Asha Akselsen Raynor—Trailblazer.

Jeremiah was called next and when his name was announced, Asha nodded once, and he gave her a wink in reply. As Jeremiah took his place on the platform, the Major stared at him for a moment longer than necessary, as if he had seen him before in another life.

Bardick broke his gaze and proceeded to read through the remaining four names, adding two more Valhollians to the group of sixteen. Asha let out a soft sigh when Rhume Meraki, one of her close friends from Kappi training, made the cut.

"Those who were not selected are expected to report back to your respective Forts immediately." A shuffling of boots and soft, disappointed murmurs filled the air as the unselected officers made for the long corridor leading to the Barracks. Asha and the fifteen other Soturi candidates stood in silence until the last of the Kappi departed the courtyard.

"Congratulations," Major Bardick bellowed, his tone sprightly and bright. "The sixteen of you will have the privilege of participating in this year's training academy. And as you embark upon this new journey, always remember that many warriors enter this house, but few will stay. Leadership wishes each of you the best of luck."

Asha forced herself to hold back another eye roll. The pride she had felt moments ago vanished. *Privilege?* she thought, mentally scoffing at the idea. *They think forcing us to skirt the line of death for the next six months is a privilege?*

As if she didn't already toe the line with Anubis on a regular basis, Asha didn't need more run-ins with the Angel of Death.

But it was all a means to an end, she knew that. She knew the edge the Soturi Mark would give her, the doors it would open while she sought out the truth.

"Captain Kage," the Major called, and a tall man with dark, short-cut hair appeared at his side.

He moved like shadows in the wind. With two long swords strapped against his back and a plethora of knives hooked on his belt, the captain looked like the picturesque embodiment of afflicted pain and torment. But the warrior's gentle, almond-shaped eyes contrasted with the brutal appearance of his weaponry. The sleeves of his uniform were rolled up to his elbows, and Asha caught a glimpse of the remarkable ink marked on his fair skin—the tattoos were only interrupted by a single obsidian bracelet fastened against his wrist. Symbols from the Kochi people stretched from the tips of his fingers all the way up his entire left arm before halting beneath his jawline. The inscriptions were beautiful.

"Will you please inform the other Leaders that they will be expected to attend the Division assignments while I escort these students to the West Wing?"

The captain nodded once before exiting the courtyard. The two golden bars fixed onto each of his shoulders glinted in the morning sunlight.

The sixteen candidates, herded like cattle by Major Bardick, shuffled through the winding colonnades in the direction of the Administration Building. Before they reached the towering oak doors that led into the stone foyer of the building's Central Wing, Major Bardick veered off to the left and escorted the group into the prohibited halls of the West Wing. They twisted and turned down an array of arched hallways, lined with iridescent chandeliers, before coming to the base of a grand, marble staircase. Without pause, Major Bardick climbed the steps and passed through the singular set of gold-plated doors resting at the top.

A small gasp escaped Asha's lips as she followed him into the room. Cream walls, cloaked with golden trim, encircled her. Open windows, outlined with intricate golden designs, wrapped around the room. Each opening joined together into a pointed arch, rimmed at the top with sculpted white marble that had been carved into phoenix wings. Perched above each archway sat a shining statue of a gold phoenix, its wings stretched out high towards the vaulted ceiling. And set before the feet of each golden firebird, lay seven torches filled with burning fire.

The room looked as if it were crafted by the Seven High Gods.

As Asha tore her gaze from the golden wings above, she saw the translucent, glass-like rock shimmering in the center of the marble floor. An infinite, colorless flame burned within the center of the monolith, and a swelling of imbued magic radiated from its core.

The Stone of Gilgal.

The Stone had been brought to Sveaborg nearly two thousand years ago by Elisha Gilgal, one of the first riders chosen by the Odyssey, after he had completed his spiritual journey. For many months, Gilgal had been tested, enduring trial after trial, until the Odyssey deemed his commitment was sufficient. Only after his acceptance did Eloi, the most powerful phoenix of his time, bond with Gilgal.

When the Bonding took place and Gilgal's power was bestowed upon him, the skies shook and the earth quaked as Ianoda, once again, after many millennia, allowed magic to return to the hands of humans. It was the end of the long-existing separation between the peoples and the God of Life; an establishment and reunification with Ianoda; and a renewed spiritual desire and appreciation for the powers he gifted them.

Gilgal, the only Oracle over the ages to be blessed by Ianoda with the gift of prophecy, had been given visions to travel to the island and erect the Stone. With guidance from Ianoda, the Stone was imbued through the fire of Eloi, and in the two thousand years since it had been ignited, the flame had never once gone out.

"The next order of business," the Major uttered, interrupting the group's gaping, "as soon as our Division Leaders join us, will be the assignment of Divisions for each of you." As if listening beyond the doors for the signal, four warriors entered the room. The first to enter was the captain from the courtyard—Kage. Followed by another captain and lieutenant that Asha had never seen. The fourth, and last, to enter through the golden doors was none other than Lieutenant Eros.

Asha swore to herself. She prayed she wouldn't be assigned to his Division.

The Major proceeded to introduce the four Leaders and

their respective Divisions.

Heading the first sector—Destroyer Division—was the new captain, who answered to the name of Balor. His domineering presence and overbearing build seemed to suck the life straight from the room. His russet hair, cut short on the sides, fell just below his brow. The fair skin of his arms was covered in scars, and the knuckles of his hands looked as if they had recently been used to crack someone's skull. His unforgiving, onyx eyes peered down at the sixteen officers like remorse was a foreign word.

The Destroyer Division was notoriously known to be the most cutthroat and unforgiving of sectors. The place where the warriors who were most expected to wreak havoc on their enemies through violence and brutality were assigned. Their vicious and cruel fighting style often had people questioning if their level of savagery was warranted, but their success in battle spoke for itself.

Captain Kage led the second sector—Inquisition Division. Home for the questioners and gainers of information, no matter the cost. These warriors usually ended up in the Interrogation Branch of the Soturi, and although they were often a little twisted in the mind, the Kingdom would never deny the necessity of their skill set.

Leader of the third sector—Tactician Division—was Lieutenant Vivek. His unbound, snow-white hair was cropped at his shoulders, with streaks of black strewn throughout, and a few loose strands fell in front of his wide, gold ringed eyes. His gaze seemed as if it held the answers to every question in the Kingdom. Unlike the other Leaders who had opted for shoulder cut tops, most of his rich, dark-brown skin was covered by long uniform sleeves. Asha figured it was due to the extensive time he spent in the cool, underground record rooms of the Administrative Building.

The Tacticians were the warriors who bore the strength of the mind. Well-versed in strategy, they often became the presiders over battle, arranging numbers and plans of Soturi warriors—complete masters of war design.

The Major introduced the final Leader of sector four—Valorous Division. Those assigned to this section were the valiant, the daring, the brave. These loyal warriors were often the most determined of fighters, maintaining a tenacious appetite for justice and a relentless craving for truth.

Asha stifled a laugh as the description of Valorous Division was explained. *Eros? Valiant?*

She figured the Stone must be broken for the lieutenant to have been assigned to such a sector.

After the Divisions were explained, the Major ordered the officers to form a line before he continued his instructions. "One at a time, you will approach the Stone of Gilgal and place your right hand on top. The Stone will read the intentions of your mind and your heart. A specific assignment may seem right in your own opinion, but the Stone of Gilgal, blessed by the power of Ianoda, will evaluate your motives. Once the Stone has made its choice, the flame within will burn the color of your assigned Division."

One by one, the officers proceeded towards the Stone. And one by one, the Stone issued their assignments.

Before Asha reached the stone, six officers had already been assigned to their Divisions. Two crimson flames ignited for Moros and Fordon, both excitedly assigned to the Destroyer Division. Another two emerald flames burned for the officers assigned to the Tactician Division—Alvis and Feivel. And a single sapphire flame had burned for Oslac, designating him to the Inquisition Division.

No officers had yet been chosen for Valorous.

Asha stepped up to the Stone and placed her palm on the

smooth surface. It was surprisingly cold beneath her fingers, and underneath the chilled stone, buzzing waves of magic rippled to the surface.

A moment passed. Then another.

The flame did not alter, no color seeped inside the steady blaze.

Just as Asha was about to remove her hand, the fire flickered, then the flame burned white.

"Our first Valorous Division," Major Bardick trilled.

Asha's heart dropped. A bittersweet feeling washed over her body as she lifted her eyes to the glaring Leader of her Division.

From the expression on Eros's face, she knew they were both thinking the same thing—how Mathieson had also been assigned to Valorous Division.

The Stone of Gilgal sorted the rest of the officers into their respective Divisions, four per sector. Captain Balor and Destroyer Division gained officers Konran and Nyoka; Captain Kage added three more officers, Meraki, Daigo, and Rydel, to Inquisition Division; and Vivek obtained officer-Tacticians Boman and Kendry.

Anselem's Division was the last to be composed, with Jeremiah Greystone as the final officer to be assigned. He joined alongside Asha, Caleb Ronin, and Gage Varrick.

Alone in their private meeting room, Anselem watched through the glass window as the sun melted down over the horizon. He turned away and raked his gaze over the group of officers gathered before him. Dawning the Commander's voice he had used so often, he addressed his Division:

"First order of business. Don't call me lieutenant. I am

your Division Leader; I'm not your supervisor. So don't get all formal with that rank bullshit. I am a Soturi of Valorous Division just the same as each of you will be once you make it to the end of training—and everyone in this unit *will* make it to graduation, I will see to that myself." He chanced a glance at Asha, whose eyes were narrow slits. He offered a smug smirk. "I have a reputation to uphold after all." Her jaw clenched, and her narrow eyes darkened.

"Who will we report to if you are not our supervisor?" A question from Varrick. Even seated, Anselem could tell he was tall. His onyx hair fell just above his shoulders and was tucked behind his ears to reveal strong, angular features. His fair skin had been tanned from the sun, with light freckles crossing his nose and cheeks. The tattooed symbols on Varrick's arm told him he likely hailed from a village outside of Kochi, the same as Kage.

"You will report to me for your daily training, but your commanding officer is ultimately Major Bardick. There are a few administrative ranks scattered throughout the middle, but my suggestion would be to avoid having any of those meetings."

Varrick nodded.

"And how shall we address you if not by your rank?" Ronin.

His voice was low, but held a tone filled with command and respect. His snow-white hair contrasted against his deep, dark brown skin, and his silver eyes glowed with a brutality Anselem had not seen from many soldiers. He knew the ferocity would serve him well if it was properly controlled.

"Eros is fine." A small grin pulled at the corner of his mouth. "And if you're good enough to beat me in the sparring ring, I might even consider letting you use my first name." Ronin let out a small laugh, but Anselem caught the glimmer of excitement the challenge brought to his eyes.

"As I was saying, you will report to me for your daily training. Every two weeks, our Division group will participate in an assortment of benchmarks. The tests change every year, and we will not be given the specifics in advance—so don't ask me." As he spoke, Anselem's tone was stern, but not cruel—the Commander incarnate. "In the weeks between our benchmarks, we will participate in the Division Wargames. Don't worry about the name, it's just a way for Leadership to try and make the Division competitions sound intimidating."

The Greystone kid let a soft smile tug at his mouth at the bluntness of Anselem's comments.

"And lastly, everyone here better take their superior-thinking heads out of their asses because we *will* be working with the Amarok and Pontos candidates, and my unit will *not* be the type of warriors who think their title makes them better than someone else."

"And what if we are better?" Her voice was pure venom, slicing through the room's air. Greystone, Varrick, and Ronin went still.

Anselem looked down at her, pinning her with a glare that often left men quaking in their boots. She didn't flinch. "Then you better show up and prove it," he bit back.

She rolled her eyes but did not say anything else.

"Our Division will start every morning with group fitness, beginning tomorrow. We will meet at the sparring rings at the top of the mountain on the South Island. And Seven"—he glanced over, addressing Asha, and watched as recognition spread across her face as she recalled the number he had used when he tightened her iron bands—"since you seem so inclined to prove your skills, you can show up thirty minutes beforehand to ready everyone's equipment."

"Do *not* call me that." The hottest fires always burned blue, and her eyes were no exception, as rage poured into her bones. He only flashed a maddening smile in response.

"As far as I am concerned, you have yet to earn the esteem that accompanies your name. So, until you prove me otherwise, you better get used to it." A flicker of pain flashed across her face before she quickly schooled it back into the lethal, unmovable mask she seemed to always wear. Anselem almost felt bad, but he did not waver from his words, knowing the only way he would be able to help mold her into a powerful Soturi would be to break down the walls of arrogance she hid behind and rebuild them into an impenetrable fortress of bravery and prowess.

"Now, unless anyone else has something they need clarified, you are all dismissed."

Asha ground her teeth as she exited the meeting room. She didn't know if she could spend one more minute in a room with *him*, much less six more months.

A number? He had diminished her value to a mere number?

Maybe she had deserved it after that unsavory comment she'd made. She hadn't truly believed it. Asha knew there were many things that the Amarok and Pontos cadets were better at than her, but she also knew she would never shy away from acknowledging that she truly was better than them in some of the skills she possessed. She'd simply made the comment to get under Eros's skin; she didn't realize it would elicit such a strong response. She figured someone with his reputation would have jumped at the opportunity to boast about his superiority. His reaction was surprising.

A scuffle of boots kicked up behind her as she stormed down the alabaster halls of the Academic Building, aiming for the exit.

"What was *that* all about?" Jeremiah asked, jogging to catch up to her quick pace.

She flashed him a glare and his eyebrows arched. She was not entirely sure what she and Jeremiah were to one another at this point; she felt like friends was a strong word for two people who had merely been connected by a life debt. And, in reality, she didn't really want any friends. Caring about people had only ever resulted in loss and pain. It was so much easier to just detach herself, to keep everyone at arm's length and avoid the inevitable loss that had accompanied every person she had ever cared about. Every person she had ever loved.

She shrugged him off, "Nothing."

"It was clearly *something*." They continued down the corridor, turning towards the oak doors that led to the outside steps.

"You're really not going to tell me?"

"I don't see why it would matter."

"Because there is clearly some unresolved issue between the two of you, and I would like to know what I'm about to be stuck in the middle of," he replied, his voice matter-of-fact and contemplative.

"*You* are not going to be in the middle of anything. It's none of your business."

She pushed through the oak doors and descended the stone stairs, heading in the direction of her room.

"It *is* my business. It's *all* of our business when we have to work together every day. When we have to sit there and watch the two of you go at each other's throats for the next six months while we try to survive this place."

"Let it go, Jeremiah."

He grabbed her wrist and turned her around, forcing her to face him.

She looked down at the hand he held against her arm before she slowly dragged her gaze up to his face, fire burning in her eyes. Her voice was low and cold as death, "I suggest you take your hand off me now, unless you would like to become familiar with the idea of it no longer being attached to your arm."

To his credit, Jeremiah did not flinch at the threat. Wisely, he dropped his hand to his side, fully aware of her ability to carry out the warning, but he did not shrink away from her gaze.

She let out a long sigh, realizing he would never let it go. She was quiet for a long moment, staring across the courtyard into the twilight sky. Jeremiah did not say a word.

She could feel his eyes on her as he patiently waited, but she continued to stare into the distance as she took in a deep breath and spoke the words she had never before allowed herself to say: "Anselem Eros killed my brother."

Jeremiah did not make a sound, and Asha forced herself to meet his eyes. Nothing but stunning shock and confusion resided on his face. She turned and headed towards her room, the words still hanging beside Jeremiah in the air where she had left them.

CHAPTER SIX

The Valorous cadets were already drenched in sweat as the sun broke over the horizon. To Anselem's surprise, Asha had arrived early, and he took the time to explain her duties and how to arrange the equipment.

She hadn't said anything, only nodded and went to work on her tasks. But Anselem caught the Darkness filling her eyes.

"No smart ass remarks this morning?" he asked, trying to draw her out of the abyss. She didn't even react, simply continued setting up the equipment. He walked over to where she was and helped her with one of the stations.

"Not a morning person, I take it?"

Silence.

He set the weights down. "You could at least act like you want to be here."

She cut her eyes over to him, fire replacing the darkness. "Do I get bonus points if I pretend to care?"

He looked at her for a long moment.

"If you don't want to be here, then leave."

Gods, it was such a risky statement. Anselem had no clue what he would do if she walked away, if she shut the door completely. He would have no way to reach her, to pull her through, to get her to graduation—to help her survive. But he knew the words were a gamble he needed to make. To show her that she had to fight, even when the Darkness was raging. And that he would not allow her to stay in the gloomy shadows, even if that meant being the monster she believed him to be.

She looked back down and continued setting up the space. She did not speak another word for the rest of the morning.

After the rest of the Division arrived, Anselem put them through a grueling workout circuit, joining in after he explained.

He took mental notes on the strengths and weaknesses of each of his cadets, creating a plan in his head of how to get each of them to a place where they would be successful.

When they had finally finished their exercises, sweat pouring down their backs, the sun broke over the horizon and lit the sky a pale shade of pink.

"Good first day, everyone," Anselem called out, his own breath still returning to normal. "Now head back to your rooms, get washed up and changed, and I will see you in the Main Auditorium in an hour." They nodded and made their way to the stairs on the far side of the mountain top, leading down to the lower grounds. After his cadets left, Anselem stayed behind to finish one more set of exercises before heading down himself to get ready for the day.

❖ ❖ ❖

Asha made it a quarter of the way down the stairs when she realized she had forgotten her jacket. She had worn it in the cool, early hours of the day when she was setting up the equipment, but as Eros ran them through a gauntlet of exercises, she threw it off as sweat began pouring down her body. Her legs felt like lead as she forced them up one step after another. She finally made it to the top ledge and paused. *He was running through the circuit again?* She swore he must enjoy pain. As she took a step towards the sparring ring where the equipment had been laid, she noticed he had removed his shirt, and his muscles were glistening with sweat. She looked over his body, staring at the sculpted muscles that flexed with each movement. A tiny flutter flickered in her chest, and her cheeks went red. She cursed at herself for having such a reaction.

Unfortunately, Eros's gaze flipped up to where she stood, and he undeniably saw the heat on her cheeks. A pleased grin spread over his face. She reluctantly crossed the field and grabbed her jacket, turning quickly back around, ready to leave without a word.

"Enjoying the show, Seven?"

She stopped in her tracks. Heat flushed her face again. She didn't want to turn and meet his eyes, but she forced herself into a composed, neutral expression and whipped around.

He still had that stupid grin plastered to his face. Closer now, she could see the details of his tattoos inked all over his skin. The sleeve of lightning branched up his arm and wrapped around his shoulder before branching inward to cover part of his muscled chest. On the other arm was a relic of sorts, one she had never seen before, and it stretched up from just above his Soturi brand, wrapping all the way to his shoulder before branching out into what looked like feathers at the top.

She collected herself as she replied, "I was just thinking of how many people were mourning the loss of a loved one courtesy of each bolt inked on your arm."

She had assumed each erratic line from his lightning tattoo had occurred in a similar fashion to how her own tendrils of mist were carved into her skin; judging by the swift disappearance of his arrogant smile, Asha had guessed correctly. She watched a wave of Darkness pour into his eyes, but it was gone quicker than it had appeared, as if he'd had a lot of practice shoving it down.

"I will see you in the Auditorium, Seven." His voice was curt and low, and he turned away from her to finish his workout. As he turned, she saw the rest of his relic. Branching out from his shoulder, was an intricately detailed wing made of phoenix feathers and fire, stretching down the entire right side of his back. It was beautiful.

She quickly turned to leave and headed to her room.

Anselem knew Asha's words had been from a place of hurt—hurt she held him responsible for—but that didn't make them any less painful. Didn't make them any less true.

He turned the corner of the colonnade and headed down another open hallway that led to the Base's Academic Building, nestled just past the open courtyard on the Main Island. The Main Auditorium was nestled in the center of the Academic Building, large enough to hold several hundred warriors. He knew the space would look even larger today with so few in attendance. Each year, Base Leadership held an introductory meeting for all the cadets. Soturi, Amarok, and

Pontos warriors all shoved into a confined space with one another. Anselem figured it would be a success if everyone just made it out unscathed.

For as long as he could remember, ever since Kapheria had chosen him and he showed up for his first day of Kappi training at the Elysian Fort, it had been drilled into the minds of every cadet that they were not to mingle with the other branches. And day after day, the instructors had convinced the phoenix riders that their powers and skills were superior to those of the other branches.

Anselem had never liked the idea of believing he was superior, especially if it was based on trivial matters like branches and titles. And if the last few years had shown him anything, it was that Amarok and Pontos warriors could be just as lethal as the Soturi—maybe even more so.

As he turned the last corner before the Academic Building, Anselem was nearly run over by Kage, hurrying towards the Auditorium himself.

Anselem laughed. "Damn, Kage, you know they will wait for us."

The captain cut his eyes towards Anselem. "Not all of us have a reputation that precedes us, Ans. Some of us actually *have* to be on time." Kage cut him another glance, but there was a faint light that danced across his eyes.

The captain was a few years older than Anselem, but the lieutenant still towered over him by several inches. Anselem threw an arm around Kage. "What, the cadets haven't learned yet that you're the Examiner?"

Kage rolled his eyes. "You know none of the Kappi soldiers are told."

Anselem flashed another grin as they continued their walk. "Well, forgive me if I thought our reputations were notorious enough that even the Kappi soldiers had heard."

"Oh, they've heard. They just don't know who the titles belong to."

"Pity. It would have been so much more entertaining walking into this assembly and watching the cadets shake in their boots when they realized the Examiner was among them." He laughed. "Especially those in your Division."

Kage rolled his eyes again, but a smile curled at the corners of his mouth. "You always were one for theatrics."

"One of us has to keep things interesting," he replied, a mischievous twinkle in his eyes.

They ascended the stairs, and just before Kage pulled open the door to enter the Auditorium, he looked at Anselem and laughed. "You definitely keep it interesting, Commander."

Asha sat at the end of the row, Jeremiah to her left. Varrick and Ronin filed in beside them. The Auditorium looked almost empty. The sixteen Soturi cadets sat in the front row, followed by the equivalent number of Amarok behind them, and the Pontos cadets were spread across the third set of seats.

No one spoke as the Instructors filed in. Major Bardick strolled up to the podium at the front of the room. Two other warriors, who looked similar in age, flanked him on either side. Their uniforms were slightly different from the dark-brown tunic Bardick donned, but the single gold star on each of their shoulders informed Asha they were the same rank.

"Good morning, cadets. I, Major Taiki," he gestured to the man on his left, "and Major Volodar," Bardick waved his hand to his right, "would like to congratulate you on your selection."

The man to Bardick's left—Major Taiki—shifted his weight. He was nearly the same height as Bardick, but his frame was leaner. He had long, dark hair that fell to his chest, and he had pulled the top half up into a knot behind his head. A clean-cut beard emphasized his handsome face, and his amber, almond-shaped eyes scanned across the cadets, leaving behind an unnerving feeling. He wore a deep blue tunic that covered a portion of his Pontos Mark, but Asha was still able to make out the tattoo. Inked onto the sun-tanned skin of his right forearm was a circular, swirling wave that looked as if the waters were in motion when he moved his arm. Surrounding the brand were patterns and emblems hailing from Takama.

On the other side of Bardick, Major Volodar kept his exposed, deep brown arms crossed over his chest. He was the oldest of the three warriors, and she was not sure whether the silver streaks in his braids were a consequence of his age or if they were more than likely a result of his Lorcan heritage. He wore a light gray tunic that was cut high on his shoulders, leaving the myriad of ink swirling around his arms exposed. His Amarok brand stretched down the entire back of his right forearm—a line containing the progression of lunar phases surrounded by flecks of sprinkled stardust.

Major Bardick continued his address, "It has been brought to our attention by some of our new Instructors that there is a need for more integration between the branches. The other Majors and I have discussed the idea and have agreed that this year, rather than the branches only working together on two of the benchmarks, you all will be expected to join together for half—three with each branch."

A few groans were heard among the crowd, but the Soturi cadets stayed silent, trained and bred to be unremittingly composed and controlled.

As the majors took turns prattling on about the changes to the cadets' scheduling, Asha overheard two feminine voices behind her trading hushed whispers.

"Is that Anselem Eros?" the first voice purred. Asha shifted her eyes from the podium over to the corner. As if he could feel her gaze on him, he looked up and caught her staring at him. He grinned and then winked. Heat flared through her body, and she told herself it was from rage.

Arrogant ass.

The girl behind her giggled, and Asha's face went hot, realizing the wink had not been meant for her.

"I'd let that man wear my legs like a belt any day." Asha heard a shifting movement and then the first woman's voice let out a muffled yelp. "Damn, Kaira, it was just a joke... kind of." From her tone, Asha could almost see the smirk the woman was likely flashing.

The second woman's voice, slightly lower than the first's, replied, "Get yourself together, Lana, and pay attention. The last thing we need is to give them a reason to think the only job we are capable of doing is opening our legs."

A huff from Lana, "What if I am capable of doing my job *and* opening my legs for the gorgeous Soturi?"

Asha rolled her eyes. Lana was naive as Hells.

"If you think that is true, Lana, then you're naive as Hells," Kaira said, echoing the sentiment ringing in Asha's head.

A small smile grew on Asha's face. She had no clue who the Amarok woman sitting behind her was, but she knew she already liked her.

"Because you already know they are looking for any excuse to dismiss you," Kaira continued in hushed whispers, "they are already looking for a reason to believe you can't cut it. So, if you're going to be stupid enough to walk that path, don't come crying to me later when it all blows up in your face."

Lana went silent, likely sitting beside her classmate seething.

Kaira was right, though. As harsh as it seemed, Asha knew the game too well herself to disagree. Leadership could sit and preach about inclusivity and offering equal chances, but Asha knew first-hand how much harder she had to work to get the same opportunity to be selected for Soturi tryouts, and she didn't want to think about how much harder she would have to work for the next twenty-four weeks to make it to graduation.

The Major's voice cut through her thoughts, "You are all dismissed, please report to your respective Leaders for the day's instructions."

There was a shuffling of feet and creaking of chairs as everyone rose from their seats. Asha turned around to glimpse at the Amarok woman she surprisingly held a small fondness for, but when Asha looked back, there was no one standing in the row behind her.

She glanced around the room once and then followed her Divisionmates over towards Eros.

Gathered with his Division in a third-story classroom of the Academic Building, Anselem looked over the folded piece of paper in his hands once more, purposefully reading each of the scrawled letters, before shoving the note in his pocket.

"At the end of this week, we will have our first Division War. Leadership does not give us any specific details when it comes to the competitions, but they do tell us the general skills that will be needed and tested. This week is archery." His gaze intuitively turned towards Asha, and he could see the faintest spark light her eyes.

"So, we will be focusing on that this week, along with exercises we could potentially encounter for our first benchmark next week."

Anselem pulled the crumpled paper from his pocket.

"I thought you said we weren't told what our benchmarks will be?" Ronin questioned.

Anselem nodded. "We aren't. But Leadership does give us hints towards what could likely take place, so our instruction as Division Leaders can be guided and have some semblance of structure." He held up the piece of paper. "We were given two clues for next week."

He set the piece of paper down on the table where the group had gathered. They squeezed in close to one another to read the scribbled writing:

1. THE FIRST LABOR SHALL SYMBOLIZE VICTORY OVER THE EGO
2. SOME ARMOR IS IMPERVIOUS TO EVEN THE GREATEST OF WEAPONS

Jeremiah laughed, breaking the silence. "Cryptic notes and trials of death? This is going to be an exciting six months." A wide grin broke across his face.

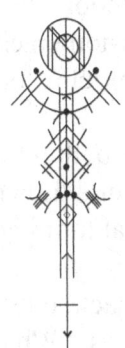

CHAPTER SEVEN

Asha let out a frustrated sigh. They had been practicing for days, and not one of the Valorous cadets seemed any better at wielding a bow.

"Did they not teach you anything in Elysia?" she ground out, pushing Ronin's elbow slightly higher. She had started to help Anselem instruct her classmates after the first morning of practice made her want to rip her hair out. Anselem could shoot fairly well—*very* well if she was being honest with herself—but Jeremiah, Varrick, and Ronin? They looked as if they had never even held a bow.

"Not everyone can be Valhol's Arrow, Asha," Varrick replied. The term would have made her smile if she didn't already want to strangle him.

She whipped her gaze over to Eros, who had been quiet for most of the morning, observing what she said, what she changed.

"What about you? How are you so good if none of the

Elysians ever learned to shoot?"

Eros's neutral expression cracked the slightest bit as he let a small grin tug at his mouth. "Is that a compliment I hear, Seven?"

Jeremiah and Varrick both released muffled laughs.

Asha rolled her eyes and turned back around to Ronin.

"I had some additional training," Eros said, vaguely answering her question.

She turned her eyes back to him as her three classmates continued firing their arrows. "What kind of additional training?"

He stared at her for a moment. "The kind of training that makes me a decent shot." He waved his hand back to Ronin, a silent command to continue correcting his form.

"What about you, Asha?" Varrick asked, pausing his continuous firing.

"What about me?"

"How did you get so good?"

She was quiet for such a long time, Varrick figured she would not answer him and returned to his target.

"My dad taught me a long time ago," she uttered, her voice barely above a whisper.

Jeremiah turned his gaze towards her, and she met it. Understanding blazed in his tawny eyes.

"Stop," Eros thundered, his voice carrying through the Division. "I think I figured it out."

Confused looks swept across the group.

"Just… indulge me for a minute." His eyes were jutting between the group and landed on Asha. His mind looked as if it were flying a million miles an hour.

"Seven, can you please step up to the line with your bow?" She gave him a weary look but grabbed her bow and quiver and sauntered over to the line.

"I need the three of you to come over and circle behind her." The cadets did as they were instructed. Asha flashed another confused look at Eros, but he ignored it.

"I want you to watch Seven as she shoots." He circled around, facing her. "Your first shot will be at normal speed. The second arrow, I want you to slow down every motion, exaggerate it. And for the third, I am going to have you walk through it, pausing with each change and explain it to them. Explain how you feel, what you're doing."

She nodded, surprised he was giving her authority and responsibility to teach her Divisionmates.

She picked up her golden bow and nocked a steel-tipped arrow into place. She glanced over at Eros, and he nodded. She felt the wind on her face and then pulled the string back, aimed in, and let the arrow fly. It sang through the air and landed at a target roughly seventy-five yards away.

Ronin let out a whistle, and she realized the only person in attendance who had seen Valhol's Arrow in action was Jeremiah, and those shots had all been less than thirty yards.

She picked up the second arrow and closed her eyes as she felt the slight change in the wind, letting the breeze brush against her cheek. She slowed every movement down. How she nocked the arrow into place, how her fingers brushed against the string. She even elongated her pull as her arm brought the string backward. She slowed where her fingers grazed against her cheek, bringing the sights into alignment. She took in a slow, deep breath. Then another. And at the bottom of her second breath, she let the arrow soar.

It hit the one-hundred-yard target.

There were no whistles or comments this time around, just pure, inquisitive silence.

She grabbed the final arrow from her quiver.

She closed her eyes once again and felt the movements

of the air, the steady breeze of the wind, the direction of its flow.

Eros's voice was quiet, but close. "Tell them what you feel."

"You have to feel the wind. Wind is the great equalizer when it comes to far distances. You can be the best shot in the world, but if you don't read the wind correctly, you will miss." She opened her eyes and looked over at Varrick. "That is how I am the best. My dad taught me when I was very young how to read the wind, how to become one with it. And once I was able to do that, the skills themselves were easy."

She turned back towards her target. "First, you must feel the wind, know the direction it is moving. Next, make sure you properly place your arrow. We have been going over that for the last three days, so all of you should have that down. Next," she said, brushing her fingers against the string, "make sure you have a proper grip and then pull back in a fluid motion." She slowly worked through the steps as she brought the arrow up towards the target.

"Lastly, you need to make sure your sights are in alignment. This is the second most important part. I can't get behind the sights for you. I can't see what you see. Neither can Lieutenant Eros, so this is the part that falls fully on your shoulders as the archer." She aimed in her sights, and just before she was about to release, she felt the smallest shift in the air.

"That—that right there," she explained, as the breeze changed directions, "those are the small shifts I am talking about that you need to feel, understand, and account for. Make changes to your aiming point based on the wind." She aimed in once more, her breathing steady, and she waited one last time for the breeze to whisper to her.

And she fired the arrow, hitting dead center at one hundred fifty.

She turned back to her Division, and all four men were staring at her wide-eyed.

"Asha… you just hit one hundred and fifty," Jeremiah breathed with awe-filled words.

She glanced over her shoulder and then looked back with a swaggering smile. "What? Like it's hard?" They all laughed in response.

The three cadets took their spots back on the firing line to continue practicing with their newfound knowledge, and each arrow that soared from their bows slowly crept closer to the center.

It had been a full week, and Anselem was no closer to understanding Leadership's hints for the benchmark. He had gone over it time and time again in his head, searching for an answer or for anything that would guide him in the right direction.

Every time, he came up short.

But he didn't have time to think about the clues today. His Division had finally arrived at the end of the first week, and they were about to compete in the first Division War.

All four Divisions were gathering in the grassy fields of the Archery Ranges, the open space resting at the base of the mountain leading up to the sparring rings.

"Good morning, Soturi cadets," Major Bardick trilled. His spritely voice at such an early hour irritated Anselem to no end. "I hope you are all equally as excited as we are," he gestured to the group of instructors gathered behind him, "for the start of Division Wars."

"This week, seeing as though all our Divisions are still fully equipped, we will be splitting off into two separate ranges to accommodate the numbers.

"On range one, the Destroyer Division will be matched against Valorous. And on range two will be Inquisition and Tactician."

Anselem swept his eyes across his cadets, but not one of them dropped their steel-faced expressions. A smile tugged at his mouth, but he kept his face composed.

"Since the teams are all equally numbered, each member will compete against one other cadet from the opposing Division. Each cadet's score will then be added to their Division's total. At the end, the team totals will be weighed, and a winner will be declared."

From the corner of his eye, Anselem saw Moros, standing among the other members of Destroyer Division, slide his gaze towards Asha. Anselem stiffened.

"Once the competing pairs have been chosen, an instructor will flip a coin to determine who goes first."

Bardick rambled on about the details of the competition, explaining how the first cadet would take a shot of their choosing at any target on the course, and the competing cadet would then have to follow up with the same shot, until a target was missed. The game would end one of two ways: the first option would be for the primary cadet to make a shot that the secondary cadet could not follow, or the second option would be, if the primary cadet missed a shot, and then the secondary cadet was able to make a shot that the primary cadet could not replicate.

Overall, the concept was simple and straightforward, but Anselem knew that if two cadets were paired together and both were strong in archery, this Wargame could last a long while.

"You have ten minutes to select your opponents, and then we will begin," Bardick concluded.

Anselem watched the Destroyer Division whip around and face his team. They held their heads high, unwavering.

Moros stepped forward from his group and growled out, "She's mine."

Anselem almost laughed at the words. He was certain Moros had no clue who he was dealing with. She belonged to no one but herself. She was Valhol's Arrow. She was a storm, a calamitous force of nature, and Anselem knew that once she finally unshackled her full power, she would be unstoppable.

Asha's face remained unmoved as Moros's words echoed through the air, but the faintest twinkle flashed through her eyes. She grabbed the worn leather bag resting beside her feet, threw it over her shoulder, and swaggered over to the first lane of the range, leaving Moros behind.

The rest of Valorous broke off into their competition groups and spread out along the range's lanes.

Placed at the front of each lane sat two rectangular stands, each holding a myriad of steel tipped arrows. And resting upright, beside each of the eight mahogany boxes, were an equal number of beautifully crafted white oak bows.

Scattered down the range were dozens of targets, filled with rings to delineate distances from the target's center. The targets themselves varied in size, distance, and height. Several were suspended high in the air to challenge the archer's skill with angled shooting, held in place by the help of lesser magic.

Asha and Moros stepped in front of their bows, and Anselem followed behind them, coin in hand.

"Moros, since you were ranked higher in the initial selection, you will get to call it—head or tails."

Anselem glanced down at the silver coin in his hand. A crowned lion stared back at him. Without flipping the coin over, he could envision the imprint of the feathered wings on the other side. He had seen it etched on his own skin every day for the last several years.

Moros nodded and smiled, the expression looking wicked and misplaced on his cruel face. "Heads," he stated.

Anselem flipped the coin in the air, caught it in his right hand, and flipped it onto the backside of his left. A pair of feathered wings glared up at the three warriors.

"Your choice, Seven. Would you like to shoot first or second?"

She looked up at him, and the same delighted twinkle flashed in her eyes.

"Second."

Anselem wasn't sure why he was surprised. He should have known she would choose the more difficult option. He should have known she would pick second, even though it was the position that created more pressure. He almost laughed to himself when he realized that was likely the exact reason why she did—she wanted to send a message. She wanted everyone to know she could handle the pressure. She could handle anything they threw her way.

Moros laughed loudly. "I didn't think you would be much of a challenge, but I didn't think you would be stupid enough to make it so easy for me." He let out another laugh. "At least this will be over quickly."

He just stared at her, and Anselem thought she would give him one of her snappy one-liners, the kind that would cut deep and kick his feet out from under him.

But she was silent. The calm before the storm.

She stepped up, grabbing the bow and one of the steel arrows. She ran her fingers over the smooth metal. Every movement was filled with lethal grace. Moros followed suit, visibly still unaware of who he was competing against.

The horn blew, and down the line, arrows began to fly.

"Maybe I should go easy on you at first, Raynor. Give you some hope." Moros donned another sly smile. Anselem restrained himself from ripping it off the cadet's face.

Moros nocked his arrow against the string. He pulled the bow into place, and his first shot soared twenty-five yards.

He hit the left side of the center-most ring. A near-perfect bullseye.

Asha pulled her bow up and aimed in, closing her eyes. Her words from earlier in the week suddenly filled Anselem's mind. That was when he felt it—the slightest bit of breeze, blowing from right to left across the field. Almost unnoticeable.

She opened her eyes and released. The steel arrow sang through the air and landed mere inches from Moros's—in the dead center. A perfect bullseye.

Anselem couldn't control the wide grin that spread across his mouth when Moros turned to Asha with fury and shock pooling in his eyes.

She was the picturesque model of composure.

Anselem turned and walked down the rest of the range, assessing how Jeremiah, Ronin, and Varrick were faring.

But as he lingered towards the other end with the rest of Valorous Division, Anselem kept one eye on the first lane.

Arrow after arrow flew.

Ronin was the first to drop out—just missing a seventy-yard, high-angle target off the right.

Jeremiah was next—besting a Destroyer cadet with a tricky, eighty-five-yard shot straight down the center of the field. The Destroyer cadet—Fordon—hadn't accounted for the change in wind when Jeremiah switched the shooting direction. Fordon was still steaming when he took his place behind the line with the growing number of cadets who had already completed their competitions.

Varrick held out the longest, matching shot for shot with Nyoka. Anselem thought he would pull through with another win for the team, until he went to follow up on Nyoka's shot and rushed the release, not taking into account the gust of wind that blew the moment before he released the string. The arrow grazed the side of the target but did not hit.

They took their places behind the line.

Anselem made his way back down to the first lane. Asha's teammates had all gathered behind her position, in a declaration of support and solidarity, but as Anselem approached, he also noticed the large group of Inquisition and Tactician cadets who had gathered behind the first lane, instructors and Leaders included.

Everyone watched as the battle between the archers unfolded.

As the Wargame continued, the sun rose in the sky and hung high above them, its rays beating down on the open field below, warming the brisk morning.

Anselem could see the sweat beading on Moros's brow.

Asha looked unbothered, as if she commanded the cooling winds herself.

Moros sent another arrow down the range. Ninety yards. He hit the ring second closest to the center.

Asha followed up with her own. She missed the center ring. But as Anselem took a closer look, he saw that she had instead stacked her arrow over Moros's, the steel arrowheads touching.

Someone behind him cursed when they realized the precision with which she had guided the arrow.

She was messing with him. A predator toying with her

prey before she went in for the kill.

The frustration on Moros's face was visible to the entire crowd. His nostrils flared as he grabbed another arrow and nocked it against the string. His hands gripped his bow so tightly his knuckles turned white.

He aimed for the one-hundred-yard target. He released, and the arrow soared through the sky.

He missed an inch off the right. The blood drained from his face as whispers broke out among the crowd.

Asha said nothing. She only picked up another arrow.

Anselem glanced over to Kage, standing off to the side with several Inquisition cadets. He saw a small smirk tug at his mouth as he mouthed silently to Anselem, "Let the show begin."

A soft smile grew on Anselem's face as he turned his attention back to the first lane.

Every movement she made was with deliberate and perfected purpose. She brought the bow up, her fingers grazing against her cheek, and aimed in her sights. She closed her eyes, and the wind blew some of the strands of her ash blonde hair that had fallen loose from her braid.

Her burning, sapphire eyes opened, and she released.

The arrow soared through the sky, but Asha did not watch it.

She turned towards Moros, her arrow still floating through the winds above, and bent at the waist, taking a dramatic bow. She pulled herself back upright, a swaggering smirk resting on her face, grabbed the bag lying beside her range position, and sauntered to her place behind the completion line.

As she stepped across the line, her arrow struck center on the furthest laid target, sitting two hundred yards down the field.

Murmurs broke out among the cadets, and the instructors exchanged shocked looks. Moros dropped the arrow back into the mahogany holder and walked behind the line, settling in next to the rest of Destroyer.

"Congratulations to Inquisition Division on their victory today. Your team will be awarded one point for the First War," Bardick announced to the gathered crowd. "We have a tie between Destroyer and Valorous Divisions. Valorous will be declared the winner and is awarded one point for their performance. Congratulations to cadet Raynor for securing today's longest shot."

The Major continued to give comments on the events of the day, which cadets had won their individual competitions, and how long the matches had lasted.

As he drawled on, Anselem noticed two cadets, Fordon and another cadet from Destroyer Division, move closer to each side of Moros. The trio began whispering amongst themselves.

Moros raised his voice a fraction higher, just enough for the cadets to hear, but kept it low enough that the instructors lining the front would not be able to make out his voice.

Anselem, standing slightly closer than the other Leaders, heard Moros's voice carry over the cadets, "Yeah, well, I'm sure she only won because she got extra instruction from her Division Leader. Spreading your legs does wonders for receiving extra help."

Asha's whole body went rigid. Anselem made a move towards the cadet, rage flooding his body, but before he even took a full step, Jeremiah, Varrick, and Ronin all whipped around.

And then, all Hells broke loose.

Fists went flying, curses and yells were barked between the groups. Inquisition and Tactician cadets stood on the edge, their eyes burning with excitement to join in.

But a single look from each of their respective Leaders kept them from throwing themselves into the middle of the brawl.

After brushing off the initial shock, Asha eagerly threw herself into the midst of the chaos, a wave of lethal calm spreading across her face. She went straight for Moros.

He was strong, but she was quick—unnaturally quick.

She dodged his barreling swing and ducked under his arm, coming up on his back. He towered more than half a foot taller, but she kicked the back of his leg in a swift motion, sending him to his knees. Anselem heard the gruesome impact as his knees smacked the ground. She wrapped her arm around his throat and began to squeeze.

"Everyone, stop!" Bardick yelled from the front of the crowd, trying to push his way through the cadets circling the mayhem. No one ceased. No one moved out of the Major's path.

As each second passed, Anselem could see the air dwindling in Moros's lungs.

He stepped up, the cadets before him parting to each side.

He donned the domineering voice of the Commander and growled, "That's enough!"

The fighting cadets immediately halted, as if a violent fire had been instantly snuffed out. Asha's eyes, filled with pain and Darkness, met Anselem's, and he nodded once, a barely visible movement. She let go of Moros's throat, and the only noise that filled the air was the exasperated gasps of the cadet attempting to fill his lungs once again with air.

"You bitch," he croaked.

Anselem turned his gaze to Captain Balor. "I suggest you get your cadet in check before I do."

The captain merely shrugged and nodded. Every cadet glanced around wide-eyed, and Anselem realized his rank alone should not have allowed him to speak to Balor in such a way. He didn't care. He turned to address his Division. "You are done here. Unless Major Bardick has anything left for you." He glanced over at the Major, who tensely shook his head, irritation evidently layered on his face. "You will come with me. Now." Anselem turned to exit the archery ranges.

The Valorous cadets, all bruised and bloodied, walked forward to grab the leather bags they had left lying on the grass and followed their Leader.

"What? No bitchy remark to make, Raynor?" Fordon, snidely commented, blood dribbling down his chin. Captain Balor cleared his throat, and Fordon glanced back at his Leader.

Asha turned her head back to face him, smiled, and replied, "I'd insult you, but I'm afraid you're too dense to notice it."

His brow furrowed, and Varrick let out a deep laugh.

Jeremiah, with an already darkening black eye, looked over to Asha and then the two other Valorous cadets and replied, "Like I said, it's going to be an exciting six months."

Then he winked at his Divisionmates—his newly forming family.

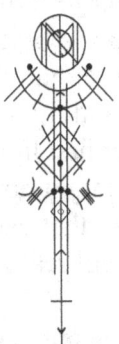

CHAPTER EIGHT

Asha and her Divisionmates followed their Leader all the way through the Soturi training grounds to the center of the South Island. They wove their way through rocks and trees until they stopped in a small opening, just east of the building the Inquisition instructors called the Tartarus. A chill ran down her spine. No one spoke a word as they walked.

Asha gathered glimpses of the Tartarus through the tree line, and the building looked like it was filled with every bit of the horrors and doom it was rumored to impose, as if it were built of bones and suffering. A dungeon of nightmares.

Anselem let out a heavy sigh before he faced his Division. "What happened today... I do not look at it lightly."

The cadets stiffened, readying themselves for the verbal lashing.

"Most people don't get to choose their family." As his words reached each of them, their shoulders loosened the slightest bit. "But here? Here you do. Every day you get to choose each other; you get to fight for each other. You get to choose this family if you want it. And once you do, know that it will be yours, for life. Family is not always blood; it is those who accept you, and fight for you, and sacrifice for you. Today? That was your first fight. Your first time fighting for your family. And you might not see it yet, but at the end of this academy, I promise that each of you will look back at this moment, and you will realize this is when you found your people.

"So, I did not bring you out here to yell at you or punish you. In reality, I'm glad you kicked their asses." A soft laugh from Varrick and Jeremiah crawled out. "But I brought you out here to have a moment together. A moment to savor the new foundation of your family, and a moment you can look back on a few months from now and realize this was when it all started. You need only to choose it." His voice was quiet but firm.

Anselem kneeled down and brushed dirt off one of the rocks. As he brushed aside the dust, it uncovered a large, smooth, onyx stone. It was embedded in the ground and shaped in a perfect circle with a large Rune carved into the center. "This is one of the three Mother Runes—the Othala. The rough translation means 'Tribe'—family," he explained, referencing the symbol. "No other Divisions know about it. It belongs only to us. Our small, hidden piece in the world meant only for the Valorous."

As Asha took a closer look at the stone, she could see, carved within the midnight black rock, were hundreds of names. Her heart skipped, and a lump formed in her throat when she came across one of the names engraved near the bottom: Mathieson Raynor. Her brother's name was grouped with three others—Eros's included in the bunch.

"Whenever you make the choice to join this family, the

Othala will be here, ready for each of you to etch your names into the rock and join the hundreds who have come before you."

No one said a word as the gravity of the moment took hold.

Asha swallowed another lump in her throat. She glanced first at Jeremiah, then at Varrick, and lastly at Ronin. Her Tribe—her family.

No one had ever told her about the brutality of healing. The Darkness that overwhelms, the loneliness that engulfs. But in that moment, standing with her Tribe, she felt it. Happiness. She didn't realize it at first; the feeling was so foreign she hadn't remembered what it was like. But there it was, shining in the depths of her shadowed soul—a warm flicker of light, a glimmer of hope. When all she'd known for years was Darkness.

Anselem looked over the cadets once more before he concluded, "You will know when it is the right time to come back here. Until then, go back to your rooms, clean yourselves up and I will see you all tomorrow. There will be no group fitness tomorrow morning."

The group nodded and began heading back towards the Barracks.

Before the cadets were too far away, Anselem called out, "Seven, will you please stay for a moment?"

Asha stopped her pace, her Divisionmates all glanced back at her, but continued on.

Once the other cadets were out of sight, she slowly turned around to face Anselem.

He looked her over once. No signs of the brawl touched

her—not even a scratch.

"Are you alright?" he asked.

The glimmer of light he had seen in her eyes moments before vanished, and the unholy Darkness returned.

"I'm fine," she seethed between clenched teeth, as if speaking to him caused her physical pain.

"I don't mean from the fight. I heard what Moros said," Anselem replied, focusing on keeping his tone level and calm.

Her cheeks flushed. "I said I'm fine."

"You're not."

And that's when her restraint snapped. "Stop trying to act like you care. Like you aren't the reason for *everything!* You're the reason he's gone. You're the reason I don't have a brother anymore! So, stop acting like you are concerned." The words came out in growls and snarls, as if she had been waiting years to scream them. As she said the word *brother*, she choked on a sob escaping her throat.

And there it finally was—the truth laid bare. Asha truly believed Anselem left her brother alone in a prison cell to die. Rage ripped through his body, and his unending patience splintered.

"On my Word, I did not kill him." Anselem's voice was harsh and brassy. And as the words left his lips, he wasn't sure if he was trying to convince her or himself.

"Well, your *word* doesn't mean shit to me. You might as well have been the one to shove the knife into him yourself," she snapped.

"You have a really special talent for finding my last godsflaming nerve and dancing all over it, Seven."

Fury raged in her eyes.

"You think you're the only one who gets to mourn him? You think you're the only one who gets to miss him? You're not."

She blinked, confusion replacing the rage.

"You can believe whatever you want. I don't care. I'm not going to stand here and try to convince you of the truth when it is clear you have already dismissed the idea of any other possibility. But just know, he would be pissed if he knew you had your head so far up your own ass that you didn't even consider that there are other sides to the story."

Anselem made to leave, his body shaking with anger, but forced himself to turn back and face her. He had failed on so many promises in his life, but there was one promise he would not falter from fulfilling, no matter how angry the woman standing before might make him. "And don't forget, we have our first one-on-one tomorrow morning. I'll see you in the courtyard at dawn."

If looks could kill, Asha's glare would have sent him straight on his way to meet Anubis in the Hells. "I hate you," she spat, the words filled with more venom than a thousand vipers.

"Yeah, well, that makes two of us."

If Anselem was honest with himself, there were many days he felt he didn't deserve love. Many days, he looked at himself, and nothing but hate-filled eyes stared back. He had a lot of qualities he was not proud of, and there were too many promises he'd made that he had walked away from. Promises that ate at him. All he truly wanted was to one day be able to look into a mirror at his own reflection and know the face staring back would love him harder than he hated himself.

Asha only blinked. For once, unsure what to say. He took a deep breath and forced his rage to subside, if only for a moment.

"Look," he said, "I know you have no reason to trust

me, but I'm not here to hurt you, okay? I'm trying to help you. And things would work a lot better if you let me."

She rolled her eyes. "You're right. I don't trust you. And I don't need your help. I can handle everything myself, or were you not watching earlier?"

He clenched his fists so tight that his knuckles turned white. He took another breath and relaxed.

"You may have everyone else here fooled with the bravado and swaggering arrogance, but not me. I see the anger that resides inside you. The Darkness. I know it very well. And I promise you that if you do not address it, I don't care how good you think you are, or how much skill you might have, you *will* fail. It will eat you alive, slowly, and you will not make it out of here. So do what you need to, hate me if you need to, but fix your shit, Seven. Until then, I can't help you."

He turned to leave, and she barked back, "Mark my words, *Lieutenant*. I promise I will be the one to ruin you."

He spun back and stepped up to her, so close they could share breath, and he stared down into her flaming sapphire eyes. A smirk crossed his lips, "I look forward to it."

He sauntered out of the opening, leaving Asha to simmer in her rage.

Fury still pulsed through Asha's veins hours later as she lay on her bed, staring at the ceiling. She wanted nothing more than to go find Uriel and head straight to the skies. That was where she had always done her best thinking.

Eros's words about Math had eaten at her since she'd left the Othala. She wondered if he had been lying or if there truly might be another side to the story. She knew there was truth in the fact that Math would have expected her to consider every possibility, especially since reading his journals and knowing things were not always as they seemed. But considering the idea that Eros might not be the one to blame for Math's death? Asha hated herself for even thinking it.

She pulled out one of the worn, leather-bound journals from her bedside table and began reading.

"THERE IS FREEDOM WAITING FOR YOU ON THE BREEZES OF THE SKY; YOU NEED ONLY BUT TO CONQUER IT."
—FLYING: A GENERAL GUIDE FOR PHOENIX RIDERS

CHAPTER NINE

Asha had been up for hours when a powerful fist began pounding on her door. The noise broke through the early morning silence of the Base, and she shot up from her lounging spot on the bed, leather journals flying onto the wooden floor. She let out an annoyed grunt as she pulled herself out from under the onyx blanket, still dressed in her black silk tank top and shorts from sleep. She leaned over to collect the fallen books.

The maddening fist met her door once again, and she felt the anger stored inside every strike.

"Seven, you better open this door, or I will rip it from the hinges."

She would know that deep, husky accent anywhere, and the sound of it made her roll her eyes.

Dramatic men, she thought, as she drifted over to the door. She flung the door open wide, just before his fist made contact once again.

His hand was still in the air as he took in the sight of her. She watched his narrowed gaze travel up and down once before settling on her eyes. Anger raged behind the emerald oceans.

"Get dressed," he commanded.

"I told you I don't want your help."

"And you don't give the orders here, *cadet*. So, you can either get dressed or you can freeze your ass off in the air. Either way, we are heading to the Aviary in five minutes." His tone was filled with such seriousness, she didn't press her luck. She simply closed the door without a word.

And with the wooden barrier between them, Asha let out a wide grin. She threw on her flying leathers with haste and quickly re-braided her hair. She threw Mathieson's journals into the mahogany side table, grabbed the small bag hanging on the back of her door, and flung the door's hinges open.

Eros took up nearly the entire door frame. His striking features were set in a harsh expression, and his normally flowing locks had been twisted together in a braid that kept any loose strands from falling in his face. Asha figured he had likely done it for the same reasons she kept her hair tightly fixed when flying—because the knots the winds created in the skies took *days* to wrestle out. She angled her head up at him and muttered, "A bit of a dramatic wake-up call, don't you think? I'm pretty sure you woke up half of the hall."

"If you had shown up when you were supposed to, I wouldn't have to make house calls."

"And if you listened to what I wanted, you wouldn't have to make house calls at all." She swept past him and headed towards the Aviary.

They weaved their way through the alabaster colonnades in silence until they arrived at the guard outpost. The two warriors stepped out and saluted Eros. He nodded, and the two Soturi stepped back inside.

"You don't have to check in or sign the log?"

"No."

"Because of your rank?"

"Something like that."

Asha let out a huff of irritation. His short-winded answers grated on her nerves, but she said nothing. She figured he had every right to be pissed at her for not showing up on time.

Uriel and Eros's firebird exited the shelter, sensing their arrivals through the Bond. The phoenixes looked like night and day, light and darkness. But no matter how opposing their feathers may appear, the birds seemed to get along much better than their riders as they pranced across the field side-by-side.

Eros pulled down two saddles from the nearest shed. Asha walked over to grab it, but he did not hand it to her.

"Wait."

His one-word commands were starting to make her feel like a house dog. He saddled up his firebird, and Asha watched the gentleness with which he cared for her, the kind voice in which he whispered. Her midnight black feathers sparkled against the dawning sun, as if stars were scattered throughout her wings.

He walked back over to the saddle he had grabbed for Asha, and he explained, "You might have better skills with fighting and archery, but the Elysian Soturi will fly laps around you in the skies if you don't take the time to learn more than what they taught you in Valhol."

She opened her mouth to argue, but he cut her off. "It's not up for debate. I have seen plenty of Valhollian Soturi come through my camps, and not one of them is able to out-ride a warrior from Elysia. So that is what we are going to focus on for the next six months. Every week. Until you are just as good as them."

"Better," she replied. His brow lifted. "I want to be better than them."

The corner of his mouth turned upward. "Better," he agreed. His grin was always halfway a smile, halfway a threat, and Asha matched it with her own.

Anselem laughed to himself. It was almost humorous to see her struggle at something, like the feeling was a foreign concept she was unable to fully wrap her mind around.

They had been in the skies for nearly an hour, and Anselem had run Asha and her firebird through some simple drills he learned back in Elysia. She was able to keep up… barely.

He tugged once on the reins, compelling Kapheria to slow her pace as Asha and Uriel caught up. Kapheria let out an irritated huff, and Anselem laughed, patting her on the back.

"We will go on a flight of our own later, and you can fly as fast as you want, I promise."

Kapheria replied with a noise that sounded something like a purr of acquiescence.

Uriel pulled up next to Kapheria, their wings almost touching, and Kapheria snapped her beak in his direction. Asha moved the reins on her saddle and guided Uriel a few feet away.

Her ash-blonde braid whipped in the wind and Anselem could see the redness growing on her wind burned cheeks.

"Just a few more drills," he called over to her through the whipping air. She nodded. He knew she would continue to fly for as long as he did, even if she wasn't conditioned for it. The last thing he needed was for her to run herself into the ground with exhaustion. Or, if she passed out from elevation sickness, *actually* run herself into the ground looming below.

He would have to work her up to extended exposures in high altitudes. He looked over and could faintly make out the nearly imperceptible pale green glow around her head. He had used his magic to fix an orb of air around her head, identical to the one he fastened around his own, so she could breathe as they ascended higher into the skies. He shook his head at the fact that Valhol refused, even for the instructors, to utilize lesser magic for the Kappi cadets during training. He knew his flying skills would never have advanced to the level they were at without his Elysian instructors utilizing their powers to create orbs of air around the cadets while their own magic was still locked by their iron bands. He still had no clue how Asha had been able to fly with the wind rushing through her eyes; that was perhaps Anselem's favorite benefit the orbs provided—a shield from the whipping winds.

Anselem looked off into the distance, peering at the approaching mountains jetting out from the ocean below. A grouping of abandoned land masses, with crossing ridges and peaks that created a wide variety of swirling wind currents, loomed on the horizon.

"Fasten the belt I attached to your seat," he called over to Asha. She whipped her gaze to him, and her eyes narrowed at the insult.

"Uriel needs to know he's not going to throw you from the saddle if he has to take control and guide you out."

A flush of red brushed over Asha's cheeks and Anselem knew it was not from wind burn. The woman may be arrogant, but she wasn't stupid. He watched as she fastened the belt across her lap.

"This is what we will be working towards. By the end of training, you will be able to keep your seat and guide Uriel through the path on your own."

Asha tore her gaze and focused on the nearing mountains.

"Are you ready?" he called over. She looked on for a long moment, and he could see her mouth moving as if she were whispering something to herself, then she turned her attention over to Anselem and called back, "Let's do it."

He nodded and pulled the reins once more and Kapheria dove down quickly towards the water.

As they approached the abandoned island, Anselem could see the mist-filled cloud clinging to the bottom of the rocky grounds. On the outer border of the land mass, monolithic, gray pillars shot straight into the air, looking like jagged, stone blades just waiting to slice through flesh. Further towards the center, the peaks of the sharp gray stones smoothed out, and a mossy green foliage sat along the walls and tops of the mountains. Murky seawater flowed through cracks and crevices on the ground, and even from a distance, Anselem could see the half-destroyed bridges that arched between a handful of the closely set peaks.

No one knew when the barren island had been inhabited. Remnants of previous occupants had been washed away for centuries, and the only remaining signs of the past inhabitants were the slowly decaying stone bridges that connected several of the mountain peaks to one another. The Perseisian citizens who knew of the abandoned archipelago speculated that the denizens from the Desert Isles were likely the ones who had ventured far from their native lands in the east to settle within the mountainous shores in pursuit of territorial expansion; but nature and sea roving pirates had killed off the majority of the ambitious pioneers, and the survivors were forced to return east, across the Seidon Sea, to their foreign lands.

The shore was a mere hundred yards off and Anselem glanced one last time at Asha. Her normally composed features looked strained, and her eyes were wide. It was intimidating, he knew that. The isle itself did not give off a warm and welcoming aura, but having to fly between the close-set walls of rock and glide through the whipping canyons slots...Intimidating was a kind word to use.

Anselem went first, passing through a small break in the jagged monoliths jetting up from the water on the isle's edge. He had to slightly twist his reins, pulling Kapheria to an angle so her wings would not scrape the walls. He heard Asha and Uriel follow in behind.

As soon as they slipped past the exterior walls, the pair was immediately met with a whipping current of air that thrust the birds straight upward. Anselem shifted his weight, his legs flexing as they held him in his seat. He already knew Asha would have fallen out of her saddle if the leather belt had not been attached. He coasted higher until he neared the ridge line. Kapheria drifted in the air for a short time while Anselem waited for Asha to guide Uriel up. Once she reached the same height, he gave a quick kick to Kapheria's side, and she tucked in her wings and plummeted down to the winding canyon below. It felt like free falling as the pair plunged through the sky, the ground growing closer and closer. When they were only one hundred yards away from crashing into the rocky terrain below, Anselem gave another swift kick of his heel, and Kapheria splayed her wings, stopping their fall just before they struck the ground.

Another pull on the reins and Kapheria slowed, giving Anselem a chance to look behind him as Asha and Uriel free-fell. Even from the far distance below, Anselem could see her hips were no longer seated, and the only thing keeping her from tumbling off the firebird was the belt he had made her fasten.

He took a mental note of the drills they would need to work through to strengthen her legs and other exercises he would run her through to build the trust between the bonded pair.

Anselem found that to be the most important aspect of success in flying—Kapheria had to trust him to make the right calls at the right time before she would give up control of where they went and what they were doing. Until she trusted him to guide them through tough courses without crashing, Kapheria had never truly relinquished control of where they flew.

As Uriel approached the ground, he spread out his wings much higher than Kapheria had, and Anselem was certain the phoenix had been the one to make the call, not the rider.

Asha glided over to where Anselem hovered, falling into formation behind him as he turned and headed through the canyon. He began to weave his way around gigantic rocks and obstacles. Each turn changed the direction of the winds barreling off the canyon walls. They neared the end of the canyon, and Anselem could see a narrow slit between two large rock walls leading out to the center opening of the isle. He guided Kapheria towards it, and as they approached, the winds channeling into the slot picked up speed before they entered. Anselem yanked the left rein and Kapheria rolled, entering the slit completely sideways. She glided through the rocks, unable to even beat her wings within the narrow space. Towering stone walls caressed them on each side. When the pair broke out and soared into the open area beyond, Kapheria returned upright, straightening her wings.

He slowed the firebird down once more, landing in the grass in the center of the valley, and waited for the second pair to join. Several moments passed, but they did not appear. Anselem was nearly about to turn back and head through the narrow passageway to ensure nothing had happened, when snow-white feathers of the firebird emerged from between the stones.

He let out a held breath.

Asha flew over to where he waited, huffing in air as she landed.

"Are you trying to kill me?!"

Anselem stared at her with amused eyes as she gulped down another breath.

"I've nearly fallen off ten times!"

Anselem's eyes went wide. He hadn't expected it to go quite *that* badly. A wave of something resembling guilt washed over him. Kapheria huffed beneath him, clearly disapproving of the rider.

Asha's eyes narrowed on the midnight firebird, and Anselem could feel a rumble growing inside the phoenix beneath him. He rubbed a hand over her feathers to calm her.

"That was only the first half," he said plainly, glancing to the other side of the mountains surrounding them in the open clearing.

Her face went pale.

He let out a frustrated breath and ran his hand through his hair.

"Look, I never said it was going to be easy. But unless you get better at reading the winds and your surroundings, he is never going to trust you enough to give you control."

"He does trust me."

"Not with flying, he doesn't."

She was silent. Her cheeks burned bright, and she

dropped her gaze to the snow-white bird beneath her.

"I can give you some specific things to work on to strengthen your legs during our morning fitness, and each week we can continue to go over more flying drills. But Seven," he waited until she looked at him, "you are the one who must trust yourself to make the right choices. Confidence in your decisions cannot come from anyone but you."

She did not reply, but he could see the words as they sank in. He gave her another moment to collect herself before he said, "Ready?"

She looked at the towering rock walls on the other side of the central valley and dragged her gaze back over to him. She nodded once.

And with Asha's agreement, Anselem patted Kapheria on the back, and she launched into the air, the second pair following close behind.

CHAPTER TEN

Valorous sat circled around a grand oak table in one of the large classrooms on the third floor of the Academic Building. Asha glanced up at the clock, five minutes past the hour.

"They're late," she snipped, breaking the silence in the room.

"And we will wait," Anselem replied, his voice controlled, but Asha caught the air of annoyance that seeped into his words.

Varrick let out a deep sigh, and Jeremiah ran his hand through his unruly hair.

Ronin was the only one to remain unmoved—patience of steel.

A small rap sounded on the door, and it opened slowly. Five Amarok strolled in.

"My apologies, Anselem, the schedule sent out this morning had us meeting an hour later." *First name basis with Eros? He must be their group's Leader.*

"No apologies necessary, Captain Mispar. We were happy to wait."

Happy seems like a strong word. Asha's eyes met Varrick's, and a grin tugged at the corner of her mouth as she read the same thought in his onyx eyes. He gave her a wink as the Amarok cadets took their seats around the table.

Two of the cadets looked unremarkably plain. Both were lean, with ordinary brown hair that they kept cropped high above their ears. They notably styled the neat cuts in slightly different ways. Their short sleeves revealed no distinct ink or markings on their fair skin. Their faces looked similar too, both with long, narrow noses and boyish features. The most defining difference between the men was their eyes—one with charcoal gray and the other with a dull brown. They were mildly attractive, in a bland type of way, and Asha guessed the two were brothers—twins perhaps.

The third man, with rich auburn hair, also cut above his brow, stood taller than the brothers, closer in height to Ronin and Jeremiah. He looked lean but built, and his tawny brown eyes glimmered in the sun's rays pouring through the window.

Asha's attention at last landed on the Amarok woman taking her seat. She had to force herself to refrain from sucking in a sharp breath. The woman was beautiful. Absolutely striking. Her rich, deeply tanned skin was mostly covered by long sleeves and light gray leathers. Her long, dark hair was pulled back from her face, and several small braids were intertwined throughout the waves. Her stunning face held full lips and strong brows, but the most striking aspect was her eyes—a gold so bright and rich it was as if the sun had been poured into them. The woman's gaze lifted, meeting the burning sapphire that filled Asha's, and she nodded once, curt and short, before returning her focus to the Leaders.

"Let's not waste any more time. All of you know that our groups will be paired together for this week's benchmark. Let's make quick introductions and begin the discussion of our plans," the Amarok captain mumbled. He gestured to Eros and the rest of the Division.

Each of the Valorous members introduced themselves by name and where they hailed from.

Jeremiah went first, claiming the Kingdom's capital of Brienza as home. Varrick was next, affirming his Kochi heritage, and Asha followed, asserting her allegiance to Valhol. Ronin went last for Valorous, declaring his attachment to Lorca. At Ronin's assertion, several of the Amarok nodded in approval at the familiarity, having spent their time as Fenri cadets at the Citadel.

The Amarok cadets went next.

The brothers—twins indeed—hailed from Orevein, a small mining town north of the Capital, nestled just outside of the Iron Mountains. The charcoal-eyed cadet went by Jasper, and his twin introduced himself as Kano. The auburn-haired man claimed Brinehaven as his home, the small fishing village located between Takama and Brienza, and went by the name of Flynn.

The golden-eyed Amarok was last to introduce herself, and when she spoke, her voice was low but strong, "My name is Kaira Samson. I hail from Velsen."

Kaira. The woman who sat behind Asha in the Auditorium. Asha left her face neutral, but a smile threatened to pull at the corners of her lips as a relieving feeling washed over her. Asha was finally able to put a face to the name, and it felt like an unmanageable itch was finally scratched.

Asha cued in right away that Kaira's strength was her intelligence. Not that she looked incapable of holding her own, but Asha already knew the Amarok's mind was by far the greatest weapon she wielded, and Asha also knew, more often than not, the mind could out-battle the sword, without ever having to raise a blade.

There was only one other person Asha had known whose brilliant mind was sharp enough to be so lethal.

A flash of dripping blood and lightless, silver-flecked eyes flashed across her mind. Nausea rolled in Asha's stomach, and her body went rigid as she shoved the memory back down into the Darkness forever lurking in her head. She focused on keeping her breathing even. Ronin and Jeremiah flashed her looks, but she did not meet their eyes.

Asha didn't allow herself to look at Kaira again.

At the other end of the table, Anselem had seen Asha go rigid after the last Amarok cadet introduced herself. He tucked the information into the back of his mind as he stood, addressing the group, "Our groups will be paired for this benchmark, as well as for the other two benchmarks where our branches will work together over the next few months, so I suggest you all get comfortable with one another quickly."

He pulled the folded paper from his pocket, the same paper he, nor any of the Valorous cadets, had been able to decipher. He placed it flatly on the table, his scribbled writing facing the group.

"This is the only information we have regarding what we could potentially face at the end of this week. Any ideas from the five of you would be greatly helpful."

Ronin and Asha shifted in their seats, uncomfortable with having to ask for assistance with the matter.

The Amarok cadets and their captain read the creased

paper over and over. Captain Mispar shook his head, followed by Flynn. Jasper and Kano desisted in sync.

The golden-eyed Amarok stared intently at the paper; her brow creased in concentration. After a long consideration, she looked up at Anselem, her eyes wide.

Her voice was low but strong, "I'm not sure of the second part... but 'Victory Over The Ego,'" she said, pointing to the first clue written on the page, "typically ego is always associated with or in reference to pride."

Anselem nodded, encouraging her to continue.

"And pride... what's the one thing we always associate with pride?" Anselem's eyes went wide as he put it together.

"Lions," a calm voice broke in. Anselem glanced back to find the voice belonging to Jeremiah.

A collection of curses rang through the group.

Asha was silent.

"How do we plan against a lion that can't be killed with..." Varrick leaned in to read off the note, "*Even the Greatest of Weapons?*"

Silence swept over the group for an extended time. Anselem chimed in, "I guess you are going to have to get creative."

Asha brushed Uriel's feathers as the tension in the field grew with each passing moment. Five firebirds, five wolves, and ten warriors all stared at one another across the open space. Rumbles and throaty growls drifted from the row of Amarok, snapping beaks and the scent of smoldering sulfur wafted across the line of Soturi.

The two groups had been flickered by a transportation stone imbued with stored magic to an unknown location for their first benchmark. Based on the surroundings, Asha suspected it was one of the smaller abandoned isles just east of Sveaborg.

Varrick leaned over to his Tribe, peeking up at the gathered firebirds. "I'm going to be pissed if my hair gets singed off."

Asha huffed out a laugh. "Between you and Ronin, I'm not sure who's vainer."

Ronin glanced over and shrugged. "There's nothing wrong with looking nice." He glanced down at his bare arms, and Asha swore he started to flex.

She rolled her eyes. "My two pretty princesses."

They laughed, and Jeremiah chimed in, "And what does that make me then, Ash?"

Asha cut her eyes over at him, a wide grin spreading on her face. "You can be the court jester, Jeremiah."

Ronin and Varrick laughed again, but Jeremiah leaned over and gave her a soft shove. "I shouldn't have asked."

Asha let out a small chuckle and gave him a wink.

"And what courtly position does that leave for you then, Seven?" His deep, husky accent chimed in from behind as he approached Valorous.

She whipped around, eyes narrowing as she gazed up at him. He was so tall. So annoyingly tall.

A swaggering grin crossed her lips. "I suppose that leaves me as the queen."

His brows raised. "Someone thinks awfully highly of herself."

Asha looked down and picked at her nails, seemingly unfazed. "Don't be upset, *Lieutenant*, I'm sure we can find you a place in our royal court. Perhaps a food taster so you can be the first to be removed."

His eyes narrowed, and a cocky smirk crossed his lips.

"Don't be surprised if I'm the one who ends up poisoning your wine, Seven."

She looked him dead in his emerald eyes. "If I'm forced to spend any more time with you, don't be surprised if I drink it."

She spun back around, leaving Eros with a blank look on his face. The three men standing beside her schooled their faces into neutral expressions, but Asha caught the humored twinkles in their eyes.

Kaira watched the group of Soturi cadets laughing with one another from across the field. The tall, domineering lieutenant standing behind them had an unamused expression on his face. Eros—the one Lana had said she'd let wear her legs as a belt. Kaira rolled her eyes once again at the recollection.

But Eros wasn't the Soturi who had caught Kaira's attention. No, that distinction belonged to the silver-blonde cadet standing in the center of the warriors. She carried herself with a swaggering confidence Kaira wished she could own, like a queen hoisted high upon her throne. But there was also an alluring quality about her that Kaira couldn't quite pinpoint, like the Soturi wore the forces of strength and darkness equally well.

She was stunning, as if she had carefully crafted her beauty to be honed as another useful weapon. And her eyes— they *burned*. Within the depths of the flaming sapphire, there lived an otherworldly flame that blazed like wildfire.

And when the warrior glanced up from her place across the field, those burning eyes narrowed, and it seemed as if she wanted to throw daggers straight into Kaira's chest.

The warrior looked half goddess, half Hells.

Tala shifted her weight beside Kaira, a low snarl building in her throat. She reached up and stroked the wolf's crisp white fur. She tilted her head down and looked at Kaira with those all-knowing ice-blue eyes.

The two warrior groups had been intermingled all week, working together to figure out different strategies for the benchmark, and just as Kaira had, Tala also noticed every jeering glare and every spiteful glance that the Soturi woman had thrown her way throughout the week.

At first, sitting inside the East Wing classroom, Kaira had been so caught off guard by the leering look that she almost thought she'd imagined it. But as the week carried on and the warrior continued to adamantly avoid working with her, Kaira's surprise had turned to indignation.

"You will have three hours to complete your benchmark," Captain Mispar called to the groups. "Here is the map." Mispar held up his arm, and a curled piece of paper was rolled in his hand. "You will meet back here once your task has been completed, or the time runs out."

No one asked how the groups would know once the time ran out, but Kaira figured Leadership had concocted some dreadful way of informing them.

"Lieutenant Eros and I will wait here until you return."

With those concluding words, Flynn walked over and took the rolled paper from the captain.

"Good luck, your time begins now."

Valorous walked to the center of the field to join their Amarok counterparts. They were already gathered around the map, deciphering the best course. The Soturi cadets allowed them to discuss and debate, conceding that the land navigation skills the Fenri learned were far superior to those of the Kappi, whose expertise lay in the skies.

It did not take long before the four Amarok cadets turned their attention to Valorous.

"What is it?" Varrick asked, dread filling his tone.

It was clear Flynn was heeding the charge of the Amarok group, but it was the golden-eyed woman who addressed Varrick, "How much weight can your firebirds carry?"

Varrick's brow furrowed. "What do you mean?"

Irritation flashed over the Amarok's face.

"They can carry us with one other rider." Asha's voice broke through the air, and she saw the gold eyes flash wide, surprise washing over her face that the Soturi had spoken to her.

As much as Asha wished to avoid Kaira, she knew she had to shove her emotions aside if they were going to make it through this benchmark in time—and *alive.*

Kaira nodded, and she spread the map out before the Valorous cadets.

"We are going to have to pair off," she explained. She pointed to the central, southernmost opening on the map. "This is where we are." She dragged her finger to the far north corner. "And this is where we need to go." She moved her hand to a spot on the paper a few inches below their objective. "But there is a large canyon that splits through the center of the island."

Asha stared at the scribblings and painted lines as the Amarok continued.

"We do not have the time for our wolves to run all the way around to where the lands connect on the western side. And the gap is far too wide for them to jump."

"They can't run down and through it?" Jeremiah asked, and his cheeks blushed bright red as both women cut their eyes at him.

But it was Ronin who replied, patting him on the shoulder, "Gods am I glad to not be the one on the receiving end of those glares."

Varrick snorted.

"If you three aren't going to say anything helpful, then keep your mouths shut," Asha snipped, staring back down at the inked paper.

The Amarok men let out stifled laughs, and Kaira cut in, "I don't see you three being any more useful."

The women exchanged a silent look before turning their attention back to the map.

"So, I'm thinking that we can pair off and your firebirds can carry us over to the northern edge of the canyon, where we can land and get our bearings instead of heading straight in."

Asha nodded her agreement. "I think that works, but I would have the wolves stage here," she pointed to the near-sided edge of the canyon roughly halfway across the island, "in case anything goes wrong, and we need to get someone out quickly. It would make for a much shorter distance for the phoenixes to carry them before heading back for the others."

Kaira's eyes scoured the map, and then she nodded.

"Anything to add?" Asha asked, turning to face the men.

Asha and Kaira were met with blank stares.

"Alright," Asha said, heading over to Uriel. "We will meet the four of you at the center opening at the southern edge of the canyon."

Kaira nodded, and the four Amarok cadets headed over to the other side of the field to meet their wolves.

Asha climbed into the pommel atop Uriel and waited for her Tribe to mount their firebirds. Once her Divisionmates had settled into their saddles, Asha grabbed the reins, patted Uriel once, and launched into the skies.

It took Kaira and the other Amarok cadets over half an hour to reach the meeting point. Mounted atop Tala, Kaira led the charge, weaving through the densely packed trees. The forest had an eerie feel to it, as if it were alive, watching the pack as they raced through the woods. Kaira held a disquieting suspicion that if the pack were to be separated, the lone wolf would possibly never be seen again, swallowed up by the surrounding gloom of the forest.

She pushed the thoughts from her mind and let out a high-pitched call, advising Tala to go faster. The wolf obliged, and the wind racing past Kaira's face burned her cheeks. Several strands of her hair were pulled loose from the braid she had fastened, but the whipping wind pushed them back, keeping her vision clear.

Tree after tree darted past, becoming a combined blur of browns and greens. She did not dare to look back, but she could hear thundering steps echoing behind her, and she knew the other three Amarok were keeping pace. Sweat began to drip down her back, and her muscles began to cramp as the pack finally neared the forest's edge and entered the open space before the canyon. She looked to her left and found the Soturi and their firebirds roughly two hundred yards away. She turned to head in their direction, but the warriors were already airborne with their birds, crossing the distance in a fraction of the time it would have taken the Amarok.

They landed only a few yards in front of the pack.

The wolves let out feral snarls, and the growls were

met with responding snaps from the phoenixes' beaks. Every warrior in the opening pulled the reins on their bonded beasts.

Kaira slid off Tala, and her Amarok teammates followed suit. The wolves stayed seated, having already been informed what the battle plan was on the way over. Tala had given a disapproving grumble in response, but eventually gave in.

Jasper, Kano, and Flynn quickly hurried over to pair up with the three men, admittedly intimidated by the daunting blonde warrior and her snow-white firebird. Kaira rolled her eyes and walked over to Asha.

"What? Afraid I'll bite, boys?" Asha drawled.

The three Amarok men's faces turned bright red, and the Valorous cadets chuckled.

The golden blonde warrior with bright, tawny eyes leaned back and called over to Kaira, reassuringly, "Don't worry, she doesn't bite."

The tall one—Varrick—chimed in, "No, but she does like to stab and shoot, Jeremiah."

Kaira glanced up at the warrior who looked like the type of woman who never ran from her demons; instead, she would learn their names.

She swallowed once and hoisted herself onto the back of the saddle.

I am a master of my fear. I have power beyond measure. I am unbreakable.

Asha repeated the mantra over and over, as the cadre threaded their way through the north side of the Isle. Asha was admittingly thankful for the Amaroks' abilities to navigate the terrain, but she kept a note in the back of her mind

of the lesser training their branch experienced when it came
to bloodshed and battle, for she knew there was impending
carnage awaiting them at the end of their trek.

It took another half hour of wandering through dried forests on foot and climbing over rocky hills before the group
finally reached the border of the expansive area that housed
the objective of their benchmark.

Asha slowed her pace, and the group mimicked her
change in speed.

She paused before exiting the cover of the forest and
stared out into the rocky hills. The rocks were lined with
caves, and streams flowed through the bottom of the gorge,
collecting in a large pool at the base of the cliff.

A figure moved inside the shadows of the cave, and as
it emerged, Asha noted the carved-out sections of rock were
not caves at all—they were a network of connecting dens.

Out of the shadows stepped the Lion with the Impenetrable Hide.

The group collectively sucked in a sharp breath as the
creature stretched to its full height. Its majestic yellow-gold
mane encircled a large head with teeth and jaws made for a
singular purpose—shredding its prey. It had a strong, dense
body with powerful forelegs and a tail that swished back and
forth with the wind. But the most paralyzing feature was not
the beast's shredding teeth or its gutting claws, nor was it the
way the cat moved with feline prowess. The most terrifying
trait was the two fierce eyes that stared at Asha as if the beast
could see straight into her soul. Golden pools filled with unnerving courage and pride.

The Lion let out a deafening roar that shook the trees,
and Asha knew they would have to fight their way out, for
they had already lost the element of surprise.

Asha stepped out from the tree line and into the sunlight. She knew there was no time to waste if the cadre was going to make it back in time.

The beast prowled nearly one hundred yards away, perched atop the cliffside as it stared down at the group of warriors.

Asha tracked the Lion with her eyes, watching each move it made as it stalked back and forth on the large rock. She unlatched her bow from her back and drew an arrow from her quiver.

"What are you doing?" Kaira hissed.

Asha did not take her eyes off the beast.

"It isn't going to work."

"I would at least like to try before we run headfirst into impending carnage," she snapped back, her voice a viscous whisper.

"How are you even going to hit the beast from this far?" one of the twins asked.

A smirk twitched on Asha's face, but she did not respond.

"Valhol's Arrow," Jeremiah replied simply.

"That's you?!" Flynn gasped.

"Keep your voice down," she barked.

She nocked the arrow against the bow and pulled the string back, her hand brushing her cheek. She felt the wind on her face as she locked eyes with the Lion. She released and had another arrow ready before it reached the cat.

She sent the second arrow flying just after the first, aiming for two different spots.

The arrow found its mark, but just before it went through the beast's eyes, a giant paw, claws fully extended, came up and swatted it away like a pestering fly.

The second followed too closely for the beast to react in time, and it struck center—right in its heart.

Asha's own heart sank as she and the rest of the cadre watched the steel arrow ricochet off the Lion's chest.

A growl ripped through the beast's throat, and it jumped from the rock face and landed on the platform level with the warriors.

"Any other brilliant ideas, Raynor?"

"I'm all ears if you have an idea, Ronin."

Silence.

The beast began to lurk towards them.

"We can't shoot it or stab it, but maybe we can beat it to death?" Kaira answered, clearly having thought through some ulterior ideas in the last several days.

Asha swallowed a lump that rose in her throat from witnessing the woman's bright mind.

She nodded, fastening the bow to her back and pulling out a smooth club. She would normally have opted for a version fixed with spikes, but when she chose the weapon, she figured if she was going to have to use it, it was because her arrows truly had failed to penetrate the Lion's hide.

The rest of the cadre followed her lead, and then the group charged towards the Lion.

Ronin struck first, then Varrick and Jeremiah. Asha fell in, swinging the club hard against the beast's jaw.

A fractured crack ripped through the air, and she felt the wood in her hand splinter.

Shit.

The Amarok cadets filed in just as the Lion's roar tore through their ears.

Asha screamed her warning, but it was too late for Kano to move. His eyes went wide as a clawed paw swiped across his torso. A piercing cry rattled the skies, and it was echoed by Jasper, as if the pair could feel one another's pain.

Kano fell to the ground, his dark, crimson blood already

pooling beneath him. Jasper was by his side in an instant, pulling his body away from the sharp canines of the cat. Flynn ran toward the twins and threw his hands onto the open gash, applying pressure in hopes of slowing the bleeding. Valorous continued beating back the beast.

Asha knew from the wound that he would bleed out soon if he did not get help.

"Varrick!" she screamed. He swung his club again, and the beast retreated a step. He flashed her a look. "You need to take Kano and fly him back!"

His eyes flashed as he took in the scene behind him.

"Now!"

He gave one final swing of his club and then stumbled backward, his feet moving faster than his body was ready for, and he raced to Kano.

Jeremiah and Ronin continued to push the beast back, their clubs doing no true harm to the creature.

Asha stepped up to fill in Varrick's open space. The Lion let out another loud growl. Its eyes were filled with irritation, as if it were playing a simple game of cat and mouse with the cadre and was quickly growing tired.

"I won't leave him!"

Asha chanced a glance behind her to see Jasper clinging to his brother's pale body. His chest was rising, but his breaths looked more and more shallow by the second.

He didn't have time.

"Jeremiah, go with Varrick, fly Jasper with him," she ordered. Jeremiah hesitated for only a moment before he quickly realized there was no time to argue. Kano was going to die if they didn't leave. Now.

He rushed past her, slowing down as he arrived next to the group, and in a flash, they were all up and running, Jasper and Jeremiah carrying Kano on their shoulders.

And just like that, their cadre had been cut in half.

Flynn fell into the place Jeremiah had abandoned, and the three warriors exchanged blow after blow with the Lion, dodging its lethal claws with each swing.

Asha glanced to her right, then to her left.

Where in the Seven Hells did Kaira go?

Sweat dripped down Asha's body. They weren't going to make it. The beast was barely phased, its strength and stamina endless.

A high-pitched whistle sounded high above the Lion's head.

Asha's gaze followed the sound, landing on the Amarok woman perched on the landing, standing before the opening to the den.

She was holding something in her hands that Asha couldn't make out. She followed Kaira's pointed hand to the other side of the ledge, and everything clicked.

Kaira wanted them to lure the Lion into one side of the den and ambush it from the other direction. Asha still had no idea what advantage ambushing an unkillable beast would give them, but she was willing to trust Kaira's mind.

Asha quickly relayed the information to Ronin and Flynn. They grunted in acknowledgment, their clubs still swinging.

"On three, we run!" she yelled to them. Both warriors nodded.

"One!" Asha struck the beast, and it stepped backward.

"Two!" She turned her hips in the direction of the cliff as Flynn dodged a swiping paw.

"Three!" Ronin's club made contact with the Lion's mouth, and the trio took off in a sprint. Asha's legs had never moved so fast in her life.

She led them to the rocky path she had seen on the far

side of the hill. She could hear the storming steps of the men behind her, followed by barreling paws on top of rocks. Her lungs burned; she felt they would rip from her chest.

Step after step, she climbed the path to the den's landing, her heels digging deeper into the loose rocks. As she crested the wall, throwing herself onto the platform before the cave opening, she heard it. The noise sounded more animal than human. It was the noise of life itself venting its terror and shock into the thin vapors of the uncaring air. A noise that served no purpose but to express pain in all its forms. The noise was so shredding, even the forest heard and understood.

Asha looked over the edge of the rock to see the Lion's jaws clenched around Ronin's leg.

"No!" she screamed, the high pitch filled with dread and agony.

A colossal, dark form whipped past her face, and she did not register the boulder Kaira had shoved over the side until it collided with the side of the cat.

It released its hold and tumbled down to the bottom of the cliff. A flapping of wings sounded, and a loud screech clamored through the skies as Ronin's cobalt firebird landed on the cutout in the rocks beside where he lay.

He looked up at Asha, fear filling his eyes, and he shook his head, refusing to leave her behind.

"Go! Flynn, take him and go!"

Flynn looked up at Kaira and paused. "I've got her, now go!"

The Lion was scrambling to its feet only a few stories below, and even from her height, Asha could see the fury raging in its golden eyes.

Flynn nodded, and hearing the rocks clattering below them, he quickly threw Ronin, fighting and yelling, onto the back of Tonalli, and the firebird launched into the sky.

The beast was halfway up the cliff when Asha scrambled to her feet and looked into Kaira's fear-filled eyes. She grabbed her hands, looking down to see a rope curled around them, then pulled her sapphire eyes up to meet the oceans of gold.

"I am a master of my fear. I have power beyond measure. I am unbreakable."

Kaira's eyes went wide.

"Say it."

"I am a master of my fear. I have power beyond measure. I am unbreakable," she repeated. Asha nodded, and she swore a faint bit of bravery poured into the shining gold.

The beast's claws scratched against the stone directly below them.

"Get it to follow you and run in that way." Kaira pointed to the far opening of the den. "I'll go in here, and when we meet in the middle, we are going to have to tie this around its neck and strangle it." She lifted the rope in her hands.

Asha's eyes went wide. Not in questioning disbelief, but in awe of how beautifully brilliant the Amarok woman's mind could be. It could not be killed with weapons, nor struck with blades and arrows, but no beast could live without air.

Asha nodded as the Lion's claws broke over the edge, and it pulled itself up onto the landing. Kaira ran. Asha paused for a fraction of a moment, waiting for the beast to step towards her. It pounced, and Asha took off in a sprint, heading into the darkness of the den, away from the Amarok.

She had a good lead, but the Lion was quickly gaining. Her legs pushed and pushed, propelling her as far forward as each step could take her through the shadowed cave.

A thunderous roar grumbled behind her, and it was so

close she could feel the vibration inside her bones.

"Duck!" a voice screamed, and Asha obeyed, scarcely missing the rope tied across two sides of the den.

She spun around, watching the rope twist around the beast's thick neck. But the sides of the wall where it was tied did not catch, and the Lion continued to barrel towards her, dragging the rope along behind it. Asha gasped and turned as the beast closed in on her. She was too slow, and the ravenous claws swatted at her stomach. A hand grabbed her arm, yanking her away from the shredding nails. But Kaira had not been able to jerk her far enough away from the reach of the beast's paw, and its mangling claw slashed through her shirt, ripping through the fabric and into flesh. Like metal screaming against stone, her cry pierced the darkness and her shirt hung from her arm like shredded ribbons.

The cord, still wound around the Lion's throat, sprawled out to each side. And with an unspoken glance, the women leapt from their space through the darkness, and grabbed each side of the rope, pulling in opposing directions. They tugged and yanked with every scrap of strength left inside them, ignoring the powerful, shredding claws mere inches from their skin. They pulled and pulled, as sweat dripped down their faces and blood trickled from their torn palms. Asha's muscles began to cramp, but she did not waver. Neither did the Amarok across from her.

The beast thrashed, but the women both held on tightly until the last of the air was choked from its lungs and the Lion crashed against the cold stone ground.

The women took in gasping breaths, gulping down air as their hearts returned to a normal rhythm. Asha's hands burned. She stared down at the suffocated beast, and its lifeless eyes blankly stared back. Blood dripped down her arm. She pulled her Elysian knife from her waistband and began to saw off one of the creature's claws. After a few moments, she detached the claw from the beast's paw.

Kaira stared at her quietly.

Asha took the claw in her hand and pressed it against the lion's pelt.

It sliced straight through.

She cut off the beast's impenetrable hide and slung it over her shoulders and turned to face the Amarok warrior. She said nothing and instead tossed the claw over to the woman, a token of remembrance for all they had accomplished.

Asha, with the Lion's pelt around her, walked out from the cave and climbed atop Uriel.

The Amarok followed suit, and within moments Uriel lifted the pair into the sky—ingenious warriors of both strength and mind.

After they returned to the southern side of the isle, the cadre stared at Asha, donning the beastly cloak, with wide eyes.

The group was swiftly congratulated on their accomplishment by the Leaders and quickly flickered back to Sveaborg by the awaiting instructors.

Once the group was alone, the questions swarmed.

"Tell us everything! How in the Seven Hells are you *wearing* that?"

"How did you kill it?"

"Are you two alright?"

Kaira told the story of how the Lion was slain and explained that the only weapon capable of cutting through its skin was the beast's own claws.

The group, still battered and broken, stood in awe.

And with her low, kind voice, Kaira added, "As chaotic as today was, it was very nice to work with all of you. I'm extremely glad we were paired with such fearless fighters."

Asha looked up and met her golden eyes. Her heart sank. Every time she looked into the gold pools, all she could think about was the brilliant mind that was behind them and the lightless, silver-flecked eyes it reminded her of. Her body went cold.

"Well, I for one will be more than happy when these joint benchmarks are all completed, and we can go back to our own responsibilities." Asha pulled the pelt tighter to her chest, grabbed her bag, and sauntered off, happy to be away from the accusing golden eyes.

She had walked a good distance back to her room when she heard the storming steps following from behind.

"What the Hells is your problem?"

Asha whipped around at the accusatory tone the Amarok brandished. "I have no problem. What the Hells is *your* problem?"

"You are. You and your bitchy attitude and unrestrained arrogance," she bit back. It had been a long time since someone had been brave enough to go toe-to-toe with Asha's unrelenting fury. She would have admired the woman if she hadn't wanted to slap her across the face.

Asha bared her teeth but said nothing, still refusing to meet Kaira's damning eyes. She turned away and began to storm off, but Kaira's words stopped her in her tracks. "Who was it? Who broke you so badly you refuse to let anyone else in?"

The words came out with a tone of irritation, but she caught the hint of understanding behind them, as if the Amarok warrior could see the brokenness inside Asha because she knew it well herself. Asha slowly turned around to face Kaira, her burning sapphire eyes holding nothing but hate.

"I saw your tattoos." Her golden eyes were softer now, and somehow the pity made Asha angrier than the condemning words she had thrown her way moments before.

Kaira sighed. "Unless you learn to face your own shadows, you will continue to see them in others."

Asha did not say a word, but the fiery rage continued to burn behind her eyes. Kaira stared back at her, unflinching, then slowly, she pulled both sleeves of her shirt up, revealing winding ink that looked like shattered rays of sunlight. A small gasp escaped from Asha's mouth, and the kindling flame behind her eyes winked out. There had to be dozens of rays stretching over her deep tan skin.

"The first ones came when I lost my parents."

Asha again said nothing, but as her eyes raised to meet the golden pool staring back at her, she nodded, an acknowledgment of an unspoken relatedness.

"Most of the others came in the following years. When I went to live with my uncle. He was... he was a cruel man, with a twisted idea of what love was."

She was quiet for a long moment. Asha's eyes were lined with silver as understanding filled her mind. When Kaira raised her gaze back to meet hers, a darkness so similar to Asha's danced behind the gold.

"Fenri training... It's not the same as how the Kappi operate. We did not stay at the Citadel all year round. So, I was able to escape him for most of the year, but during the summers, I would be sent back to Velsen.

"When I was seventeen, I met Lysander. He was nice and kind. He was a good man. And he loved me."

She was quiet again for a long moment. Memories flashing through her mind. She let a small smile cross her face. She dragged her thumb across a deeper-lined ray on her forearm. "He was killed in a battle south of the Strait a year after we got married."

"I'm so sorry," Asha whispered, the words coming out thick.

Kaira smiled. "I held a lot of guilt for a long while after."

Asha's brow crinkled.

"I think at first I believed it was love. He was so sweet, and at the start, there was excitement and passion. But I think, more than I longed for him, I longed for the promise of escape. And as the months went by, I think even he knew the love I had for him was more from what he had given me than for who he was. I'm not proud of that. He deserved better."

Asha searched her face, now staring down at the grass beneath her, but found nothing in Kaira's blank stare.

"I would have stayed with him, and he knew that too, but I think he also knew it was over long before he left for war."

"Did you know it was over?"

"Yes."

"How?"

Kaira lifted her head and looked into Asha's eyes. "I think you know it's over when you feel more in love with your memories and the idea of someone than the person standing in front of you."

Asha swallowed a lump in her throat. Kaira's gold eyes burned into Asha, but she remained quiet as the Soturi gathered the words buried deep inside her.

If Asha was honest with herself, she truly wasn't sure why she answered the Amarok warrior. She didn't know if it was because the woman had just bared her soul to her, or because there was something in her golden eyes that told Asha she could trust her, or simply because Asha had held the Darkness inside for too long and it was hungering to crawl out; but she took a deep breath and said, "Her name was Nina."

And Asha, for the first time in her life, told the story of her best friend. She told her of the Kappi soldier who had stood by her side every day for fourteen years, of the woman who had held her in her arms and cried with her as she learned of her brother's death, and she told her of the culminating test in the Inferno—*The Final Testing of Algae*—when she had to plunge a dagger into her heart of gold and watch the beaming light leave her silver-flecked eyes.

And as Asha told the story about the woman with a heart of light and a mind of steel, tears slid from her eyes, and the Darkness lurking deep inside her heart receded the smallest of steps.

CHAPTER ELEVEN

Sweat poured down Asha's back. They had been sparring for hours in the midday sun, and she was drenched beneath her leathers. Eros had instructed them through one-on-one fights throughout the morning, and Asha had won each of them with ease.

In an effort to increase the challenge, he had her fight not just one, not two, but all three of her teammates at once, just to see how she would fare. She was initially pissed when he gave Valorous the instructions, thinking he was simply trying to create a scenario in which she would fail. But as she stepped into the ring with the three warriors, she saw Eros's stare locked in on her, watching every movement she made; and Asha had the keen awareness that he might actually have been trying to help construct a situation where she would have a chance to learn—a situation, she realized, she might actually have to face one day when she made it out of training.

She quickly removed Varrick from the equation as soon as the match began, pinning him to the ground swiftly, before the other two warriors even had a chance to register the move. After she sprang back up, Varrick swearing as he sulked to the outer perimeter of the ring, she assessed Ronin and Jeremiah. She knew she could not take both on at once, so she decided she would need to split them up, take care of one, and then the other. Ronin was a bigger challenge, so she baited Jeremiah first, taunting him until he leapt towards her. She quickly spun out of his reach and grabbed him from behind, flipping him over her shoulder. He landed on his back, the air knocked from his lungs. She knew she only had a split second before he would be back on his feet and lunging towards her, so she took the opening to deal with Ronin.

She pulled a dagger from her waistband. Ronin's eyes went wide as he palmed the blade on his own waistband, knowing full well she could end him before he even pulled the knife out from its sheath. Asha chuckled.

"Calm down, Ronin, I wouldn't actually stab you." A mischievous glimmer flicked in her eyes.

"Well, excuse me if I don't particularly believe you, Raynor. Sometimes you get that devious spark in your eyes, and I swear the flames inside you start to burn a little brighter. And I'm not dumb enough to stand here and get torched. I know my own limits."

She laughed, and he flashed a smile.

She heard Jeremiah scrambling to his feet behind her.

"How about this? If I hit the center of the wooden pole beside you, we can both pretend it was between your eyes, and I will spare you the embarrassment of wrestling you to the ground. I wouldn't want to dirty up your pristine-looking leathers, Ronin." She flashed another grin and sent the dagger flying. It plunged straight into the center of the wood.

Ronin's eyes grew even wider as he looked over to where the blade landed, mere inches from his head.

He let out a relieved laugh. "You walk a fine line between brilliantly lethal and absurdly psychotic, Raynor." She gave him a wink, and he shook his head, still laughing to himself as he stepped out of the ring.

"One on your back, Fletch!" a voice behind Asha yelled from across the open yard.

Asha froze in the ring, her whole body going still.

There was only one person who still called her that...

Feeling an approaching presence, she whipped around, dodging the dagger of the final fighter. Grabbing Jeremiah's arm, she twisted it behind him and pulled up until he dropped the blade. A yelp escaped from his lips. She turned her weight and pushed him face-first onto the ground; his arm still twisted behind his back as she shoved a knee into his spine. She unsheathed a final dagger that she'd kept hidden in her boot and pressed it against Jeremiah's throat.

Leaning over him, her knee still pressing him hard into the dirt, Asha looked up from her spot in the ring, eyes searching the crowd hastily before locking in on the man across the field. A scarce smile spread across her face.

There he stood, tall and broad, his skin more sun-kissed than she had seen it a few months before—likely a result of too many hours in the sky. His blonde hair was cut shorter now, and his body somehow looked even more muscular than she remembered.

Asha pulled her blade from Jeremiah's neck, tucking it in her belt, and took off in a run clear across the open training field. A voice called after her, but she paid it no mind.

When she finally reached the man on the other side, without pause, she leapt into his arms, throwing her body against his and grabbing him tight.

He wrapped his arms around her and laughed. "Not bad, Fletch."

Her head was tucked under his chin, and she breathed in the familiar smell of patchouli and pine. She leaned her head back slightly, pulling off his chest to better look at his face; neither of them let go of the other.

"Dolion," she whispered. The name came out soft and low, as if she couldn't believe it was him. Her childhood best friend. The one person who had been there through every-thing, who knew everything. He had been by her side every day since Math died, until last year when he had to leave for Soturi tryouts while she stayed behind in Valhol to finish out her final year of Kappi training.

"Hi, Ash," he smiled back, a full, genial grin.

She had missed that smile. It reminded her so much of simpler times, of better days—a smile that would always make her think of Mathieson.

"What are you doing here?" Her eyes began to rake over him, surveying to ensure he wasn't injured.

"Just my routine training week, no need to fuss."

Asha let out a sigh, and her shoulders untensed. Had it already been three weeks that she had been here? She'd memorized Dolion's unit number months ago and made sure to look up the rotational schedule for the active Soturi war-riors when she first arrived at Sveaborg to ensure no chang-es had occurred—six-week rotations; five weeks at a des-ignated war camp, followed by one seven-day assignment of in-service training at the Base. Usually, anywhere from three to four units were assigned to training at a given time. After their assigned week, each group headed back to their respective stations across Perseis.

It was midway through his schedule when Asha arrived at Sveaborg. She couldn't believe the three weeks had already passed. *Time flies when you're sidestepping death every day,* she mused.

"Couldn't survive another week without seeing my beautiful face?"

Dolion let out another lighthearted laugh. "I missed you, too, Fletch."

Asha peeled herself from Dolion's arms and walked back across the field to the ring, Dolion glued to her side. She grabbed her bag, lying on the ground just outside the fighting ring, and turned to head towards the Barracks.

"You're not finished here," Anselem barked at her.

She whipped around. "Yeah, and who else is there for me to fight? I'm pretty sure these *boys* have had their asses handed to them enough for one day." She glanced over Eros's shoulder to look at each of her teammates; not one of them dared counter her claims.

"Well then, perhaps you should fight someone new. I'm sure Sergeant Laeradur wouldn't mind, would you?" Eros turned his gaze over to Dolion, who stiffened at Asha's side.

Asha did not remove her leer from Eros.

"I'm not fighting Dolion," she replied.

"Fine," Eros growled. A wicked grin spread over his face as he turned his eyes back to Asha. "Then you get to fight me."

Anselem had watched Asha fight every day for the past three weeks. He had watched the way she carried herself, her poised posture, the gentle sway of her hips as she sauntered into the ring to meet an opponent, already confident of the win.

He had observed the gracefulness of her movements,

the contemplative assessment she made each time she approached her rival, and the incredible speed in which she disarmed her adversaries.

He had noticed the light feet, the tucked chin, the loose shoulders—every cue he had ever been taught to look out for in a fight.

And Anselem also knew from his years in training that most of the time, he never really had to worry too much about the soldier who was talking smack. Those men were usually pretty easy to take care of. But the one who *didn't* say anything? *That* was the warrior he knew he should think twice about before tangling with him.

And Asha? She was as silent as the grave.

So Anselem could admit to himself that she was good—great even. It would be ignorant not to.

But he was better.

He stepped into the ring and positioned himself on the far side, waiting for Asha to join. A large group started to join the Valorous cadets gathered around the ring's edge.

As she stepped towards the circle, Dolion grabbed her wrist, and Anselem had to strain his ears to hear what he said.

"Do you have a death wish?"

She ripped her arm from his hold, and even from his corner of the ring, Anselem could see the icy rage glossing over her eyes.

Did Laeradur not know her at all? Did he seriously think implying she couldn't *do something was going to get her to back off?*

Watching as Asha sauntered into the circle, Anselem picked up on the tenseness in her shoulders, the uneven rise of her chest beneath her leathers. She was nervous. For once in her life, Asha Raynor looked nervous for a fight. *Good.*

Anselem unsheathed the knives from his belt, un-strapped the swords from his back, and dropped them on the ground outside the ring. The long steel blades glinted in the sunlight.

One of the swords shimmered with beauty. It had been handcrafted in Elysia, specifically for Anselem, and was made by the finest swordsmith in Perseis, and Anselem had paid handsomely for it.

But the second one was simpler, with an obsidian hilt fixed with a single gold stone at the pommel.

Soulmaker—The Blade Which Cries Through the Veil.

It was rumored that the sword possessed a voice of its own, and its whispering words could not be heard by anyone but the one who commanded the blade's path. He earned it on his first mission, and the stories claimed it was crafted of the only material stronger than Elysian steel—dragon glass. But the dragons had been wiped out millennia before, in The First War, and Anselem had never been one to listen to the tales of old.

"No weapons," he stated, turning back to face the center of the ring. He knew she only had one dagger left from her last fight, hidden somewhere on her body. She hadn't replaced the others when she walked back over from her off-putting tangle with Laeradur. Anselem had no clue why the whole scene bothered him so much. He shoved the thought from his head and focused on the warrior before him.

Asha pulled the dagger from her waistband, palming it in her right hand. But she didn't move to the edge to discard it. Anselem stared deep into her icy, sapphire eyes. A moment passed, and then he saw it—a simple, swift flick of her wrist.

He heard the collision against the frame of the sparring

ring behind him before the pain radiated up his arm. He heard the gasps from the group gathered around the circle, and a slow trickle of blood started to dribble down his tricep.

He looked down at his arm. Just a scratch. It wouldn't even leave a scar.

He whipped his eyes back across the ring. "You missed."

"Just discarding my weaponry, *Lieutenant*. It must have slipped." He had seen her with those daggers—he knew she didn't miss.

She really might have a death wish, he thought. She was fearless and daring—it reminded him so much of Mathieson that a small grin formed on his lips.

"Let's see what you've got, Seven."

The two warriors broke into a dance, circling one another as they searched for an opening to take. He watched as the patience in her eyes slowly ran out, overtaken by ice and fury. He turned his body, slightly opening his left side, just enough to bait her. He hoped she would be smart enough to sense the trap. With the frost coating her veins, blocking out her sense of reason, she wasn't.

She took the bait—lunged straight for his left side, he easily spun out of the way, avoiding the twisting punch she had intended for his ribs. He smirked, and the ice in her eyes dissolved, replaced by roaring fire.

She lunged again, quicker this time, her moves powerful and fast.

Damn. She really was good. He had always assumed her reputation as one of Valhol's greatest soldiers had been predominantly due to her sharpshooter skills, but as they grappled, he realized firsthand her skills were not just limited to a bow.

Anselem deflected each blow, twisting and turning and blocking with ease.

"Fight back," she growled, her eyes dark and filled with flames.

He let out a small laugh. "I thought you were here to hand all of the *boys* their asses," he drawled, "or is that everyone but me?"

She looked like she would explode. Her breath grew heavy with rage as she lunged at him again, and he moved with ease out of her grasp. He whipped around and grabbed her, pulling her against him, her back pressed to his chest. He swept an arm under her throat and pressed down, leaving the pressure light enough for her to still breathe. Her hands shot up to her throat, clawing at his forearm. She tried to kick, but he moved before she made contact, leaving his arm still wrapped around her neck.

He leaned his chin down, his mouth close beside her ear, and whispered so low that no one else could hear, "Calm down." She thrashed more in his arms, trying to break free from his grasp. "Seven, listen to me and calm down. Think. Think through it."

Asha's body slowed as the words registered. She might hate him, and he didn't blame her for it, but he could still teach her. He could still give her every possible chance at surviving. Her breathing started to slow down, the gears in her mind turning as she worked through her options. She dropped her hand down to her waistband, and, as she reared it back up, Anselem caught the flash of metal at the last second. He dropped her from his arms as she twisted back, slashing the hidden dagger towards his torso. He was able to twist out of the way from the blade sliding through his stomach, but she caught the end of his arm, ripping a gash through his forearm.

He could feel the blood dripping down his fingers, but he didn't take his eyes off his opponent.

He wondered if she would do it, in front of the crowd, if she would truly try to kill him here.

He wondered if he would let her.

He didn't think about the idea long before she lunged again, blade singing as he dodged slice after slice. They fell back into another rhythmic dance. He defended, she attacked.

He watched each movement, timing it, learning the pattern of the swings.

Until she cut for him one last time, and he dodged to the side, kicking his feet underneath hers as he took her off balance, and she fell to the ground.

He didn't waste a second before he was on top of her, pinning her against the ground below, blood still dripping from his arm. Her arm was sprawled to the side, pinned on the ground with the dagger still in hand. Her breathing was rushed, sweat beading on her forehead.

Anselem's breath was barely raised. He leaned in close, his voice lowered again, "I don't care if you hate me. I don't frankly care if you want to kill me, Seven. But you *will* show up, you *will* learn, and you will fight for your life every day until you leave this Base." Asha blinked, the only sign that she had heard him. Then he realized how close her body was pressed up against his own. How he could feel the rise of her chest with each breath and smell the radiating scent of jasmine and vanilla. He noticed the small, crescent -shaped scar on her left cheek and wondered when she had gotten it. And then he noticed the dip of her eyes, how they, for the briefest of moments, trailed down to his lips and lingered. And then he became too aware of his position between her legs, the placement of her legs around him. His unwavering breath hitched. Her eyes shot back up to his, and a fraction of a moment passed before the world was shifting. And he realized too late that she had tucked her foot behind his legs and pushed her hips up, twisting the two of them over until she was on top of him, dagger plunging toward his chest. He grabbed her wrist, holding it off as she leaned in, those sapphire blue eyes twinkling. "Didn't anyone ever teach you that you should stay focused, *Lieutenant*? Distractions can be deadly, even if they are wrapped up so beautifully."

And as she spoke, Anselem had moved his other hand down to his side, the motion so small, it was almost unnoticed. Until he pressed his own hidden blade to the side of her throat, "Looks like I'm not the only one who can be distracted," he replied. The light in her sapphire eyes went dark. "And it looks like I'm not the only one with something to hide."

Asha let go of the dagger, and it dropped into the dirt, thudding against the ground. She flung herself off him and strutted across the ring to her bag, grabbing it without breaking her stride. Even from a distance, he could see the steam leaking from her ears.

Anselem cut a lethal look towards the silent crowd, and they dispersed, no words spoken among the group.

His scent of amber and citrus was still wrapped around her as she stormed across the yard. She did not know where she was headed, her head spinning with fury.

"Fletch, slow down."

She didn't stop, her steps heading towards the staircase that led down the mountain towards the lower fields of the Soturi training grounds.

"Fletch," Dolion ground out again, his steps catching up to hers.

She made it all the way across the field, far away from the rings, when he was finally able to reach her side.

"Asha, stop." He grabbed her elbow to stop her from descending the stairs. She whipped around.

"What Dolion. What in the Seven Hells could you possibly have to say that would somehow make it better? Make *that* any better?" She waved her hand towards the ring across the field from which she had stormed away. He looked at her, giving her a chance to collect herself before he spoke. As the moments passed, her breathing began to slow, returning to normal.

"Do you realize how stupid that was?"

Asha glared at him, ice filling her eyes once again.

"You're lucky to be alive after going toe-to-toe with him."

She scoffed. "Yeah, like he would have actually done anything."

"Asha, he is part of the Septant! They don't play by the same rules as the rest of us!" His voice was strained and exasperated, as if he truly believed she had a death wish.

She was quiet for a moment, forcing her face to stay neutral, and she responded with a lowered voice, "I know who he is, Dolion. I know exactly who he is and what he has done and what he belongs to."

His eyes softened a bit. "I know you do, Ash. But that doesn't make it any less stupid to go up against him."

"He wouldn't have hurt me."

"You don't know that."

"I do."

"How?" he asked, annoyance returning to his tone.

"I just do." She cut him a glance to let him know the conversation was over, and she headed back towards the descending staircase. She didn't wait to see if he would follow.

He didn't.

As she plunged down the steps, rage fueling the speed of her downward climb, she worked through all her moves in the ring, ran through each of her decisions, and what she had done wrong. She made herself consider Anselem's words. She tried to process what she should make of them. Had he actually tried to help her? She didn't want to think about the idea of it and what that would mean.

She instead forced her mind to what Dolion had revealed. *The Septant.*

She had lied. When she entered the ring, she had no clue Anselem was part of the Septant—Perseis's top seven warriors, hand-picked from all three branches. To be chosen for the Septant was not only a privilege, it was the highest honor one could achieve. It was the most elite unit a warrior could join, and only the best of the best—whether Soturi, Amarok, or Pontos—were ever selected. They were the most lethal, proficient, and powerful warriors of the Perseisian Army, and they held honor and loyalty in the highest esteem.

But their promise—their Word—was the most valuable asset they wielded. They were realm-renowned for *always* following through on their promises and for always paying their debts. A warrior did not get chosen for the unit without displaying each of those attributes—repeatedly.

Asha had never known Anselem was part of the unit. She never would have guessed it. She had assumed he was well-known for his brutality and cunningness. She never once thought his reverence amongst the warriors might have actually been warranted.

She tried to swallow the information, make sense of it, but before she was able to shove the knowledge down to digest later, one more thought popped into her head.

If Anselem had been in Aaru on a mission with the

Septant, what in the Hells was Mathieson doing there with them? And if she was missing *that* key part of information, what other details had been lost along the way?

Anselem's words from weeks ago came rushing into her mind. *There are other sides to the story.*

CHAPTER TWELVE

The rest of the week had gone by in a blur. Each day, Valorous met, and each day Anselem ran them through drill after drill, sparring with one another until their bodies went limp from exhaustion. But, at the end of the week, Anselem's unending drills paid off, and Valorous won their Wargame against Inquisition Division, three to one. Varrick was bested by Asha's old friend from Valhol, Meraki, but she smiled and gave him a pat on the shoulder for the significant improvement he made throughout the week in the ring.

Asha spent the remainder of her time sifting through Math's journals and the handful of books she requested from the Base's archives. She first tried her luck in the Base's library, but when the scrolls and books she found produced nothing of significance, she decided to test her luck and head to the Archives. Lieutenant Vivek gave her an inquisitive look when she wandered down to the Academic Building's lower level and requested to borrow any of the scrolls within the Archive's collection that were related to the history of the Perseisian Army. He hesitantly handed over three scrolls he pulled from among the shelves, and Asha departed with nothing more than a swift 'Thank you, sir,' as she gathered the leather-bound documents in her arms and exited the Archives.

She brought the documents back to her room, and with gentle hands she untied the strings of leather and laid the fragile papers out on her desk. The first two scrolls, *A Complete Timeline of Perseisian Battles* and *The Great Strategies of War*, offered her no insights.

Asha woke early to read through the final scroll, knowing she would have a little extra time before she needed to meet Anselem down at the Aviary.

As she read through the final scroll, *Unrivaled Warriors of Bloodshed*, that was when she found it.

The Septant. The Lords of Carnage.

Asha's eyes widened, and a smile pulled on her mouth.

The scroll did not provide much information apart from confirming a lot of what she already knew—the Septant was composed of the Kingdom's seven most elite warriors, chosen from all three branches of the Perseisian Army. It was the highest honor a warrior could achieve, and once a warrior was chosen, they were bound to their Vow for life. Asha also learned that honor and loyalty were not only renowned attributes for the warriors but required. And, because a Septant warrior's most valuable asset was their Word, if one was found to have broken a Vow or was incapable of repaying a debt, the warrior would be stripped of his title, and the remaining six members would deal with the traitor accordingly.

Asha learned quickly from the text that *accordingly* always meant death.

She unrolled another portion of the scroll, and a small gasp escaped her lips. Painted across the crinkled paper was a near duplicate replica of the tattoo Asha had seen inked on Anselem's back—a pair of widely spread wings made of feathers constructed from fire, moondust, and mist.

She had heard rumors about the Septant's Wings—long-held speculations that the warrior's Marks were not merely symbolic ink sketched onto their backs.

Many speculators believed that the warriors—through whatever god had found favor with their warfare—were not only endowed with extraordinary enhancements in their powers, but they were also gifted with a set of Septant Wings. Legend claimed the wings could be retracted and hidden within the warriors to preserve their identities whenever they were not in the midst of bloodshed, but Asha had never bought into the stories of old and thought the idea of winged men waging war sounded absurd.

A knock rattled against Asha's door, and she startled. She quickly rolled the scroll back up, fastened the leather tie around it, and placed it inside the bottom drawer of her desk before walking over to the door. She turned the iron knob and swung the door open. Surprise spread over her face when she saw who was standing outside.

"Morning, Fletch."

"What are you doing here?" She looked down the hall to ensure nothing was wrong, but the early air of the Barracks was still quiet with sleep. She glanced back at Dolion.

"I'm heading back to Brienza tonight, and I wanted to come say goodbye in case you were busy later." Dark circles sat beneath his amber eyes, and a hint of sadness floated within them.

She had only seen Dolion one other time this week, after her sparring fight with Anselem. She had been so exhausted after drills, she could hardly stand upright as she walked to her room. She ran into Dolion on the way back, and he had been eager to follow her to make sure she didn't 'fall asleep in the colonnade walkway.' Asha had barely been able to summon enough energy to laugh, but she let out a small chuckle and allowed him to walk with her to her room. When they got back, she collapsed straight onto the bed. All she remembered was the faintest part of a conversation, and then the enveloping blackness took hold. When she woke an hour later, he was gone.

A wave of guilt washed over her. "Sorry I haven't been around much this week," she replied.

He offered her a small smile. "You don't have to apologize, Ash, I get it."

She smiled at him, happy to have a piece of home nearby for once.

"You'll be back again in six weeks, right?"

It seemed like a lifetime away.

"As long as I don't get sent out on a mission, yes."

"Tell them if you go too long without seeing my beautiful face that you'll wither away and die."

Dolion chuckled. "Yeah, Ash, I'll get right on that. I'm sure it will go over super well with my command."

She flashed him a smile, and through his light laughter, he looked at her with eyes that said so many words she wished they didn't.

She loved Dolion. She had loved him since she was ten years old. And there was a time, years ago, when she even believed she may have even been in love with him. But she was not that girl anymore, and the gods of fate and time had never been on her side when it came to matters as frivolous as the ones inside her heart.

She had resolved in her mind, even before she had lost

Math and Nina, before the Darkness had taken root in her heart, that love would never be a luxury she would have the chance to enjoy. So, she had shoved the thoughts away until they turned platonic, until there was nothing in her that looked at Dolion with anything but friendly eyes.

They had never discussed it. She knew he was aware of how she felt. But it did not make her blind to the longing, hopeful looks he still flashed her way from time to time.

"I have to leave in a few minutes, or I will be late."

"For what?"

"Training."

"You have training this early?"

Asha didn't mention that her Division usually had fitness training this early every morning, and that today was the only day their group *didn't* have it. Just her. She nodded. "I have my one-on-one training with Eros."

He raised his brows, and a wave of something that looked like loathing washed over his face. "You're training with him? Alone?"

"I don't have much of a choice, Dolion."

"There's always a choice, Asha." She hated when he used her full name; he made it sound so bitter in his mouth.

She sighed. "And what exactly would you suggest I do?"

He was quiet for a moment and moved his eyes to the corner, as if he couldn't look at her with the thoughts he had racing in his mind.

"What is it?"

He looked back at her. "Nothing."

"Just say it."

He was silent.

"Say it."

"I think you should leave Soturi training."

The silence that followed was suffocating. Asha felt the fire inside her beginning to burn through her veins.

"What did you just say?" Her voice was cold, and it sliced through the room like shards of ice.

Dolion's voice was a whisper, "I said I think you should leave."

The words ripped through her like splintered thorns, and her heart dropped.

"Why?" she asked. Her voice sounded timid, small, and she hated herself for it.

But before he even responded, she knew. She knew deep down that Dolion had never really thought she could do it. And maybe a part of her had always seen that. A part of her had always known he didn't believe in her. And that was why she had never been able to fully give him every last part of her shattered heart.

He let out a long sigh. "Fletch, you know how I feel about you. I don't—I can't lose you, too."

Her heart felt heavy at his words. But rage overcame the hurt as she snapped back at him, "Did you ever think I could do it?"

His eyes went wide as she finally voiced the unspoken truth that had always hung between them.

"Asha—"

A knock sounded at Asha's door, cutting off his words. Dolion's brow crinkled. Asha ignored him and walked over to open the door.

Anselem, taking up nearly the entire opening, looked at her for a fraction of a moment before his gaze moved over her shoulder and landed on Dolion. His jaw clenched, but he turned his eyes back to Asha and said with a playful tone, "I'm glad to see you're dressed this time." She did not move her gaze from his burning emerald stare, but from the corner of her eye, she saw Dolion stiffen. She stifled a laugh before it escaped her mouth.

She wasn't sure what came over her, maybe it was the fact she had spent the entire morning considering the possibility that Anselem was not the monster she believed him to be, or maybe it was because she had started to realize Anselem had not lied when he told her he was trying to help, or maybe it was because her mood always lifted on the days she was able to fly with him, but Asha replied in the most innocent of voices, "I'm glad to see you still make house calls."

His unalterable composure shifted the slightest bit, and Asha saw the flash of surprise in his eyes, the slight twitch of his lips. She grabbed her bag hanging on the back of the door, looked at Dolion with narrowed eyes, and replied, "We will finish this discussion later."

"Fletch—"

But Asha had already turned for the door, her sapphire eyes meeting Anselem's as she sauntered past him, and she led the way towards the Aviary.

Anselem was quiet for the entire walk from her room, for the entire time they saddled up Uriel and Kapheria, and for the entire time they circled Sveaborg. He led them once more around the Base, allowing the firebirds to stretch out their wings before flying into a variety of new flight patterns.

She pulled Uriel over close to Kapheria and called over to Anselem, "What's up with you? You're more grumpy than usual." Asha started to second-guess the comment she had made in the doorway, and she was thankful her cheeks were already red from the wind as a wave of embarrassment flushed over her.

"Nothing."

The wind whipped the braid flowing behind his head

from side to side.

"Obviously not nothing."

He didn't respond.

"I'll trade you," she said. His eyes turned, and his brows bunched.

"A truth for a truth. Whatever question you wish."

As soon as the words left her lips, she regretted them.

He pulled back on the reins, slowing Kapheria down to a leisurely glide, and the whipping winds tapered off.

"Fine."

"Why are you mad?"

"I'm not mad."

She rolled her eyes. "Then what has your panties in a bunch?"

He rolled his eyes in response but said nothing. Several moments passed without a word, and Asha began to pull on the reins to create space between the pairs, when Anselem broke the silence, "Why does he call you Fletch?"

Asha was so caught off guard by the question, she didn't even hide the wave of confusion that spread across her face.

"You know that's not how it works, right?"

"What?"

"You have to answer the question first before you ask your own."

His lips pursed, but he did not reply. A gust of wind pulled a few strands loose from Asha's braid.

She let out a sigh. "I used to make my own arrows when I was younger."

He raised an eyebrow.

"After my father taught me how to shoot, I wanted to be able to practice on my own. But he wouldn't let me have my own arrows or bow. He told me I had to earn the one I would carry over time with practice and by honing my skills. But I was impatient." A small smile turned upward on Anselem's lips, as if to say *some things haven't changed*. "So, when I was old enough to go out on my own, I did, and I found all the materials I needed to make my own arrows. It took a few tries to get the balance and weight right, but eventually I figured it out."

Asha smiled at the memory. "I found out later it was my father's plan all along. He knew I wouldn't wait, and he wanted me to learn the skills of forging a bow and carving arrowheads on my own so I would always be able to fight my way out of a situation. As long as I had time."

Another smile pulled on Asha's lips. "Math was the first one to call me it—Fletcher. I think, at first, he did it to tease me when my bow and the arrows were rickety and crooked. But as I fixed them and learned how to perfect it, I think he kept calling me that because he was proud I didn't give up. That I figured it out."

Silver threatened to line Asha's eyes, and she pushed the tears back down.

"Eventually, it just stuck. I met Dolion a year or so later, and I'm pretty sure there were a few weeks at first when he thought it was my actual name," she laughed. "He would never admit it, but he didn't call me Asha for almost two months, so I'm fairly certain." She let out another small laugh.

"So, it's really Math's name for you. Not Laeradur's."

It was the first time she had heard her brother's name from his mouth. Somehow it didn't hurt quite as much as she had expected, and Asha wasn't sure what to do with that.

She cleared the lump in her throat. "Yeah, it was Math's."

He was quiet. "I like it." She swallowed again.

"From Valhol's Fletcher to Valhol's Arrow," he mused. She said nothing as they continued gliding through the skies.

"That is the kind of tale songs are written about."

She flashed a grin, and with her swaggering tone on full display, she fired back, "Would you expect anything less from such greatness?"

Anselem rolled his eyes but laughed.

They rode in unexpected, comfortable silence until they neared the final curve of the Base's exterior, approaching the air above the Aviary. Anselem broke the stillness in the air, "Do you want it now or later?"

Asha looked over to him, but he was still facing forward. "Want what?"

"The answer I owe you."

She said nothing, contemplating as they approached the starting place of their flight.

"Later," she replied, filing away the debt until a time when she found a true question she needed answered.

He nodded and pulled on the reins, guiding Kapheria quickly downward. Asha and Uriel fell in behind the pair, and their morning lesson began.

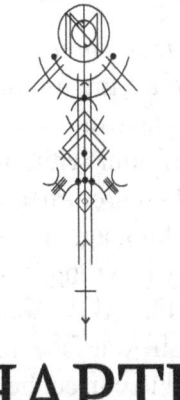

CHAPTER THIRTEEN

Valorous waited on the eastern shore of the North Island, not far from where the Pontos Aquaria was located. The Division had arrived early to try to work through their understanding of how the sea warriors operated.

When the Division members arrived on Base a few weeks prior, Valorous possessed very little knowledge about the specific duties of the two other branches. But in comparison to their understanding of the Amarok, the knowledge the Soturi cadets held about the Pontos was nearly nonexistent.

Asha tried for the third time to tie a compound sailing knot, often used when anchoring ships that held non-seafaring warriors fighting alongside the Pontos and hippocas.

"That's not how you do it," Anselem stated.

She whipped around, fury pulsing through her. "Oh, splendid, now you're going to educate me. Very well." She waved her hand in front of her, gesturing for him to proceed.

"You don't seem like you actually want to know," he replied.

"On the contrary, *Lieutenant*. I'm always thrilled when a man wants to tell me all the important things he knows." Irritation seeped into the words as she realized he let her struggle for the last half hour without providing any advice.

He shook his head and returned to sharpening his knife.

She attempted the knot again.

"You're still doing it wrong," Anselem said, his voice filled with a smugness that irked Asha to no end.

"I'm going to smash your face in," she barked back, irritated that he *always* had to correct her with such satisfaction.

A smirk twitched on his mouth. "As if you could reach."

She cut her eyes back at him.

Muffled laughs crawled out from Varrick, Jeremiah, and Ronin, and she ripped her cutting eyes over to them. The laughter halted, but her Divisionmates still had humored smiles on their faces.

The water just off the shore stirred, and Valorous watched as four men and one woman emerged from below the water. The light blue orbs around their heads vanished as soon as they broke above the waves and into the fresh air. The Pontos cadets and their Leader were all mounted on the backs of their hippocas.

Asha had never seen one of the beasts up close before, and her eyes flared wide as she took in the aquatic creature.

Through the crystal-clear water of the Gulf, she was able to make out the hippocas' beautiful details. The upper portion of the sea-beasts resembled the head and fore-parts of a colossal seahorse, with bony, sea-green scales and fish-fin manes and appendages. The lower half of the creature morphed into the serpentine tail of a fish, and even in its still state, the fin visibly held great strength and force, endlessly capable of propelling the hippocas and their riders through the ripping ocean waters.

The creatures were beautiful and fierce. And, similarly to the firebirds surrounding the shore, each hippoca was unique in its own fashion. Two were covered in blue scales, one of a light, sky color, the other a deep navy. The three others were all wrapped in various shades of sea green.

The Pontos men were all shirtless, donning nothing on their upper half except their iron bands. Each cadet had a different shade of deeply sun-tanned skin, and they wore their hair cut closely against their scalps. The woman, whose hair was also shaved down nearly to the skin, had beautiful, light brown skin that was covered in dark freckles. She wore a fitted dark-blue top with cut sleeves that exposed most of her toned arms.

As the group dismounted their hippocas and swam to the sand to greet Valorous, Asha caught a glimpse of the Pontos Mark on the woman's wrist, signifying her role as the group's Leader.

The circular swirl of a detailed wave curled on the inside of her left forearm. The Mark looked as if it had been crafted from the deep waters of the ocean.

"Hello, Anselem," the woman called over as she made her way across the sand. A bright, fierce smile was plastered on her face, and the look she gave Valorous's Division Leader made Asha's jaw involuntarily clench.

The woman was pretty, in an unconventional type of way, and she appeared to be only a few years older than Anselem. Her amber eyes seemed to brighten when she greeted the warrior, and a wide smile broke across her face.

"Good to see you, Meri." His voice was calm, but Asha caught the slightest bit of strained discomfort in his tone.

"It's been a while," she replied, the fierce smile still

hanging on her lips.

He nodded. "It has."

The tension between the two Leaders was so thick, Asha wasn't sure even an Elysian blade would be able to sever the air. She stared at the two warriors, wondering what type of relationship the pair must have shared to cause such a cold, rigid reaction from Anselem. As she tried to read whatever unspoken strangeness was passing between them, Anselem broke his gaze with Meri and turned to Valorous.

"Let's begin with quick introductions before we discuss this week's benchmark."

Anselem motioned to Valorous, and the Soturi cadets launched into the same informal introductions they had declared to the Amarok cadets two weeks prior.

The Pontos cadets followed suit, working their way down the line as they announced their names and hometowns.

Brizo went first, and with an accent that matched Anselem's, he claimed Elysia as his home. The cadet had deeply tanned, honey-brown skin, and his amber eyes held flecks of gold. He had a kind face with a strong jawline and a long, silver scar cut across his bare, broad chest.

Yoko introduced himself next. A tall, lean-muscled man with naturally pale skin that had turned tan from many days in the open water. He hailed from Takama and explained that reporting to Sveaborg was the first time he had ever traveled outside of his city.

Dylan and Zale were last, both from Valhol. Even with how closely cut Zale's hair was, Asha could see the traditional Valhollian ash-blonde color attempting to peak through. Dylan donned a short, dark-brown cut, but, unlike his hair, his eyes did not abandon the typical Valhollian hazel color. Both men matched the other Pontos cadets, with deep, sun-kissed skin earned from spending many days uncovered under the sun's rays.

"Any idea what's in store for them?" Meri asked, turning to Anselem.

He shook his head as he pulled out a folded piece of paper from his pocket. He read the note out loud to the gathered cadets:

If you wish to claim victory over the vices of your heart, you must sear your ties at the root; or else the evil desires within will bii th many more.

Asha huffed out a breath. She had only been at Sveaborg for four weeks, and she was already tired of riddles and enigmatic puzzles. She was drained, and her head hurt. But despite the irritation rolling through her body, she took a piece of paper from her bag and wrote down the abstruse words, determined to run the cryptic words by Kaira whenever she saw her next. Asha figured if anyone would be able to solve the riddle, it would be the steel mind of her golden-eyed friend.

Asha smiled softly as the thought flashed through her head, glad to admit that the word *friend* was one she was able to use once again.

"Any ideas?" The Pontos Leader questioned.

The group all looked around at one another, their faces blank.

Anselem sighed. "Then the most we can do for now is try to figure out how our two groups are going to work with one another while we solve it."

The cadets nodded and walked towards their firebirds and hippocas, intent on discovering some type of common working ground between the beasts of the air and the creatures of the sea.

❖ ❖ ❖

"Did she really say that?" Varrick asked, his usually sun-kissed skin looking pale.

Asha nodded. "She was away all week for a land navigation trial for Amarok training and just returned last night. It was the first moment I was able to ask her."

Ronin shook his head.

The Pontos and Soturi cadets spent the entire week working through drills and other exercises to familiarize themselves and their bonded beasts with one another. No one had any idea what the benchmark clue meant until Asha was able to ask Kaira the evening before the benchmark took place.

Jeremiah let out a loud breath. "And she said it was a what?"

"Ocean Serpent," Anselem cut in, joining Valorous on the far side of the beach, away from the choppy ocean water where the Pontos cadets were wading with their Leader.

"Please tell me that is not what I think it is," Jeremiah replied, dread entering his voice.

Asha swallowed a lump in her throat. She was so tired of water-bred snake monsters.

"And how exactly is that different from the one Raynor killed in the Lake?" Ronin asked, voicing the question Asha herself had wondered since the night before.

Anselem turned his gaze to Asha before he replied, "It's bigger."

Her face did not waver, set in a calm, stone-like expression, but her heart began to race, and her chest felt tight.

"You should go inform the Pontos cadets. Even a small heads up will help."

Valorous nodded, and the four cadets trudged across the sand, meeting the Pontos at the shore's edge.

Anselem wondered if Asha had always been that way—Unshakable.

She made strong look invincible and walked with the weight of the world on her shoulders, making it look as if it were a perfectly fit pair of wings.

She was a warrior. Not because she held no fear, but rather because, in the middle of the fear, she still chose to take a step forward, with sparked flames burning in her eyes, and was fully determined to make it out the other side.

"An Ocean Serpent?" a familiar voice trilled from behind him. Anselem turned around to see Meri shuffling across the sand. He nodded.

"That ought to be interesting for them to figure out."

Anselem gave an affirmative grunt.

She rolled her eyes. "Are you going to hate me forever, Anselem?"

He cut his emerald gaze to her. There had been a teasing tone in her words, but Anselem caught the flicker of hurt that flashed in her amber eyes. It was gone a moment later.

He scoffed. But he wasn't surprised the warrior had the audacity to be hurt by her own choices.

"I don't hate you, Meri," he snipped, "I just can't stand to be near you."

"Ans..."

"Don't." His voice was sharp, and it cut like glass.

She pursed her lips. But ignoring his warning, she continued, "It was a mistake."

He rolled his eyes. He could feel the electricity begin to

flow through his body. He took a steadying breath.

"I didn't mean to…"

"What?" he cut in. "You didn't mean to sleep with him? Or you just didn't mean to get caught?"

The Pontos's face turned red with shame.

"He told you?" she asked, her voice a near whisper.

He sneered at the warrior, "Of course, he told me. Why do you think I have avoided you for so many months?"

She shook her head. "I just thought you were still grieving and that you knew we ended things…"

Anselem had never heard her voice sound so shaky.

"Well, when you're trapped in a cell for six months, you start to run out of conversations to discuss."

She was quiet for a long time before she turned her sad eyes to the cadets on the shore.

"It's really her, isn't it?"

Hot rage pumped through his body as he saw Meri's eyes lock in on Asha.

He dropped his voice low, letting the lethal tone of the Commander enter, "You don't get to screw around on her brother and then think you get to grieve him in the same way as his family."

Meri's eyes flashed back to Anselem and went wide.

"I just thought…"

A crack of thunder boomed in the distance. He could feel the gazes of each of the eight cadets burning into the side of his face. He kept his stare locked on Meri as he growled through gritted teeth, "If you say anything to her, Meri, I promise you, you will be praying for Anubis to save you from me. You don't get to choose him now that he is gone."

Silver lined her eyes, but she did not let the drops drip down her cheeks or fall to the sand below, for she already knew they would be wasted tears. She said nothing more as she turned away, wading across the sand towards her cadets.

Asha took in a deep breath as Valorous glided through the air. Far below, she could see the shadowed outlines of the Pontos cadets saddled atop their hippocas as they swam through the Gulf's water.

The two groups were given pointed directions for reaching the small isle where the benchmark was to take place. They traveled a little over an hour north of the Ponto's Aquatica when they reached the circular island. A large, deep blue lagoon rested in the center. Rocky terrain surrounded the dark oceanic pool, and tall trees were scattered further back, just outside the rigid ground.

From a quick aerial loop around the landmass, the Soturi cadets found a narrow opening connecting the central lagoon to the surrounding ocean.

Prior to leaving, Asha had given the Pontos cadets as much detail on the Lake's Sea Serpent as she could remember, hopeful that the water snake they were about to encounter would be similar, aside from its size.

The groups made a swift plan for attacking the aquatic beast once Valorous found a way for the hippocas and their bonded soldiers to enter the lagoon. The Pontos cadets would take point on the attack, as they were likely to have better access to the beast, and Valorous would provide overwatch, looking out for any other creatures likely to crawl out from the caves below once the Ocean Serpent was slain.

Hovering high above on the back of Uriel, Asha looked on as Yoko took point, his sky-blue hippoca leading the rest of the Pontos cadets through the narrow opening and winding their way through the salty waters towards the lagoon.

Asha's heart thudded against her chest as the shadowed figures, one by one, entered the deep-blue pool.

Several moments passed.

Then several more.

Nothing happened. The water did not move, the air above the lagoon did not stir.

Asha saw one of the shadows below the surface creep to the top. Brizo's head broke through the water a second later.

Asha pulled the reins, guiding Uriel towards the edge of the lagoon. The rest of Valorous followed suit.

Uriel landed gracefully on the side of the rocky ground, and Brizo's hippoca swam over to meet them.

"There are several caves below. I think we are going to have to lure it out."

An uneasy feeling crept over Asha. "Are you sure?"

Brizo nodded. "Dylan and Zale have already headed down. Yoko is holding anchor halfway in between so he can relay any information."

Asha nodded. "Okay. Do you need us to do anything—"

Before she could finish voicing her question, a violent splash sounded on the far side of the pool, and the Soturi cadets whipped their heads up to see Yoko breaking through the surface.

"It got Dylan!" he screamed, his voice filled with pain and terror.

As soon as his fear-filled words rang through the air, Asha looked down to see red and blue blood saturating the deep-blue water. A second later, Zale broke through the surface, gasping for air.

"What the Hells is it?" Brizo screamed over to him, his voice shaky and distressed. Before Zale had the chance to respond, a colossal water-creature crashed through the surface of the lagoon and landed on the rocky ground.

Jeremiah went pale, and Varrick and Ronin's eyes flashed wide with fear.

Staring down at Valorous were nine serpentine heads, all locked in on the Tribe.

"It's not an Ocean Serpent. It's a Hydra," Asha breathed, her voice nearly stolen from shock.

The phoenixes screeched, and the Hydra released a ghastly hiss in response. Asha and her Tribe threw themselves onto the backs of their firebirds and launched into the air, her heart beating so fast she thought it would rip through her chest. The Pontos cadets made their way towards the edge of the lagoon and hastily crawled out of the water, aiming to help attack from the ground.

Circling in the sky, Ronin pulled a long blade from his back, and Tonalli swooped down towards one of the beast's necks. He swung his sword, slicing straight through the black scales. The severed head tumbled to the ground, blue blood spraying across the white rocks beneath the beast. The Hydra let out a screeching roar, and its remaining eight mouths opened wide, lunging for Ronin as Tonalli darted around the long, swinging necks. The firebird maneuvered swiftly, careful to avoid the plethora of fangs ready to sink into Ronin's skin.

He barely escaped the chomping jaws of the final serpent head as he flew past, Tonalli banking low and right to avoid the collision.

The tension in Asha's body relaxed the slightest bit as she realized they might be able to defeat the dark beast and make it out alive.

But the relief was short-lived, as a rumble stirred within the depths of the Hydra's body.

Asha watched in awe as the severed neck of the serpent,

still dripping blue blood, began to thrash; a moment later, out of the sliced hole grew three additional heads.

Asha's stomach dropped. Her mouth turned to ash, and she forgot how to breathe.

Before she could scream her warning, two more heads fell to the ground, one cut down by the Pontos cadets battling from the rocky ground, and one by Varrick, mounted on the back of his crimson firebird. He twisted his way through the winding, scaled necks as another rumble sounded and the Hydra let out a menacing hiss. Six more heads grew from the severed spots.

"Stop!" Asha screamed, praying her voice would carry through the carnage raging around them. She pointed to where Varrick had just chopped off one of the heads, and as Valorous followed her finger, the eyes of the Soturi cadets went wide as realization struck.

Think. She needed to think.

She circled the Hydra once again, and Uriel let out a piercing war cry, followed by a flare of flames from deep within his throat.

Dozens of cobalt eyes, surrounded by midnight black scales and razor-sharp fangs, flared wide at the sight of the fire pouring from Uriel's mouth. As soon as she saw the roaring flames, Asha remembered the words Anselem had written down on the folded paper days before:

Sear your ties at the root.

They needed to burn it.

She relayed her plan to Uriel and was met with the echoing of an affirmative screech. She turned towards Jeremiah, hovering in the air beside her. He sat saddled atop his golden firebird, Khalfani, holding a long, sharp blade in his hand, unsure what move to make next. She called over to him, ordering him to slice through the beast's neck on the outer left side.

Jeremiah's brow furrowed, and he narrowed his eyes, but he nodded hesitantly. Lifting his sword high as Khalfani dropped low, Jeremiah headed straight for the Hydra.

Asha gave a small kick to Uriel's side, instructing him to follow closely after the golden-feathered firebird drifting towards the midnight sea monster.

Dozens of eyes locked in on Jeremiah as he swung the blade, fangs chomping and biting all around him. The Elysian steel cut through the serpent's neck as if it were water, smoothly and easily slicing the scales with a single strike of the sword.

Uriel followed directly behind the pair, blue blood spattering on his snow-white feathers. Another piercing war cry escaped his throat, and a roaring fire trailed after it.

Before a rumble even commenced, the Hydra's neck, singed by the white-hot flames of the firebird, closed, and no additional heads sprang from the sealed wound.

Celebrations were still far off, and as Asha turned Uriel to the side, guiding him swiftly with the reins, she did not see the frenzied thrash of the Hydra's remaining heads until it was too late. One of the long, scaly necks knocked her clean off Uriel's back, and she tumbled through the air, crashing into the deep-blue waters of the lagoon below.

The water was cold, but not nearly as icy as the inky depths she had encountered when submerged in the Lake. The lagoon was surprisingly quiet, and the short reprieve she found below the water's surface felt rather peaceful. But as quickly as the solitude and respite had come, it vanished, and she found herself drawn back to the air above by a strong, ceaseless yank down the Bond.

She made a mental note to have a discussion with Uriel about control and his incessant need to make sure she was alright in the middle of battle.

She yielded to the tug, swiftly kicking her feet as she rose higher and higher in the water. Light from the midday sun filled the pool as she rose.

Her head broke through the surface, and she felt strong hands pull her out of the lagoon and onto the rocky ground, hauling her a few yards away before one of the last remaining heads of the Hydra fell from the skies and landed lifelessly on the ground where she had lain. Blue blood dripped from the severed neck.

She looked up to see Ronin, still gasping for breath, sprawled out on the white rocks beside her. He crawled to his feet, tugging Asha up with him as he raised himself. Once he made it onto his feet, he looked at her, she nodded, and he turned to jump back onto the back of his cobalt firebird.

They launched into the air, and Asha's eyes followed the pair upward as they flew across the space to join Varrick and his crimson phoenix, Zeno, both battling against the remaining serpent heads.

Uriel was by her side seconds later, barely stopping long enough to give her time to climb into the saddle before he was off once more.

Valorous, their firebirds in tow, raged in the skies, following closely behind for each of the black scaled necks the Pontos cadets severed, searing the open wounds before they were able to spawn more cobalt-eyed heads.

It did not take long for the two warrior groups to find a routine, and one by one, the Hydra's endless heads fell to the ground, until only one remained.

The long, onyx-scaled beast roared, the sound blasting through the space. But as menacing as the thundering cry had been, the Hydra's half-lifeless body was not able to intimidate the cadets as it had before.

Asha, still soaked from the lagoon, pushed up her sleeves and pulled an Elysian blade from her back. Just as she shoved the fabric of her shirt further up her arm, the silver scar she had received from the Lake's Sea Serpent, now wet, began to glow.

The final pair of piercing cobalt eyes locked in on the glowing scar, as if the creature knew where she had received it. Asha swore, and in the split second between when the beast stared her and when it lunged towards her and Uriel, its sharp, clamping mouth wide open, Asha pulled the sword strapped to Uriel's saddle and thrust it upward, splitting through the jaws of the beast.

A screeching wail reverberated through the air as Varrick swept in on the back of Zeno, severing the Hydra's final head clean off. Jeremiah and Ronin finished the job, their firebirds searing the open wound with blue fire.

Then the black-scaled beast crashed to the rocky ground with a thunderous boom, blue staining the alabaster rocks beneath it.

Standing on the shore, Anselem could only see seven warriors returning from the benchmark.

One less Pontos cadet and hippoca sailed through the water.

Even from far below on the sand, Anselem could see that Valorous was exhausted, and he could make out the dripping clothes clinging to Asha's body.

Meri took off from beside him, rushing into the water towards her three remaining cadets.

What the Hells happened?

The firebirds landed on the shoreline, the beasts looking

equally as spent as their riders. He walked towards them, meeting his Division halfway.

"What happened?" he asked, relief filling his body as he took in the minimal injuries the Division had sustained.

His brow creased as he once again surveyed the sopping wet clothes hanging on Asha.

"Hydra," she breathed, her voice weary and fatigued.

His heart dropped as the word hit his ears.

"What?" he asked, convinced he had not heard her correctly.

She tossed an onyx-scaled tail at his feet, and with an exhausted, but triumphant smirk spread over her lips, she called out in that swaggering tone she loved to wield, "Next time, send me to fetch something other than another serpent tail, *Lieutenant*. I think my collection is starting to get rather full."

Anselem looked down at the Hydra tail resting at his feet, and he could not stifle the pride-filled smile that crept onto his face.

He dragged his gaze up to his cadets, looking each of them in the eyes as he declared with rare, unfiltered impression, "Well done, Valorous."

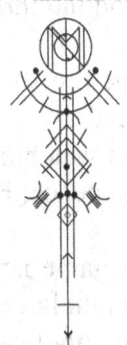

CHAPTER FOURTEEN

Several weeks passed, and the Divisions gathered around the Lake for the fifth Wargame.

With the threat of the Sea Serpent extinguished weeks before, the eerie feel of the waters had dimmed, but a menacing presence still hovered close by, as if a new creature had been birthed in the inky darkness and was patiently waiting, lurking just under the glassy surface of the body of water. Or perhaps it was skulking along the trees that lined the banks of the Lake.

A being that was dying for the opportunity to meet with the living.

"If it isn't the Kingdom's biggest insult to the name of warrior."

Asha rolled her eyes. That voice. There would never be a day when that voice didn't make her want to strangle the breath that gave it life.

"If I throw a stick, will you leave, Moros?"

Her Tribe laughed, and the three men following behind Moros glared.

"Shut your mouths before we shut them for you," the cadet beside Moros growled.

"It's kind of hilarious watching you try to fit your entire vocabulary into one sentence, Fordon," Jeremiah called. Asha smirked.

"Too bad today's Wargame isn't just shooting little arrows across a field; you might have actually had a chance."

"If you plan on testing my waters, Moros, you'd better know how to swim." She glanced over at the Lake before cutting her eyes back to him.

"Everyone here knows they never should have let you in. You don't belong here. You never will."

Asha narrowed her eyes as ice ripped through her body. "I hope Anubis uses your backbone for his ladder when he tries to crawl back out of the Hells. Gods know you won't be using it, you spineless prick."

She kept her voice steady, but his words had hit her in the gut. Hard.

Moros smirked, knowing he'd struck a nerve. "You deserve whatever end comes to you, Raynor." He turned and ambled off towards Destroyer's starting position, but before he made it too far, he glanced back at Asha and added, "And I'll pray to Anubis that your end comes soon."

With those parting words, Moros and his posse paraded off to the other side of the Lake.

"What a chauvinist ass," Varrick interjected.

Asha said nothing as she met Ronin's rage-filled eyes. He stepped past her, heading after Destroyer. She grabbed his arm. "Caleb, don't. He isn't worth it."

Ronin stopped quickly and dragged his eyes back to Asha, his brows raised. "Caleb? Have we finally advanced to first names, Raynor?"

She laughed, the heaviness of Moros's words leaving her body. "I'm pretty sure *I* earned that right when I saved your sorry ass from the Lion."

He chuckled, and she released his wrist. "Then I earned it when I pulled you from the lagoon, *Ash*."

She smiled. "Fair enough."

"Everyone gets to call you by your first name except me?" Varrick complained.

Asha chuckled. "Apparently, life debts earn a first-name basis, *Gage*."

"What about the life debt from last week?" Varrick offered, desperate to be included.

"If I recall correctly, *I* was the one who saved *you* from being gutted by that wild boar's tusks."

"Then I saved you from the golden hind, the benchmark before!"

Asha blinked. Ronin and Jeremiah both stared at Varrick, and then the entire group burst into laughter.

"Okay, we can say you saved me from a little deer if it makes you feel better," Asha coughed out through bent-over laughs.

Varrick stood with a smile plastered on his face, unashamed of his silly claims, but happy to be included in the inner circle.

The group was still laughing when a deep voice cut in, "I hope all this laughter means you are all prepared to start the Wargame."

"Oh, don't be so tightly wound, Anselem." Asha was still laughing, wiping a few tears from her eyes, when the rest of the group went silent. She looked up and saw wide eyes flashing between her and their Leader. She glanced towards him, and his brows were raised, a humored smirk on his face.

Her face went hot as she realized what she had done.

She had never said his name out loud, not to him, and especially not in front of the others.

She twisted on her heels and began heading over to the edge of the Lake. "Come on, let's go get set up," she mumbled, her cheeks red. Her Tribe followed behind her and said nothing.

Valorous was paired against Tactician, who appeared one cadet short of their original starting four. Anselem did not know what benchmarks the other Divisions had battled in, but he was fairly certain the difficulty of the tests must match his own Division's if Tactician had already lost a cadet.

Valorous took their place on the edge of the Lake, and Tactician mirrored the group on the opposing side. A thick, long rope stretched across the water between the Divisions.

The Wargame lost a great deal of its threatening nature once Asha slaughtered the Lake's Sea Serpent, but Anselem still felt an otherworldly presence lurking close by. He prayed the current inhabitants lacked the malevolent temperament of the Lake's former ruler.

As the two Divisions lined up, rope in hand, a figure crept along the water's edge, hidden by the shadows cast off from the trees hugging the rim of the Lake.

Valorous dug their boots into the muddy ground, gripped the rope with as much force as they could muster, and then the horn rang out. The two Divisions began ripping the rope with all the strength inside their bodies.

Asha was at the front, with Jeremiah and Varrick behind

her. Ronin held the anchor for the group at the rear.

Minutes passed, and Valorous was able to make a small headway, inching away from the water with each choreographed step.

Ronin gave out another call, and the group, in unison, stepped back, pulling the rope and Tactician along with them.

As Asha stepped backward, her boot snagged on a loose rock and she lost her footing, her shoes sliding through the mud.

Valorous was hurtled forward, now dancing on the edge of the Lake.

Ronin strained to keep the entire Division from being thrust into the water as Tactician yanked them forward. He was able to hold his ground until Varrick and Jeremiah regained their footing, but Asha had already been launched ahead.

From the corner of his eyes, Anselem saw the shadowed figure dip beneath the surface, and for the second time, he had to stand by and watch as Asha crashed into the inky water.

The icy water ripped through her leathers. She did not fight against the Lake's current this time; she had learned from the last time that it would be useless.

She was not entirely sure how far down the tide pulled her, but she assumed it had dragged her close to the bottom, as the inky blackness blotted out nearly all the sky's light.

The darkness felt different this time.

Asha was not sure if it was from the Sea Serpent's absence or because the Darkness inside her own heart had lessened, and this space no longer felt like home.

She was not alone—that much she did know. But the presence she felt did not hold the same viciousness as the last beast she had encountered in the murky depths.

She waded in place, waiting.

The shadows around her stirred, as if some aquatic being was quickly circling the space where she floated, until it stopped in front of her, pausing to take in its prey.

The creature's upper body looked like a human's, with no hair and eyes that held nothing but a deep abyssal black, no white surrounding the center. Its skin was a cool gray color, and a cluster of gills sat behind each of its ears. A shark-like tail formed its lower half, and a horned spear grew out from the center of its head. Its fingers were tipped with long black nails, and what appeared to be a golden collar rested around its neck.

If there was air with which to fill her lungs, Asha would have swallowed a gasp.

An Adaro.

The creatures were believed to have vanished long ago, destroyed by other malevolent water creatures even more savage than they.

The Adaro, holding a spear-shaped weapon, cocked his crowned head to the side as he stared at Asha, his endless eyes locked on her face. Through the murkiness, she saw a small army of Adaro surround her, all awaiting a signal from their leader to strike.

And then, through a kind of old magic Asha had never encountered, the King of the army opened his mouth, exposing razor-sharp teeth, and a deep oceanic voice traveled through the inky water to her ears, "Are you the Serpent Slayer?"

Her eyes went wide, the salty water stinging as it entered, and she forced herself to nod, her head bobbing up and down slowly.

The Adaro King, held in place with preternatural still-ness, narrowed his murky eyes, as if he was searching over Asha for a sign of validation. His dark eyes glanced down at her arm, focusing on the long, reflective scar.

She tried her best not to move. Her lungs began to burn.

The leader lifted his smooth, gray hand, motioning over another Adaro. The female glided to his side and placed something Asha could not see in the leader's hand. She swift-ly returned to her place behind him in the surrounding army.

Asha's body began to thrash as it longed for air to fill its lungs. A moment later, a light blue orb appeared around her head.

She gulped down the air.

"Thank you," she gasped through choppy breaths.

The Adaro King did not reply.

Once she caught her breath, the creature continued, "You have freed my kind from the Serpent's dominion."

She blinked, grateful her eyes no longer stung from the salty water flowing through them. Shock filled her veins as she processed the fact that she was in the presence of an army of Adaro and still alive.

"Take this as a token of our gratitude." The King stuck out his gray hand, dropping a key fastened on a worn, golden chain into Asha's palm. The key stretched nearly the entire-ty of her hand and was crafted from a worn, brushed gold. The top was arranged in intricate swirls that curled around a light teal stone fixed in the center. A faint light glowed from within the gem.

From tales of old, Asha had always known the Adaro to be vicious and cruel being; never once did she expect the creatures to be... kind.

"We are in your debt, Serpent Slayer."

She tore her gaze from the key and looked up into the dark eyes of the Adaro and nodded once.

The leader did not waste time with the formalities of a farewell before he turned and swam off into the inky blackness of the Lake. His army followed behind him, and as they disappeared into the lightless space beyond, the orb surrounding Asha vanished, and she quickly kicked herself to the surface.

Her head broke through the surface, and she sucked in a deep breath. She wiped the water from her eyes and looked up to see four pairs of eyes staring down at her. She glanced across the Lake. Three soaking Tactician cadets were pulling themselves from the water.

She gazed back up at her Tribe and stretched out a hand.

"If you three couldn't wait for me to celebrate the win, you can at least get me out of this freezing water."

They all blinked, but Ronin quickly stretched out his arm and pulled her onto the shore.

She shoved the oceanic key into her pocket as she scrambled to her feet.

"Are you alright?"

Asha looked up to see bright emerald eyes staring down at her. She nodded.

He looked at her for a long moment, as if he could see the key burning through her pocket.

He nodded once. "Then get back to your room and change."

She stared into his eyes and realized he knew something had happened beneath the water's surface.

She said nothing as she passed him, shivering the entire way to her room.

❖ ❖ ❖

Asha had finished peeling off the last of her dripping wet clothes and threw on a sweater and pants when a soft tap sounded on her door. She walked over, still towel drying her unbound hair, and flung the oak door wide open.

Anselem stood in the doorway, his wide frame blocking the entire opening.

"Hello, *Lieutenant*."

He looked her up and down, his gaze lingering on her unbound hair. She realized he had never seen it down before. It fell nearly to her waist. He dragged his eyes back up to hers.

"I just wanted to check in and make sure you were alright."

Asha raised her brows but then narrowed her eyes.

He had never once come to check on her after any of her other close encounters with Death.

"Why are you really here?"

Anselem's brow crinkled, but then he sighed.

"Grab a jacket and walk with me." He nodded in the direction of the courtyard beyond the Barracks and turned to head down the hall.

"You can just come in…"

"Hurry up, Seven."

She rolled her eyes but quickly grabbed the dry jacket hanging beside her door and followed him.

He stopped walking once they were far enough away from any listening ears or snooping eyes.

"Tell me what happened."

Asha tilted her head back to look up at him. His emerald eyes were bright, and, in the sunlight, she could see the remnants of a faint scar that stretched across his left cheek. She wondered how she had never noticed it before.

"Nothing happened."

He stared at her, deep into her eyes, but she held firm, refusing to drop his gaze.

"Don't lie to me, Seven."

She hated how he did that. How he somehow always knew what was going on in her mind.

"How did you know?"

He ran his hand through his hair. "Because you were down there too long. And I knew you were running out of air... so I sent my magic out, to find you, to try and give you an orb, or something to give you time to find your way out..." he was mumbling, and Asha wasn't sure she ever heard him speak in a manner other than self-assured and confident.

"But when my magic found you... There was something else there. Something I had never felt before. I don't know how to describe it. It felt old. And... other."

Asha kept her face composed, but her heart thudded in her chest.

"You can't do that," she whispered.

"Do what?"

"Interfere. You know that it's against the rules."

"First off, I didn't actually interfere. Whatever was... down there prevented me from doing so. Secondly, burn the rules. If one of my cadets is in trouble, I'm going to do whatever is necessary."

Asha looked at him, trying to read his face, but he had schooled it into the unphased mask he always wore.

"It was an Adaro," she answered, keeping her voice soft and low.

She expected him to dismiss her, to laugh at the statement and tell her she must have gone without oxygen for too long because she was clearly seeing things that had not existed for millennia.

But he did none of those things. He simply let out a whooshing breath and stepped closer to her.

"Do not tell anyone," he urged, his normally composed voice full of distress.

She hadn't planned on telling anyone, not even him, but the concern on his face made her ask, "Why?"

"Seven, there are things I cannot tell you right now. But on my Word, I promise to tell you when the time is right."

His cryptic nature and lack of openness annoyed her to no end. But she was also understanding of the fact that secrecy was part of his job, and soon would be part of hers. And as much as she hated the lack of candor, she believed he would tell her when she needed to know.

"Alright," she replied. His eyes went wide, clearly shocked she was so agreeable.

She rolled her eyes. "Don't act so surprised that I am capable of civility."

He smirked. "I wouldn't go that far, Seven."

She narrowed her eyes. "It's a wonder no one has killed you yet, *lieutenant*."

"Many have tried, but no one has yet to succeed."

"Perhaps one did succeed, but Anubis himself couldn't even endure your company."

Anselem laughed. "The Angel of Death sends his regards."

Asha smiled, wondering when her hate for him had so blatantly turned into a genuine desire to be around him, even if he did irritate her to no end. Of course, she told herself, she would have to be near him to throttle him, so perhaps it did make sense.

"Do you need anything else from me?"

He looked into her eyes, the smirk still lingering on his face, and she watched as his eyes trailed down to her unbound hair once more. She ran her hand through the loose strands, twirling the ends. He swallowed, bringing his gaze back to her face. Her heart fluttered, but she did not move.

"Nothing else, Seven."

She had not realized how close they had been standing until he took a step back.

He took a deep breath, still staring down at her. "I will see you tomorrow morning."

She nodded but did not move. She could see the rise and fall of his chest muscles, and she prayed he could not hear how quickly her heart beat.

He waited a moment longer than necessary before he turned around and walked across the courtyard, heading up the stairs, leaving Asha alone in the open space.

He did not look back as he disappeared around the corner.

Asha crossed the yard, heading back to her room, and swore to herself, realizing the hate she had held in her heart for Anselem Eros was hanging on by a desperately frayed thread.

"WARRIORS ARE MADE BY THE PATHS THEY CHOOSE, NOT THE POWERS RESIDING IN THEIR VEINS."

—ARTICLE 2, SECTION 3 OF THE VALOROUS DIVISION CODEX

CHAPTER FIFTEEN

The four cadets circled silently around the Othala, staring down at the Mother Rune. Varrick held a chisel in his hand.

It had been nine weeks since Valorous stood before the rock, and the four cadets had endured enough encounters with Death to last a lifetime—many lifetimes.

They had fought lions and hydras; captured a deer with golden horns and hoofs of bronze, ensnared a wild boar with tusks growing from its mouth, and battled their way through Wargames.

The evening before they met at the Othala, Valorous slayed an enormous flock of birds gathered at a Perseisian lake, using arrows tipped with poisonous blood they had stored in vials from the slain Hydra.

A soft smile tugged on Asha's mouth as she reminisced on all the trials her Valorous Court had accomplished together.

"Should we say something?" Jeremiah asked, and the

men glanced at one another, their eyes landing on Asha. She looked at each of them, one after another, until she dropped her gaze to the rock before them. She took a breath.

"I think nothing ever truly ends poetically. Things end, and we search for a way to twist the pain into something beautiful, something worth enduring. But all that blood, all the scars and the hurt, it was never once beautiful; it was always just crimson pools and cruel marks and grueling agony." She broke her gaze from the rock as she spoke, and looked first into the eyes of Ronin, then Varrick, and last Jeremiah. "But sometimes, in the middle of all the unpoetic pain and Darkness, we are given someone to walk by our side. In the midst of the suffering, we are given a lifeline. A friend. A family.

"And I vow to each of you, no matter where the winds may take us or the seas may carry us, you will always be my family. The one that came to me unexpectedly, in the middle of the night, when I thought there was no room left in my scarred heart for love. And all that I ask is for each of you to promise we will make it out of this together. As one Tribe. Because this fractured heart of mine cannot withstand another breaking of my family."

The men were quiet, each of their eyes lined with tears at her candor, at her openness, and her willingness to drop the swaggering charade and pour out her heart to her family. Their Queen of Valorous.

Each of the men nodded as she met their gazes, their eyes full of genuineness and promise and love.

As Asha's cracked heart filled with the vows of her Tribe, she took the chisel from Varrick and carved the four names of her family beside one another into the rock, forever imprinted on the Othala.

"LET YOUR APPROACH BE VEILED AND SILENT, LIKE SHADOWS IN THE NIGHT. WHEN
YOU STRIKE, CRASH LIKE THUNDER AND LIGHTNING."
—THE GREAT STRATEGIES OF WAR

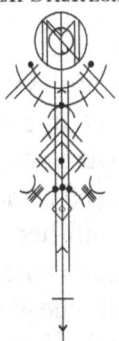

CHAPTER SIXTEEN

The sun was just beginning to dip behind the horizon and disappear into the emerging night sky when Asha finished her evening run on the Cliffs that rested high above the Academic Building, overlooking the stretching sea. The Cliffs were the rock formations encircling the northern side of the Main Island and appeared as if they plunged straight up from the sea below. They towered higher than any other place in Sveaborg, and with an abundance of trees scattered amongst the rocks, the whipping winds dwindled into a gentle breeze that made the cliffside rather peaceful in the dusk light. She stared out at the setting sun, breathing in the cool twilight air, and let her heartbeat return to a rested state. Several peaceful minutes went by as she stared off at the crashing waves below, and then a dark voice came from behind her.

"You really shouldn't be wandering out here alone."

A chill ran down her spine, and her mouth went dry. She forced herself to swallow the lump in her throat as she turned

CAMERON L. JIMENEZ

around.

Shit.

Moros, Fordon, and a third Soturi cadet whose name she could not remember gathered in a half circle around the edge of where she stood. They were no more than ten yards away.

She quickly, but discreetly, moved her hand to feel for the daggers strapped beneath her shirt. She always carried them on her runs in case she came across any wild animals stalking through the forest; she figured this encounter was essentially the same—a pack of feral wolves.

She only carried two blades.

Asha had seen each of the men fight before. She might have a chance. *Might.*

A vicious laugh escaped Moros's mouth. "I guess you don't have much to say when your Division Leader isn't around to protect you, huh?"

Asha could feel the ice as it settled in her veins, the lethal calm overtaking her frantic thoughts.

Her eyes cut over to Fordon first, the burly cadet from Destroyer Division who followed Moros around like a lost puppy. He had never been shy of hiding his chauvinist views. Asha always figured that was why Moros had put up with Fordon's lack of intelligence for as long as he had. He truly gave the idea of *Brawn No Brains* a whole new meaning.

Moros stood in the middle, his eyes filled with disgust and rage, but a flicker of pleasure sparked across them as she assessed his stance, as if he got some sort of sick, twisted high off the idea of ripping people apart.

Asha flashed her gaze towards the last man, standing furthest to the right. Alvis. That was his name. She did not know much about him aside from his affiliation with the Tactician Division. She would save him for last. If there was one she could beat one-on-one without a weapon, it would

232

be him. She could see the hesitation, the questioning uncertainty in his amber eyes.

Asha wrapped her hand around the hilt of the dagger, and she watched Moros's eyes flicker to her waist. She did not take her eyes off Moros, and with the quickest flick of her wrist, she flung the first dagger.

It plunged straight into Fordon's thigh, and he let out a loud wail. Not exactly where she had intended, but she didn't want to sacrifice removing her eyes from Moros to ensure perfect accuracy.

"You *bitch*," he growled.

Asha chanced a glance at him and rolled her eyes. "Misogynist name-calling, how original, Fordon."

Moros let out a laugh that whipped her attention back to the ringleader.

"There's that smart mouth of yours. Maybe we can put it to a more enjoyable use before we let your friends bury you in an early grave."

A wicked smile curled on her lips. "Just make sure they bury me shallow—I'll be back."

The three warriors' gazes all drifted from Asha to something lingering behind her. She heard the scrape of boots against the rocks but did not turn her eyes away from Moros. If there was a fourth in the group sneaking up from behind, she would have no chance.

Asha's eyes darted around, looking for a possible exit, a potential place to run.

"By all means, don't let me interrupt the party."

Gods, she had never in her life felt so relieved to hear his voice. Never thought she would have wanted to. But standing on the Cliffs, surrounded by warrior eyes filled with wishes of death, she had never heard a sound so beautiful.

"Look who came to the rescue once again. Your own

personal little knight in shining armor."

Anselem scoffed, and his voice came out amused, "Little is a word that has never once been used to describe me." Asha knew there was a smirk sitting on his face. "And I have no doubts she can handle you all on her own. I'm just here to enjoy the show."

Moros's eyes narrowed.

At the sight of the lieutenant, Fordon and Alvis began slowly backing away, Fordon limping with each step.

Once they were close enough to the tree line, both warriors turned and ran.

"Cowards," Moros sneered.

"You might as well follow them, Moros." Asha nodded her head towards the tree line.

He stepped closer with each word, a disparaging smile forming on his mouth. "Scared?"

Her heart thudded in her chest, louder and louder with each step he took towards her. She saw nothing but death in his onyx eyes.

She inhaled a deep breath. *I am a master of my fear. I have power beyond measure. I am unbreakable.* As she exhaled, she entered the place of lethal calm, and Moros quickly crossed the last remaining steps between them.

He lunged for her. She tried to dodge him, but his hands reached for her throat, and he clasped his fingers around her neck. Her air instantly ceased. As Moros began to pick her up off the ground, his hands clenching tighter and tighter around her throat, she remembered the words Anselem told her the first time they ever sparred together in the ring. She willed herself to remain calm, to think through it. Her mind raced, and as her vision began to blur, she reached down to her waist, remembering the final dagger she had strapped under her shirt. She palmed the blade, twisted her hand, and watched the shock—the fear—ripple across Moros's face as she drove the knife upward. In the split second her blade crossed the short distance between them, he released his hands, but she could see in his eyes that he knew it was too late.

Asha thrust the dagger straight into Moros's heart and watched the life drain from his eyes. She pulled the dagger out, and Moros dropped to the ground.

She looked down at her hands, covered in dark, red blood, and the world went silent around her—numb. She didn't hear Anselem's footsteps as he walked over to her, lingering a few steps away. She simply continued staring at the wet blood as it dripped off her fingers and fell onto the rocks below.

Blood on your hands—that was the phrase she had always heard, as though it stopped there, at her wrist, like a crimson glove. As though she could do these things and there would be any part of her left that wasn't stained and dripping.

The ringing in her ears continued. Her face was twisted into a blank and lifeless expression.

"Seven," he said softly, almost a whisper.

She didn't look up from her hands as a new ribbon of wind and smoke carved into the skin beneath her leathers.

"Seven," he tried again, stepping towards her.

Her knees buckled from the weight pressing in on her—from the Darkness trying to break through her walls. The same Darkness she had dwelled with for so long, it had become a close friend.

Before she fell, Anselem swiftly closed the gap between them, catching her underneath her elbows before her knees crashed into the rocky ground.

She started shaking. The blank, lifeless look was still

fixed on her face. Anselem pulled her against his chest, holding her tightly to help stifle the shaking.

"You're okay," he assured, "it's over, you're alive."

Asha's body wouldn't stop trembling, tears threatening to form in her eyes before she shoved them back down. Haunted memories flashed through her mind before she could suppress them. *The Inferno. The Final Testing of Algae. Nina.*

Waves of Darkness crashed all around her, but all she did was watch them. She was paralyzed by the numbness swallowing her, shoving her deeper into the depths of overwhelming blackness.

Underwater, sinking slowly to the bottom, she was suffocating, running out of oxygen.

She was stuck inside a shrinking box, with walls closing in on each side. But she had been the one who locked the door; she was the one who'd twisted the key and thrown it in the sea, letting it drift deep down to the sandy floor below.

"You're okay." Anselem continued holding her tightly against him. "Everything is going to be okay, Seven."

But she didn't believe him—because it was too hard to forget her past when it was written all over her body.

And then, everything went black.

Asha woke up and had no clue where she was. Morning light was beginning to peek in through the windows, and her heart began to race. She shot straight up in the unfamiliar bed. It only took a moment for the memories of the day before to begin rushing back into her mind. She was still dressed in her clothes from her evening run, but as she looked down at her hands, not even the faintest stain of blood remained.

She could still feel the sticky wetness on her fingers—like a bloody, phantom glove she was unable to remove.

As she took in her surroundings, the smell of amber and citrus clung to every surface, but he was nowhere to be found.

His room was large, with two floor-to-ceiling windows that covered a majority of the east-facing wall and provided a view of the Gulf beyond. The style and colors were the same as her own—onyx with accents of gold and rich mahogany pieces. His room additionally held a large cognac couch in the corner. A deep imprint was set in the leather, and Asha assumed Anselem had slept there last night.

As her eyes grazed across the room, he burst in through the door, as if her awakening had summoned him. His abrupt entrance startled her, and she grabbed the sheets, pulling them up against her chest.

His emerald eyes softened as he entered. "Sorry, I didn't mean to scare you... There is a meeting in the Auditorium in an hour." His voice was soft, gentle.

She stared at him for a long moment before she nodded. She slowly pulled the sheets off and, as she dragged herself out of the bed, she caught a glimpse of herself in the reflection.

Her eyes went wide.

She looked like a complete *wreck*. She quickly attempted to run her hands through her hair and pulled it back from her face, tying it up in a knot atop her head with a thin piece of leather.

There was nothing to be done about the dark, purple circles underneath her eyes, but she prayed a bath would help wash away the dirt and grime from the previous evening—*and the lingering feeling of dried blood.*

She glanced over and saw Anselem watching as she

fixed herself into a semi-presentable state. His eyes still held the air of seriousness, but she could see a flash of humor cross through them at the idea she felt there was any need to straighten herself up after such a grim night.

She cut a glare at him, and the corner of his mouth twitched.

"What."

He shook his head and pressed his lips tightly together.

She huffed out a breath. "You are the only person I know who can make silence insulting."

With that, he let out a small laugh but did not respond.

"I don't have the energy to pretend to like you today."

"When have you ever pretended to like me, Seven?"

She narrowed her eyes, but no flaring rage seeped into her veins. He held her gaze unflinchingly, and staring into his eyes made her heart begin to race.

She broke his stare. "I need to wash off," she mumbled. Anselem turned to the side, making space for her to pass.

She quickly headed to the door and paused a moment before opening it. She leaned against the wood, listening for any movement outside.

"No one is in the hall," he stated. She turned her head back towards him, but left her hand on the doorknob.

"I made sure the rest of the instructors had a reason to be gone early this morning. You don't have to worry about any lingering eyes or fear any circulating rumors."

She blinked as a wave of surprise washed over her. She never would have thought he would care about her reputation, or that he would even realize the implications of her leaving his room at such an early hour. She nodded. "Thank you."

He flashed a grin and replied, "Now there are two words I never would have believed I'd hear from you."

She rolled her eyes. "Don't expect to hear them again."

"I won't hold my breath," he laughed.

She turned the knob but paused before pulling the hinges open. She looked back at him once more, her eyes holding nothing but sincerity. "For last night too," she added.

The laughter in his face faded, and earnestness filled his emerald eyes. "Anytime, Seven."

She pulled open the door and headed down the hall towards her room.

Asha managed to avoid every potential prying gaze as she coiled her way through the winding corridors. She made it back to her room without running into a soul.

She pulled her door open and found two wide eyes glaring at her from the desk as she entered the room.

"You look like you had a fun night," Kaira called over to her.

Asha said nothing as she pulled a set of clean clothes from her wardrobe.

"Are you not going to tell me where you just came from?"

Silence.

Asha peeled her top off and threw it into the bottom of the wardrobe. She avoided the hanging mirror as she gathered her things and walked towards the bathing chamber.

Kaira grabbed her wrist. "Ash, what's wrong? You told me to meet you here this morning so we could go over some more of the journals..." Kaira's voice trailed off as her eyes met the newly printed ink on her wrist, marked just above The Brand.

"Who?"

A lump grew in Asha's throat, and silver lined her eyes. "Moros."

Kaira nodded, no blame in her eyes. She did not even know what had occurred, but no sign of judgment swam through her golden oceans.

"Good," she whispered.

Asha nodded, and Kaira gently dropped her wrist.

"Bathe quickly, and then we will figure out what to do."

"I have to be in the auditorium in an hour."

Kaira's brow bunched. "Anselem told me a few minutes ago that there is a meeting for all of the Soturi cadets."

Kaira's brows raised. "You were with Eros?"

Asha caught the flicker of intrigue cross her face as she realized the time; the early morning sun was just beginning to creep through her window. She quickly added, "Not like *that*!"

Kaira laughed. "I wouldn't blame you if you were!"

Asha knew her friend was just trying to distract her, to keep her mind off the phantom blood covering her hands and the dark ink wrapped around her forearm.

"You can catch me up after the meeting. And I'll fill you in on what I found."

Asha nodded and headed into the washing chamber, unable to process any information her friend might have found.

"I'll come find you later today."

Kaira nodded, grabbing her bag off the floor.

Asha pulled open the door to the washroom but paused. "Take them with you, you seem to have better luck figuring out my brother's cryptic messages than I do."

"You sure?"

Asha nodded. "I'll let you know when I need them back," then she slipped into the chamber to wash off the feeling of blood and death still clinging to her skin.

"Do any of you know what this is about?" Jeremiah asked, leaning forward in his chair to ask his Tribe. Asha shook her head, but her chest felt tight.

The Soturi cadets were all gathered in the Main Auditorium, but none of the instructors had entered the room. No one asked about Moros's absence. Asha searched the room for Alvis and Fordon, but they were nowhere to be found. She figured Anselem had reported them for breaking the Sacred Rule on Base, the one that prevented them from killing another warrior while at Sveaborg.

The subdued chimes of the clock rang through the room. On the last ring, the doors flung open, and the Leaders and instructors poured into the hall. Asha's eyes found Anselem's, and he gave her a reassuring wink. Her heart still raced, but the weight that was perched upon her chest abated the smallest bit.

The Major took the center of the stage.

"Good morning, cadets. Apologies for the early assembly, but we have a few announcements that need to be brought to light."

Asha swallowed the growing lump in her throat.

"First, we wanted to pass along Leadership's decision to grant you three days off for your midway break, following the completion of your sixth benchmark. You will be permitted to leave Base during your break, and you will not be expected to attend any training activities, barring any orders you may receive from your Division Leader."

The gathered cadets, bred to be controlled and composed, said nothing, but the feel of the room shifted from tired and worn to expectant and cheerful.

"Secondly, we have gathered you here to issue a warning. Three cadets were found dead this morning at the Cliffs. We are not entirely sure what occurred, but it appeared to be a tragic accident. Likely a wild animal attack."

Asha's ears were ringing.

Fordon and Alvis were dead?

Her eyes dragged over to the side of the Auditorium, locking on Anselem's face.

As if he could feel her glare burning into him, he slowly pulled his eyes to meet hers, his face locked in the ever-composed expression it always held.

But when he looked at her, for a split second she saw it—the flicker of Darkness in his emerald seas—and Asha undoubtedly knew.

It had been no accident at all.

Just as she had, Anselem Eros broke the Sacred Rule. He killed two warriors on Base. She couldn't bring herself to admit it was because of her. That he had done it *for* her.

She tried to swallow the lump in her throat, but her mouth had gone dry. He inclined his head and then turned his attention back to the Major.

Asha sat there, unable to find the words in her mind for what had unfolded.

But as she stared at the warrior from across the room, something inside her cold, dark heart shifted, and for the first time in a long while, it finally began to beat again.

"The Great War has carried on for centuries, a ceaseless Battle of the Kingdoms. But, before it began, long ago in a time before the Gods of New, the First War was waged."
—A Complete Timeline of Perseisian Battles

CHAPTER SEVENTEEN

"Three whole days!" Jeremiah shouted as the Tribe landed in an open area outside of Reyka.

"I can't believe they are giving us an entire three days off to do *nothing*!" His voice was full of so much cheer, Asha couldn't help but smile.

"Don't get too excited. I'm sure Eros will find something to make us do for the halfway break," Ronin chimed in.

"Yeah, like early morning fitness," Varrick added.

Asha laughed, knowing it was very likely something their Leader would do.

"But we have been crushing it in Wargames, and we absolutely dominated our sixth benchmark yesterday!" A touch of concern entered Jeremiah's voice.

The group began walking through the trees towards the quaint port town, leaving the firebirds free to roam.

Jeremiah was right, Valorous truly had dominated in their benchmark the day before. There had been a rogue bull rampaging through a Perseisian town, destroying farmland and terrorizing the citizens. The Division was directed to capture the bull and present it to their Leader and the other instructors present for the benchmark. When they finally tracked down the creature, they found it was no ordinary bull. It was the great white bull of Kochi, rumored to have slain many warriors who had attempted to seize it. And it was a sacred figure of Varrick's people. The Tribe had taken a note from Kaira's handbook and used their strength and wits to strangle it until the beast lay unconscious. They then tethered it, rode it across the town to the meeting location, and presented it to Leadership. After they were congratulated on their success, and the bull had fulfilled its purpose, Valorous released the beast, unwilling to bring dishonor onto Varrick's home.

"Worried you won't be free to spend all weekend with Tahira?" Varrick teased.

Jeremiah had gabbed nonstop all week about how he couldn't wait to leave Sveaborg. When the Tribe asked why, he hesitantly admitted that he had a woman back in Elysia who was coming up to Reyka to meet him. The pure excitement that leaked into his voice when he spoke of Tahira was enough for the men to grab hold of and run. And when he accidentally let the word *love* slip from his lips? They tormented him endlessly for the rest of the week.

Jeremiah flashed him a glare. "Perhaps."

Varrick and Ronin both laughed.

"Is she coming up tonight?" Asha asked.

Jeremiah tore his glare from the mocking men. "Yes, but it will take her a little while longer to get here."

"What is the name of the place she's meeting us?" Varrick asked.

"There will be no *us*, just me. I refuse to expose her to you savages."

"Aw, come on, Greystone," Ronin pleaded, "we will be on our best behavior." A mischievous glimmer sparked in Ronin's eyes, and a playful grin spread over Varrick's face.

"Absolutely not."

Asha cut in, "You're really not going to introduce her to your family, Jer?"

The laughter of the men fell silent. It was the first time she had said the word after the Othala.

Jeremiah looked over at her, the joking tone having left his voice. "I will." Then he glanced back to Ronin and Varrick, the teasing nature having reemerged, "Even if you are a bunch of barbarians."

Asha laughed and added, "We can find her an honorary spot in our Valorous Court."

Jeremiah smiled. She had never seen his eyes so bright. "Tahira would love that."

"So… where exactly are we going?" Varrick asked again, looking both ways down the quiet street.

"The Golden Sail. It should be a corner tavern at the end of the road, a street away from the shore."

Varrick turned to his left, and the group headed towards the Gulf.

When Ronin opened the door and the group stepped inside, Asha was shocked at what she was met with. So contrary to the quiet streets they had curved their way through, the tavern was *alive*. There was a group of men playing music in the corner, patrons laughing and dancing in the open floor space. Asha's eyes flared wide and bright, and a huge smile broke across her face.

She turned, grabbing Ronin by the hand. "Please tell me

you know how to dance!"

A smile broke across Ronin's face, but he shook his head. "I'm sorry, Ash, I never learned the steps to any of the dances."

She turned to Jeremiah and Varrick. Varrick shook his head, but a wide grin spread over Jeremiah's face. "I never would have thought Valhol's Arrow loved to dance."

Asha met his smile with her own. Dancing was the only time, other than flying, when Asha felt free. She could lose herself in the music, in the songs, and feel as if nothing else mattered for the short time the instruments played.

"Please tell me you know the steps, Jer."

"You really think I could call Brienza home and *not* know the dances?" He offered her his hand, and the two took to the floor, joining in with the half-drunk patrons already swaying along to the music.

Song after song played, and Asha danced with Jeremiah, the pair laughing and spinning until their lungs burned and their mouths ran dry.

They were still giggling like children when they left the floor and made their way over to the table Varrick and Ronin had claimed.

"Who would have thought the two of you could actually dance?" Varrick teased, and Asha grabbed the glass of warm ale sitting in front of her chair. She quickly gulped it down, quenching her thirst.

"Who would have thought the two of you couldn't!" she replied, shaking her head.

"When would we have learned, Ash?"

She shrugged. "You two never went out during training?"

"Of course we did. I just usually had... other things on my mind," Ronin replied, glancing at the table beside them full of beautiful women.

Asha rolled her eyes. "No excuse."

"Valid excuse," Varrick chimed in, and the table laughed.

The group talked about their time in Elysia and asked Asha about her time in Valhol. She told them of the underground tunnels that threaded their way beneath the city, and they told her how full of life their city had always been.

They talked for an hour or so when Jeremiah jumped up from the table, knocking over his near-empty glass. His chair flew back behind him, rattling against the ground.

"What the Hells, Greystone!" Ronin barked, but Jeremiah was already gone.

The Tribe followed him with their eyes as he ran across the tavern and scooped a petite golden-blonde woman into his arms.

As she watched their embrace, Asha's heart felt so full she thought it would burst.

"Tahira," she breathed, and she could see the merriment flickering through Ronin and Varrick's eyes at the happiness that radiated from their brother.

Jeremiah held onto Tahira for a long time before he finally let the woman breathe, but he did not release her hand as he guided her through the crowd and over to the table, as if he thought she would vanish into thin air if he wasn't touching her.

She was pretty, with shoulder-length hair that fell in loose curls and dainty features and full lips. Her skin looked sun-kissed, same as Jeremiah's, and even from afar, Asha could see the innocent twinkle in her doe-shaped eyes.

Jeremiah's face looked full of worry as he approached the table.

"Everyone, this is Tahira." She smiled, the grin soft and kind.

Ronin spoke first. "Hello, Tahira, we are the barbarian savages."

Jeremiah's face dropped, but the woman's smile grew wider. "Nice to meet you, barbarian savages. I have heard a lot about you."

"It's all true," Varrick added, smirking.

Asha rolled her eyes, grabbed Tahira's hand, and patted the chair beside her. "Please sit next to me, and save me from the company of these brutes."

Tahira smiled and took the place beside her, but Asha caught the surprise in her eyes, and she wondered what exactly Jeremiah had told Tahira about her.

"So, what position do we think would be a good fit for you in our court?"

She looked across the table to Jeremiah, and there was so much thankfulness in his eyes. Asha flashed him a reassuring wink and turned back to the golden-haired woman.

Her Tribe went off in different directions as the night dragged on. Jeremiah left with Tahira, and Varrick and Ronin took off with companions of their own.

Asha found herself sitting atop a high table alone. She finished the last of her drink and thought of calling it a night when a gorgeous face across the room caught her eye. She told herself it was because of the alcohol, but a grin pulled at the corners of her mouth. It was wiped away as quickly as it appeared when a man standing in front of his table, blocking the view, moved to the side, and she saw a stunning woman sitting beside him—*on him.*

She was beautiful. Striking. With long dark hair and full lips painted a deep red. Her fox-like eyes sparkled even from across the room. She wore a midnight black dress fitted tight against her fair skin, displaying every generous curve.

But what unnerved Asha the most was the thin, delicate hand the woman had placed against Anselem's chest as she leaned in close and whispered something in his ear. He laughed, and his smile sent a delicious shiver down Asha's spine. She shook her head and turned away, realizing his smile was not meant for her. Her cheeks burned, and she told herself again that it was from the alcohol.

She stood up to leave, and the room tilted. She held onto the edge of the table to steady herself when an unfamiliar voice broke through the noise around her.

"Heading out?" a handsome man with curly dark hair and deep amber skin asked across the table.

His gold-flecked eyes were warm, inviting, and his smile looked kind. At least from what Asha could tell from the blurriness in her own.

She wondered why he was swaying back and forth until she realized it was her. She blushed.

She looked around for her Tribe but found no trace of her friends. She knew she was in no shape to walk out, much less climb atop Uriel and have him fly her back to Base.

She shook her head at the man. "No, not yet. I think I am going to stay for a little while."

He flashed a pretty grin.

She pulled the chair out and sat down. The room stopped tilting when she was seated.

"Can I buy you a drink?"

She stared at him again, forcing herself to focus on his face. He was very handsome, and she could tell there was a decent amount of muscle packed beneath his well-fitted shirt.

She glanced back over in the direction of Anselem, but

he was still tangled up with the stunning woman. She moved her gaze back to the man across the table.

"Sure," she replied, a soft grin pulling at the corners of her mouth.

"Perfect," he answered, and headed towards the bar.

Several paces away, he turned back around. "I'm Manasseh, by the way." A wide smile was perched on his face.

"Asha," she replied, matching his grin with her own.

He had seen her the moment she walked in. Her white-blonde hair and grace-filled movements overtook the space as she entered. She seemed unaware of her overwhelming effect, as if she didn't notice how heads turned, and gawking gazes stared. And her eyes—*those damn eyes*—Anselem could see how they burned like a living fire even from across the tavern.

Tucked back in a corner booth, while he waited, he watched her dance with Greystone, laughing and spinning to the music, watched as she smiled and joked with her Divisionmates, and watched as the irksome-looking man plopped down beside her and showered her with dreamy eyes and flashy smiles.

Anselem had never considered himself a jealous man. But for some reason, seeing some worthless, philandering Kappi lean in close and whisper in Asha's ear made him want to put his fist through the soldier's face.

He knew it made him a hypocrite, with how he was sure his own situation must have appeared from outside eyes, with the woman beside him still hanging on his lap. Yet there he was, lost in his thoughts regardless.

Anselem turned his attention back to the dark-haired woman next to him.

"So can you get it done?" he asked in Elysian. He took a sip of his ale.

She leaned in close, her fox-like eyes piercing into him. "You know I always deliver," she purred, her strongly accented voice sounding like honey. "It just may take me some time."

He nodded. "Take whatever time you need, just get it done."

She pressed a hand against his chest. "So tense tonight, Anselem. Pretty little blonde got you all worked up?"

He cut his eyes to her, and they darkened. "We're done here."

The dark-haired woman pressed her lips together in a pout. "Aw, and to think I hoped we could take the party elsewhere." Her hand began to slide down his chest.

Anselem wrapped it in his own and chucked it into her lap. "I said we are done here," he snapped in the common language of Perseis.

She rolled her eyes and let out a honeyed laugh. "Fine. But be careful with that one," she replied in Elysian, nodding towards Asha. "The people who consider her powerless and irrelevant have not yet seen the wolf prowling behind her eyes, nor the flames buried inside her soul. But I promise you, one day, that girl will do what wolves and fire do best, and she will strike when they least expect it." As she spoke, her typically sultry voice had turned earnest, genuine, as if the Spinner herself knew a thing or two about strong women and the darkness that lurked inside their souls.

❖ ❖ ❖

"Another?" Manasseh asked.

"Sure," she offered, already knowing it was not the best decision. He flashed her a grin, got up from the table, and walked to the back of the tavern.

She was glad to be rid of him for a moment of quiet. The entire evening, Manasseh had mumbled on and on about himself. He had bragged about the monumental achievements he had attained and never failed to mention his successes as a Kappi. Asha had barely been able to get in a word about herself, so the man never learned that she not only outranked him, but she had already surpassed him in every 'achievement' he felt so inclined to boast about.

She did not mind that she passed him in skills and experience; what bothered her to no end was his self-obsessed personality.

Asha's head spun, and she rubbed her temples. She glanced over to the table across the room and locked eyes with Anselem.

She swallowed, his emerald eyes never once leaving hers. She moved the stray pieces of hair out of her face, tucking them behind her ear. She continued to look at him, realizing the woman who had been sitting with him was nowhere to be seen. He took a sip from his glass, but his gaze still refused to leave Asha. She narrowed her eyes. Why was he staring at her?

Before she realized what she was doing, she was up and swaying across the room on unsteady feet. He never once took his eyes off her as she walked up to his table.

"Having a good night?" she asked.

"Even better now."

"You're drunk." The irony of the words was not lost on her as she assessed her own state.

"I'm still sober enough to kill you, darling, so don't

push your luck." He flashed her a wink.

Her cheeks flushed. She told herself it was because of the alcohol, but before the thought fully crossed her mind, she knew it was a lie.

"That was months ago. It would be a much different outcome now." Her voice was full of baseless arrogance.

It wouldn't have been different. It would've been exactly the same, and Asha knew it.

He laughed. "Look at you, you're just begging for someone to put you in your place."

She scoffed, stepping towards him. "And you think you can handle that?" she snipped back, "I could have you on your knees in a heartbeat."

She brazenly dragged her eyes down his body, the ale having given her a spurious confidence. "It would suit you," she added.

His brows raised at the brazenness of her words. His voice dropped lower than before, the tone turning wilder as he leaned forward on the table, his weight pressed on his forearms, "Do you think about that image a lot, Seven? Me on my knees before you?" A twinkle flashed through his eyes, a flicker she had never seen before.

Her cheeks burned, and she shifted her weight.

He rose from his seat, towering above the other patrons in the tavern, and crossed the short space between them. She had to lean her head back to stare into his emerald eyes. The mischievous twinkle still lingered, and he smirked as he leaned towards her ear and whispered, "It's getting harder, isn't it? To quiet that feeling late at night that tells you I should be there."

Her heart leapt in her chest.

He pulled away; a cocky grin stretched over his handsome face. His face was still so close to hers, and it took all her willpower not to lean in towards him.

She wished her head wasn't spinning from all the alcohol. If her mind had been clear, she would have found a witty remark to throw back his way.

She knew he didn't mean it. She knew he was just messing with her. Just continuing the game of back-and-forth banter they had played for so many months. The game that had eased the endless tension of wanting to kill him. The game that had helped distract her from the inevitable brushes with Anubis she met each week.

He laughed softly when she did not respond.

"Are you at least having a good night with Mr. Self-Absorbed, Seven?" Asha had no clue how he had known Manasseh had boasted all evening about his 'accomplishments,' but Anselem's smug look irked her to no end.

"Yes, actually. A wonderful time."

Anselem flashed a grin. "I'm sure. He seems like a real charmer."

Asha rolled her eyes. "Charming enough for me." The words came out slightly slurred, and she cursed at herself as she tried to regain her composure.

His eyes darkened the slightest bit as he took a step away from her and reached down to the table. He grabbed his glass and finished the last sip of his ale.

"Enough?" he questioned, placing the empty glass back on the table. "Well, if *enough* is what you believe you should settle for, then you have every right to that decision. As long as you're clear-minded enough to consent to it."

"I do," she spat back, unsure what else to say. "And I *am* clear-minded," she added. He raised his brows at the latter part.

Gods, he knew how to get under her skin. He knew how to make her angry in a way no one else ever had. Her head started to spin, but not from the ale.

He looked over her shoulder. Something resembling pain settled in his eyes as he said, "I just figured you would know you deserve something more than *enough*."

A lump rose in her throat, but she masked the pain with indignation as she scoffed, "And what is wrong with enough? You seemed quite comfortable to indulge your desires all night; why shouldn't I?" She cursed at herself as soon as the words came out. She knew how it sounded. She knew there was no other way for it to come across besides jealousy.

He shook his head, clearly not thinking jealousy was the place from which her words had stemmed. "I wasn't *indulging* in anything, Seven. I was getting information. She gives that look to every man. Whether she wants to take him to bed or not."

Asha rolled her eyes, but her cheeks burned.

"But that's the difference between someone like me and someone like him," he nodded in the direction of Manasseh, who was winding his way through the crowd towards them.

"What's the difference?"

Anselem began to walk towards the exit, but stopped just before he passed her and leaned in close, his lips nearly grazing her ear, and said, "The difference between me and him, Seven, is that I can make you feel things with your clothes still on. And I would never, even for a moment, let you believe you should settle for *enough*."

Her heart leapt into her throat as she glanced up into his emerald-green eyes, their faces so close they shared breath. "Jealous, Anselem?" It took every ounce of willpower to keep her voice from wavering.

"If you want a distraction, Seven, that's your choice. I don't care who you sleep with. I only care about you."

Then he pulled back and stood up straight, glancing over

her shoulder. "Enjoy your night." She turned and watched him as he exited the tavern, never once glancing back.

And Asha stood there, in the middle of the noisy space, and realized she had made a complete mess with nothing but the idea that she was not enough.

"Knowledge is always revealed through the secrets one is willing to share. But first, you must be welcomed into the game. To receive an invitation, you must be willing to play. The Keeper of Secrets holds the Key."

— Excerpt from Journal Entry 66 of Mathieson Raynor

CHAPTER EIGHTEEN

"I think I'm dying," Asha moaned. The sunlight pouring in through her window made her head pound even louder. She threw a pillow over her eyes.

"From all the ale you drank last night, or from how you embarrassed yourself?"

Asha pulled the pillow slightly back from her eyes and glanced over to see an amused look on Kaira's face.

"It was bad, wasn't it?"

"Tragically calamitous."

Asha groaned, throwing her head back onto the bed.

"It could have been worse, I suppose."

Asha looked across the room once again to see Kaira flipping through the journals sprawled out on the desk. The two of them had spent the last several weeks combing through Math's entries together, attempting to find any leads.

"In what world could that have been worse?" Asha whined.

Kaira's hands stopped, and she turned her eyes to her

friend, a teasing twinkle in her eye. "At least now you know the man is perceptive enough to see that he makes you feel things even *with* your clothes on. Imagine what he could do without—"

Asha chucked the pillow at Kaira, cutting off her words. She let out a roaring laugh.

Asha's face was hot. "Do *not* finish that sentence."

Shortly after Anselem left the Golden Sail, she stumbled her way through Reyka until she found Uriel and convinced him to fly her back to Base. When she landed, she went straight to Kaira's room to tell her how she had made a complete fool of herself. Kaira listened to her slurred story and then walked her back to her own room, tucking her in for a few hours of sleep before she returned the next morning to check on her.

Kaira rolled her eyes and turned her attention back to the journals. "I don't know why you fight it so much. You obviously know he's not the reason Math is gone." She gestured to the journals and pieces of paper Asha had used to copy the most useful information from the *Unrivaled Warriors of Bloodshed*. "Not to mention that the man definitely looks like the type to know exactly what he's doing."

Her cheeks flushed hot once again, and she was thankful Kaira did not turn her gaze from the papers.

She made her voice neutral as she replied, "I know he isn't the reason Math is gone. But it doesn't change the fact that he is my lieutenant."

Kaira cut her eyes over towards the bed. "You are just making excuses. He isn't your commanding officer. There would be absolutely nothing wrong if something happened between the two of you, and you know it."

Sometimes Asha hated how brilliant her friend was, always able to find a way around a problem.

"What happened to the Amarok warrior who thought it was naive as Hells to *open my legs for the gorgeous Soturi?*"

THE DOMINIONS: ASH AND EMBERS

This time, Kaira blushed. "You heard that?!"

Asha laughed. "That was when I decided I liked you. For that comment alone."

Kaira smiled, but then her face took on a more serious expression. "I meant that for *Lana*. You're different."

"How would that situation be any different for me?"

Kaira turned, giving her full attention to her friend. "Because I can see you for who you really are instead of the person you have lied to yourself about being."

Asha blinked, and Kaira let out a sigh before continuing, "First of all, you wouldn't just be sleeping with him because you wanted to get laid. I can see the way you look at him, even if you can't. And I'm fairly certain your entire Division can see that he looks at you the same way, so that automatically makes it a different situation.

"But even if you both didn't look at each other like you awakened one another's souls, it would still be different for you. People don't look at you and question whether you can cut it, Ash. People look at you, and they shake in their boots.

"You are *Asha Raynor*. Trailblazer. Valhol's Arrow. Queen to the Royal Court of Valorous. You have fire in your eyes and ice running through your veins. You have been through the Hells and have come out the other side. You are the Warrior."

Asha hadn't realized tears had formed until they fell from her eyes and dripped onto the blanket beneath her. The onyx covering swallowed up any trace of the drops.

And it was in that moment, when Kaira's profession hit her ears and nothing but love and support and pride filled the words, Asha knew, sometimes a person's soulmate can be found in their friends.

"ONLY THE WORTHY SHALL BE SELECTED. SEVEN WARRIORS, ALL DESTINED FOR GREATNESS. SEVEN WARRIORS CHOSEN TO ALTER FATE."

—UNRIVALED WARRIORS OF BLOODSHED

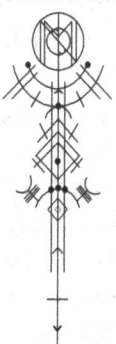

CHAPTER NINETEEN

The weeks passed quickly. Between preparations for Wargames, flying lessons, and readying for benchmarks, Asha had seen Anselem every day, but he remained distant, even more than before. He avoided having any prolonged conversations; he never responded to her mocking jokes or witty banter. After several days of rejection, Asha stopped trying to mend the small progress they had made and returned to ignoring him.

It was for the best, she told herself. There was no need to begin caring for someone she wanted to kill mere months ago, even if the way he avoided looking her in her eyes gave her an unsettling feeling she couldn't shake.

She rolled over in her bed, still irritated with herself that she was bothered by Anselem Eros. She shook her head to no one but herself.

A knock sounded on her door. She sprang to her feet, her heart fluttering in her chest, but as she opened the door, a wave of disappointment washed over her.

"Hi, Fletch."

"Hi." She assumed her face must have shown every emotion rushing through her body because Dolion's smile turned into more of a pained grimace. She composed herself.

"Can I come in?" He motioned to the room behind her.

"Oh, yes, of course."

She moved to the side, and he slid into the room. She walked over to the bed and quickly shut the journal she had been reading and placed it in the top drawer of the mahogany side table.

"How has it been going?"

"Good," she replied. An odd, uncomfortable sort of tension filled the space between them.

He sighed, running his hand through his blonde hair.

"I wrote to you while I was gone."

"I know," she answered, glancing over to the desk drawer that held his unanswered letters.

"Fletch, I hate this," he said, his voice filling with a crushing pain she had only heard one other time. Irritation rushed through her veins.

She did not respond.

"Ash, please say something."

She looked at him for a long time before she responded, "For how long?"

He blinked, and then his brow furrowed.

"For how long did you stand by my side, as my oldest friend, and not believe I could make it? Was it the entire time or just when I tried out to be a Soturi?"

"Ash, it's not that I…"

"Don't you dare insult me by lying," she cut in, her voice cold and filled with daggers.

Dolion took a steadying breath.

"Asha, I do believe in you. Look at everything you have done. Clearly, I was wrong. I think… I think I was just scared to lose you. So, I said something stupid, and I'm so sorry."

The words should have made her feel better. They should have mended the chasm-sized rift floating between them, but as they hit her ears, the truthfulness behind them fell flat.

He stepped towards her and tucked a strand of hair behind her ear; her body tensed at the gesture. He noticed the rigidity of her frame and dropped his hand to his side.

"Tell me what I need to do to fix it," he pleaded.

The pain in his voice softened something in Asha's heart. He was her oldest friend, and no matter how much hurt he had caused her, she never wanted to see him in pain.

"You can tell me the truth."

His brow crinkled.

"Stop telling me what you think I want to hear. Tell me the truth. That is the only way we can move forward. I can handle it. I'm not some fragile little girl, Dolion. I am a warrior."

Not soldier, not cadet—*warrior.*

She looked at him as he tried to find the words.

"No, Ash. I didn't think you could do it. But I do now. I truly do. And I am sorry for doubting you."

She nodded and grabbed his hand. "Thank you for telling me the truth."

He nodded and looked down at her hand holding his and laced his fingers between hers. "I'm sorry, Ash."

The sincerity in his voice pierced through her hard heart, and she squeezed his hand once before letting it go. "I forgive you."

And she did. Asha would let it go. But it was in that moment that she realized why it had never worked with him.

Why she had never been able to give her heart to him. Because even though he believed in her now, she knew she needed someone who believed in her always. Not only when it was easy, or convenient, or once she showed him she was capable; she needed someone who would believe in her when every odd was stacked against her.

She needed someone who would look at her with assured eyes, without a single doubt wavering inside of them, and know that she would conquer. She needed someone who would see her shadows and weather the storm raging inside her. Someone who understood that there were times when she was a calm day and times when she was a raging hurricane. One who would see stars in her darkness and love her in all places, like the moon between the earth and sun. One who would not pick and choose the parts of her to love but would love her wholly.

Because she was broken, and her soul had been shattered into dozens of pieces. But she was also fierce and loyal, and the love she had buried deep inside her heart would wage wars for the people she loved.

So, Asha would forgive her friend, and she would move past the disbelief and the disappointment, but she would continue to wait for her person, because she knew deep down, she deserved the kind of love that could level kingdoms.

CHAPTER TWENTY

Asha's heart raced as they approached the abandoned island. It looked the same as it did every week, with mist-filled clouds eerily clinging to the rocky ground, and the ominous stone pillars that looked like carved blades surrounding the edge. As they neared the gray pillars, she could see the flow of murky seawater through the valleys and the mossy foliage that crept up the walls of the mountains, connected by half-demolished arches.

She took in a deep breath.

I am a master of my fear. I have power beyond measure. I am unbreakable.

Anselem and Kapheria slowed before her, allowing her to come to his side before entering the wall of rocks.

She guided Uriel over to Kapheria's side, their wings steadily beating as the firebirds hovered in the air.

"You're ready."

Asha nodded.

She knew it would be today—she knew it was time.

After the months of training and the endless lessons, she knew it was her time to finally fly the course completely.

"I will follow directly behind you."

His voice was serious, but not unkind. It was strictly professional. A Leader with his cadet.

She nodded once more.

Asha went to buckle the belt, but as she reached down, she noticed that the clasp had been detached.

She picked her head up and looked into Anselem's emerald eyes. She saw the faintest twinkle of amusement in them as she realized he had been the one who had removed it.

This man truly does want me to die, she thought.

She shook her head but said nothing and grabbed the reins.

She took one last steadying inhale, then gently kicked her heel into the side of Uriel, and the phoenix soared down towards the wall of stone.

Just as they approached a small break in the jagged monoliths, she slightly twisted her reins, and Uriel angled his wings to avoid scraping the walls. Once they slipped inside the towering exterior walls, Asha was prepared to meet the whipping current of air that would thrust them upward. She shifted her weight, flexing the strong muscles she had spent months building, and Uriel launched skyward. Asha's legs strained, but she managed to keep herself in the saddle. A small grin tugged at the corner of her mouth.

She guided Uriel up to the ridge line, Anselem and Kapheria close behind, and as soon as his wings brushed the crest of the mountain top, she gave a swift kick of her heel into Uriel's side, and the firebird tucked in his wings and plummeted towards the canyon below.

Her leg muscles tightened again as they free-fell, the ground growing closer and closer with every passing second. Asha's heart raced. They were nearly two hundred yards from the rocky terrain, but she did not pull the reins. Not yet.

One hundred fifty.

Her heart launched into her throat, but she waited.

One hundred.

Another swift kick and Uriel's wings splayed wide.

Her arms strained against the saddle reins, and her legs began to shake as she held on for dear life, the full force of the free-fall abruptly halting just before they crashed into the ground.

She lightly tugged, and Uriel slowed, giving Asha a moment to catch her breath. As she gulped down air, she gave a slight pat to Uriel's back, proud of the progress the pair had made with their trust over the last several months.

She heard the beat of midnight wings close behind her, and she continued towards the canyon ahead, not once looking back.

Her mind was focused, locked in on the obstacles before her. They had run this course so many times, but she had always been able to fall back on the leather belt across her waist or on Uriel's ability to make up for her lack of skill.

But not today.

Today, it had to be all her. And even her firebird knew that.

She guided him between the rocks, weaving through the ever-changing winds barreling off the canyon walls. In and out, she twisted and pulled on the reins, around obstacle after obstacle. Monolithic rocks swept past her head, one after another.

As she neared the end of the canyon, she saw the rock wall with the narrow opening that led into the center of the canyon.

Sweat beaded on her brow, and she took in a deep breath.

This was it.

This was the one part of the course she had not yet been able to master.

The opening barreled closer and closer.

And just as she neared the narrow space, she held her breath and yanked hard on the left rein. Uriel rolled, entering the slit sideways as the channeling winds threw them forward, the speed of their flight picking up as they entered the gap.

As she guided Uriel in, his wings held steady, she released her breath, but the sweat on her brow began to pour, and the muscles in her legs and arms shook as she strained her entire body to hold on.

The gap between the walls felt as if it lasted for miles, as Asha hung on for her life with everything she had.

Just as her grip was beginning to slip, light seeped through the rocks, and they broke out into the open space beyond.

She carefully pulled Uriel back upright and slowed his speed until he hovered in the center of the field. She patted him twice on his back, and he landed effortlessly on the grass below.

She took in deep breaths as midnight feathers momentarily blocked out the sun above and then softly landed beside her.

Asha stared at the snow-white head of Uriel for a moment, not quite able to believe she had done it.

She made it.

As her heart began to slow, she felt a single tear escape from her eye, and then a wide, wholesome grin stretched across her face.

She pulled her head up and slowly turned her gaze to the warrior sitting beside her.

Pride filled the emerald green, and a genuine smile spread over his face.

Before she knew what she was doing, she slid off Uriel, Anselem following her lead, and she crossed the distance between them and threw her arms around him.

"I did it!" she screamed with an excitement and happiness she had not felt for herself in a long time.

Anselem wrapped his arms around her waist and spun her in a circle, equally as excited for the triumphant feat.

"I knew you would," he murmured against her ear.

He softly set her feet back down on the grass, and she blushed, realizing she had just, quite literally, thrown herself in his arms.

She glanced down, noticing he hadn't yet removed his hands from her hips, and she recognized just how close they were standing to one another. She slowly moved her gaze back up to his eyes, drowning in the emerald oceans. Her heart fluttered, and her breathing deepened.

As she looked into his devastating eyes, her heart pounding against her chest, Asha realized she had never truly known desire until she felt his hands around her waist. Her mind went blank of every thought, every reason, and her eyes settled on his lips.

He quickly dropped his hands, as if he had seen something in her gaze that had revealed the thoughts racing through her mind.

She took a small step back, breathing deeply to calm her heart and mind. Heat flushed on her cheeks once more. She tried to flush the thoughts from her mind. What the Hells was she doing?

But her embarrassment quickly faded as she saw the

pride and excitement fill the eyes of the warrior standing before, bringing her back to reality, and she knew he was just as thrilled about her success as she was. And another wide smile broke out on her lips.

It was that smile.

He had never seen her smile like that before. And the first time he saw it, he knew he wanted to see it for the rest of his life.

And as soon as he realized *that*—Anselem Eros knew he was irrevocably screwed.

But Anselem also knew there were too many secrets he would have to keep hidden from her to ever venture down that path. He knew he was not what she needed. And he was not sure he ever would be.

Hells, he wasn't even what she *wanted*.

He didn't blame her for that. He knew how truly flawed he was. Broken. He knew she still blamed him for Math's death. Still hated him the majority of the time. Some days, he still blamed himself, too. Hated himself, too.

Most days.

But he would do what he could to be there for her, in the only way he knew how—protection.

He would not cross that line, no matter how much he wanted to. She deserved so much. And he would not let her settle for *enough*. No, Anselem knew Asha deserved the very stars that hung in the sky, and even if it broke him, he would make sure she found what she deserved, what she wanted— even if it wasn't him.

They stayed in the field on the abandoned isle for a long while, resting and coming down from the adrenaline rush.

Asha lay on one of the large rocks, soaking up the midday sunlight while the firebirds lounged under the shade of the nearby trees.

Anselem was perched on the rock beside her, conscious to keep a professional distance between the two of them after their embrace and whatever moment had happened when their eyes locked.

After his excitement for her success on the flight path had worn off, he seemed to have returned to being angry with her, ignoring her. Keeping a wide distance.

She pulled her mind from the warrior by her side and let her thoughts drift off, closing her eyes and embracing the warmth of the rays beaming down.

"Do you think I will be a Soturi?" The words came out of her mouth unexpectedly—accidentally—as her mind had drifted to the earlier conversation with Dolion, and she remembered his pleas from months ago.

She wasn't sure why she asked him. She wasn't even sure why she was speaking to him, besides the faint voice inside her head that reminded her of his words in the tavern. That he cared. Even if it didn't seem like it the last several days.

His brow furrowed.

"Of course I do. Why would you ask such a question?"

She sighed.

"I knew you would make it through the academy since the moment I saw you chuck the Sea Serpent's tail at Moros. Nothing has changed my opinion since then. Nothing will."

From the unwavering conviction in his voice, she knew he was telling her the truth.

"Dolion told me to quit. Week three, he told me I should

leave training. He said it was because he couldn't bear to lose me, but I know it was because he didn't think I could do it."

She expected him to brush it off, to dismiss it. She expected him to simply tell her that he was ignorant and then to move on, but his response surprised her.

His voice was calm, sincere. "Some people get really uncomfortable when you grow out of the box they put you in. And sometimes, people don't want to see the truth that's right in front of them because they don't want their illusions destroyed."

She looked at him, into his kind, emerald eyes, and nodded. His gaze burrowed deep into her, towards the darkness she wanted to hide, and she broke his stare and looked away.

"Can I ask you something?"

"Sure, Seven."

Her usually assured, swaggering facade faded, and her voice came out so low it was almost a whisper, "You are part of the Septant."

There was only silence next to her, and she forced her eyes back to meet his.

"Is there a question in there, or are you just making a statement?"

Her eyes went wide. She had known for months, but hearing it from him, hearing the lack of denial running from his mouth, it hit her like a stone wall.

"Who told you?"

She looked over at him but did not open her mouth.

Anselem let out an irritated huff. "Godsflaming Laeradur," he grumbled.

She nodded, letting out a breath she did not realize she had been holding. "I thought you would have denied it," she replied, her voice still low.

He shook his head. "I am many things, Seven, but I'm not a liar. At least not with you."

She blinked, still fully wrapping her head around the confirmation. She glanced down at the Septant-black cuff fixed around his wrist—the one he never removed.

"How long have you known?"

Her cheeks burned. "I found out in the third week."

Anselem's emerald eyes went wide. "You knew for months and never said anything?!"

A soft smile tugged on her lips. "What was I supposed to say? Hi, I know I hated you and tried to kill you yesterday, but I think I changed my mind. Whoops."

He shook his head. "So, you *did* try to kill me when we sparred."

She rolled her eyes. "Don't remind me of my lack of success."

He grinned. That stupid, beautiful grin that she hated. "But if you had killed me then you never would have had the opportunity to stare at me longingly from across a tavern or become acquainted with my dashing personality."

She scoffed. "You wish, *lieutenant*." She waved her hand dismissively.

He looked down at her, his eyes trailing to her lips and back up to her flame-filled sapphire eyes. "Maybe I do."

Her cheeks heated, and she hated how he was the only person able to elicit a reaction from her expressionless face.

He grinned again. "So, what else did Laeradur tell you?"

"Was there something else he should have told me?"

Anselem looked at her for a long moment, and his cheerful, teasing grin disappeared from his face. He ran his hand through his hair, brushing the loose strands from his face.

Asha's chest tightened.

"Math was also part of the Septant."

She nodded slowly, taking in the information. She had suspected it. Kaira had even proposed the idea at one point when they were rifling through the journals, attempting to find any confirmation on the reason he was in Aaru. But hearing the words from Anselem's mouth still felt like a gut punch, like the air had been ripped straight out of her lungs.

How had she not known? How had he not told her?

"He couldn't have told you, Seven." She whipped her eyes back to him. How did he always know what she was thinking?

He huffed out a laugh. "Because it's written all over your face."

She opened her mouth, then closed it. Her feelings were not written all over her face. She had spent endless years ensuring they were not. Anselem was the only person to ever know what was racing through her mind.

She would make sense of that later.

"So that was why he was in Aaru. He was there with all of you."

"Yes," he answered softly.

She nodded, still sorting it all out.

He sighed. "There are four others. You know Kage." Asha's eyes flared, but she let him continue.

"Then Blaidd—he's up in Lorca and is also General of the Vanguard. Einar and Sacha are Pontos, so they typically stay in Takama or along the coast somewhere."

"Who is the seventh?"

Anselem went rigid, and she could see the debate waging war in his mind. "I'll tell you that story when you graduate."

"What!" she replied with fueled frustration.

Anselem winked. "Gives you something to work for."

"Isn't that what I've been doing every day for the last

five months?"

He laughed. "Fair, but I can't tell you all my secrets."

She narrowed her eyes, internally debating calling in the debt he owed her.

After an internal battle raged in her mind, she opted to wait for his answer. She could wait four more weeks. She could be patient, even if it was a skill that had never come naturally to her.

"I'll hold you to that, *lieutenant.*"

He smiled, climbing atop Kapheria, who had wandered back to his side, along with Uriel.

Over the months, the two firebirds had seemed to become somewhat friendly, as if the relationship between their bonded riders had rubbed off on them.

She pulled herself into the saddle on top of Uriel's back and adjusted the reins. Her thighs were already sore.

Anselem looked over to her, answering her statement with a taunting tone and a smirk, "You'd have to be able to catch me to hold me to it, Seven."

Then the midnight firebird launched into the skies and headed back towards Sveaborg.

Asha laughed, and a moment later, she was guiding Uriel back through the narrow gap, right on their heels.

CHAPTER TWENTY-ONE

"I wonder what the next benchmark is going to be," Varrick pondered as Valorous trekked across the Base towards the East Wing.

"Hopefully something similar to the last few. We absolutely dominated," Jeremiah answered, his words filled with pride.

"Dominated is a strong word," Ronin chimed in, eying Jeremiah from the side.

Ronin was right. Jeremiah always had a way of reminiscing on their past successes with an overly positive outlook.

The last three benchmarks had been... interesting.

During the seventh benchmark, Valorous was sent to Silversage, a small farming town north of Kochi. They were instructed to obtain the cattle of a local villager who had stolen the herd for its rarity. The cattle were magnificent beasts, with coats made red by the light of the setting sun.

When the Division arrived, the cadets quickly realized the task was more complicated than the instructors had explained, for the villager was no mere farmer. He was rumored to have immense strength, and all the men who had come to face him died in his hands, the skulls of the vanquished placed on posts around his home. Asha shot the man with a poison-tipped arrow, but it was only enough to maim him. Once the villager fell to the ground, the rest of the Tribe filed in and shackled the thief, dragging him all the way back to the instructors on the back of one of his prized cattle.

The other benchmarks went slightly smoother. The Tribe managed to stealthily sneak into a garden on the northern edge of Perseis and steal three golden apples rumored to have once belonged to the gods of old. Valorous was expected to accomplish the mission undetected, to ensure the cadets could perform missions without being caught. Varrick and Asha had been the ones to slip into the garden and steal the apples while the others stood watch.

The last benchmark had singularly fallen on Asha's shoulders. The group was sent to a remote isle off the coast of Takama, Skull's Rock, where a group of warrior women lived apart from any men. Valorous was tasked with retrieving a belt of armor from the Isle's Emir, the ruling woman of the clan that occupied the island. When the Division arrived, accompanied by the Pontos cadets, the Emir came down, with a small army following her, and met the group on the shore.

She looked as if she had been born to lead, with strong muscles wrapped in glowing tawny skin, and amber eyes that held the experience of battle and the wisdom of leadership.

Her golden-brown hair was twisted in dozens of braids, and her body, covered in golden armor that glinted against the high sun, was painted in the lines and art of the Isle People.

The Isle Emir only spoke to Asha, refusing to acknowledge the men.

She asked what brought the cadets to her lands, and with an unknown wave of trust, Asha decided to answer the Emir honestly, explaining the simple purpose of their visit.

The Emir, moved by Asha's candor, promised to give the belt to Valorous, under one condition—Asha was the sole fighter able to don the armor. Asha nodded in agreement, and the Emir handed her the belt. But before the ruler released the armor, she looked deep into Asha's eyes, watching the fire that burned inside them, and her sovereign voice drifted over the group, "Never forget you carry the mindset of a Queen and heart of a warrior inside you. With each step you take, let the earth tremble at your feet and remember you are a force of nature."

Asha, unsure of how to reply, nodded once and took the belt from the Emir. She ran her hand over the gold-plated armor. It was painted with cobalt blue lines, and a large, sapphire gem was fixed in the center.

The group left the isle and returned to the instructors awaiting them in Takama. But she kept her promise, and Asha never let anyone else touch the belt of the Isle Emir.

Jeremiah laughed, pulling Asha from the reminiscent thoughts running through her mind. "In my mind, we dominated, and that's what I'm going with."

Asha smiled as they pulled open the door to the East Wing foyer. "Well, at least one of us isn't a pessimist."

The Tribe laughed as they walked to the second-floor meeting room.

❖ ❖ ❖

Gathered around the oak table in the East Wing class-room, Anselem stared into the anticipating eyes of each of his Division cadets as he held the folded paper in his hand. He hadn't needed to write down the words; he already knew what awaited them. He crumpled the piece of paper into his fist and tossed it in a nearby bin.

The Valorous cadets stared at him with confused expressions. Each cadet except Asha, whose face had gone pale, and he knew she was already aware of what was to come.

Anselem sucked in a deep breath.

"We only have a few weeks left until graduation. And although there is still another benchmark to follow this week, I need each of you to understand that this will likely be the most difficult."

"But you don't even know what the next two benchmarks will be," Ronin cut in.

"I don't need to," Anselem replied, his voice filled with haunted memories.

The cadets looked at one another, but Asha's intent stare did not leave his face.

"What is it?" Varrick asked, his usual, joking tone nowhere to be found.

Anselem was quiet for a short moment before he replied, "The Tartarus."

Jeremiah scrunched his brow, and Ronin and Varrick exchanged a look.

"What is the Tartarus?" Jeremiah asked.

Before Anselem could open his mouth, a quiet voice called out from the other side of the table, a soft tone so foreign from the arrogant, haughty one she normally wielded, he almost didn't believe it belonged to her.

"It's your own personally crafted pit of the Hells."

"ONE CAN WITHSTAND A GREAT DEAL OF HARM TO THE BODY IF THE MIND IS WITHOUT FEAR. BUT ONCE THE MIND IS DESTROYED, BOTH THE BODY AND THE SOUL WILL FOLLOW QUICKLY BEHIND."

—EXCERPT FROM THE ARTISTRY OF INTERROGATION (AN INCOMPLETE MANUSCRIPT) BY CAPTAIN Z. KAGE

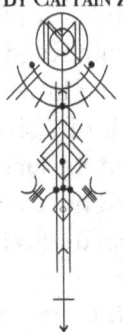

CHAPTER TWENTY-TWO

Asha stared up at the dungeon of nightmares. The alabaster stone structure had a faint yellow tint to it, and looked less like the clean, pristine walls that covered the rest of the structures across the Base, and more like it had been carved from the ground down parts of splintered bones. Asha drew in a sharp, jagged breath.

Anselem gave them most of the week off from any intense training. The Division still went through their normal morning fitness and kept up with group sparring, but he had not added in any additional drills, as if he knew there was nothing that could be done to help prepare Valorous for what they were about to face. Somehow, the ample time off had made the anticipation worse.

She watched as her Tribe all filed through the open, iron door, carved with shapes and patterns that looked like screaming mouths. She was the last to enter, and as she stepped into the Tartarus, she felt a shift in the air. Cold.

Like life refused to enter.

Death lurked so close by, it felt like a third companion as she walked beside Captain Kage, winding their way down the narrow steps and into the lower levels.

The hairs on the back of Asha's neck stood upright as the group reached the bottom landing. The Major, flanked by two other men Asha had never seen before, unexpectedly greeted them as they stepped into the open space of the underground.

The hallway stretched in two opposing directions, lined with a plethora of rooms on each side. The floors were made of gray and white checkered tile, and the walls were crafted from the same bony material as the exterior structure many floors above. Golden-white luminos lined both sides of the hallway.

"Good morning, Major. I was not expecting you."

Bardick flashed a serpentine grin, and Asha's blood ran cold. "Gentlemen, this is Captain Kage." Kage nodded to each of the men.

The Major turned to Kage. "I'm afraid there has been a slight change in plans. These two men are finishing their Examination Training and only have one more session to go before it is completed."

Kage remained silent.

"So, I'm sure you won't mind, but we will need to borrow one of your cadets," Major Bardick finished.

Kage, standing beside Asha, went rigid, but his face remained unmoved. Asha's heart began to beat harder against her chest.

Kage nodded. "Of course, sir." He turned to Ronin, guilt flashing in his eyes, and said, "Cadet Ronin is available."

Ronin went still beside Varrick.

"As you know, Captain, a lot of preparation goes into

developing a plan of Inquisition for a specific individual. And unfortunately, these men," he motioned to the two beside him, "have already researched and devised questions specific to Cadet Raynor."

Bile rose in Asha's throat, and her breath became shallow, as if the air inside them had been sucked out.

"But sir, I think Ronin would be a much better option…"

The Major's diplomatic face turned hostile. "It's not up for discussion, *captain*."

Asha tried to swallow the lump in her throat, but her mouth had turned to charred ash.

Asha looked over to Kage, but his eyes were fixed on the Major; an intense, unspoken conversation was raging between them.

"Come along, Cadet Raynor," Bardick trilled, and he turned with his companions and began to saunter down the hall.

Asha pressed her hands firmly against her sides as they began to shake, and then she forced herself to step one foot in front of the other and follow the Major down the hall.

The room was stripped, except for a bare wooden table and a single metal ring fastened in the center of the dark floor. Asha stood in the middle of the room, her mind forcing her body to keep from bolting out the door and back down the hall. Bardick and one of his companions entered after her, shutting the heavy iron door behind them.

The Major walked in a circle around the room. Asha trailed him with her eyes but said nothing.

A few minutes passed, and then she heard the handle on the door shift. The second man walked into the room, holding a pair of iron chains.

Her heart began to race, and she slid her eyes back to the Major.

He halted his circling steps in front of her and pushed up his sleeves, revealing Marked skin underneath.

Asha's heart plummeted, and she thought she might vomit.

Deeply etched into his forearm sat the Mark of The Vice—a branding eye permanently inked upon the skin.

No.

No.

No.

And as the door clicked shut, that was when she knew—she was no longer participating in a benchmark.

A serpent's smile spread over the Vice's face.

The Snake's face.

"Scream all you want, Asha, no one can hear you down here."

❖ ❖ ❖

She had fought. And fought and fought. Until the burly one struck her so hard in the back of the head, she lost consciousness.

When she came to, the iron chains were shackled around her wrists and ankles, and the Major stood before her, leaning against the wall, wholly relaxed.

She tried to keep her breathing even, but she could hear the hitch in her lungs as they drew in tightened breaths.

She would not cry. She would not give him the satisfaction.

She would not yield. She would not break.

I am a master of my fear. I have power beyond measure. I am unbreakable.

His eyes devoured her, and an ominous look sparkled in his gaze.

Three days. She just had to hold out for three days, and someone would come find her. They had to come find her.

But as he pressed himself off the wall, stepping towards her, the Darkness inside her began to stir.

Her demons, calm as they had been for months, had not disappeared. They had simply been waiting for a reason to wake, patiently biding their time until they were able to take a long overdue breath, and crawl back into her ear, whispering to her of all the Darkness she still held within.

She shoved them back, pushing away the dark voices in her head, hoping she could hold them off long enough for someone to come.

Someone had to come.

He laughed, and the oily sound made Asha's stomach turn. "Chained and beaten, but in your eyes, I can see the hope you hold onto." He made the word sound foul, as if it disgusted him. He scoffed. "You truly think someone will come rescue you, don't you?" He shook his head, and another sinister laugh left his mouth. "Well, if there is still an ember of hope burning inside you, it won't take very long for it to be winked out. No one is coming. No one will come. It is just you and me and the demons we dance with."

He spoke of hope as if it was a fragile, fleeting thing; made up of hushed murmurs and gossamer threads and broken dreams. But that was not the hope Asha knew. It was not the hope she had been taught and promised. The hope she knew had bloodstained knuckles, scraped skin, and bruised bones. The hope she knew had been beaten down, burned alive, and trampled on; yet she still fought, still raised herself up, always ready for one more round.

"Although, you Raynor women seem to hold out much longer than most."

Asha's stomach turned, and she looked up at the Major.

The Snake's smile grew wide, and his eyes darkened. "Yes, your mother dearest held out for a long while. We had a lot of fun together."

Asha's stomach dropped, her head spun, and the room tilted. Her ears rang.

"But," he sighed, "all good things must come to an end."

She vomited onto her shirt.

"But thankfully not before I was able to get some *very* useful information."

Asha stared at the floor in front of her, trying to focus on her breathing.

She breathed in and out. In and back out.

The Major let out an exasperated sigh. "Asha, this will be a much more enjoyable time for everyone if you do something other than sit there with a blank stare."

Enjoyable? She nearly ripped the chains off the hinges at the word. But instead, she let that cool, lethal calm spread through her entire body as she looked up to him with flames burning in her eyes.

"Go to Hells," she spat.

He cackled, the sound wicked and unsettling, and replied, "Haven't you heard? The Seven Hells are empty and all its demons are here."

Asha stared at him with promises of death in her eyes.

He snickered.

"Now, dear Asha, this can go very smoothly. Painless. All I need is a little information from you, and we can move on, like nothing has even happened here."

Silence.

The Major began to saunter in a circle around her as he spoke. "I just need you to tell me where it is."

Asha realized the Major had no idea how well acquainted she had once been with silence. No words left her mouth as she stared straight ahead at the stone wall.

"Where is the book, Asha?"

What in the Seven Hells was he talking about?

"The journal. Tell me where it is, and you can walk out right now. And we can consider this... a misunderstanding."

Math's journals.

Asha kept her face unmoved, but sweat began to bead on her back.

"We know your mother gave the book to Mathieson before we brought her in for questioning. And I have been informed that your brother's belongings were brought to you before they were sent to be burned."

Mom had a journal? Asha's mind began to race.

"But we searched the entire boat before it was set aflame, and your mother's journal was nowhere to be found. So, I'm going to ask you one last time, Asha, where is your mother's journal?"

Asha barely heard the Major's question as her mind darted in a million directions.

He did not want Math's journals; he wanted her mother's? Why? And where was it if it hadn't been with the rest of Mathieson's things?

A movement flashed beside her. She heard the slap ring through the room before she felt the heat sting over her cheek. Her head whipped to the side with the force of his hand against her skin.

She slowly brought her face back to meet his. "I don't know anything."

Half-truth.

Asha had no idea what he was talking about regarding her mother, but she certainly did know *something*. Even if Math's journals were not what the Major truly desired, she still held knowledge of something connected to what he *did* want.

Knowledge that would implicate Kaira.

And Asha was many things, but mindless was not one of them. She would not tell him. Could not tell him. And she would allow him to think she held more secrets than she did, because as soon as he got the information he sought, Asha knew she would be dead.

But above all, she would never give up Kaira. She would join Anubis in the Hells before she ever let another friend die at her hands.

"Now we both know that isn't true, is it?"

Asha's stare was blank, but rage began to boil inside her.

"What do you even want with something of my mother's? She has been gone for years. And let's not pretend that we both don't know that she was denied the opportunity to work on anything of value." Asha had meant to keep her tone neutral, but displeasure had uncontrollably seeped into her words.

The Major clicked his tongue. "Is that what she told you? That we didn't let her?"

Asha's eyes narrowed.

"Did you ever think that perhaps she just wasn't good enough to cut it? She didn't have the talent? The drive?"

The demons in Asha's ear made another effort to crawl back out, to feed her the lies about herself that she had bought for so long, to tell her that she would never make it, that she wasn't enough.

But she knew her mother. She knew the type of woman she was. The type of woman she had taught her to be, even if Asha had forgotten it for a long while.

Asha opened the door in her mind that held the memories of her mom. A room that she did not like to visit much, for the pain it brought of missing her was often too much to hold. But as Asha thought of her smile, of the sapphire blue eyes that gifted her, her own, Asha felt a wave wash over her. But it was not sadness that the wave brought; it was comfort and pride and love. And it was rather beautiful, the way the memories of her mother put her insecurities to sleep. The way she starved all her fears and knew all the dreams she kept coiled beneath her bones.

And Asha smiled as she remembered the silver-blonde woman who held her in her arms so many years ago and told her she could be anything she wanted to be.

"You're a liar."

The Major cocked his head.

"You know she made it through the Soturi Tryout. You know she deserved to be chosen. And you found a way to deny her, to silence her voice and force her out."

The Major's eyes narrowed the faintest bit. "Not just a pretty face, are you?"

"I know what you did, what you have all done—for decades. But not anymore. You lost. I made it. I am here. I will be a Soturi. The first of many women who will follow after me. The road you have traveled for so many years, the one full of dreams and hopes you hunted down and extinguished, has reached its end. The dreamers will be the saviors of this world you have broken."

The Major's eyes went dark, as if night had entered them. "The stories you read as a child, the ones filled with fairytales and dreams coming true—the storytellers forgot to mention that nightmares are dreams too. And unfortunately for you, Asha, you've just entered the beginning of the darkest kind."

Asha stared at him, the fire in her veins burning brighter. A sneer spread over his face.

"Just like your mother, it looks like you and I will be

having a lot of fun together." He stepped towards the door and grabbed the iron handle. But before he opened the door, he looked back with the serpent's grin and added, "And unlike her, there's nowhere for you to run and hide."

Asha stared at his sinister smile and prayed one day she would be the one to rip it from his sickening face.

She forced the swaggering smile to spread across her face. "Unfortunately for you, I don't run from my demons. I learn their names. And I may have a long list of them, but when I leave here, yours will be underlined in red."

He pulled down on the handle, and a terrifying smile crossed his face. "The only way you will leave here is in fragmented pieces."

Then he sauntered through the door, leaving Asha alone in the dungeon.

An hour or two passed before the door reopened. Bardick sauntered into the dim room, the two men trailing behind him. The blood drained from Asha's face as she saw what the men carried.

In each scarred hand was a variety of knives and other metal tools that looked specifically crafted to inflict pain.

Asha's heart began to race, and sweat beaded above her brow.

"It is so unfortunate it has come to this," the Major trilled, his voice upbeat and excited. It sounded so contrary to the surrounding grimness of the room.

"But, since you insist on playing games and refuse to tell me what I need to know, you leave me no other options."

Asha stared into Bardick's eyes—the Snake's eyes, for there was no other fitting name for a man so sinister, so conniving, so cold.

Her head whipped to the side with blunt force, and it took her a moment, before the pain had radiated up through her cheek, to realize she had been hit. Hard.

Blood pooled in her mouth from where her teeth had been slammed against the inside of her cheek. She spat it on the ground before her, droplets of crimson splattered onto Bardick's boots.

"Where is the journal, Asha?"

She glared at him through burning eyes.

Another fist swung, this time meeting her side. The air was punched from her lungs, and she took in a gasping breath.

"You think I don't know about your little excursion to the Archives?"

Asha's hands, shackled behind her, began to shake.

The Major laughed, a cruel, oily sound reverberating from his throat. "I know everything, Asha. Every move you have made for the past five months, ever since you stepped onto this Base."

She tried to calm her breathing, tried to maintain a semblance of control, but her body failed her, and she drew in ragged breaths.

She racked her brain, her mind traveling a million miles an hour, as she tried to recall if she had given anything away, if she had made any other mistakes aside from visiting the Archives. The only thing she was grateful for now was that she had never left the Base on her own. Every time she had left, it was with Anselem, and not one of those times had been logged.

A sickening feeling crawled into her mind, from deep within the Darkness, and a wave of nausea accompanied the thoughts. What if the Major already knew about Math's journals? What if he had found them? Or worse—what if he had harmed Kaira to find them?

She took in a deep breath, trying to calm herself and shove the thoughts away before they took root.

No. He would have taunted her with that discovery; he would have known that was the best way to break her, to force her to give up the information he was convinced she held.

Another cracking fist swung across her face. This time, the pain was immediate, and a small cry escaped from her lips. She blinked, but her vision was spotty. She could already feel the blood rushing to the skin around her eyes, swelling it shut.

"I told you, I don't know anything about my mother's journal."

The Major clicked his tongue. "Perhaps," he replied, seemingly unfazed by the beaten woman who knelt before him. "But you do know something. And no matter how long it takes, I will find out what it is you know."

A chill waved over her body. Three days. She just needed to last three days, and they would have to let her go. People would start to ask questions... Her Tribe would wonder where she was.

She just needed to hold on for three days.

As she kneeled there, convincing herself she could hold out, that she could make it, the Major peered down at her, a serpent's smile slithering over his face, and said, "I told you before, no one is coming."

She looked up at him, fear spreading over her face. "I can still see it in your eyes—that useless hope."

He looked down at his jacket, picking off a piece of dust. "But don't worry, before you leave here, that hope will be gone."

He turned and sauntered to the door.

"Do whatever you want, just don't kill her yet. I still have a few more things I need answered." He opened the latch and disappeared into the hall on the other side of the door.

Asha's hands began to shake, and she took in a deep breath.

A boot collided with her back, shoving her onto the stone floor. Her face scraped against the rock as it impacted.

Then the two men were over her, fists and feet impacting against flesh and bones. She heard a crack as one of their boots crushed into her side, and a loud cry pierced the air. It was met with maniacal laughter and an enlivened desire to elicit a similar wail.

They hadn't even gotten to the knives when she lost consciousness.

Asha had no clue how long she had been left alone. Hours? Days? Time seemed endless as she drifted in and out of consciousness.

There were moments when she opened her eyes and her pain was so endless, the salt of her tears did not taste of her own, but like that of the women who had come before her, enduring shattered dreams and broken hearts, filled with nothing but the sorrow of lost hope.

She could taste the blood pooling in her mouth. She drew in jagged breaths, but with each inhale, shards of glass ripped through her side.

She was so tired. So, so tired. The hinges on the iron door clicked open, and her body began to shake. A tear slipped from her swollen eye.

She didn't know how long she could hold out. How much longer she could endure it. But she would try for as long as she could. For them, she would hold on. For her mom, for Math, for Nina. And for her new family, her Court of Misfits, and for Kaira. Asha would keep holding on until there was nothing left of her but the Darkness of her memories.

And as she lay there, curled up on the cold, stone floor, those dark memories she kept locked away for so long called to her to let them out. They invited her back into the mansion she had built in her mind, and she no longer had the will to fight against them, so she walked through the front door.

Inside her mind resided a home that she had been trapped in for years. It was full of walls covered in holes she had created with her fists—beating out the anger until her hands bled. The mansion was full of many rooms she refused to enter, terrified to face what lurked behind the doors. There was a part of this house that she hadn't visited in months, tucked far in the back corner, away from the safe room she'd built downstairs. She never let herself return to that room after she left it.

A single tear escaped from Asha's eyes as she walked up the stairs and down the hallways of her mind, knowing exactly where her footsteps would lead. She came to the end of the corridor and stared at the final, locked room. Her heart raced and her breathing hitched as she watched the door slowly crack open. Her shaking hand grabbed the knob and pushed the door inward. Asha forced herself to walk across the threshold and into the lightless room. The air in the room was thick and smelled of loss and decay. There were no windows, just an endless darkness that closed in all around her. It was cold—icy—like life itself refused to reside there. Asha forced herself to take a breath. This place reminded her of drowning, without ever being allowed to die.

She remembered the first time she ever came to the room, how she lived in there for such a long time. The Darkness had sunk its claws into her so deeply, she thought she would never rip free from them. It was in the days after she'd heard of Mathieson's death when she created the space. She'd built it slowly, and the Darkness had silently spread out from the room's corners the longer she stayed inside. Asha didn't even try to fight as the shadows grew and grew. It was so hard to continue to turn the pages when she knew he wouldn't be in the next chapter.

So, she didn't—she stopped turning the pages and closed the book altogether.

The room was born from chaos and pain. It felt as if she was living in a body that was fighting to survive, with a mind that was trying to die.

When Math died, it was like everyone else continued to move on with their lives, but Asha was still stuck in a hole she couldn't climb out of. A hole she had dug too far and too deep into the Darkness, that even the piercing light under the door seam wouldn't dare venture into its depths.

So that was where she stayed—for months. Just wandering aimlessly in the dark. She didn't sob or wail. She just existed. She simply went through the motions—numb to the world. Her grief was horribly discreet, but it was persistent, like bleeding from an unstitched wound.

Until one day, an unknown hand reached for hers and dragged her out of the room. She never saw who saved her, who pulled her from the depths of her anguish, but she still sent a prayer up to Ianoda every morning to thank him for whomever he sent.

Asha knew she would always dedicate a piece of her mind, a part of her heart, and a section of her soul to the endless possibilities of the man she knew her brother would have become. But, after she was pulled out of the Dark Room, each day, she forced herself to walk past it in her mind, keeping its doors locked, and she remembered how far she had come from the brokenness that once swallowed her whole.

Until her Final Testing of Algae. When her fractured heart shattered all over again. But instead of returning to the Dark Room in her mind and letting herself be swallowed in the endless shadows, Asha had walked up to the Dark Room, twisted the knob, and unleashed the darkness inside her soul on the world.

And then she threw away the key.

"Welcome back," the Snake trilled. He leaned against the wall several feet in front of her. She could barely see him through her swollen eye, but with the other, she was able to make out the sinister twinkle in his eyes.

"I really thought you would have been more agreeable, Asha."

She wondered how slow she could make his death if he dared venture close enough to where she knelt.

"But, since you seem reluctant to do so, I'm afraid you leave me no choice but to become more... creative."

Her stomach rolled.

"Are you sure you don't have anything you would like to share with me, Miss Raynor?"

Asha stayed silent. For Kaira. She would stay silent for Kaira.

The Major clicked his tongue. "Pity."

She watched his serpentine eyes glance over to his companion standing behind Asha, and he nodded once.

Then she felt his hands on her shirt as he pulled it away from her skin. She heard the blade as it swiftly cut through the fabric, and she felt the material fall to the sides, exposing her bruised back.

Her heart raced, and she held her breath. *For Kaira,* she whispered to only herself.

The whip cracked a moment later, and her ears were filled with the shattering sound of her curdled screams as the skin was ripped from her back.

Over and over.

Snap after snap.

The whip did not cease. It sliced through her body until her throat was raw, and the only noise she made came from the dripping trickle of her blood against the stone.

Blow after blow. She felt every agonizing slash.

Then her veins began to burn. And as the last snap of his whip sounded, she felt the iron bands beneath her shirt begin to crack.

Anselem had been fidgety for three days. He knew that the Tartarus was never an enjoyable experience, so he forced himself to keep busy by reviewing battle plans for the ongoing war across the Strait.

The instructors had implemented the benchmark into Soturi training years ago, insisting the warriors needed to endure exposure to the elements of imprisonment in case they were ever captured. They roughed the cadets up a bit, deprived them of sleep, but they didn't kill them. They rarely ever broke bones. Just enough pain to ensure the warriors could handle captivity without exposing any of the Kingdom's secrets.

Anselem hated the entire concept, and he was grateful his Division would be released today. As he waited, he was able to find a small amount of comfort in knowing Kage was the instructor who conducted the examinations.

He brought his attention back to the maps and papers before him. As he stood hunched over his desk, his hands bracing his weight against the wood, his door slammed open, and a figure burst into his room.

Anselem whipped around, fury filling his words, "What the Hells do you think—"

His voice went silent as he looked over to see Kage standing inside the doorway.

His heart plummeted.

"Where is she?" Anselem's voice was darker than night.

Kage gulped down air, as if he had run all the way to Anselem's room from somewhere far across the Base.

"They took her."

Silence burned the room.

"What do you mean they took her?"

Kage's voice came out in exhausted, fear-filled gasps. "They wouldn't let me conduct her assessment. They had her on the other side of the Tartarus for the entire benchmark, and now the room is empty. She's gone."

A darkness crawled into Anselem's eyes, overtaking the emerald hue, and a crack of lightning sounded in the distance. He grabbed the twin swords hanging above his desk and strapped them to his back.

He fastened a smaller blade to his hip and threw a belt covered in an assortment of sheathed daggers over to Kage, who had managed to bring his breathing back to a steady rhythm.

He looked over to his friend, nothing but the face and voice of the Commander on display, and said through clenched teeth, "Let's go."

CHAPTER TWENTY-THREE

Asha opened her eyes, and everything felt... different.

The air was colder, and a musty stench burned her nose. She cracked open her eyes, and they began to slowly adjust to the dark room. The only light in the space was a pair of luminos hanging on each side of the iron door.

She had been moved. To a new room, or a new building, or a new world, she was not sure.

She was also unsure how many days had passed since she had been locked away. There were no windows in this new space either, and she was still bound by iron chains.

She blinked. Slowly. Her eyes and head felt so heavy. Her tongue felt like sandpaper in her mouth, and her throat burned.

A shadow moved in the corner, and she forced her gaze to drag over to the figure.

When the silhouette stepped out of the darkness and into the faint light, a sob escaped from Asha's torn lips.

Her auburn hair and sun-kissed skin glowed. She was beautiful, radiant. And when her piercing, silver-flecked eyes met Asha's, the tears she thought had run dry, once again began to fall onto her bloodied cheeks.

"Nina," she croaked out. The word felt like splinters in her throat.

"Hi, Ash." Her voice was just as she had remembered. Soft, kind, filled with love.

Another quiet sob left her lips. "I'm sorry, Nina. So, so sorry."

She stared back at Asha with only kindness in her silver-flecked eyes. "Why do you continue to carry a burden that never belonged to you?"

More tears left her sapphire eyes. "I killed you," she whispered.

"We both know that isn't the whole story."

Asha looked down at the cold, stone ground. "I shoved the blade into your heart." Her voice cracked as the words escaped.

"I asked you to. We both knew I was not going to survive. We both knew that the creature's claws had poison in them that even phoenix tears could not heal."

Asha was silent as bright flashes of memory flickered through her mind.

The reeking smell of the beast burned her nose as she and Nina wandered into an open field with dead grass and drained flowers, both searching for the answer to complete Nina's Final Testing of Algae.

Asha had shown Nina her note as soon as The Test began, and Nina had promised to complete her own Test and make it through Kappi graduation so she could go on and attend Soturi training in Asha's place, vowing to help her finish what Math had started.

As they stood in the field, the creature came out of the trees and barreled towards the women.

Before they had time to react, the creature's claws ripped through Nina's side, and Asha watched as her friend fell to the ground below.

The shriek she cried rang through Asha's ears, and she held her friend in her arms as the black poison spread through her body. Nina looked up at her, with labored breaths, and told her she needed to be the one to do it. She wanted it to be her—so Asha could continue, so she could pass her Test and keep fighting.

Tears slid down Asha's face as she honored her friend's final wish—her final sacrifice—and plunged the dagger into her heart of gold.

Tears poured down Asha's face as the memory blasted through her mind.

"Let it go."

"I can't."

"You can."

Asha raised her wet eyes to look at her friend.

"Just because you carry it so well does not mean it isn't heavy. Let it go, Asha. It was never your sin to bear."

"I miss you."

"I know," she replied.

"And I am so tired, Nina."

She offered a soft smile to the warrior.

"I don't understand. I don't understand why I am still here. I don't know anything. Why won't they let me go?" The words were nearly a sob as they fell from her lips.

Nina was quiet for a long moment before her delicate, unwavering voice replied, "Sometimes people will try to destroy you because they fear the power within you. It is not because they don't recognize it, or because they do not notice the fire burning within your soul. Sometimes, it is precisely because they *do* see it, and they do not want it to continue to burn."

Asha heard the footsteps on the other side of the door. Her body involuntarily began to shake in response.

Nina moved beside Asha and kneeled next to her, her voice kind but strong in her ear, "Get off the ground," she commanded her friend. "Spit your blood and bare your teeth. Go down savage, go down fighting."

The latch on the door unlocked, and the iron hinges swung open. The Snake sauntered in; a cruel smile fixed on his face.

"Ah, it looks like the dreamer has finally awakened." His voice was slick with oil.

She glanced over to Nina and slowly stood on her shaky feet, spitting out the blood that had pooled in her mouth.

The Major let out a wicked laugh. "Oh? Have you kindled the last bit of fire left inside of you, Asha? You think you can outlast me? Beat me?"

She glared at him with fire-filled eyes.

He scoffed. "I truly don't know who you think you are. We both know how this will end—with your name added to a long list of forgotten warriors who came before you. And you will be nothing more than that."

She forced her voice to remain steady as the words ripped through her scream-torn throat, "I am one of the heirs of the women you dismissed. I am one of the voices you thought would forever stay silent. And if you hadn't been so confident in your ability to shatter our hope, you would have been smart enough to sift through the ashes of every woman's dreams you'd ever burned. Because all it takes is a single ember to spark a whole wildfire back to life. So yes. I *will* be my own fire. And I will be the fire for every one of the women before me whose dreams were snuffed out by your hand. And if I am burned by my flames, I will continue to fly forward on scorched wings. Until *you* are the one who is nothing but a forgotten memory."

A serpent's smile washed over his face. "Scorched wings? How poetic. I'm fairly certain we can find a way for that to be arranged."

She glanced once more to the corner of the room, and Nina smiled back at her, pride filling her eyes, and her voice was soft as the edges of her image started to blur. "I love you bunches, Ash. Forever." And with her parting words, a single tear slid from Asha's eye.

Asha had always been told that people die twice. One time when they stop breathing, and a second time when someone they love says their name for the last time.

Then a whipping fist cracked across her jaw, echoing the sound of her shattering heart, and blackness filled the world once again.

There was a ringing in her ears as Asha woke to a deep voice in the hall. She had no idea how much time had passed. Days? Weeks? It felt endless.

She had woken several other times since Nina left, each time met with more whips and fists the moment her eyes broke open. She had learned to keep them shut.

She lay in the middle of the room, curled on the stone floor. Something wet covered her face, her hair. She didn't know if it was blood or sweat. She didn't care.

"Where is she?" the voice whispered. Or perhaps the voice screamed it, she was not sure. Her head felt like it was submerged under water; every sound around her was muffled and far. She thought she heard thunder in the distance.

The iron hinges swung open, but her body was too exhausted to shake.

"Asha?" A husky, accented voice broke through the silence. She forced her eyes open. Her name sounded so foreign on his lips. She wasn't sure if she had ever heard him say it.

She forced herself to look up. Pain and fury were wrecked across his emerald-green eyes. She could see the ink shaking on his honey-brown arms. She wasn't sure if he was real. She hoped he was. He took a step closer and kneeled beside her. She heard a noise that sounded like a wounded whimper, and she realized it had come from her own lips.

"Is it okay if I touch you?" he asked. His voice was soft and calm, one she had never seen him use before, but his expression was serious, and Asha noted how it softened slightly when he looked into her eyes. Like the way he looked at her was different from how he looked at everyone else.

Her throat was too raw from the screaming, she knew no sound would come out. She nodded once. She vaguely felt his hands on her wrists, then again on her ankles. She barely heard the click as the shackles were unlocked. She was numb. Everything was numb.

He wrapped her up in his arms, careful to avoid the parts of her skin that were covered in gashes and half-healed bruises. She was surprised he was able to find any place left undamaged. "You're safe now, Seven."

Her head felt so heavy. She lay it against his body, burying her face in his shoulder as he held her. Darkness threatened to take hold, and the only thoughts she could hear swimming through her numbed mind were the ones that whispered she needed him. She needed his arms around her, needed him to hold her and tell her that everything would be okay.

And as he carried her out of the room, Anselem told her exactly that.

The darkness closed around the last bit of light left in her eyes, and the faintest of smiles twitched on her lips because, this time, when he said those words, she realized she believed him.

"LARGE, DEEP LACERATIONS STRETCH THE ENTIRE LENGTH OF THE PATIENT'S BACK. ACCOMPANYING CUTS TO BOTH THE ARMS AND LEGS. BROKEN LEFT ARM, DISPLACED SHOULDER, CRACKED RIBS. HEALED BY PHOENIX TEARS. CURRENTLY IN THE INFIRMARY FOR MONITORING. UNKNOWN HOW PATIENT SURVIVED."
—EXCERPT FROM THE PATIENT CHART OF CADET A. RAYNOR. LOGGED BY RAPHA BRIGHID CHIRON

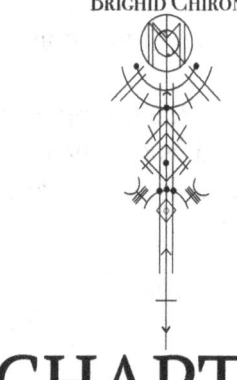

CHAPTER TWENTY-FOUR

Nine days. That was how long she had been in the Tartarus. Or, rather, three days in the Tartarus, like each of her Divisionmates, and another six in the spiraling depths of an unmarked building on Base. *Dungeon*, she thought. There was no other word for the Nameless Place.

After Anselem broke her out, Asha was never left alone, not even for a moment. Either Kaira or her Tribe were present with her for every minute of the day. They took rotations by her side while she slept, holding her hand when she awoke to her own screams. It had been three days since she left the Nameless Place, and she was finally able to stand on her own, Uriel's tears having healed the majority of the more severe injuries. Most of her body was still sore, and when she took too deep a breath, a shooting pain would slide up her side.

They had broken several of her ribs.

It was midday when her Tribe strolled into her room in

the East Wing. Kaira was lounging on the chair closest to the window, flipping through a book, and the Rapha who cared for her every day left shortly before Valorous arrived.

"How ya feeling, Ash?" Jeremiah chirped.

Varrick punched him in the arm. "How do you think she feels, bonehead?"

Ronin rolled his eyes and sat in the chair beside her bed. "Hi, Ash."

Asha grinned.

"A little better today, Jer."

Jeremiah flashed a look at Varrick. "See? I'm not a bonehead."

"I wouldn't go that far, Jeremiah," Ronin chimed. Jeremiah narrowed his eyes at Ronin.

She smiled at her Tribe, her Court of Royal Misfits.

"Catch me up. What did I miss while I was… gone?"

The men all winced at the word, but Jeremiah, ever the peacekeeper, quickly piped in, "You would be super proud. We won our Wargame."

"It wasn't pretty, but we managed," Ronin added.

The three men all held proud grins on their faces, but she could see the smiles did not meet their eyes. She knew they still held a lot of guilt and worry in their hearts.

Asha forced the swaggering tone into her voice as she replied, "My Princesses and Jester stepped up to fight for their incapacitated Queen; how noble."

A laugh escaped from the corner Kaira was curled up in. The men blinked before they joined in, the darkness in their eyes lightening the faintest bit.

For the next hour, the men told her of how they bested Destroyer Division in a dagger-throwing challenge. Asha laughed and smiled as they told the story, chiming in with her mocking commentary.

A knock sounded at the door, and the group went quiet. Kaira walked over to open it. "Good afternoon, lieutenant." She pushed the door open wider, and Asha saw Anselem standing in the doorway.

Kaira glanced back at Valorous. "They were actually just leaving." Varrick opened his mouth to interject, but a stern glance from Kaira kept his lips sealed. The men stood, gathered their belongings, and said their goodbyes to Asha. Each warrior nodded as they passed Anselem. He did not say a word.

"And I was going to step out for a moment myself," Kaira added after Asha's Tribe disappeared down the hall. She looked back at Asha. "I will be back before he leaves. I just need to check in with my Leader and rearrange some things for this weekend." She flashed Asha a wink before she turned back to the door and strutted down the hall.

Anselem stepped through the door and gently closed it behind him.

He stared at her for a long moment before he opened his mouth.

"How are you?"

"I'm good." He raised his brows at her.

"How are you?" he asked again. Her brow furrowed.

"I said I'm good."

"I know what you said, Seven. I was giving you another chance to not lie through your teeth to me."

She sighed. Her voice went low. "I don't know how I am."

It was the truth. She didn't know how she felt; all she knew was that she no longer felt like herself. Not anymore. Now she felt like a watered-down version of who she had been. Less bright. More cracked.

He nodded and walked over to the seat beside her. Amber and citrus folded into the air around her.

He sighed. "I couldn't find him. I searched the Base over twice, but Bardick is long gone."

She nodded, unsure if his disappearance caused her more anxiety or relieved it. She knew the other two men, Bardick's companions—the ones whose names she had never learned—had been killed by Anselem in the hall. She hadn't asked where the bodies had gone, but when Anselem mentioned Kage had come with him, she had a fairly good idea what the Examiner had done to dispose of the wicked souls.

He stared intently at her, as if he could see past all the healing the phoenix tears had done and still recalled every scrape and bruise that wrecked her face just days before. She dropped her eyes to her hands folded in her lap.

"Never again," he murmured. His voice was wild, with an edge of fierceness she had never heard before.

She raised her gaze back to his face. The intensity of his emerald eyes made her heart flutter.

"He will suffer a thousand deaths," he whispered, "before he ever touches another hair on your head." And with that fatal promise still reverberating through her heart, he concluded, "I give you my Word."

She unfolded her hands and reached for his. He interlaced his fingers with hers, and they sat like that for a long while, without words, as the sunlight creeping through the window began to fade.

And as they sat in comfortable silence, Anselem stood strong in the middle of the storm raging inside her—dead center in the chaos of it. And when she glanced over into his emerald oceans, his hopeful eyes silently whispered back to hers, *I promise you, Seven, there is no place I'd rather be.*

❖ ❖ ❖

Asha woke in the middle of the night to Jeremiah's muffled snores wafting over from the corner couch where he slept. She was exhausted, but she was grateful for a reprieve from waking to her own nightmare shrieks.

As she stared at the ceiling, Asha heard the soft squeaking of hinges. Her heart began to thud in her chest as the door slowly opened.

She let out a relieved breath when Brighid, the Rapha who had cared for her the last several days, slid in through the small opening.

She was a petite woman, only a few years older than Asha, with kind, amber eyes and pale skin that was covered in delicate freckles. Her bright red hair was braided back from her gentle face, and she worked with careful, tender movements.

Her eyes spread wide as she caught Asha's gaze, pinned on her.

"Oh, I'm so sorry, I thought you would be asleep."

Asha did not reply as she stared at the Rapha. She raised a bundle of fabric in her hand. "I just came to restock the bandages... I can come back later if you would prefer."

Asha raised her hand and motioned towards the cabinet, inviting the healer to continue with her work. She nodded and moved towards the wooden storage case. Asha caught the faint glint of fear in the Rapha's eyes; she had seen it often enough from others when they realized how lethal she could be.

"You don't need to be afraid of me."

The healer stilled for a moment before turning to Asha. "I'm not afraid of you."

Asha raised her brows. Even in the dim moonlight, she

could see the blush flush across the healer's face.

"I'm not afraid. I... You're inspiring." Asha's raised brows turned into a twisted crinkle in the middle of her face.

"It's embarrassing to admit, but I admire you. You seem so... fearless. So strong. And you can clearly endure... a great deal." Her voice came out in hushed whispers.

Asha shook her head. "Do not admire me, Brighid."

The Rapha's face went blank, and she blinked.

Asha sighed. The healer was right, at least about some of it. She *was* strong. But in the back of her mind, Asha didn't think she was ever meant to be so strong for so long.

"Some of us were put here to destroy. To kill and to shatter," she glanced down at the tendrils of smoky mist inked all over her arms, so many more than there had been merely a week ago. She looked back up at the healer. "And some of us were put here to heal. To fix and to mend and to put all the broken pieces back together. Never take for granted which side of the table you sit on. There are many destroyers whose only dream is to piece back together all the parts of their broken souls."

The Rapha was quiet, but her eyes were sincere as she nodded, her gentle voice filling the room, "It is both a blessing and a burden to feel everything so very deeply."

Asha only stared back into her amber eyes, knowing a truer statement might never before have been uttered.

❖ ❖ ❖

Three pairs of demonic eyes stared down at Asha as a wet trickle began to drip down her face. It smelled metallic and sickeningly bitter. She wiped her nose as the stench smothered her senses, suffocating her breath. Asha glanced down to find a spattering of deep crimson staining her fin-

gers—blood. Her blood.

A low, menacing snarl escaped from each of the beast's throats, and she whipped her gaze back towards the three sets of fiendish eyes peering down from atop the stairs. Their teeth were barred, attention focused singularly on her, and a low growl rumbled in their mouths. Asha's heart raced, threatening to rip itself from her chest. She turned to run, sending a prayer up to Ianoda to ask for help she knew she did not deserve. But as her body twisted to make a bolt for the arched entryway, she saw him *emerge from behind the marble pillar. She froze.*

"I've been waiting for you." The words dripped with venom.

A sinister sneer spread across his face, and Asha watched a spirit of malignity extend out from where he stood, seeking to devour anyone within its reach.

Her feet slowly set out to creep backwards, but as she attempted to move, she found them stuck—locked—as if they had been nailed into place. Asha looked down at her boots, ripping at them, willing them to move, but they stayed fastened to the stone floor. Her gaze shot back up, locking in on dark, empty eyes. She watched as he lightly placed his foot on the top stair. Her eyes flared wide, panic wiping over her entire body, as he took the first step towards her.

Asha awoke gasping for air. Anselem was up in a flash, crossing the distance from the couch to the side of her bed. "You alright?" She gulped down more air but managed to nod.

Dawning sunlight filled the room. She looked up at him with confused eyes and then back over to the couch.

"I swapped out with Jeremiah an hour ago." She nodded again, her breathing returning to normal.

"I'm here," he said. "We can talk about it or not talk about it, but I'm here." She nodded once more, not knowing what to say.

She leaned back against the top of the bed, adjusting herself so she was more upright.

"How's Uriel?"

A flash of surprise waved over his face at the sudden turn in conversation, but it quickly disappeared.

"He's fine. I have to quite literally give him daily reports on how you're doing, or else I'm afraid he's going to break through the East Wing foyer and batter his way through the halls until he finds your room to check for himself. But other than that, he's fine."

A small smile curled on Asha's lips. "He's such a mother hen."

Anselem scoffed. "You think?" Asha's small smile grew wider.

She was quiet for a moment.

"I missed seeing Dolion when I was... there."

Anselem's eyes narrowed the slightest bit, and Asha wasn't sure if it was from the warrior she mentioned or from the reference to the Nameless Place.

"Yes," he replied.

"Did he ask where I was?"

Anselem paused for a moment, seemingly trying to find the right words. "He did. He tracked down Jeremiah to ask."

"What did he say?" Asha could tell there was something he was trying not to expose by the careful choice in his words.

He huffed out a breath, and in the corner of her eye, she caught the way his hands curled into fists. "When Jeremiah told him it had been a week and that he didn't know where you were, Laeradur... He told Jeremiah that Leadership must have a reason to keep you there, and there was nothing to worry about."

Asha's face went pale, but the sudden shock was quickly replaced with rage. "He said I *deserved* to be there?"

"No, Seven, I don't think he understood what was really happening."

"He said they must have had a *reason* to keep me. Seems pretty clear he thought I deserved whatever they decided was fitting punishment for my supposed crimes." Disgust laced every word.

"Please don't make me the one who has to defend him. You know better than anyone, I'm not exactly his biggest fan."

Asha cut her eyes back to Anselem, and she could see the darkness wading within the emerald waves.

"Fine. But he's getting an earful next time I see him about his deficiency in proper word choice."

Anselem snorted. "I would expect nothing less."

She rolled her eyes and glanced back down at her uncovered arms. She stared down at the dark coils for a long time until Anselem broke through her thoughts with a whispered voice.

"Seven?"

She turned to him.

"I need to talk to you about something, and it isn't going to be pleasant."

Her heart skipped a beat, but she nodded.

He released a breath of air, and it came out in a quick whoosh. "Your bands," he said, his voice low as he gestured to the iron rings fastened just above her elbows, "they're not real."

Asha broke his gaze and glanced down at the rings encircling her arms. They looked the same. Felt the same.

"When I found you in... that place, your bands were cracked." Flashes of memories rushed back into her mind as she recalled feeling the iron bands begin to splinter under her shirt. Her breathing quickened, and she pushed the memories down, locking them away.

She nodded. "I remember. But they didn't break." She looked back down at the bands for the cracks she had felt, but the rings looked solid, fixed.

"They didn't break until I took you out and rushed you to Uriel. I'm not sure if you remember, but you came to for a moment... I think he might have tugged on the Bond to wake you, to make sure you were still there. Still fighting."

She didn't remember anything but darkness.

"When you woke up, I think your magic surged... just like it had when you were in the room and they first cracked."

She remembered the scorching feeling of fire burning through her veins. It felt like shredding thorns and splintered ice and raging flames all ripping through her body at once. But the fire inside her was winked out as quickly as it had surged, the iron bands swallowing the embers. But as the magic pulsing through her subsided, she felt the bands begin to crack.

"I replaced them with fake bands. They're only for show, they do not have iron in them."

Asha looked once more at the rings around her arms. They looked nearly identical to the ones she had worn all her life. She tried to feel for the burning magic within her, but no ripping thorns or splintering ice lurked beneath the surface of her skin. Not even a spark.

"It hasn't happened yet." She looked back at him.

"The manifestation. I think your magic only flared those few times because... because of everything you had endured. But your powers have not manifested yet."

"When will it happen?"

"Soon," he replied, "it varies for each person, but likely in the next couple of weeks."

She nodded, unsure of what to say.

"Ans?"

"Yes, Seven?"

"I'm calling in my debt."

His eyes narrowed in contemplation, but he nodded.

She took a breath.

She was ready. She needed to know.

"Tell me what happened in Aaru."

His eyes looked tired, rimmed with dark circles, and his stubble was thicker than he normally kept it. He ran his hand over his chin and let out a long sigh. Then Anselem finally told Asha the story of how her brother died.

"I HAVE PLAYED IT OVER AND OVER IN MY MIND, WONDERING WHERE IT ALL WENT WRONG. WHAT I COULD HAVE CHANGED. THE DEMONS IN MY HEAD NEVER REST. SOME DAYS I FEEL EVERYTHING AT ONCE. OTHERS, I FEEL NOTHING AT ALL. AND I'M NOT SURE WHICH IS WORSE: DROWNING BENEATH THE WAVES OR DYING FROM THE THIRST."

—QUOTE FROM COMMANDER ANSELEM EROS OF ASSIGNMENT 858, ANNOTATED IN THE LORDS OF CARNAGE: REDACTED OUTLINES OF THE MISSIONS OF THE SEPTANT

CHAPTER TWENTY-FIVE

His grief was like the ocean; it ebbed and flowed. Some days it was calm, like a silent shadow lingering in the back of his mind, and others it was an overwhelming typhoon, pulling him down underneath the crashing waves.

Anselem had discovered over the years that all he could do to endure it was to learn how to swim.

It started the same as any other mission. Anselem received orders, he hashed out the details, and he commanded the directive.

He never gave it a second thought, never questioned what the warriors were walking into; he simply accepted the assignment and plowed forward.

That was his first mistake.

The Commander led the Septant west across the Smaragdus Sea, soaring over the emerald waves with Mathieson, Kage, and their firebirds. Einar and Sacha traveled by sea, their hippocas quickly gliding through the open waters. Blaidd and Balam departed earlier than the rest, needing to commandeer a ship in Brienza to sail them and their wolves across the waters dividing the rival Kingdoms. Once they landed on the shores of Montu, Blaidd and Balam reconvened with the rest of the Lords of Carnage.

That was when Anselem made his second mistake.

He ordered the group of warriors to split into two factions as they entered Aaru's capital, heading for the Midnight Castle, home to the Obsidian Throne.

Anselem's plan was well thought out, and each of the warriors knew their objectives. But even the most wellstitched plans can fall apart when players begin to pull strings.

Anselem wore Septant black on the day he was called to kill a Queen. Fitted black leathers, with a dark belt fixed at the waist, donning a single iron dagger. His obsidian jacket was tailored to closely hug his wide shoulders and taper in at his waist, giving no room for loose pieces of fabric to snag on his surroundings or for his weapons to catch.

A single, long Elysian-steel sword was fixed across his back, and a large hood draped down in front of his eyes, hiding the upper portion of his face. An onyx mask was fixed against the bottom half, a customary tradition for the Septant to ensure the identities of the warriors stayed hidden.

And, in customary tradition, each of the other men was also covered wholly in black.

Black for its silence. Black to blend into the darkness. Black to avoid detection.

Assassins of the night.

For if one was going to kill a man, it was best to ensure he never saw you coming.

The orders were straightforward—get in, kill the queen, and get back out undetected.

The Septant waited until nightfall to make their move.

Anselem, flanked by Sacha and Blaidd, crept through the dimly lit halls. It hadn't taken much effort for the trio to incapacitate the handful of castle guards monitoring the southern wall. After they quickly hid the bodies, they slipped in through an exterior side door and down to the castle's lower level.

They wound their way up through the floors, silently removing any threats along the way, until they reached the top level that housed the queen's chambers.

The trio stuck to the shadows, skulking their way past the hung luminos and avoiding the portions of the floors illuminated by the moonlight crawling in through the wide, open windows.

Once they made it to the end of the hall, the three warriors swiftly removed the large group of guards standing post outside the queen's door. Sacha and Blaidd took out two with the shortened blades they carried for close-quarter combat; Anselem summoned lightning into his hands, sending jolts of lethal electricity from his fingertips into the hearts of four others. He finished off the final two guards with twin daggers he unsheathed from his waist, thrusting the blades into the guards' throats before the bodies of their electrified comrades had even hit the floor.

Anselem pulled out the long, Elysian sword from his back. His heart raced as he reached for the knob.

That was Anselem's third mistake.

There was a fraction of a moment between when his hand twisted the knob and the door cracked open, when the Commander felt deep inside his bones that something was wrong. It had been easy—perhaps too easy—to kill the Queen of the Obsidian Throne. And Anselem Eros was a seasoned enough warrior to know the difference.

The steel door creaked open, its hinges squealing, and the trio quickly filtered into the room.

Anselem halted as his eyes took in what lay before him.

Balam, standing beside the queen's bed, had a long blade pressed against the throat of a shadowed figure kneeling before him. He brushed his straight, dark hair out of his gray eyes, and his hollow cheekbones, which had always given an ominous edge to his pale face, looked even more grim in the dim light.

To his right stood two more castle guards, each with his own blade pressed against another hidden figure.

Anselem's eyes dragged to the corner of the room where a tall woman with waist-length obsidian hair and a crown studded with onyx and ruby gems stood, a spider's smile fixed upon her face. Her bone-colored eyes, filled with black where white should have been, looked as if they held the wrath-filled secrets of Anubis.

His heart plummeted as he cut his gaze back to the hidden figure kneeling in front of Balam. The queen waved her pale hand, tipped with blood red nails, and the cloud of darkness around the men vanished. Anselem's mouth went dry as he saw Mathieson kneeling in front of Balam. Einar and Kage were both forcefully knelt next to him.

Anselem's heart shattered, and fury rampaged through his veins. Electricity crackled in his hands, and from the corner of his eye, he could see swirling darkness begin to rip from Blaidd's hands. Sacha gripped his sword tighter, his own magic only able to be wielded within the sea.

"Unless you would like to see your friends' blood

poured out onto the ground before them, I suggest you stop the theatrics." The queen waved her delicate hand back and forth between the two warriors, seemingly unthreatened by their displays of magic.

Her voice was filled with loathing and ire, but she masked the wrath with a delicate sweetness that was sickening to Anselem's ears.

He could see a faint, transparent glow hanging like a wall between the two groups. An impenetrable shield of magic, courtesy of Balam, prevented the warriors from attacking. A shield that had been used so many times to protect the Septant—to protect the brother whose throat he now held a blade against.

The crackle in his hands ceased, but he kept his power in reach, ready to strike as soon as the opportunity presented itself. Blaidd's shadows coiled back in towards his hands. Sacha did not move.

The spidery smile on the queen's fair face grew wider, and her onyx eyes glimmered.

"Wonderful," she crooned, "already such obedient pets."

She snapped her fingers, and a swarm of guards poured into the room—all entering from the halls Balam was instructed to clear out.

Anselem cursed to himself, and the look Blaidd burned into Balam was darker than any Anselem had ever seen the warrior bestow.

"Bind them," she ordered, her venomous voice coated with spoiled sweetness.

The guards brought in six pairs of iron shackles. Anselem's power flared, and Blaidd threw his darkness towards the men.

It was no use. Balam's shield blocked each attack with ease.

A yelp escaped from Einar's mouth, and a trickle of blood began to drip down his throat.

"Stop!" Anselem roared.

The queen sauntered over in front of the men, tucked in safely just behind the shield.

"You and your pretty friend," she stated, glancing over to Blaidd, "seem to enjoy a flair for the dramatic. If you would like to avoid any unwelcome endings to the night, then I suggest you put these on before I lose the last of my patience, Commander Eros."

Balam spat at the title.

The guards flung the chains across the invisible line where the shield stretched.

He stared down at the chains before him. When he looked back up, across the space at his three brothers with swords pressed against their throats, Anselem made his final mistake.

"Don't," Mathieson demanded. He swallowed.

"Don't!" he cried again as Anselem picked up the shackles. He forced his shaking hands to still and clasped the iron chains around his wrists.

He felt his magic lock. The Bond with Kapheria went quieter than it had been in years.

He did not need to turn to the warriors beside him. He knew they would follow his unspoken command, no matter how dark the path might be that it sent them down. The click of clasping chains echoed through the room.

The castle guards quickly bound the three warriors kneeling behind the invisible line in iron, and Balam dropped the shield.

The queen and rogue warrior stepped forward, but Anselem did not look at the monarch; his attention was locked on Balam.

"Why?" he seethed, fury overtaking the betrayal he felt ripping through his chest.

Balam snarled at the Commander, "You never should have been appointed to command. Look at the peril you lead them into."

Anselem swallowed a lump in his throat as the warrior he would have gladly given his life for spat at his feet. And as he stared at Balam, standing beside the Queen of the Obsidian Throne, he wondered how many scars he had excused simply because he loved the person holding the knife.

The guards, their eyes all darker than the onyx gems covering the queen's crown, pulled Mathieson, Einar, and Kage to their feet. Three more fell in behind the remaining warriors and shoved them forward, ushering them to a side door with an unlit, descending staircase inside.

Anselem walked across the room, following behind his brothers, and entered the door, crossing through the gates into his own, personal version of the Hells.

Six months passed.

They were beaten, mentally tormented, and abused. Everyone except Mathieson, who was pulled from his cell and dragged to an unknown place each day. He would be gone for hours before his brothers saw him again. He never spoke of what happened when he was away. No one asked. But he never once returned with scars or bloodied bruises. In the endless dark, Anselem was thankful for at least that much.

He thought Blaidd had it the worst. For the first few weeks, the queen forced each of the men to spend the evenings servicing her in her bedchambers. But as the weeks went by, she grew particularly fond of Blaidd, until the other warriors were no longer brought to her room, and the guards came at night to retrieve only Blaidd.

Each time he was brought back to his cage, the light in his silver eyes was a little dimmer.

Over the months, the six warriors found various ways to communicate with one another between their cells.

So, they planned.

And planned.

Until they masterfully developed a way to escape.

The day they broke out, that was when Anselem's heart shattered for the second time.

The Septant managed to collectively disarm and kill the entire group of guards standing post in the lower-level cell block.

Unable to find keys to unlock the shackles, the warriors stripped the guards of their weapons and made for the stone stairs.

Blaidd led Kage, Einar, and Sacha towards the exit, killing their way through the halls.

Anselem and Mathieson broke off, heading to the upper levels. The cages they had been kept in held no windows, and the sunlight pouring in through the open archways was near blinding.

Turn after turn, they charged down the long, vaulted halls. They slit throats and snapped bones along the way, letting the fury from the past six months fuel them as they transformed into weapons.

The Lords of Carnage incarnate.

Mathieson and Anselem made it to the end of a final hall in one of the middle levels of the castle and crashed into the room, nearly ripping the oak door from its hinges. They found Balam sitting at a desk in the corner of the bedchamber. The former warrior's eyes went wide as he saw the Lords of Carnage before him. His shield rippled out, but the two warriors, still bound by their iron shackles, slipped through the shield like a blade through water.

Balam had already palmed a dagger, but Anselem could outfight the man on his worst day, magic or not. Having Mathieson by his side simply made the task easier.

He quickly disarmed Balam and shoved him against the wall, his hand wrapped around his throat. Rage stormed through his veins.

Mathieson stood by his side as Anselem donned the voice of the Commander and growled through clenched teeth, "Svikari."

Traitor.

And with the spoken decree of the Commander of the Septant, Balam cried out in pain, and the brothers knew the inked wing on his back was being burned away from his flesh.

Anselem took the dagger he had stolen from a castle guard and thrust it into Balam's heart. Still holding the man against the wall, Anselem watched as his onyx eyes glazed over and his head fell to the side, no life left in his perfidious body.

Anselem's hands shook as he released Balam, and the slain warrior dropped to the ground in a crumpled pile, crimson blood still dripping from his chest.

Anselem and Mathieson wasted no time as they fought their way to the southern wall, where they had agreed to meet Blaidd and the others.

The men flung themselves from the castle doors and into the manicured gardens, their feet darting for the castle wall. They were nearly across the open field, lined with flowers and bushes, when they heard the horn ring out.

They were twenty yards away from the stones when the doors crashed open, and hundreds of guards poured from the castle.

Ten more yards.

Five.

The duo hurled themselves onto the wall, clawing at the indentations and grooves within the stones to propel themselves upward.

Anselem's nails cracked as they dug into the rocks, and blood trickled down his hand, but neither of the warriors stopped their climb.

His heart pounded against his chest, and he dragged in rapid breaths. The men paused for a moment, catching their breath, their muscles fatigued from months of disuse. The boots beside him scraped against the wall, and Mathieson moved closer to Anselem.

"Promise me," he huffed out.

"Promise you what?" Anselem replied, his voice ragged.

"That you will see it through. You are the only one who can make sure she does it."

"Make sure who does it? What do you mean—"

"Anselem, promise me right now. Swear it." Mathieson's voice took on a tone of urgency as boots began to scrape against the rocks beneath them. There was such gravity in his words—in the words of his brother who had never once asked him for anything. His brother, who somehow always knew, in his own cryptic way, how things would unfold. Anselem reached out his hand, grasping Mathieson's shoulder, and looked into his sapphire eyes. "I give you my Word."

And with those final words, Anselem felt his brother push himself from the wall, and watched as he tumbled to the ground, tearing down the guards approaching from below.

A piercing cry escaped Anselem's lips, and he stared at Mathieson's crumpled form below. But his heart leapt in his chest as the warrior crawled to his feet.

Still hanging halfway up the wall, Anselem saw the queen exit the castle doors, a spider's smile set upon her face. Mathieson limped his way towards her, pain wrecking his face with every step. And as he approached the queen, he watched her wrath-filled eyes glimmer as she pulled an obsidian blade from her waist. The world went dark around the monarch, like all the light around her had been snuffed out, and Anselem watched as a delicate hand emerged from the darkness and plunged the knife into Mathieson's chest.

Anselem couldn't breathe as he watched his brother collapse to the ground. His ears rang and his mind went blank.

A muffled scraping of boots against stone sounded below him, but all he could hear through the deafening silence was the crash of Math's body against the dirt.

A screech bellowed from overhead, and it pulled Anselem from the Darkness seeping into his mind.

He felt the ink burning into the skin beneath his jacket, and it forced his body to move. Forced him to leave his fallen brother behind and honor his promise.

Anselem scaled the rest of the wall, tears streaming down his face. When he pulled himself onto the ledge, a wave of midnight feathers landed next to him. Numbly, he climbed onto the back of Kapheria, and she launched into the skies. And as Anselem exited the obsidian gates of the Hells, he left behind a portion of his shattered heart that he knew would never heal.

Anselem went quiet once he finished telling Asha the story. His chest felt tight, and he refused to meet her burning eyes.

He felt her hand move until it was placed in front of him, palm facing up. He took it in his and raised his eyes to hers.

His chains were broken, but many nights, startled awake from nightmarish dreams, Anselem wondered if he was truly free.

She smiled softly at him, and her voice was kind as she replied, "You carry a burden that never belonged to you. Let it go."

It sounded so simple, but it was so much easier said than done.

He nodded. "I will try."

She squeezed his hand and loosened her grip, but he wrapped his fingers more tightly around hers, unwilling to let go.

Because, for the first time, as he stared down at his scarred hands intertwined with hers, life made sense.

CHAPTER TWENTY-SIX

The all-consuming Darkness ripped through her veins.

Air.

I need air. She screamed inside her head.

Asha threw open her bedroom door and raced down the hallway, running towards the central courtyard. The cold, night breeze ripped tears from her eyes as she rushed down the stairs and into the opening. Streaking tears burned her cheeks as she continued to gasp for air that was not there. She pushed her back against the cold, stone wall that surrounded the center lawn, and her tears continued to flow.

What in the Seven Hells...

Asha's legs gave out, and her back slid down the hard, smooth marble. As she sat on the ground, she tugged her knees to her chest and began to count, her breath uneven and catching.

One, two...

It felt like a colossal rock was perched on her chest.

Asha tried to sip in tiny breaths.

Three, four...

With each passing second, the Darkness continued to rage, to grow. It slithered its way into every corner of her mind. It was unbearable. She needed to make it stop. It *burned*.

Five, six...

Anything to make it stop.

The tears continued to roll down her cheeks, and the Darkness started to swallow the last bit of light left inside her. Asha let her head hang between her legs, and she closed her eyes, accepting its demise.

Seven...

Strong hands were lifting her up, a deep voice ringing in her ears.

"Seven!" it rang again.

Asha's eyes broke open, meeting the two deep emerald ones staring back. Confusion spread across her face, and the place between her brows bunched together.

"Asha, fight back. Control it."

His voice sounded far, like he was a million miles away.

"You have to control it, and then you're going to have to build up your mental walls."

What the Hells was he talking about? Build what?

As the Darkness made its last run towards the final glimmer of light inside her heart, Asha realized what was happening.

"Oh *shit*," she replied, no other words appearing on her lips.

So much for having a couple of weeks.

Asha tried to push back at the Darkness, but it did not ease. It was too strong, too powerful. Her efforts against it were futile. As useless as trying to push over the stone wall behind her, currently keeping her from collapsing.

She could feel Anselem's hands under her arms, balancing her against the wall.

Asha looked up at his face. His jaw was clenched, and his deep green eyes, narrow and focused, scoured every inch of her face.

"Focus on controlling it, ground yourself," he stated.

"How?" she breathed, barely able to keep her thoughts straight as the Darkness overwhelmed every sense.

"Close your eyes," he answered, "focus on feeling your feet on the ground."

She obeyed, digging her boots into the stone beneath her.

"Feel yourself connected with the earth. It will help you balance and stabilize your power." A light breeze brushed across her cheek. "Now, search through your mind's eye, look for the light, feel for it."

Swirls of ebony sparks flashed in mixed directions through Asha's mind, nearly indistinguishable from the shadows of the Darkness. The deep, black tendrils raged after the shimmering onyx, swallowing the painted glimmers. She could hardly tell the difference between the two shades of black.

But the *feel* of the two was different.

The Darkness seemed as if it was built of Death and ruin, lurking silently in the gloom, ready to devour.

While the obsidian shimmers ripping through her veins felt… *alive*, as if a sparking ember was still fighting to stay lit amongst the ashes. The onyx glimmers were the darkness of a warrior—a dreamer—and they appeared to have emerged from the brokenness harbored in her heart from years of loss and tragedy.

But they were also made of a darkness that was ready to

burn Kingdoms.

A darkness ready to wage war.

She nodded.

"Good," he replied simply, "now you need to visualize a shield, build a wall up around the light. Close out the Darkness. You can make it from anything you want. You just need to focus on containing the light inside it."

She slowly began to build up walls around the glimmering black. Her face strained against closed eyes as she focused.

Anselem kept talking. "The human mind is absolute chaos. Trying to filter what is automatic, what is instinctual, what is secondary, and what is primary thoughts is nearly impossible without a lot of work. Right now, just focus on getting your wall built around the light."

Asha realized Anselem had no clue how much practice she'd had at building walls and rooms inside her mind. The mansion she avoided visiting flashed before her eyes. She pushed it aside and focused on constructing a new foundation. A few moments passed as she began building the new walls, attempting to secure the light inside the frame.

"The Darkness..." Panic ripped through her voice.

"Tell me what you see," he responded, only calm, reassuring tones leaving his lips. Forever the essence of composure.

"The Darkness... it's everywhere..." Tears began to slide out of her closed eyelids.

"Focus, Asha, where is the light in the Darkness?"

But as she searched, Asha realized there was no light to be found. There was only blackness hidden within the walls. She concentrated more closely, keeping her mind open, and as she searched, a shimmering onyx flash jetted across her eyes. The dark shadows ripped at its heels.

"I found an onyx light," she told him.

His hands tightened under her arms. A moment passed before he responded.

"Okay, good," he uttered, his voice lower than it was before. "Ground yourself again, and now I want you to focus on the onyx light. Allow yourself to feel it, embrace it. As it grows, start to push out the shadows and replace the space with the light."

Asha grounded herself again and internally pushed back at the Darkness, willing it to be exchanged with the enticing ebony light roaming deep within her mind. In the sea of blackness, she was not entirely sure which darkness she was forcing out, and which she was begging to stay. She kept pulling at the sparkling ebony, willing it to overcome the Dark.

Anselem's body stiffened next to her, and Asha's eyes flared open in response. She searched his face, her gaze landing on his slightly parted mouth. She kept her eyes focused on his lips, imagining the way they would feel against hers. The distraction of her thoughts forced the Darkness to recede, just an inch, glimmering light continuing to take over in its place.

"Good," he rasped, "just like that." His voice sounded like velvet.

More light encompassed the shadows.

"Good, Asha," he whispered.

She thought of his hands underneath her arms, how close his body was to her own. She felt the warmth of his breath against her cheek.

Shimmering ebony enveloped the entirety of the Darkness inside her, and her power began to emanate from her; her palms began to illuminate.

"*Shit*," he swore, his voice straining on the words.

Anselem started to pull away from Asha, but her fingers curled around his muscular forearms, holding him close. She didn't trust her legs to stand. She didn't want to do this alone. He didn't fight against her grasp.

"Seven..." he trailed off. His breathing grew heavy, and Asha felt his pulse quicken under her hands. She needed him to stay; she didn't want to fight the Darkness on her own.

"Don't leave me. Please." She knew her voice wavered; knew the terror she was feeling coated the words.

He held her tighter. "I'm not going anywhere."

The light continued to radiate out of her.

"I've never seen a first-time manifest this strongly..." he muttered, his eyes raking up and down Asha's body.

She tilted her head up to him, their faces only inches from one another.

"Anselem," she breathily said, and his eyes buried deep into her. It *burned*. She could feel every scorching ripple of the magic as it whipped its way through her veins.

The onyx light continued to rage through Asha's mind, menacingly laughing at the struggle she was losing within herself to control it. She was so scared. Aside from the Tartarus, she couldn't remember the last time she had been so scared.

Burning light poured from her body, tumbling towards Anselem, reaching.

He closed his eyes and pressed his forehead against hers, wincing, like he was taking every blow of her magic and willing himself to hold still. To not break. To not leave.

"Anselem," she said. Her voice sounded far; she barely recognized it as her own.

He continued to keep his eyes closed, like he couldn't face looking at her. "Control it, Ash."

He held her still while several more moments passed.

The shimmering obsidian slowly started to dissipate as Asha fought to harness any semblance of control over it.

He loosened his grip on her elbows, fingers barely pressing against her arms. As the last of her power settled inside, Asha felt a wave of exhaustion swarm over her.

Anselem released her arms and took a step back, creating what felt like an enormous rift in the space between them. He finally opened his narrowed eyes and looked at Asha, pain wracked across his face. He quickly tried to hide the grimace. Asha glimpsed the burns on his arms before he could tuck them away.

She reached out a hand, but he pulled away. Her arm dropped back to her side.

"I'm fine."

Asha opened her mouth to speak, but words didn't come out. A single tear slid down her face.

"Anselem," she whispered, her voice breaking.

"Don't. Not right now, Asha," was all he said, his voice so low it was barely audible. There was no anger behind his words, only pain.

He turned and began to walk away, knowing her initial rush of power was over and she was safe from whatever danger the Darkness had threatened to unleash.

Anselem paused just before he reached the stairs and looked back. He opened his mouth as if to speak, but shut it again without a word, as if he thought better than to express what was on his mind. He turned and headed up the stairs.

As she watched him go, Asha felt the Darkness start to creep back in. She forced herself to ground and mentally shove it back, keenly aware of the origin and roots from which the Darkness grew—fear and despair.

CHAPTER TWENTY-SEVEN

A week passed, and Asha did not see Anselem once. Not even when Valorous completed their eleventh benchmark, which consisted of an entire day of cleaning the Base stables. Asha didn't complain; she was happy to have a week off from fighting for her life, even if the belittling benchmark was meant to 'build character and develop a respect towards the helpers who keep order in the Base.' Asha simply thought Leadership was likely projecting their own guilt onto the cadets for how poorly they treated the staff who kept the Base running.

Her bruises and cuts were mostly healed, courtesy of Uriel and the Rapha, but her mind still raced, and she woke herself with harrowing screams each night, her throat raw and burning.

Valorous went through their typical drills each day, fitness in the morning, sparring in the afternoon, and a mix of other training activities in between. But not once did Anselem show up. Asha figured he was either on an assignment or actively avoiding her.

Staring off at the horizon, Asha heard the near-silent steps approaching as the ghostly feet climbed the last few stairs to the clock tower's roof, where she had escaped. She palmed a dagger as the door swung open. Her shoulders untensed as Anselem ducked through the opening. She said nothing and turned her gaze back to the distant horizon. She could almost hear the gears in his head spinning as he decided what to do.

"Sorry, I didn't realize anyone else would be here." She did not respond. A moment passed. "I'll leave you to it then." She heard his feet scuff against the rooftop.

"You can stay," she said, not moving her eyes from the water, and gestured to the spot beside her.

She could almost hear the hesitation of his thoughts before his feet moved and he settled down beside her.

"I didn't think anyone else ever came up here," he said. She broke her gaze from the setting sky and turned to look at him.

"You come up here, why wouldn't anyone else?"

He shrugged but said nothing more.

She was quiet for a long time. "I figured you were still avoiding me."

His brow furrowed. "I wasn't avoiding you, Seven." She smiled to herself at the name. He made it sound almost endearing at this point, as if he liked the idea of having a name only he could call her.

"Why do you still call me that?" she asked, genuine curiosity filling her voice. She often wondered if she would ever live up to her last name, ever earn the distinction.

He looked off at the horizon, avoiding her burning eyes. He let out a long sigh and ran his hand through his hair.

"Honestly?"

She nodded.

"It never had anything to do with you not being able to live up to your name. The moment you won the Minos Maze, I knew you would always work hard enough to honor it. The truth is," he took in a steadying breath and turned his eyes towards hers, "it hurt too much."

Asha blinked, and her chest tightened.

"It hurt too much to think about having to say his name every single day. And I know it doesn't just belong to him; it is every bit as much yours, but for me, that was how I knew him. And the thought of having to say it every day and not look up and see him… a small part inside of me broke at the idea. So, I didn't. I know it's unfair, but I just couldn't." He shook his head at himself.

A laugh escaped her lips, and his brow furrowed.

"I'm sorry," she said, "I don't mean to be so insensitive. I just thought you named me that because you thought I was worthless. Not even worthy of a name, only a number. I was upset about it for days—weeks."

She laughed again, more softly, relief filling her mind. "Come to find out you're just a sentimental bonehead," she teased, attempting to lighten the seriousness of the conversation.

The distressed look on his face vanished, and he let out a soft chuckle at her words. The sound was like music to her ears. "I guess I am." A huge grin was plastered across his face.

"So why Seven?"

He pulled his eyes from hers, as if he couldn't bear to look into her gaze, as he continued. "You were my seventh reason," he confessed.

"Your what?"

He let out a long breath.

"You were my seventh reason. It's… something they teach us when we join the Septant. You should always have seven reasons."

"Seven reasons for what?" she whispered.

He turned his burning emerald eyes to her.

"To live," he replied.

Her face was blank, and she went still. "You're my seventh reason, Asha."

"Why?" she asked so softly that she nearly mouthed the word.

He turned his gaze back to the horizon, and his shoulders softened the slightest bit.

"Because when Math died, I didn't have seven reasons anymore. I only had six. And six is not enough to keep living."

Her stomach dropped, and she felt the urge to reach out and touch him, to feel him and make sure he was still here, he was safe. She did not move as he continued to speak.

"And without that seventh reason, I went to a very dark place. A place I did not want to come back from. But when I saw you, it just… clicked. And I knew you were my seventh reason. I knew I had to stay, at least a little longer, and fight to make sure you made it through. That you survived. For Math."

He stopped speaking, but Asha could tell he had more words he wanted to say. More words to add to the confession he laid bare before her.

She stayed quiet for a long while, pushing back the tears threatening to pool in her eyes.

When it became clear he was not going to add anything more to his admission, a soft smile curled on her mouth and she asked, "So you weren't avoiding me?"

He shook his head. "I may be a bonehead, Seven, but I'm not a coward."

"I wanted to give you space," he continued, "after your powers manifested. It's... a lot. I know that. And I was also battling with myself about it, so I figured I needed to sort through my own mental shit before I dragged you into any of my mess."

"Why were you upset with yourself about it?" Asha's face was twisted with confusion.

"Because I blame myself. I should have tightened your bands. If I had, you never would have experienced that."

"I would have experienced it eventually."

He only nodded.

"Why didn't you?" she asked.

He looked away again, as if contemplating how many secrets he was willing to divulge in one night.

"I thought it would help. I thought they would have broken earlier, and it would give me time to help teach you how to wield them. I believed that if you had access to your magic, it would help protect you. But then everything happened with Moros, and then the Tartarus, and I realized you were going to be Marked when your powers manifested, and I panicked. When your bands broke last week, I literally lost it. I had no clue how to protect you from... *that*."

She did not mention that she had more misty Markings than the ones she had earned from Moros and the Nameless Place. She took notice of how many times he had mentioned protecting her, but she did not say anything as he continued to speak.

"So, I just kept a close watch and made sure I would be there when it finally happened."

"How did you know what was going to happen?" she asked quietly.

He did not say anything, but instead pulled up his sleeve and pointed to a dark bolt of lightning stretching down his arm. "I got this one when I was ten."

Asha sucked in a breath. *Ten.*

He pushed his sleeve back down as he continued, "So I knew what happens to those of us who are Marked before our powers are released."

"Was it the same for you?"

A small, soft smile appeared on his lips, as if he were recalling the memory. She assumed his experience must have been incredibly different from hers if it elicited anything other than a grimace.

"I think it was probably pretty similar," he said. She tilted her head.

"I think everyone has slightly different experiences, but overall, it's the same. Mine manifested a few weeks after graduation, the first time I was back on Base. It started with the burning in my veins as the power was finally unleashed, then I could feel it—the light of my magic—as it tore through me." He paused for a moment, reflecting. "I think the biggest difference is that the ones who are not Marked before the manifestation don't have to deal with the Darkness barreling after the light of their magic."

He sighed. "It feeds on it—the Darkness. As if the shadows we hold inside our souls have been anticipating the moment of release, patiently waiting to swallow the gifts of life and light that Ianoda has granted us."

Asha let his words settle in the silence before she asked, "What does it look like for you?"

Anselem stared off into the waves beyond. "It's like flashes of crackling silver. When it first happened, I could see the life-filled electricity as it snapped across my mind and illuminated the Dark."

He was quiet for a moment before he continued.

"But it was also like an ocean of shadows, and I was in the middle of the Dark sea, swimming. I kept trying to fight to get to shore, but every crashing wave brought me out further and further, away from the silver lights. And then I was pulled under and started drowning in the Darkness."

Asha's body tensed, but she stayed silent.

"I had no clue how to find my way back." Anselem's face grew grim from the memory.

"I wound up here," he gestured to the clock tower roof. "The Darkness... I let it win. Let it consume me."

Asha held her breath.

"It led me here, and I knew what it wanted me to do. Knew what *I* wanted to do, as I floated beneath the surface of the inky ocean."

It took everything in her not to reach out and touch him, comfort him. He continued to stare off into the sinking sun.

"And I would have," he said plainly. Then a large grin replaced the grim expression sitting on his face. "But Mathieson showed up."

Asha's jaw dropped, and her heart skipped.

"What," she breathed out.

Anselem turned his face towards hers once again. "He found me, saved me. And helped walk me through it."

Tears formed in Asha's eyes.

"That's why I come up here every now and then. Whenever I think about him, whenever I miss him. It helps remind me of everything he did for me, helps me feel close."

Tears spilled over the edge and streamed down her face.

His voice dropped to a whisper, "I would have traded places with Math if I could have. If he had told me."

As she thought about her brother, the tears continued to fall down her cheeks and dripped onto the hands placed in her lap. Gods, she missed him.

And from the silver lining Anselem's eyes, Asha knew he did too. She believed every word that left his mouth.

They sat in uninterrupted quietness for a long time.

"Thank you," she said, breaking the silence between them.

"For what?" he replied.

"For not moving past it like everything is the same as it was before. Like it can go back to the way it was before."

He nodded, knowing no words were needed.

"You know it's okay to still want things for yourself, right?" She moved her gaze back over to him, confused by the sudden change in direction.

"It's okay to want something for yourself. You walk around like you hate the idea of being a Soturi, like you're only doing it for Math, but I can tell deep down you really want it for yourself."

She let out a long breath. "Is it that obvious?"

He released a small chuckle. "No, not to anyone else."

Asha wasn't sure how she felt about Anselem reading her so well.

"I'm just saying, you should know it's okay to still want things. Even if he isn't here to share them with anymore."

She knew he was right. She knew Math would want her to continue living. Not just surviving—living. But knowing it and doing it were two different things.

"How did you get it?" she asked, trying to change the subject. He softly smiled, understanding she was done discussing the idea, at least for tonight.

"Get what?"

"Your first Marking."

She studied his face as he contemplated how to word his response.

"I didn't grow up in the best of situations. My father... had a temper. He would beat me and my mom. As I got older, it only got worse. One day, my mom had pissed him off for gods know what reason, and he lost it. He slammed her into the wall, and she cracked her head on the floor when she fell. He began beating her when she was on the ground... There was so much blood. I thought she was dead, or close to it. I grabbed the knife off the kitchen table, walked over, and shoved it in his back."

This time, without truly knowing what she was doing, Asha reached over and grabbed his hand as he spoke. When he felt her fingers, he flinched. Anselem was not used to being touched with such kindness, not since his mother was alive. He was no stranger to women; over the years, he had felt many different hands on every part of his body, but Asha's touch was different. It was gentle and caring—it made him feel safe, like he belonged.

She quickly pulled her hand away, but he grabbed it softly and held it in his. It was warm, intimate, but not in a sensual way, in a way that felt like two broken souls had been wandering in the Darkness for so long, and they finally found someone else who understood the night.

"I don't regret it," he concluded, "maybe that makes me a piece of shit, I'm not sure. I don't really care if it does. I'd do it again."

Asha squeezed his hand. "But your mom was okay?"

A flicker of pain flashed across his face. "No. She... she didn't make it. It took the healers too long to get to her. She had lost too much blood; even phoenix tears couldn't save her."

Asha wondered if that was why he had sat beside her bed in the East Wing after she competed in the Maze, if the circumstances had aligned too closely with his memories.

"I am so sorry," Asha said. And she was. No child should ever have to experience that sort of pain.

He offered her a small smile in return.

"What was she like?"

Another smile. And then he told her. About his mother's kindness, her limitless love. Her quiet disposition and heart of gold. Asha listened to every word. His mind was intoxicating. He was sincere and so strong and so broken; she wanted to sit with that and know more of that, not in a way that demanded, but in a way that understood.

He went quiet for a long moment after he concluded, staring off into the distance as he reflected on the memories of a lifetime ago.

Anselem turned to Asha, a quiet curiosity filling his eyes. "Tell me about you."

"What would you like to know?"

He studied her face with such intensity, she almost turned away.

"Tell me everything," he said.

Asha broke his gaze, her turn to now stare off into the twilight sky, and she thought through everything she had lived through. Everything she had endured. Everything she was.

"Long ago," she said, a soft smile forming on her lips at the familiar words she had heard so often in her childhood. The same words her mother would whisper to her late at night while she was curled up in bed, quietly listening to the secret tales of old. "In a world forged from flames of Darkness, there was a warrior whose heart of Light fought to stay lit inside the shadowed sea of ash and embers."

And Asha told him her story. She told him about her past, about her pain and her loss. She told him about her walk through the Abyss and how she'd fought her way to the other side. She told him about the days after she lost her brother, and about the faintest ember that battled to stay sparked inside her burning heart of fire.

Anselem sat beside her, long after the sun had dropped from the sky, and listened to her story, listened to all she had lost and all she had overcome. And once she was finished, he took her hand and held it—a friend who understood how hard the walk through the Darkness had been, how much she had to fight to crawl back into the Light.

They sat like that for a long while, hand-in-hand underneath the silence of the stars, the sea in the distance the only sound between them.

And as they sat, their hands intertwined, they drowned under the waves of the words they left unspoken.

CHAPTER TWENTY-EIGHT

"You have to stay focused, Seven."

"I am," Asha seethed back, her eyes focused on the open palms before her.

Every morning since her powers had manifested, Anselem had woken early, before the other warriors on Base were up, and met Asha at the sparring rings. He chose the location in case any instructors happened to stumble upon them, knowing it would be easy to pass off their training as additional sparring lessons.

He took a step towards her and placed his hands in front of her, laying them on top of her own. A small, controlled bolt of lightning crackled in his hands.

"Show off," she sneered, cutting her eyes up at him.

"Watch," he ordered.

Her eyes narrowed, but she focused her gaze back onto his hands. The electricity in his palms grew, flashing brighter.

"Can you feel it?"

She nodded, pressing her hands harder to his own. He released another controlled bolt, this time holding the electric light in his hands. The power within his palms radiated between his fingers.

"I can feel it," she breathed.

"That is what you must focus on. The feeling. The difference between the two. You must understand the power coursing through you. Learn it. Understand it. Become one with it. And then you will have to learn how to harness it."

Anselem further released the leash on his power, the bolts within his hands rising towards the clouds above.

Power was like the ocean. It was all interconnected and derived from the same waters, but there were separated levels.

His lesser magic, the power he was able to quickly access, rested along the shore, restricted in the amount it could provide.

But his specific power—his Kratos, as warriors and Leadership often referred to them—had to be found. Discovered. It was the magic that dwelled deep within the center of the sea, its limit dependent upon how far the wielder dared to dive.

Anselem had spent the last several days teaching Asha the difference between the two. She quickly learned how to control her lesser magic, able to light luminos and fix an aerial orb around her head.

But she had yet to tap into the depths of her true power. Had yet to discover her Kratos. As if a subconscious part of her was afraid to plunge into the chasm for fear of what it would find.

Anselem focused on the magic pulsing through his veins, diving deeper into the well of power. He held the increasing power for a short moment, allowing it to radiate from his body, giving Asha the opportunity to feel the pulse of energy harbored within his hands. Then he released it.

An angry, bursting bolt of lightning struck the sky. A crackle sounded in the distance.

"I felt it," she whispered, glancing up at him, "I felt the change as you dove deeper into your well of power. The shift when you pulled it back up to the surface with you."

He removed his hands from atop hers, placing them back at his sides.

"Good. Now you need to find yours."

"You make it seem so easy."

Anselem chuckled. "Trust me, there were plenty of days when I went to sleep to the smell of scorched bedsheets."

A smile twitched on Asha's mouth. "The great Anselem Eros actually struggled with something?"

He let out a soft laugh. "Don't tell anyone, my sterling reputation would be ruined."

He winked at her and nodded at the hands she had rested back at her side. "Again."

Asha let out a sigh and raised her bent arms back in front of her.

"Close your eyes," Anselem instructed. Asha did as she was told, her eyes softly closing.

"Now feel it. Don't look for it. *Feel* it."

Asha was unsure how much time had passed, likely an hour or two, as the dawning sunlight attempted to creep through her closed lids. Anselem remained patiently silent by her side as she focused on the magic running through her veins.

He told her that power was like the ocean, the same as every magic wielder had told her before.

But as she stood atop the hillside, surrounded by sparring rings and the Commander of the Septant, Asha did not wade through an ocean of power within her mind. She did not find a sea of magic waiting within her veins, nor deep waters to sift through.

No, when Asha sifted through the power living in her body, the magic that had resided within her for her entire life, all she was met with was endless dark.

No ocean. No sea. No waters.

Boundless, undulating darkness.

She did not say anything to Anselem. She figured her soul might have simply been too broken to see things the way the rest of the world did. So, instead, for hours she waded through the uninterrupted darkness, searching for her Kratos she prayed she would find.

And just as she was about to give up, to quit searching and wait for another day, that was when she felt it.

Like a whisper in the night, a devouring abyss summoned her. She followed its cry, wading through the lightless space inside her, as if the very darkness had beckoned her to its home, and her shadowed soul had no choice but to answer the call.

Asha opened her eyes to a wide grin set upon Anselem's face. She looked down at her outstretched hands, and a small sparking of flames rested within each palm.

Anselem's voice, bursting with pride and delight, filled the morning air. "Fire wielder."

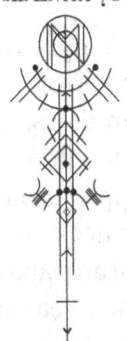

CHAPTER TWENTY-NINE

"How do I look?" Asha asked, spinning in a small circle.

"If I didn't have to compete with Eros pining after you, I'd take you home with me." Kaira's voice carried through Asha's small room.

Asha lightly slapped her on the arm, rolling her eyes. "There is most certainly no *pining* happening." She glanced over at Kaira and winked. "But I'm glad to know I can turn heads, even yours." The women both let out laughs.

Asha's week had been eventful.

Along with discovering her Kratos, Valorous won their final Division Wargame, placing them in the lead over the three other Divisions in points. The Leaders declared Valorous the victors and gifted each of the cadets a small, silver ring, engraved with various runes, as their prize.

After the conclusion of Wargames, Asha returned to the East Wing for her final healing, and in the morning, before Kaira came to her room, Asha had her weekly flight with

Anselem.

As the last of the sun's light faded in the window, Asha glanced once more in her mirror.

Her snow-white, satin dress, adorned with shimmering pearls, stretched down to the floor. Sheer tulle, studded with various-sized pearls, wrapped around the bodice. The fabric was tied high around her neck, with long sleeves specially constructed to cover her iron bands—*fake* bands. The dress was fashioned with cut outs, leaving her tattooed shoulders and the skin between her breasts exposed. The form-fitting gown hugged her curves, leaving little to the imagination. Asha's mask, ornately embellished with matching cream-colored pearls, twinkled in the moonlight. The covering shaded her ocean-blue eyes, painted with black outlines and shimmering blue powder.

Her silver blonde hair, sleek against her head, was arranged into two intricate braids that joined to form a crown around her head before falling down her exposed back in a single, woven waterfall, plunging to the waist.

She stared at the bare skin on her back, lingering on the long lines of silver. Her hair covered most of it, but she still saw the thick scars peeking through.

"I'm sorry... I had it made before everything happened. If you want, I can look for something to cover them..." Kaira rambled.

Asha shook her head, still staring into the reflection at her scarred skin.

"Don't. I'm not ashamed of what I have survived."

And she wasn't. She was different now, changed. But her scars were a reminder of the battle she had fought and won. They were proof of her survival and, through it all, even in the depths of the endless dark, she had chosen life. She had chosen to fight. And even though the fire that blazed inside of her burned a little dimmer than before, Asha was proud to have kept the faintest spark inside herself lit. So, she would wear her scars as if they, too, were another stunning dress, made straight from Hellsfire.

She broke her gaze from the mirror and looked once more at her friend, whose face held a smile that did not meet her eyes.

"What?" Asha said.

Kaira looked into her sapphire seas. "Just be careful, Ash."

Asha reached out and squeezed her hand, nodding. She took a deep breath, that mischievous smile spreading across her face. "Time to break out of the alabaster cage."

As Asha approached the Aviary, a long dark cloak thrown around her, hiding her dress beneath, she sent a warning down the Bond to Uriel, advising him to be ready. Ever since her powers had manifested, the Bond between her and her firebird was stronger than it had ever been before.

She turned the last corner of the colonnade and entered the open space. Uriel was already standing in the field, ready to leave. She knew every moment counted if she was going to escape without notice. Or, more importantly, without a record.

She had learned that leaving any sort of trail was how one could get caught—and subsequently tortured for nine days.

A shiver slid down her spine, but she pushed back the memories.

She nodded at the guards as she walked over to the shed next to Uriel, grabbing a saddle. She ran through the story she had made up in her mind once more, knowing the guards would ask why she was there so late.

"Heading out with Lieutenant Eros?"

She nodded, offering a soft smile. She was just about to open her mouth to explain that the lieutenant would be here shortly and instructed her to begin without him when the guard chimed in, "I'm surprised he didn't wait for you."

Asha kept her face neutral as her mind raced. *Anselem isn't here?*

"He left not long ago. I'm sure if you're quick, you can catch up." He winked.

Asha smiled again. "Thank you." She threw the saddle onto Uriel, fastened the straps, and climbed into the pommel. She pulled the hood over her head and patted him once on the neck.

The firebird launched into the night sky.

Uriel landed a short distance from the Manor, in a small opening buried within the surrounding trees. Asha straightened the two stray pieces of hair that had come unfastened on the flight over from Sveaborg and secured her mask in place.

"I'll send a call if I need you. I shouldn't be long." Uriel huffed a breath in her outstretched hand and nuzzled into her side.

She chuckled. "Don't mess up my dress, you fireball." Uriel looked down at her again, and she scratched his head.

"I'll be fine." He let out another huff that smelled like smoldering embers. She turned towards the nearby dirt path, picking up her dress to ensure it did not drag on the ground beneath her, and began walking. She steadily made her way down the road connecting the small, nearby village of Reyka to the tucked-away premises of the Manor.

She did not need to travel for very long before she reached the outer gate of the Manor grounds. It was tall and made of iron, with the property name carved in jagged letters at the top: *Boeotian Manor*. Asha passed through the opening, and as she stepped onto the estate's property, she felt a shift inside her veins. A damper on her power. Deep inside her mind, she still felt the tether of the Bond, but it was faint, like a thinned strand that would snap if tugged too hard. But even with confirmation of the Bond, Asha knew the rest of her magic was locked, unable to be accessed. She smelled it in the air, tasted it in her mouth—a metallic, bitter reek of ferrous and salt, emanating from the cloud of iron-filled air surrounding the grounds. She choked on the foggy air as she sauntered down the cobblestone path leading to the main doors.

The Manor looked every bit as cursed as Math had described in his journal. With towering peaks made of dark, onyx stone, and sinister beasts sculpted inside the stonework, all illuminated by blood red luminos, the Manor gave every indication that Asha should turn back and run—fast. Even the murky air surrounding her felt sinister, as if haunting creatures were lurking within the encircling gardens. The castle looked like it was filled with skeletons and haunted spirits, or perhaps crafted by their very bones. A shiver ran down Asha's back as she wondered what horrors the Manor's walls had witnessed.

She made it to the base of the stairs and climbed her way to the top, appearing unfazed as her heart pounded against her chest with each step. She slowed her jagged breaths as she made it to the landing.

A pale man with an eerie smile greeted her. "Welcome

to Boeotian Manor." His eyes were dark and held no life behind them. He gave her a chilling grin she believed was somehow meant to be inviting. "The Lord of the Manor welcomes you to his Evening of Mystery."

Asha unclasped her cloak and handed it to the doorman's outstretched hand, along with a single golden harp string—the payment for entrance.

It had taken Kaira over a month to find a merchant in possession of gold-plated music parts. She didn't ask what type of snooping Kaira had done in order to find the merchant, but Asha was glad her friend knew where to look to find undiscoverable objects.

Convincing the merchant to trade with her was another obstacle entirely.

Asha avoided asking how much it cost and instead handed a large bag of coins to her friend when she went to procure the stringed piece. When Kaira returned with her bag of gold, Asha winced at how much lighter the sack weighed than when it had left.

The doorman nodded once and reached behind him, grasping the large iron knob on the door and swinging it open by its squealing hinges.

"Enjoy your night, miss."

Asha said nothing as she crossed the threshold.

Mathieson's journal had not given her much detail about the inside of the Manor, but as soon as she stepped into the grandiose hall, filled with hundreds of masked partygoers, Asha saw that the wicked, gothic style of the exteriors also permeated inside the castle walls. Onyx tiles spread out over the ballroom floor, and sitting high above, fixed against every wall, was a vast number of blood-red luminos, lighting the party below in a macabre and murderous hue.

Asha spent months planning this meeting. Endless nights pouring through the scribbled notes inside Math's journals with Kaira, searching every page for more insight and more details. In one of the many entries, he wrote before leaving for Aaru, Math mentioned a crucial need to come to Boeotian Manor, meet the Manor's Lord, and ask him how to find the one who was called the Adversary.

Asha was not entirely sure what Math's entry meant, or why he'd needed the information so direly, but as she scrounged through the rest of his journals and hunted down more information from the Base library, she was only able to discover a minuscule amount of information floating around about the Lord of Boeotian Manor, Raziel—better known in dark circles as the Secret-Seeker. In all her searches, she had found nothing on anyone deemed the Adversary.

And now, since she had managed to sneak her way out of Sveaborg and swindle her way into a party she had *not* been invited to, all she had to do was find the host, play his game, and ask him where she could find the *Arch of the Abyss*.

Asha circled the room, feigning interest in the tapestries and paintings hung on the walls. Each piece of art, all thematically dark and twisted, must have cost a small fortune. She neared the grand staircase fixed in the center of the back wall. A pair of deep crimson doors, tucked in the corner behind a wall of slightly parted curtains, caught her eye.

She saw a petite woman, donning a long red gown, and a short, mousy-looking man enter through the blood-red doors. From the descriptions she had read in Math's journals, Asha knew the doors led into the *Faustia Room*—the Lord of the Manor's private meeting room. A room that no guests were permitted to enter unless personally invited by Raziel himself. Asha continued to amble around the ballroom, conversing with other guests and trying her best to blend in as she searched for the Manor's Lord.

As the evening stretched on, Asha began to lose hope of finding the owner of the estate. She waded her way across the ballroom and back to the bottom of the grand staircase, the one she assumed led upstairs to a great number of spacious bedrooms and large halls. She dragged her gaze over the crowd, always keeping an eye on the deep red double doors tucked away in the corner, as if she expected the host to burst through them at any moment.

As she stood beside the stairs, a man, donning a glittering black jacket with chic, crimson embroidery, strode to her side. His eyes, the only portion of his face covered, were hidden behind an ebony mask laced with tiny, blood-red gems that wrapped all the way to the edges. The metal covering was affixed with thick, onyx details that built themselves up into three separate shards, pointed at the head. The three peaks centered around a singular, omniscient eye, glaring out from the middle of the mask. The covering looked as if it were designed by Anubis himself.

He was tall, with striking features that held an astonishing amount of seductive beauty. His long, midnight-black hair, tucked neatly behind one ear, flowed down to his shoulders in sleek waves of gloomy smoke. The darkness of his hair contrasted with the light, moon-pale skin covering his smooth face. Lines of jet-black ink crept out from under the collar of his ebony jacket. Silver rings, fastened all along his right ear, matched the two smaller loops that pierced the outer edge of his right brow. Asha centered her gaze, his fixed stare gleaming back, and she witnessed the madness that lurked behind his obsidian eyes. It was filled with hints of rabid, animal-like savagery, patiently waiting to be unleashed. Something else—she could not bring herself to call humanity—stirred beneath the jet-black depths of those beaming eyes. Asha caught his gaze as it trailed down her body, a ravenous look spreading across his angular face, and she repressed a shudder before it escaped her bones.

The man removed his mask, and a tempest's voice greeted Asha, "Welcome to my home. My name is Raziel," he purred. His hands slithered upward to secure the mask back in its proper place.

I've found you, Secret-Seeker, Asha reveled.

"Asha," she offered, letting an air of innocence saturate her tone. Raziel's eyes darkened with delight at the sound.

Too easy.

"Are you enjoying your time here, Asha?"

"It has been wonderful, thank you."

His head cocked slightly to the side as he stared intently at her.

"We have not met before." It was a statement rather than a question, and Asha's heart quickened, afraid the Lord of the Manor would realize she did not belong.

"I would remember a face as stunning as yours," he added, a tone of interest the only sound entering his voice.

She internally sighed, thankful the Secret-Seeker was too distracted by superficial beauty to notice someone had infiltrated his gathering.

She held out her hand. "I am very pleased to make your acquaintance, my lord."

He took her hand in his and brought it to his lips, placing a kiss on top. "Please, call me Raziel."

Asha smiled, letting the expression meet her eyes to hide the disgust she felt when his lips pressed against her hand.

"As you wish," she answered, feeding the desire for obedience she knew men like the Secret-Seeker always held.

The curtains beside them swept open, and a short man

burst through the onyx fabric, quickly shoving the hanging drapes back together before he disappeared across the room.

An air of nativity filled her mouth, and she took the sole opportunity she believed would present itself to ask, "Is there another party back there?" She motioned behind the curtains that she was sure Raziel had heard rip open. He kept his dark eyes on her face, never moving his gaze to the curtains hiding the crimson doors.

A sinister smile crept onto his face. "It is a meeting room."

"Oh, for business?"

"More of the entertainment variety, but yes, sometimes contracts are also drawn up."

She nodded, looking upward at him through thick lashes. "Well, I certainly did not come to such a grand party to discuss business." She let her gaze drop to his lips before pulling her eyes back up. She bit her lower lip.

"No? Then what did you come here in search of?" His tone was full of desire, hunger, and he took a step closer to Asha. She would have laughed at how predictable some men could be if the man standing before her didn't make her skin crawl.

She gave him a teasing smile, "I suppose we will see as the night continues."

His eyes grew darker as he replied with an assurance that no person should possess, "I could help you find *exactly* what you need." He looked her up and down slowly, his intentions on full display.

She laughed softly and added, "I'm not sure you're my type."

"Darling, I'm everyone's type." Another arrogant smile appeared on his lips.

Prick.

She simply smiled in response, not trusting her fiery tongue with the retort she knew it was primed to spit.

"But if you wish to be persuaded, I am happy to oblige. Tell me about yourself, Miss Asha." She pushed the fire that burned inside her eyes down as far as she could manage.

"Oh, there is not much to know, I'm afraid I live quite a simple life. I would much rather hear about you." She took a strand of her ash-blonde hair between her fingers and twirled it in soft circles, her eyes holding the most innocent look of interest.

Asha let the Secret-Seeker ramble on about his estate, his interests—namely the many, *many* lavish parties he threw—and his duties as Lord of Boeotian Manor; politely nodding and feigning interest, leaning deep into the naive, attentive persona that despotic men loved to exploit.

Right before boredom threatened to swallow her whole, a short, thin man with pasty skin and close-cut, dark hair rushed over and whispered in Raziel's ear. She recognized him as the man from earlier in the evening who had escorted the woman in the red dress into the Faustia Room. Asha's cheeks, thankful for the reprieve from the forced smiles, relaxed as the two men discussed something in hushed tones. After a brief moment, Raziel dismissed the man, and a disappointed look waved over his face.

He glanced back at Asha, "I'm very sorry, darling, but I must step away for a moment. Don't run off too far," he grinned, "I will come find you once my business is completed."

This was her only chance.

The words from Mathieson's journal rang in her head— *To receive an invitation, you must be willing to play.* Math had underlined the final word twice.

Asha stared at Raziel, letting disappointment creep over

her face, before she gently rested her hand on his arm. She moved her body closer to his. It took everything in her to force a smile up to her painted lips, suppressing a flinch as his skin brushed against hers.

"What a shame," she murmured, a saccharine tone glazing over her words. "I was having such a lovely time with you."

A salacious desire flittered in Raziel's eyes. She batted her dark lashes in response, disgust rumbling in her stomach at the gesture.

"Do promise you'll come back once you're done, and we can *play*." She leaned in close, her tone laced with suggestive implication, and she let her eyes drift down to his lips before climbing back up to his eyes.

Asha knew the word landed exactly how she intended before it even had time to snake its way up to his ears. His abyssal eyes twinkled, and a sinister grin stretched across his lips. Nausea ripped through her, but she compelled herself to stay composed, eyes still locked on his.

"Asha, darling, would you like to play a game?"

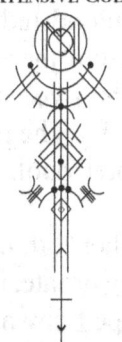

CHAPTER THIRTY

Asha and Raziel proceeded into the ominous room, and as she crossed the threshold, realization struck that she was the last player of the group to join. Her eyes scanned the space as the Secret-Seeker guided her to her place, his left hand on her elbow, directing her.

The decor in the Faustia Room matched the rest of the Manor—dark and devious, like evil lurked in its shadows. The round walls were lined with shelves of black books that stretched all the way to the high ceiling above. The floor was painted with a deep crimson carpet that paired dauntingly with the hue of the suspended luminos. In the center of the round room, a still pool of abyssal, dark water rested. An arched, glass window spanned across the wall opposite the entrance, large enough to illuminate the room with the moonlight pouring in from the outside. An ebony desk sat in the back corner. The sole occupants perched on top of it included a blank, open book, twin to the hundreds lining the shelves around the room, and an onyx quill; both sat beside a clear casing filled with blood-red ink.

Asha tore her gaze from the desk, nausea seeping into her body, and surveyed the five pairs of eyes staring at her from beneath detailed masks. The participants were all evenly spaced around the center pool, dressed in luxurious and opulent ensembles.

Standing furthest to her left, cold, harsh eyes bore into her from underneath a long ornate, mask. The covering swept across his brow and dropped down to cloak the right side of his face, leaving his left eye exposed. The lightweight, metallic base was adorned with luxurious filigree cutouts and multi-sized, silver-toned rhinestones. The surrounding metal enhanced the man's fluorescent gray eyes, standing out against his dark brown skin. His silver-white hair, half tied back, fell just above his shoulders, framing his charming, handsome face. His fitted, cobalt colored jacket, fashioned with dozens of intricate, silver threads, generously displayed the defined muscles underneath. A glimpse of royalty incarnate.

To the right of the silver-eyed gentleman stood a petite woman with brightly painted, full, red lips that strongly contrasted her fair skin. Her straight, jet-black hair barely grazed the bottom of her chin, and matched the narrow, anthracite eyes raging behind her checkered mask. The covering swept over the woman's high cheekbones before it cut upward to wrap itself around her piercing, almond-shaped eyes, outlined in thin black lines. Sprawled across the surface of the wooden mask rested a rotating pattern of crimson, ebony, and bone-white squares, each overlaid with matching gemstones. Thin, gold embellishments divided the colored sections. Her ruby gown hung tightly over one shoulder, decorated with beads sparkling all the way to the ground. Her leg peeked out from the high slit cut on the side, stopping glaringly high on her thin thigh. She looked like a raging hurricane, ready to deliver a storm.

The third player, a tall, lean woman with rich, tawny skin and striking amber eyes, donned a shimmering golden mask with tassels that fell from below her exposed eyes. The covering shaded the entire lower half of her face and connected at the bridge of her nose before climbing upward, dividing the space between her glimmering eyes with seven large, gold rhinestones extending up to her hairline. Her eyes were lined with a thick, smoky powder that sparkled like stars in the moonlight. Her deep brown hair was arranged in dozens of braids that plunged down her back, stopping at her waist. Her solid, foiled gold dress left her shoulders exposed as it hugged her curves, draping all the way down to the floor. The woman radiated the delicate structure of cultivated beauty.

To her right stood a clean-cut male, hovering several inches taller than the stunning woman beside him. His wavy, light-blonde hair fell just above his eyes. The deep green jacket hugging tightly against his chest complimented his lightly tanned skin and outlined his sculpted frame. His topaz eyes hid themselves behind his intricately fashioned mask. Similar to the woman in red, his gold mask, complemented by bright, sinister green details, covered only his eyes, leaving the remainder of his face exposed. Metallic, intricately engraved snakes slithered their way up and around the top brow portion of the man's mask. The serpents entangled themselves until they wound back and faced downward, connecting to the portion of the mask that spread over the man's nose. The bottom half of the covering was purposefully and carefully carved to reflect the etched remnants of a human skull. The menacing look plastered on the man's face matched the vicious sentiment carried by the mask, and he emitted the essence of tantalizing malice. Disgust slashed through Asha's body.

Her head turned slightly right as she assessed the last player in line, standing on the furthest side of the pool. Her eyes flared as they met the final face staring back at her, and her breath caught. Asha forced herself to keep breathing. Even hidden beneath the black, scaled mask, she would know who owned those emerald eyes anywhere. His gaze joined hers, and she saw a quick flash of fear cut across his face before he forced his features back into the permanently calm and indifferent expression he normally donned. His eyes trailed over her, and she watched as they settled on the dark, uncovered ink on her shoulder.

Anselem was dressed from head to toe in a deep, rich black. His jacket looked tailored specifically to fit his broad, muscular shoulders; it traced over every inch of his toned arms, a defined contour of his entire body. He towered a few inches above the other men in the room, and a quiet confidence emanated from him. His jade eyes appeared as if they glowed against the dark contrast of his obsidian mask. Shading the top half of his face, the covering looked like ripples of electric light, laced around shadowy billows of undulating darkness. The silver lights seemed as if they were moving, crackling with life. Dark, reflective scales adorned the lower portion of his mask, covering his cheeks and nose as they sparkled in the moonlight like stars. Asha strained to pull her eyes from him as the Secret-Seeker addressed the group in greeting.

"Welcome, my friends," Raziel bellowed. Several of the players shifted their weight as the Secret-Seeker sauntered around the room.

"Just a few rules to clarify for our newcomers before we

begin," Raziel flashed a wicked smile in Asha's direction, as if he hoped the novelty of his game would engulf the naive guise she'd carefully crafted for him throughout the night.

"The rules are simple. I will ask one question each round. One by one, you will provide your answers. Respond truthfully, and you get to stay. Respond dishonestly, and you will be removed." Raziel's eyes turned toward Asha. "And trust me," he beckoned, "I will know if you are lying." Another sinister smile pulled at the corners of his mouth, the expression such a contrast to the beautifully sculpted face on which it was displayed. Darkness crept into his ebony eyes, and Asha knew at her core he spoke the truth.

"If you wish, you may refuse to answer my questions. This will yield your turn and result in removal from the game." The Secret-Seeker continued his stride around the room. "However, you will have the option of requesting a bargain in place of answering my inquiries." A sly, wicked look spread over his face. "The deal will be made on *my terms*." His opaque eyes darkened with desire. "And once agreed, it will be binding." A flick of his wrist flashed a glimpse of the inked lines wrapping around his forearm. "We will continue our game until there is only one player left standing."

"The finalist," he grinned, his tone almost singing with excitement for what was about to unfold, "will be granted one question of his or her choosing. To which I will be bound to answer with unsuppressed wisdom." Raziel glanced once more around the room, his eyes cold as ice. "Let us begin!" he roared with enthusiasm.

"We shall allow the ladies to go first."

How gentlemanly of him, Asha thought. It took every ounce of self-restraint stored in her body to refrain from rolling her eyes.

Raziel turned to the woman in red, a vicious smile expanding across his face. "Miss Vendaval, we will begin with you."

Her eyes narrowed, and she pressed her full lips together into a thin line.

"Don't worry, Aella, we will start off easy," he promised, and his eyes danced with excitement. "What do you value most?" Raziel inquired, his voice sickly sweet.

Asha's palms started to sweat, and the air grew a little thicker, like she couldn't quite fill her lungs all the way.

Aella didn't miss a beat, as if she expected this sort of question to rear its head at some point in the night.

"Loyalty," she replied simply. Her tone let the room know she had absolutely no trouble cutting people off who didn't return the sentiment.

Raziel did not respond, but instead turned to the woman wrapped in gold.

"Calista?" he called, her name sounding like threaded silk on his lips.

The beautiful woman hesitated for a moment, contemplating her response. "Forgiveness," she stated quietly, her accented voice coming out gently.

The Secret-Seeker smiled wickedly at her answer, as if the singular word provided an insight into her private thoughts. From the corner of her eye, Asha saw the dark pool in the center of the room let out a single, almost invisible, ripple before it brought itself back to a rest.

Asha racked her brain for an answer, trying to arrive at a response both truthful and unrevealing.

Raziel turned towards her, eyes a blazing onyx. "And you?"

She studied his face for a moment, attempting to uncover any weakness that lay under his mask of confidence. She found nothing but poised composure.

"Justice," Asha declared, straining to keep her voice from shaking. She schooled her face into a neutral, un-amused expression.

Raziel's eyes widened the slightest bit, and his left eye-brow slowly rose. He did not respond as he forced his face back to complete neutrality.

There goes tonight's act of innocence, Asha thought.

The water behind him did not move.

"Gentlemen," he hummed, turning towards the man fur-thest to the left, "your turn." The Secret-Seeker glided over to the man draped in blue. "Kendric?"

The knightly man stared at Raziel, silver eyes reflecting off his metallic mask. "Respect." His voice was deep and regal. The midnight pool did not quiver.

"Casimir?" he purred, prancing over to the menacing man in green.

"Power," he hissed in reply. A corner of his mouth tugged upward, and the sly smirk reached his eyes. Casi-mir's voice slithered through his teeth, matching the spirit of the serpents circling his eyes.

Again, the pool did not waver.

Raziel turned at last to Anselem. Asha could feel her heartbeat begin to quicken. "Mr. Eros?" Raziel's snide tone wafted through the room.

Anselem kept his face in perfect neutrality, as if it were carved of stone. He answered confidently and without hes-itation. "Freedom." His deep, gravelly voice swallowed all the air in the room.

Asha held her breath as she willed the deep, abyssal wa-ter to remain still.

A second ripple waded its way through the pool.

The Secret-Seeker's smile grew wide, and he turned

away from Anselem. The faintest glimmer of satisfaction flashed in Anselem's eyes when Raziel's back was turned.

Asha internally gasped. *He wanted it to happen.*

Anselem made the water react—to make it seem like he had a weak spot for Raziel to focus on, to start tugging at. A perfectly laid loose string, just waiting to be pulled from its fabric.

He was playing the game, maybe even better than the host.

"See? I told you all we would start off easy," Raziel cooed, his crimson and ebony jacket glittering against the moonlight as he walked over to Aella.

The Secret-Seeker continued his charade, asking several more 'easy' questions to the group. Asha kept her answers short, divulging as little as possible. The cavernous pool did not emit any more revealing waves to the Gamemaster.

"Now, my friends," the affectionate term sent a chill down Asha's back, "since we have become comfortable with each other, let's make things a little more... interesting."

Asha's heart dropped into her stomach.

"What is your worst memory?" he coaxed, his dark eyes vehemently glancing around the room. Small droplets of sweat started to bead on Asha's back, and she cursed at her body for betraying the carefully crafted facade of indifference she held.

Anselem slightly shifted his weight, his only sign of unease.

Aella looked at Raziel, her face a combination of discomfort and rage. She kept her voice low as she snarled, "The morning I found that bitch in our bed." Betrayal soaked every word.

Another ripple soared across the pool, and Asha swallowed hard, knowing deep down it would not be the last time the waters shook.

Raziel skipped his way over to Calista, seemingly enjoying the secrets he was collecting. Calista's head was low, but she could not hide the fine line of tears rimming the bottom of her eyes, seeking an escape as they started to pile in the corners.

The Secret-Seeker stood in front of her without a sound, a silent signal that it was her turn to respond.

"The day—," her voice broke, and a single tear fell from her eye. An otherworldly energy buzzed beneath the water. Waiting. Anticipating. Starved for secrets to satiate its hunger.

Calista cleared her throat and started again, emptiness filling the air around her, "The day my son died."

Asha sucked in a sharp breath as the words hit.

The buzzing beneath the water abruptly halted. Asha let out a silent sigh and thanked Ianoda that another wave did not lash through the pool at the expense of such a broken woman.

Raziel did not move. He stood still, in front of Calista, staring at her face until her gaze moved up to meet his. The moment their eyes locked, the water in the pool began to violently swirl, bottomless anger raging from its depths.

Calista's eyes widened, but she did not move, frozen in place by fear.

Raziel raised his inked hand, and the swirling water ceased. He let out a disappointed sigh, clicking his tongue before he spoke. "My sweet Calista. What was our one rule?" The golden goddess stayed silent; her wet, amber eyes were streaked with sadness. "I told you to never lie to me," Raziel chastised, a hint of anger creeping into his tone. "Or did you simply believe I wouldn't know? That the Waters of Muse wouldn't tell me?"

It spoke to him? What in the Seven Hells...

"You see, sweet Calista, that's how this game of mine works." Asha's stomach twisted, bile rising in her throat. "When you lie, or in your case, withhold the truth, the Muses share your secrets with me, down to the most exhaustive detail." A nefarious look crept across Raziel's face, and his smile was crafted from pure evil.

His voice lowered a fraction of an octave as he unapologetically continued, "That's how I know your son didn't just die last year, did he?" His tantalizing tone made Asha sicker with each breath.

"No, he didn't," he replied in response to her silence. Tears poured from Calista's eyes. Raziel's voice did not waver; no emotion filled his words as he delivered the final blow, "You killed him."

Asha's heart pounded so hard in her chest she thought it would rip through her skin. Her ears rang, and her hands began to shake by her side. She scrunched her fingers into a fist as she tried to gain a grasp over her body. Her mind raced; she couldn't focus.

She killed her child?

The nausea resurfaced, and it took every bit of willpower Asha had to keep from vomiting on the crimson carpet.

Calista's eyes narrowed. Fury burned through her veins. "I don't have to explain myself to you," she spat.

The charming, wicked smile found its way back to the Secret-Seeker's face. "Oh, sweet Calista, you say that like I don't already know. As if the Muses did not show me themselves what happened on that beautiful autumn afternoon. How you were so tired of the screaming and his crying. You just wanted it to stop. How you pushed his small, beautiful head under the water and—"

Asha heard the smack before she saw Raziel's neck

twist. The slap rang through the room. The Secret-Seeker's cheek turned red from where Calista's hand struck it. The wicked smile was still sprawled across his face.

"You may see yourself out," was all he responded. Everyone watched in silence as the golden dress exited the room.

Five players were left.

Four still needed to answer the current round's question. The Gamemaster turned to face Asha, and she stared at the outline of the bright red handprint as he walked towards her.

"Asha?" he grinned. The smile contained less malice, but instead held a hint of... sensuousness. She suppressed the urge to recoil with disgust.

There were so many horrible memories rushing through her mind, it was hard to settle on just one.

"The day I found out Mathieson died." Piercing pain tore through her. She watched as waves began to slosh in the water, lapping up over the edges and dampening the carpet. Her head dropped down and she looked at the floor in front of her feet. Anselem's gaze burned into the side of her face, but she did not lift her eyes to look at him.

"Kendric?"

"The day my kingdom fell." A ruler without a crown. Small ripples waded in the water.

Casimir's response was equally as simple, but much less emotional, "When that bastard told me no."

The water in the pool didn't even stir. Raziel appeared unfulfilled but continued to Anselem.

Asha lifted her eyes from the carpet, looking over to where he stood.

"Anselem?"

His eyes lost all the light in them, his face hardened, and he looked a million miles away, as if he had been transported back in time by a dark and evil memory.

"Montu." His voice was cold and hard, pain hanging on each syllable.

Asha's heart sank, a small part of it breaking all over again. Anselem refused to meet her gaze. Worry and sorrow swept over her, and ice frosted her veins, threatening to explode. Asha could hear the onyx pool ripping harsh waves, but she focused on controlling the magic attempting to stir inside her.

"Well, this is shaping up to be a rather enjoyable night, don't we all agree?" The amusement in Raziel's tone made her want to imprint a matching red hand against the other side of his face.

She kept her face expressionless.

"Let's continue our play," the Secret-Seeker beckoned, shifting his attention to Aella. "What is your greatest fear?"

Shit.

Asha had no clue how to answer the question without lying. She wasn't even sure she knew the truth herself.

She used to know—before Aaru. Before the Final Testing of Algae. That had been her greatest fear—losing those she loved. The one thing she never thought she would recover from. Yet, here she was, still standing. Somehow.

Aella's voice drew Asha out of her thoughts and back to the Faustia Room. "I want to make a bargain."

Her eyes whipped across the room to look at Aella, shock spreading over her face. The energy deep within the pool began to hum, and excitement radiated out.

Raziel's devious eyes met Aella's as his hand gestured to the ebony desk sitting in the corner. He guided her over to it.

The players watched as the Secret-Seeker leaned in close, his mouth less than an inch from Aella's ear. He spoke in faint whispers, meant only for Aella's ears. She nodded, looking down at the open book on the table. She picked up the quill and dipped it in the blood-red ink. Asha could not see what was scribbled into the book, but the horrid look on Raziel's face told her it was something she wanted no part of. Aella set the quill back on the table once she was done. Raziel unbuttoned his ebony jacket, placing it on the back of the chair tucked beneath the desk. He wore a simple, black shirt with the sleeves rolled up to his elbows. Asha stifled a gasp.

As he took Aella's right hand and held it in his, Asha raked her eyes over the myriad of ink streaking the exposed portion of his pale arms. Hundreds of tattoos, signifying the binding nature of his bargains, wrapped around his arms like endless ribbons. Some of the lines were deep, long, and dark; others were faint, ill-defined, barely visible unless someone strained their eyes to look. The differences indicated just how much the recipient had sacrificed to make their deal.

The humming in the pool grew greater until it shook the entire room around them. Asha closed her eyes to stay balanced.

Then it stopped, almost as quickly as it had started. She opened her eyes to see a content smirk set upon Raziel's face. He guided Aella back to the rim of the pool. As he released her hand, Asha saw the fresh Marking of a single, black-lined tattoo cutting across Aella's right wrist. Asha's stomach dropped. She looked over Raziel's arms but could not differentiate Aella's from the hundreds of other lines already traced over his pale skin. As Aella settled into her place in the circle, Raziel took the quill, still wet with ink, and scribbled something along the spine.

"Asha," he called, delight spilling from his eyes as he closed the book, "you're next." Asha caught a glimpse of the lettering along the book's edge as he placed it on a nearby shelf: *A. Vendaval.*

A shiver ran down her spine. He turned towards her, and Asha's mind raced to find the answer.

Loss.

Loss.

Loss.

But that wasn't her answer anymore. It hadn't been for a long while now. That fear had been replaced by something else, something new. An unending desire for justice. A need for retribution. And a fear of...

"Failure," she growled, anger seeping out of her.

Asha feared failing many things—Soturi training, harnessing her burning magic, and she feared being unable to prove every person who had ever doubted her wrong.

But, more than any of the other daunting challenges laid before her, Asha's greatest fear was the failure of letting down her brother; of being unsuccessful in bringing justice to his sacrifice.

Asha forced herself to quiet her mind, shocked that the only response in the room was the small ripples bouncing through the black water.

The Secret-Seeker displayed a bored look, as if he expected some fantastic response from her, and her reply had left him disappointed. He slithered his way over to Kendric.

"Being forgotten," Kendric replied. A fallen king's worst nightmare. No crown, no legacy; only waste and ruin left in place of where he once reigned. The water hardly moved.

Casimir was next, a snug smile on his face, as if he believed he was immune to fear. "Death," he hissed. Before he even let the word off his lips, the pool began to swirl. The snugness on Casimir's face evaporated. "What in the Seven Hells?" he stammered; genuine confusion perched on his face.

Raziel waited a moment as the waters whispered to him. He raised his hand as he had the last time, and the Muses halted their speech.

"Ah," he replied to Casimir, "what an interesting situation."

"What are you talking about?" Casimir fired back.

"There are not many times when I have players who are able to lie to themselves so strongly that even they begin to believe the tales."

Casimir cocked his head to the side and his brow furrowed, the perfect picture of bewilderment.

"Mediocrity, yes?" Raziel hummed, "That is the true answer, is it not? You fear being ordinary. You loathe it, actually."

A flash of fury raged across Casimir's face, and the serpents on his mask looked like they were beginning to rattle.

"I suppose that makes sense. A fear of being inarguably average is ironically rather common amongst narcissists." The Secret-Seeker paused a moment before continuing, "So, I suppose in your overwhelming fear of being anything less than extraordinary... You joined the masses of all of those most similar to you and adopted the exact same fear I see from everyone like you, Casimir. Congratulations on becoming that which you fear most—common, predictable... and incessantly ordinary."

The group could almost see the heat steaming from Casimir's ears. He snarled a string of curses from behind his serpentine mask before storming out the door. His departure was anticlimactic.

Without skipping a beat, Raziel turned to Anselem.

"And what about you, warrior? What is your greatest fear?"

Anselem stood in perfected silence for a long moment, looking like he was contemplating whether to follow Casimir's exit. He chanced a quick glance at Asha before redirecting his eyes back to Raziel.

"Loneliness," he whispered, his usual confidence nowhere to be found. The Muses stood still, but Raziel's face beamed.

Asha's heart jerked inside her chest. *Loneliness? How could a man with so much confidence and an overwhelmingly successful reputation worry about—*

"Now we are down to four," Raziel interjected, cutting off Asha's thoughts before they started to walk themselves down a very slippery path.

The heinousness oozing from his body was almost visible as he blurted out the next question, "What is the worst thing you have ever done?"

Asha's skin went cold. Her heart nearly stopped inside her chest. Memories she had worked so hard to keep shoved deep in her mind, refusing to visit, raced their way to the surface, like they had been freed from their shackles.

Blood. So much blood. The deep Marks on her shoulder flared, burning deeper into her skin.

"Miss Vendaval, we will start with you," the Secret-Seeker sang, but Asha watched as his eyes surveyed all four of the remaining players, taking in the expressions that ravaged their faces.

Aella opened her red lips before quickly shutting them again, unsure of whether it was safe to divulge her secret. She narrowed her eyes at Raziel, her voice laced with poison, "I ruined that bitch's life." Raziel did not move from in front of Aella, the water behind him slowly starting to spin. Aella's eyes widened with fear as Raziel chimed in, "And which bitch would that be? The woman you found in your bed, or your wife?" The pool continued to slowly spin, as if waiting for Aella to hammer the final nail into her coffin before it released its circular twists.

Small beads of sweat formed on Aella's brow. "Both," she seethed through clenched teeth. A breathless moment passed. Time stopped.

And then the Muses unleashed their horrid swirls. Aella's face dropped, and a wide smile spread across Raziel's face. He lifted his hand slowly, urging the Muses to quiet back down as he drank in every last whisper they hummed.

"I told you the truth!" Aella snapped at him, fire and rage flying from her body.

"I warned you before, half-truths will not satisfy me, nor will they satisfy the Muses," the Secret-Seeker bit back, his tone harsher than any he had used throughout the night.

Aella moved to leave, but Raziel grabbed her wrist, not yet finished with her role in his game.

"You left out one of the people in your story, didn't you?" Sharp words pierced from Raziel's mouth as he addressed Aella. "You didn't just ruin two women's lives." His onyx eyes somehow grew even darker than before, devoid of all light. "No, you ruined three. You ran your wife's lover out of town after you found her in your bed, but you didn't end your revenge there, did you?" Raziel's words cut deep into Aella, trudging up old memories she wished to have long forgotten. "No, you decided to find your way into the bed of your wife's sister." Raziel clicked his tongue. "Shame. I never guessed you'd play the role of a hypocrite."

The icy words sliced through the air.

Aella ripped her hand from his grasp, spitting in his face before she turned and walked out the door.

Three left.

"Miss Raynor?" The growing knots in Asha's stomach

twisted again as he glided over to her, wiping Aella's saliva from his cheek. She did not want to know how he had discovered her last name. She figured the abyssal pool before her likely played a role in gifting him the information.

She answered with nausea pulsing through her veins, "I killed someone." Her voice came out quiet, loaded with guilt and shame. It sounded foreign, detached, like it belonged to someone else.

The Muses rippled but did not swirl. Anselem looked at her again, confusion hanging on his face. He was there when she killed Moros. He watched as she shoved the knife into his chest. She could almost see the thoughts flashing through Anselem's mind, thinking she was innocent and good. Believing she had taken an evil life, one unworthy of life in the first place. She didn't disagree; she held no guilt in her heart from that day at the Cliffs. It wasn't one of the memories that ripped her from sleep, jerking awake in a cold sweat.

No, killing Moros was *not* who she was referring to when the answer rolled off her lips, and Asha had a sick feeling Raziel knew exactly who she meant from the darkness fluttering in his eyes. The Secret-Seeker lifted his hand, and Asha stiffened as he lightly caressed her face. He stared into her eyes for a long moment before he dropped his arm back to his side and walked around the pool to where Kendric stood.

Raziel peered down at Kendric and angled his head slightly to the side, a noiseless invitation for Kendric's response.

"I stole my crown," he offered, a small sense of disgrace seeping into the words.

The Muses began to move into a slow swirl, and Kendric quickly attempted to recover, "My apologies, Gamemaster, let me further clarify. I stole the crown by extorting my best friend." The Waters of Muse quieted themselves back down, granting the imposter king one more chance to stay. Raziel didn't smile; instead, he simply stared at Kendric, eyes tracing over every inch of the silver masked face—searching. He narrowed his eyes on Kendric before spinning around to head towards Anselem. A sigh of relief escaped from Kendric's shoulders.

The Secret-Seeker strutted over to Anselem, attempting to peer down at him, but failing to do so as the top of his head lingered several inches beneath Anselem's. The glare his emerald eyes held could cut glass.

"Leaving Mathieson," he growled, his voice coming from deep inside his throat. Pain fastened itself to every syllable. The crack in Asha's chest grew wider when she heard her brother's name on his lips. Her heart ached with every sharp breath she attempted to inhale.

Math.

A mischievous smirk formed on Raziel's mouth. "Oh, how *delicious*," he cooed, delight reentering his eyes as he turned towards Asha. "I did not realize you two knew each other."

Asha kept her mouth shut as he stalked over to her. The light caught on his mask, and it twinkled. He whipped his eyes between the two of them. "Are the two of you together?" he mocked, his tone filled with intrigue.

"No," Anselem hissed before a heartbeat passed. His voice was low and calm, but it was filled with an unending pit of rage.

Asha's lips pressed tightly together, and a small, almost invisible ripple waded its way through the Muses. Her eyes cut over to Anselem, her brows crinkled, but his neutral face revealed nothing.

Raziel let out a soft, wicked laugh. "Very well," he continued, filing the information away for later use. "Our game is now down to three." He still stood in front of Asha, and his eyes wound their way down her body, greed engulfing the onyx glare that trailed over her. He paused a moment, contemplating his next round, before another devious grin formed on his lips.

"Who is responsible for breaking you?" It came out in a breathy whisper, like he had to force himself to contain the excitement pulsing through him. As soon as the words escaped his tongue, they hit Asha like a tidal wave. She realized each person the Secret-Seeker had brought into the room was carefully and purposefully selected. That deep within each of them lingered a brokenness they tried their hardest to mend, but never wholly fixed. She knew the Secret-Seeker, and whatever power was supplied to him by the Muses, saw through each of the players' carefully crafted masks, straight down into the depths of their broken souls. The energy in the pool began to hum with eager anticipation, as if it had been waiting for this moment—as if its hunger was satiated solely by feeding on the broken souls brave enough to answer it.

Asha's body tightened, and her heart picked up speed.

The memories of the Tartarus called to her to let them out. She pushed them down, until they grew relentlessly angry, and shoved themselves to the forefront of her mind, forcing her to acknowledge them—to remember.

For weeks, she had felt numb—paralyzed. Like she was drifting in a new abyss of Darkness, unable to escape.

She thought her Darkness had first crept in when she lost Math, when her heart shattered into an uncountable number of pieces. But over the last several weeks, Asha realized that her cold heart had been cracked long before her brother died.

But the most disappointing part of her experience was that she truly believed when she left the Dark Room in her head, she never would have entered the space again. Little did she know there was a much greater evil lurking beyond the Dark Room, in the Nameless Place. And the shadows haunting her nightmares from the space were more sinister than even Asha's dark mind could have imagined.

She no longer felt things the way she knew she should. The way she had before. She was lost inside her own mind and did not think, this time, she would find a way back into the light.

Raziel shifted his weight, and the movement ripped Asha from memories, bringing her back to the present.

"Bardick," she choked out, her voice cracking on the name.

As the words left her lips, a sudden wave of exhaustion spread over her, like the world—the Muses—drained her for everything she had. The silent tears piling on her lids poured themselves over the edges. The Muses remained still, as if they had soaked up all the brokenness inside her and had buckled under the weight.

Raziel studied Asha's face. He gently wiped the tears streaking her cheeks. The gesture was almost sweet—if the hand it was connected to hadn't been the reason they flowed in the first place. She pulled her face back from his touch. He dropped his hands without a word.

The Secret-Seeker paraded over to Kendric, his back facing Asha. She could see Anselem staring at her from the corner of her eye, and she dared a glance in his direction. Something akin to worry was written on his beautiful face. She turned away before more tears swelled to the surface.

"Mr. Vasili?"

A wave of terror swept across Kendric's face. His silver eyes flushed with panic, and he began to stammer. "I—I don't know. I don't have an answer." All sense of diplomacy and composure left his royal body. "You cannot remove me simply because I do not know the answer," he begged, desperation seeping into his tone.

"I can do precisely that," Raziel hissed back, his patience having worn thin. "You always have another option," he suggested, his hand motioning over to the ebony desk.

Kendric's eyes narrowed. "Wretched snake," the fallen king snarled. His face dropped, knowing he had lost to the Gamemaster. "Go to Hells."

Raziel laughed, the sound eerily wicked. "Oh, my friend, where do you think I came from?" A sinister grin danced across his face.

Asha's entire body broke out in a cold sweat, and her hands trembled.

Raziel turned to Anselem, dismissing the silver-haired man as he walked to the other side of the Muses.

The Secret-Seeker said nothing more while he awaited Anselem's answer. Pain and sorrow filled his emerald eyes.

"Kalevala."

A devious smile broke over Raziel's lips, and the Muses roared behind him. Anselem's head dropped, and he stared at the pool with a blank, empty expression.

Shards sliced their way through Asha's chest. *He looked so... defeated.*

Raziel spun away from Anselem, leaving him standing there as he broke all over again from the memories tormenting his mind. The Secret-Seeker began circling the pool as he spoke.

"My final two," he gleamed, his eyes glancing between Asha and Anselem. "I think this is where the fun really begins," he gushed, the endless darkness returning to his dead eyes. "Now, our game will continue as it has, with one... addition." Asha's blood turned to ice, and an air of titillation coated his words. Raziel began walking around the two finalists as he explained, "You will still have the choice to divulge the truths that you wish to stay concealed, and you will also have the opportunity to make a bargain." He nodded at the black book sitting on the corner desk, and the smirk that crossed his mouth sent a chill down Asha's spine. Her hands went clammy.

Neither of the players spoke. Neither of them moved.

The Secret-Seeker continued his dance, circling them, a predator closing in on his prey.

"But, to make our time together even more interesting, the winner of our little game will now be granted *two* questions of his or her choosing." His voice hung heavily in the air, as if his words sucked out all the oxygen in the room. He knew exactly how to win, exactly how to get what he wanted. Forever the commander of a game he had masterfully learned to play throughout the years.

His steps ceased behind her, and her body went stiff.

Asha chanced a glance at Anselem, but his eyes did not stray from Raziel. Only wrath existed behind the beautiful, deep green. "Asha," he murmured with excitement, her name sounding foul on his tongue. "Ladies first," he taunted. The Secret-Seeker stood so close she could feel the heat from his chest against her back, feel his breath against her neck as he tilted his chin down towards her ear. Raziel lowered his voice, barely above a whisper, "Shall I ask about Mathieson's journals? Or would you rather indulge my other desires?"

His voice was so low, Asha knew her ears were the only ones it reached. The blood drained from her face. Fear filled her veins. A collision of dread and terror ripped through her. She could feel her power rumbling beneath the surface.

Asha sucked in a sharp breath as Raziel's lips grazed

her neck. A wave of nausea poured over her, but she did not allow herself to move.

Raziel's body shifted, rotating in front, towards Asha's face. He placed his right hand underneath her chin and tilted her face up towards his. Tinged, black eyes with flecks of red stared into hers. His thumb brushed across her lower lip. "What a pretty mouth," he breathed, "it would be such a waste not to be able to show you what delightful things you could do with it." His eyes glimmered with the evil inside him. Asha forced herself to hold his stare as he trailed his unoccupied fingers down her side. She stifled a shudder. "So, which would you prefer?" A wicked smile pulled at the corners of his mouth, his voice still low, barely a whisper.

Asha found herself caught in the middle of a very dangerous game, and the malicious look on his face told her the Secret-Seeker knew she had run out of cards to play.

A small tear formed in the corner of her eye and slid down her cheek. Her breath began to quicken, knowing she would never let Anselem hear about Mathieson's journals. She would never subject him to the risks attached to what it contained; never involve him with Bardick and the other vicious people who desperately sought the information.

And she certainly knew she could not offer that same information to the Secret-Seeker, unsure of what sinister way he would twist the knowledge for his own gain.

"What shall it be, Asha?" Raziel crooned more loudly, his voice carrying through the room. He leaned in, his lips approaching hers. His left hand lingered on the small of her back and pulled her closer to him, pressing his body against her own; the intentions of his bargain were crystal clear.

Another wave of nausea washed over her. It took every fiber of her being to push it down.

A singular moment passed as Asha tried to find words.

"I yield," a deep voice broke through the silence.

Raziel halted, his mouth mere inches from Asha's. Disappointment and surprise stretched over his face. His eyes narrowed, growing dark with displeasure. He did not move away.

"I said *I yield*," the voice barked louder, hostility coating every word.

The Secret-Seeker pulled his face back from Asha, and she released a breath she did not realize she had been holding. Raziel turned his head slowly towards Anselem, resentment emanating from every inch of his body, vexed by the abrupt ending of his game.

His right hand still held her chin towards his mouth. She shook her face loose from his grip and took a step backward, gladly putting space between their bodies.

"Interesting," he seethed, his eyes locked on Anselem. "You may see yourself out," Raziel directed, his body tense with agitation. Asha's stomach dropped at the thought of being alone with the Secret-Seeker.

"I'm not leaving her alone with you," Anselem growled back, as if he had read her thoughts. His voice was still loaded with hostility. Asha's eyes flared wide beneath her mask, shock creeping onto her face.

Raziel's eyes narrowed in on him, and he snarled through gnashed teeth, "You don't make the rules here, *Soturi*." He spat the title out with disgust, as if he somehow meant for it to be an insult.

"Go ahead, Raziel, bare your teeth at me. I'll pluck them out one by one," Anselem threatened. He gripped his fists so tightly, his knuckles started to turn white by his side.

Raziel let out a malicious laugh, but did not step any further towards Anselem, as if he knew precisely how lethal the man before him could be. "It's almost sweet, you're trying to protect her. But she doesn't know, does she?" His eyes flickered over to Asha before resting back on Anselem. The lieutenant clenched his jaw but didn't say a word. "She doesn't know all the horrible things you have done. Doesn't know what you agreed to in Aaru. Why you were there in the first place."

Vomit rose in Asha's throat.

Mathieson.

"Ah, I can see she most certainly does not. Do you think it would make her change her mind about you?" A wicked grin appeared on his face.

"Shut your damn mouth," Anselem hissed.

"Oh, you don't want sweet Asha to know all the vile things you did for Kalevala, do you? What about all the nights you spent warming her bed? How eager you were to play her *whore?* What about all the innocent lives you took? The families you destroyed? How perfectly eager you were to play the *executioner.*"

Asha's head whirled. A million thoughts rushed around, all fighting against one another.

She watched Anselem wince as the words hit his ears. He remained calm, his eyes still piercing through Raziel's face. "I've been called worse by better." The venom coating Anselem's words was pure poison.

A light knock on the door interrupted the heated stares, and they whipped their heads towards the sound.

Raziel turned away from Anselem and walked over to the door. He paused just before passing her and turned towards her. His hand slowly moved up to her face.

"Touch her and I'll snap your neck," Anselem growled, his voice stern and full of unquestioning promise.

A flicker of consideration flashed in Raziel's eyes, but he dropped his hand and proceeded to cross the remaining steps towards the door. Asha knew he must have also believed Anselem's warning.

Asha let out a sigh. Raziel opened the door, and the short, pasty man from earlier whispered something inaudible. The Secret-Seeker nodded once before dismissing him and then closed the door behind the man.

"My apologies, Asha, I have something urgent I need to tend to." He brandished a hostile look at Anselem before returning his gaze to Asha. "I will be back momentarily, and then you and I can complete our game." He threw another nasty look in Anselem's direction before he turned to exit.

Raziel shut the door behind him, and Asha and Anselem were the only ones left standing in the silence.

Her gaze stayed locked on the closed, wooden door, as if it had the answers to the questions racing in her head. She heard Anselem's footsteps as they quietly approached.

"Asha," he breathed softly, barely a whisper.

She swiftly jerked her head at the nearness of his voice, nearly colliding with his chest. Asha's eyes cut up at him, annoyed at how beautiful his face looked in such a gruesome setting.

"I advise you to choose your next words *very* carefully," she warned. He took a small step back, as if he could dodge the bitterness woven into her tone.

"We don't have much time," he proceeded, his voice still hushed. The words poured quickly from his mouth. "And I know you have no reason to right now, but I need you to trust me."

Anger bubbled inside her at the word—*trust*. As if she hadn't just found out there were more secrets he was keeping. And some of them had to do with Aaru—with Mathieson.

"Trust you? Trust *you*? What, like how Math trusted

you? Before you left him there to die?" Her words came out fast and heated, and she watched as every single one sliced through him like shards of glass. Pain rose to the surface of his emerald eyes.

It was a low blow. She knew that. She knew deep down it wasn't Anselem's fault that he was the one who escaped and not Math. But it still hurt every time she looked into those shimmering green eyes and was reminded she would never see her brother again.

And she was pissed she had to find out from Raziel, of all people, that there were more secrets Anselem was hiding. But, if Asha was being honest with herself, there were still some secrets she had left unsaid. The night on the clock tower, she had refrained from mentioning Nina. She wasn't ready to come to terms with what she had done. She wasn't sure if she ever would be. But she knew for certain she was not ready for Anselem to look at her with pure judgment in his eyes and finally see who she really was behind the mask.

"You lied." She tried to keep the hurt from her voice, but it betrayed her, cracking as the words came out.

"I didn't lie to you."

"You don't get to get off on a technicality."

"We don't have time for me to explain everything right now. I just need you to trust me." That word again. *Trust.* But she did trust him. After everything that had happened over the last several months, deep down she knew she trusted him, even if there were still secrets between them.

"And I need you to use one of your questions to ask Raziel something for me."

She let out a huffed laugh at his audacity. "You want me to use one of my questions to ask the Secret-Seeker something for you? After I just found out you lied?"

Anselem kept his face composed, letting no emotion

wave over it. Asha searched his jade eyes for some sort of answer. She found nothing.

"I need you to ask him where to find the Empress of the Forgotten City."

Her brow furrowed again, this time with genuine confusion.

The latch clicked, and Asha's neck snapped back towards the door. Anselem swiftly moved several steps away from her as the hinges creaked and Raziel opened the door and entered.

His eyes darkened when they met Anselem. "I thought you would have had enough sense to be gone before I returned." The Secret-Seeker's steps covered the place between Asha and the door, and he arrogantly stopped beside her, gaze still locked on Anselem.

Anselem said nothing, his face unmoving behind his electric mask.

Raziel's clean-cut face turned towards Asha, avidity burning in his eyes. "And what exactly would you like to know, darling?" A sensual tone laced his words.

She hesitated a moment, contemplating her decision. She did not dare look over to Anselem as she took a deep breath, "Where can I find the Empress of the Forgotten City?"

Raziel's eyes slowly narrowed, undeniably sensing from whom the question originated. He took a long moment, his dark eyes burrowing into Asha's, before he answered. "Thotha resides in Verloren, the city hidden within the depths of the Kunlun Mountains. The White Tiger of the West will guide the way among the Eight Pillars until you reach the Hands of the Wise One."

She tried to make sense of his response but found herself at a loss. The only words she understood were the Kunlun

Mountains, the southern mountain range that split through the center of Perseis. And she recognized the name Verloren, City of the Forgotten, which she vaguely recalled from stories her mother had told her as a child. The rest was a jumble of words she did not comprehend.

Before she had time to decide if she would ask her original question, Raziel shot a look towards Anselem and added, "You know Kalevala is still looking for a way to bring you back, right? She'll never stop. Not until she has you back inside her—" Raziel's words were cut off before he could finish his sentence.

A flash of Anselem's electricity flickered, but was quickly snuffed out by the iron floating through the air, and before Asha could blink, he had crossed the gap between himself and Raziel. Anselem grabbed him by the throat, cutting off Raziel's words, and he shoved him up against the wall. Raziel's feet dangled an inch above the floor. Anselem's fingers were clenched so tightly around his pale neck, she knew no air was able to flow through. The Muses started to rage beside them.

Tears began to slide down Asha's cheeks. Not from fear—she didn't care whether Raziel lived or died, aside from the inconvenience of having to find another way to get her questions answered. No, her concern came from what she saw erupting inside Anselem. It was like looking in a mirror, watching the Darkness tearing through him, attempting to take hold. The sight choked the breath from her body, and a small part of her heart sank. She finally saw the broken side of the unshakable, forever-composed Soturi the rest of the world knew. She gazed through the impenetrable mask he put on for everyone else—the mask he had always worn around her. Asha's feet slowly made their way over to him, tears still slipping from her eyes, and she placed a soft, gentle hand on his muscled shoulder.

"Anselem," she breathed, almost a whisper.

His stiff body softened under her touch. "Anselem, let him go." In a strained effort, his gaze left Raziel, and he turned it towards her. And suddenly, the monster raging inside of him fell silent as he met her eyes.

Anselem released Raziel from his grip, letting him drop to the floor. With disgust plastered on his face, he looked down at the Secret-Seeker crumbled beneath him. He turned aside and stormed to the door, preparing to leave. But as he reached for the knob, he paused, and Asha knew he had forced himself to stay while she was still there.

"Letting the emotional little girl defend you? I thought you were a better warrior than that, Eros," Raziel rasped, his breathing ragged as he attempted to fill his empty lungs with air. Ice frosted Asha's veins.

She did not balk at his attempt to insult. No, she'd spent far too many days of her life thinking her emotions made her weak, flawed. Too much time letting other people act like they were a vulnerability.

She stepped towards him, her voice calm and colder than the ice coursing through her, "Do not confuse emotional for weak. I will slit your throat with tears rolling down my cheeks."

Raziel sneered between the gasps, "Fiery little one, aren't you?" Asha refused to drop her gaze as he stumbled to his feet, a dark bruise beginning to form on his neck. "Don't be naive enough to think you can stop it. Any of it. They are more powerful than even you know, Seal-Breaker."

Asha took a step closer, dismissing the unknown title he had thrown at her, and settled her voice into a lethal calm. "I want you to know that one day I will come back here. And when I do, I will burn every last piece of this room to the ground. And as you watch the twisted joys of your life ignite in flames, you will remember this moment. You will remember that you should have kept your damn mouth shut. You will remember you are not as untouchable as you may believe. And as the flames engulf these walls, you will know that I was the one holding the matches when your precious Room of Secrets went up in smoke."

Promise wrapped itself around every frost-bit word. Raziel only blinked, for once, at a loss for words. She turned to head for the door.

"You still have one question left," he croaked, his voice filling with disappointment as his game neared its end. Asha stopped halfway to the door but kept her body facing the exit. Raziel rubbed his hand over his purpling neck.

"You never said *when* I had to ask my questions, simply that I would get to. So, I will be seeing you again. Soon. But next time it will be on *my terms.*" She emphasized the final two words, reminding him of the ones he had used earlier in the evening.

A sly smile pulled up at the corners of Raziel's mouth.

"Clever girl," he replied, his eyes twinkling with delight, "you are welcome to play in my home any time."

Asha turned back and marched the rest of the way to the door, pushing past Anselem. Right before she crossed the threshold to exit the Faustia Room, an onyx, leather-bound book, sitting on the shelf next to the door, caught her eye. Seven letters were written on the spine in blood-red ink: *M. Raynor.*

Asha forced herself to exit the Manor before she vomited the contents of her stomach onto the perfectly manicured lawn.

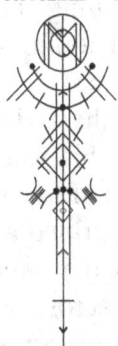

CHAPTER THIRTY-ONE

The next evening, Asha found Anselem soaking in a large, thermal spring, set in the center of an opening of trees on the western side of the South Island. The dark water swallowed all the light from the moon as it floated against his chest, hiding the rest of his body below. His strong, tan arms were draped around the pool's rim, and his head leaned back against the edge. His eyes were closed, and a peaceful, relaxed expression sat on his face. His dark hair, wet and tangled, had a few small strands sticking to his face.

Asha stood in the shadows of the oaks, staring at him for a few moments before his voice broke through the silence, "I can feel you standing there, you know."

A wave of embarrassment washed over her as she crept out from the concealing darkness. Anselem picked his head up from its resting place and opened his blazing emerald eyes.

"Didn't anyone ever tell you that it's not polite to stare?"

393

he teased, a small smile pulling at the corner of his mouth.

"Get out," she barked at him, and the smile forming on his face abruptly disappeared.

He stood in the pool, the dark water receding down his body, hovering just above his waist. He sauntered through the spring towards the side of the pool where Asha stood.

The water droplets sparkled against his deep, honeyed skin. His body looked as if it were sculpted by the gods. Hard, wet muscles flexed across his chiseled stomach as he waded through the water. His arms tensed as he lifted himself out of the spring, directly next to where Asha was waiting, revealing the lack of clothing he wore on his lower half.

Oh gods...

Asha whipped her gaze up to his beautiful, angular face, refusing to allow her eyes to drop back down. He smirked.

"Cold?" she snidely commented, fighting to keep her voice even. *He could use some humbling,* she thought, *even if it is a lie...*

He let out a soft laugh that sounded like dripping honey.

"Are you offering to be the one to warm me up if I am?" he countered back, a teasing tone wrapping his words.

A flash of heat flared over Asha's cheeks, and she prayed he couldn't see it in the midnight light. She rolled her eyes, internally straining to keep her features schooled in a neutral and unamused expression.

"Because I'm sure I could find some fun ways for us to create a little heat, Seven," he joked again, flashing another gorgeous smile.

"Arrogant prick," she grumbled back, chucking the towel at him that was hanging on the branch beside her. Another light laugh escaped his lips as he wrapped the towel around his waist.

"What do you need, Seven?" he asked simply, all teasing having left his voice. A libidinous twinkle momentarily flickered in Anselem's eyes as he looked down at her. Asha's heartbeat quickened, but she maintained her indifferent expression.

"What do I need?" she growled; all semblance of composure having left her body.

His eyes widened in response to the tone.

"I need you to tell me what you were doing in the Faustia Room," she snapped, the words rushing out like overflowing liquid, lacking any hint of civility. "I need you to tell me why in the Seven Hells you needed *that* question answered." Her voice was laced with fury, rising with every word. "I still need you to tell me why you lied, and I need you to tell me why you yielded on *my* turn." Asha's breathing came out labored as the anger inside her ripped through her veins. The respect she held for his position, which would normally have kept her anger somewhat in check, had run out along with her patience. She needed answers, and she was tired of him leaving out half of the information.

Anselem blinked but did not respond. Asha studied his face, his mind racing as he decided whether to tell her the truth, and exactly how much of it he would be willing to share if he did decide to let her in. She watched demons run circles in his eyes, recklessly playing with matches. She had never seen sparks so beautiful.

She waited in silence.

"Do you trust me?" he breathed; his voice having lost its teasing tone.

That damn word again.

Trust.

Asha stared back into his eyes, searching for a reason to say no.

"I haven't decided yet, since I just found out you apparently like to leave out important information," she replied. But she tasted the lie's bitterness as it crossed her lips.

She knew if he hadn't told her the entire story, there was a reason for it, and she knew when she looked into his eyes, in the depths of her soul, that he was good.

She knew Darkness lingered deep in the emerald oceans staring back at her, but in her heart, deep within her own Darkness, she trusted him. From the morning on the Cliffs, to the night on the clock tower, and the day he pulled her from the Nameless Place, he had never shown her anything but the trustworthy, loyal man her brother always claimed him to be. She knew everything that happened to him and Mathieson in Aaru was so closely aligned with her own experience during the Inferno that Anselem never would have chosen for things to end the way they did, and she believed his words from on top of the clock tower when he told her he would have traded places with Math if he had the chance.

She was unsure if she wished he had traded places with Math, but she was certain of one thing—that even if she was unable to forgive herself for how her own situation unfolded, she forgave him.

Anselem nodded as her words reached him, and his body loosened the slightest bit, as if her response was better than an outright rejection. He took a step forward, his body inches from hers. Asha put a hand up as he closed the distance between them, her fingers landing on his bare chest.

He let out a small laugh. "Sorry, this is probably a little... distracting. Let me throw on some clothes."

But she didn't pull her hand away. She glanced up at him, her eyes landing on his lips. He lingered for a moment, his breathing heavy, before he forced himself to step back and walk to the edge of the pool, where his clothes were neatly folded on the ground.

Distracting is an understatement, she thought.

He faced away from Asha, and the inked wing on his back glistened in the moonlight. The Mark was beautiful, and shimmering like the stars overhead, it looked alive—like life had been breathed into it by the Dominions themselves.

She watched the ink move as his muscles tensed, and for the briefest of moments, she wondered if the rumors had been true—if the Septant Wings were more than dark etchings on top of his honeyed skin.

He dropped the towel, and Asha's cheeks flushed. She quickly turned around, her back facing him as he dressed.

While she waited, she tried to shove down her impatience. Tried to sort through what she needed to ask and what they needed to discuss. Lost in her thoughts, she did not hear as Anselem returned.

"Valhol's most notorious warrior, and she doesn't even hear the approach from behind," he teased, his voice only inches from her ear.

She whipped her body around, nearly slamming into him. Anselem, now fully clothed, let out a soft laugh and his lips tipped into a smirk.

"Why do you need me to trust you for you to tell me what the Hells is going on?" she questioned.

His smile dropped. "I'm sorry," he said, and it took Asha every ounce of training she had ever learned to keep the shock from reaching her face. She would bet a lot of gold those words were ones that rarely, if ever, left his lips.

"I am sorry," he repeated, "for not finding you after you left the Boeotian Manor. I have been spending the day tracking down... some information."

"Tell me."

"I can't."

Heat steamed from her head. "You can't or you won't?"

"There is a lot more at stake than you know."

She dropped her voice low, laced with heat and anger. "I know about the Adversary."

Anselem blinked. Once. Twice.

Asha sighed. "I have known since they sent Math's belongings back after Aaru." The Darkness inside her tried to rear its head, but she shoved it back inside the Dark Room in her mind.

Anselem was silent, but thoughts flashed across his face. "You read them, didn't you?" he asked.

"Read what?"

"His journals."

Asha's body went rigid, and the blood drained from her face. *He knows.*

"Yes," she whispered.

"Do you still have them?"

He knows. He knows. He knows.

"How?" was all she was able to croak out.

Anselem's granite face turned softer, and a small, rare light lit in his eyes. "Who do you think told him to write them?"

"You... you told him to write it all down?"

"Yes."

Asha's head spun. Over and over, as reality hit her: Anselem Eros had never been the monster she believed him to be.

"But you have them?" he asked again, his voice softer than its usual commanding tone.

"Yes," she rasped, still trying to stop the spinning. "How did you know I would have them?"

Another smile as he looked into her eyes. "Who do you think made sure they were sent to you after... everything?"

"Why?" Tears started to slip from her silver-lined eyes.

Anselem lifted a hand as if he was going to brush them from her cheeks, but then lowered it back to his side as if he'd thought better of it.

He let out a long sigh. "Because I knew you were the one he would want to have them. I knew you were the one person he trusted more than anyone—even the Septant—to do what was right. I knew that even though I wanted to keep them, to do right by him and follow what he laid out, that Math would want you to have a small piece of him when he was gone. And honoring that—honoring him—was more important to me than keeping them as a guide to follow for myself. When I had the box sent to you, I made a promise to him that I would figure out a way to get it done without the journals. Never in my life did I expect you to show up to Soturi Tryouts or to be assigned to my Division; never did I think I would have to stand there every day and be reminded of the promise I haven't been able to hold." His words were frantic, as if he had been holding the truth in for too many days, and it was a relief to finally let it out. "And never in my life did I think that I would have to spend every waking moment since you arrived, worried I was going to fail my Blood Oath to Raynor."

The Septant's Blood Oath. Asha had heard rumors about it, but even after she found out that Anselem was part of the Septant, she never dared to ask him about the stories.

The Blood Oath that the seven members took bound the brothers in promise to protect one another with their lives. The Oath also extended outside the seven warriors, as each member declared one person of their choosing to be protected by the Septant with their lives. More tears streamed down her face as Anselem's words barreled into her and she realized Math's Oath had been vowed for her. And she realized everything Anselem had done for her was to honor his promise to Math.

"Why didn't you just ask me for them?" she whispered, her usual steady voice beginning to tremble.

"Because they were never meant for me," he replied, pain flashing in his silver-lined eyes.

She let out a shaky breath. "So, what now?"

"Well, if you already know about the Adversary, then you're mostly caught up to speed. After the other night in the Faustia Room, I was able to track down a little more information about the Empress, but without Math's journals, I've come to somewhat of a dead end in terms of where to look next." His voice started to trail off as he concluded.

Asha stared at him for a long time, vaguely remembering reading something in the journals about an Empress, and she responded, "I can get them. I can give them to you."

A flicker of what could only be described as hope flashed across Anselem's face before realization set in, and he replied, "I can't ask you to do that, Seven."

"Why not?" Annoyance began to pilfer its way back inside her words.

"Because I made him a promise—an Oath—to keep you safe. That was why I kept things from you about Montu, about our purpose for going there. About the Adversary. Because this road we are heading down... I think the only way this road will end is with death and tragedy."

"Then it is not the end of the road."

"What?" Anselem replied, his brow crinkling as confusion stretched over his face.

"If the road is full of death and tragedy, then we have not reached the end."

A knowing look crossed his face—the look of someone, like her, who had battled their way through Darkness. The look of someone who still held onto the faintest sliver of hope that on the other side of the dark abyss, they would find the light—the peace. A better side. A better end to the road they had traveled.

A better world.

"And it is my choice," she said plainly.

He nodded in agreement as he sorted through the jumbled thoughts in his mind, the promises he had made and was determined to keep.

Anselem stepped closer and raised his hand again, placing it on her shoulder. He brushed his thumb over her jacket, as if he could see through the leather, down to the inked skin underneath. "If we are going to do this," he said, his voice strong and unwavering, "the only way we will be able to finish it is together. And I know you have your reservations, and you do not fully trust me, so, before we go any further down this road, the choice is yours, but I need to know if you will be able to accept that—accept doing this with me."

Asha was quiet for a long moment. She looked past him, to the darkness beyond. To a different time—a different world. Anselem stayed silent, patiently awaiting her reply.

Her eyes returned, and she brought her gaze up to meet his. She focused on his tear-streaked face, and in the moment his eyes met hers, Asha realized she was no longer alone. She realized for the first time since the Darkness had entered her life, she finally found a friend to walk by her side, through the midst of it. Not only to endure it, but someone who understood. Someone who would stand with her, hand-in-hand, and look into the depths of her soul and never be afraid of the Darkness peering back.

She straightened and held her chin high, her voice steadfast, "Before I agree, you have to promise me two things."

"Anything," he breathed, and by the sincerity in his voice, she knew he meant it.

"First, you are going to tell me everything. And I mean *everything*. And I will do the same for you. No judgment. But we can't go into this with any more secrets."

"Done," he said, "and the second thing?"

"Secondly, you have to promise me once we start this, we will not stop until we see it through, until the end, no matter the cost. I will not start down this path with you only to go halfway. If we start this, we will finish it."

"I promise," he answered, "we will follow it until we meet the road's end."

"Until we fight through every last fire we have before us?"

He grinned, a long-lost joy sparking in his emerald eyes. "Until we are nothing but ash and embers."

She nodded, smiling at the words he used from her story atop the clock tower.

"Until we are ash and embers," she promised him back.

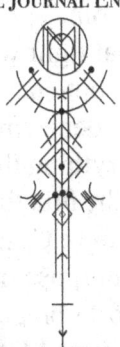

CHAPTER THIRTY-TWO

The base was quiet, dormant. Dawn began to peak into the midnight sky as Asha shuffled down the open walkway, heading towards the archery range to clear her mind of haunted dreams and restless sleep.

As she wandered her way through the corridors, Asha reflected on everything that had happened the night before. She reluctantly told Anselem about Nina, expecting disgust and judgment to fill his eyes, but when she looked into the emerald oceans, she was only met with kindness and understanding. Then she told him why she was in the Faustia Room and how she had intended to ask Raziel how to break into Montu. Anselem looked at her curiously, and Asha explained how she had every intention of flying to Aaru after graduation and burning the entire Kingdom to the ground. When the words left her lips, she thought his gaze would have turned ambivalent, but surprise crossed her face when he simply replied, "Then I will go with you, and together, we will level the entire Kingdom."

She nodded, her throat tight with emotions she was not sure how to comprehend, but she was thankful to look into his eyes and see only confidence in her ability to succeed.

Anselem told her everything that happened in Aaru—all the details he had left out the first time. He explained the purpose of going to the Midnight Castle—how the Septant had not gone for the singular purpose of killing the Queen to the Obsidian Throne, but also to break into her castle and steal the *Divulgence Key*, an object Math told the Septant would lead to the Adversary.

Like Asha, Anselem did not have much information on the *Arch of the Abyss*, but he mentioned that before they went to Montu, Mathieson told him the Adversary was a primordial being, formed of Darkness itself. He had no idea how Mathieson learned the information, and he had no clue how the *Divulgence Key* would help them understand more about the role the Adversary played; he didn't even know what the *Divulgence Key* was, but he did tell her, amid everything that happened, the Septant was not able to steal the key.

Anselem also filled her in on the information he secured earlier in the day—about the Empress of the Forgotten City. She was rumored to be an ancient, near-immortal spirit, with powers of insight and knowledge. He believed she could be one of the only beings with any understanding of who the Adversary was and where exactly he may reside. And if they were not able to retrieve the *Divulgence Key*, the Empress might be the next best option for finding the Adversary.

Asha's head swam with the abundance of information. She sorted through most of it when she returned to her room and had a moment of silence to think.

Mathieson had died—*sacrificed himself*—to ensure Anselem and his brothers got away, but not without making sure they knew about the *Divulgence Key* and the Adversary—the *Arch of the Abyss*. Even with the limited information surrounding the primordial being, Asha made the safe assumption that if Mathieson had held such grave concern for the existence of the Adversary, a concern great enough to sacrifice himself for, then there was a very good chance the Arch was a significant threat to the Kingdom of Perseis—and possibly all Darnella.

Asha continued to sashay down the halls, taking deep breaths as she once again sorted through everything they discussed. She pushed down the nightmares from the night before and the doubt that crept into her mind about all the things she needed to do. About all the possibilities for failure.

As she shoved back the threatening Darkness, she smiled to herself. Because she realized she was here. And no one really knew what that meant except for her. It was a place beyond all the blood. A place beyond all she had lost. A place with a shattered heart she had learned how to put back together. Here. Where she loved her scars and didn't quite know what would happen next, but it was okay. Because for the first time since the Nameless Place, she thought she might once again be ready for the unknown.

A cool morning breeze brushed against her cheek as she turned another corner of the colonnade, and she pulled her jacket tighter to her chest. Two steps past the turn, a hand clasped around her mouth and jerked her into the dark corner, hidden under the shadows of the receding night sky.

Asha's heart pounded, her breathing hitched, and a wave of nervous heat coursed through her body. Flashes of Moros from the Cliffs and Bardick in the Tartarus poured into her mind. Sweat started to creep onto her skin's surface. She desperately grabbed at the strong, calloused hand pressed against her mouth. Her free hand reached down for the knife in her waistband, but before she could unsheathe the blade, his other hand seized her wrist, as if he already knew what move she would make.

He pulled her all the way back into the darkness, Asha's back pressed against his strong body, and she could feel the warmth of his breath as he leaned his head down towards her ear. "A knife? Are you flirting with me, Seven?" he whispered, his teasing tone low and gravelly. Asha whipped around to confront him, annoyance enveloping every part of her.

"What the Hells, Anselem?" she grumbled, her voice slowly rising with each word. She was way too tired, and it was way too early for such nonsense.

"And to think, I would have figured you'd be happy to see me this morning," Anselem smirked down at her.

"Oh, shut up." Asha rolled her eyes and slapped his shoulder. He let out a soft chuckle.

Anselem glanced over her shoulder, down to the end of the empty colonnade.

"I *am* going to need you to be quiet, though." His voice dropped lower than before. "If you think you can actually manage that for once." The corner of his mouth twitched up slightly, his eyes still locked down the hallway.

"Make me," she snapped at him. All lingering patience left her body. Not that she had much to begin with after another sleepless night, but his charade drained all that remained.

His lips tipped into a smirk that promised something dark. He leaned in, their faces so close they shared breath. He released his eyes from the hall, and they dropped down to hers.

"I can think of a few ways." His teasing tone was sultry

and low.

Heat rose in Asha's cheeks, and her eyes widened. She internally cursed herself for the uncontrollable response.

"But the problem is," he murmured, leaning in closer, "if I kiss you, I don't think I'll be able to stop."

Asha's heart thumped so loudly, it rang in her ears.

She opened her mouth to respond, unsure of her reply, but before any noise escaped her lips, footsteps scuffed against the stones at the end of the colonnade.

Anselem's eyes snapped upward, and the grin on his face dissolved. He grabbed Asha's shoulders and turned her around, trading places. Her back was pressed against the unyielding wall, and his tall, muscled body hid them in the shadows. He put a single finger to his lips, silently willing her to stay quiet.

"She's just a girl, Soren," a muffled voice sounded down the corridor.

A hooded group of four figures rounded the corner, and Asha's body went still as the name of the Vice reached her.

"Well, that *girl* is becoming a bigger problem than we thought," a rough, masculine voice sneered.

Anselem brushed the back of his hand against hers as the slithering voice echoed down the hall.

The group stopped moving, gathering into a corner alcove. One of the hidden faces looked in both directions. Asha held her breath as the shadowed eyes lingered a moment longer on the darkened corner where she and Anselem were hidden. She prayed the Skull was not among them.

The endless moment passed, and the hooded figure turned back to the group.

"Well, what would you like to do about it, Soren?" the short, stout cloak asked.

Even from far down the hall, Asha felt the sinisterness

radiating from the Vices. The otherness of their power.

The tall one let out an aggravated sigh.

"That family has been a thorn in our side for too long. It all started with that mother of hers."

"Not to mention her inquisitive brother," another voice chimed in.

"I had hoped the arrangement Bardick made for her Final Testing of Algae would have stopped this one from being eligible to become a Soturi, yet here we are," the presumed leader of the group—Soren—growled.

Nausea rolled in Asha's stomach as the man's words hit her ears. She felt Anselem gently press a hand against her shoulder, knowing her rage was beginning to boil over.

It was him.

The Major was the one who had arranged her Final Testing of Algae. He was the one who ensured her final test was one she could never pass. He was the one who wrote the note she received on the final day of the Inferno. One sentence, just for Asha Akselsen Raynor. One sentence, written in blood-red ink, that changed everything:

KILL CADET AEROL

The Major—the Snake—was the reason Nina was dead. He was the one who ordered her to kill her best friend.

Asha's entire body began to shake.

"We cannot go against the Skia's wishes. Not again," the third man with a croaky voice chimed in.

A glance up at Anselem's shadowed face told her he did not recognize the mentioned group either.

The Skia.

"True, Tristan, we know what happened last time."

The three hoods turned to Soren.

"How was Bardick to know the Skia would have sent their hounds after her during the Inferno?"

The lean silhouetted figure replied, "It's a shame the Aerol girl was caught up in the mix." Her coaxing voice was soft and spun with honey.

Fallon Malvina—the Sparrow.

Asha couldn't breathe. Tears fell from her eyes, and the hooded figures blurred. Her magic began to flare.

Anselem took her hands in his without a second thought, never once fearing her power.

She forced the burning flames and raging frost to stay beneath the surface.

"All is fair in war, Fallon," Soren—the Spear—replied flatly.

The rage inside her was beginning to burn, and her skin turned hot.

Soren—another name she would add to her list, along with every other Vice in the Kingdom.

Fallon sighed but did not rebut.

"I will see what I can do about the final benchmark," Soren added, "perhaps we can stage an accident and get rid of this girl once and for all."

Asha felt Anselem go rigid beside her.

The hoods all nodded in agreement, then proceeded down the corridor. Asha and Anselem were silent in the shadows as they passed.

Anselem pushed away from the alcove, taking a few steps out of the darkness. He looked around, ensuring the Vices had left. When he glanced back at Asha, she simply stared at him, her eyes wide.

"If you're observant enough, people usually tell on themselves," he said.

"THE CONTINENTS OF DARNELLA ARE COMPRISED OF SEVEN DEMARCATED
KINGDOMS. ONLY SIX ARE CURRENTLY INHABITED."
—PAGE I OF THE COMPLETE GEOGRAPHICAL ARCHIVES OF DARNELLA: VOLUME I

CHAPTER
THIRTY-THREE

Valorous was flickered to an undisclosed location for their final benchmark. But, unlike the other times, the Tribe was not stationed on a small, remote island or in a commonly known part of Perseis. In fact, the group possessed absolutely no inkling of where Leadership sent them, and their surroundings gave no indication of where they were located. They were dropped off in an obscure, rocky field with hundreds of tall trees surrounding the space. A large, enchanted boulder sat in the center.

Before departing, Leadership explained that the rock was imbued with high magic and was only to be utilized once the benchmark was completed. The boulder possessed a similar power to the Golden Lever Asha pulled many months before in The Minos Maze, and once touched, would return the Division to Sveaborg.

Additionally, for their culminating benchmark, Valorous was prohibited from bringing along their firebirds.

After all that had unfolded in recent weeks, Asha had to have a lengthy conversation with Uriel before he would leave her side and allow her to go. The only way she won the argument was to assure him that her Tribe would be with her the entire time. The phoenix huffed at her sharply, but he finally gave in.

Valorous trudged through the thick forest, and even with little information to go off, Asha oddly felt like she had been here before, as if this was a place she had once visited.

The sun hung directly overhead in the sky, unable to help establish any sense of direction, so the group simply began walking in the vague direction Leadership had pointed towards when they arrived in the open field, surrounded by a thick blanket of trees.

Step after step, Asha had the keen awareness they were being followed. By beast or by eyes, she was not sure.

As they came to the edge of the forest, an overwhelming reek singed her nostrils. Her hands went clammy, and sweat beaded on her back.

Walking out from the tree line, she realized they were near the edge of a tall cliff, with rocky grounds that overlooked the sea. From the coloring of the waters far below, she believed it was the Seidon Sea, with its deep, cobalt hue and the white crests of choppy waves scattered throughout.

But the most notable aspect of the open space was the flat, stacked rocks that surrounded the vast cliffside. The rocks formed a short, enclosing wall that stretched up to Asha's waist. Directly before them sat a floating passageway of stones. The stones were arched overhead like a rounded doorframe, but even from a distance, Asha saw the spaced gaps between the rocks suspended high in the air.

The passage gate beckoned to Valorous to enter, and Asha swallowed a lump in her throat as the Division approached the opening. As she passed into the enclosed area, Asha felt a burning in her veins, a dampening on her magic, and a shift in her power. It was slightly similar to the one she experienced at the Boeotian Manor, but this time it felt different. This felt... other. As if this place disliked the magic roaring inside her and was intent on pushing it out.

Valorous slowly crept through the opening, towards the edge of the cliff. Her Tribe looked in every direction for impending threats, but Asha's eyes stayed locked on the stairs in front of her.

Alabaster stone steps shot up from the rocky ground, seemingly misplaced, as there was no building to which they led. At the top of the stairs was a landing, made of white marble, and a large, carved stone curved out from the edges to form a wide, circular opening.

In the center of the circular arch, swirled midnight-black Darkness.

Asha halted, and the stinging reek wafted once more through her nose.

She *had* been here before.

And she knew what would happen next. But just the same as last time, when she attempted to move backwards, she found her feet stuck—locked—as if they had been nailed into place.

No. No. No.

She heard a snarl rip from the portal above them, and with barely enough time to take in the entirety of the situation, a large beast stepped out from the Darkness and onto the landing above.

She heard her Tribe suck in a breath as a trio of obsidian eyes stared down at them, flecked with blood-red streaks.

A dark-coated, three-headed hound, towering more than a story high, let out a shattering growl.

Asha's heart pounded against her chest.

She took in a deep, steadying breath.

I am a master of my fear. I have power beyond measure. I am unbreakable.

She heard her Divisionmates unsheathe their weapons, taking a readying stance. She pulled *Windrunner* from her back and nocked one of her golden-tipped arrows onto the string.

The clouded Darkness behind the Hound began eddying once more, and the pit in Asha's stomach plummeted deeper as a pack of demonic creatures crawled out of the portal, bringing with them a vile stench that reeked of death and decay. The beasts looked as if they had been crafted in the deepest level of the Seven Hells.

The beasts' eyes mirrored the Hound's, with crimson flecks scattered inside pools of midnight black. The six creatures stood upright, walking with unnaturally long, blanch limbs. Their shape resembled that of a distorted man, but nothing human existed within their skeletal faces or thrashing movements.

Valorous froze.

Asha felt the magic in her veins rising with each passing moment.

"What the Hells are those?" Jeremiah whispered, his voice tight.

No one answered.

No one knew.

The creatures stepped forward, descending the alabaster stairs. The Hound did not move forward, standing guard before the marble gate.

Snarls and otherworldly sounds tore from their demonic throats. One of the beasts dragged its long, stygian nails across the marble.

A shiver ran down Asha's spine.

She raised *Windrunner* to her cheek, the golden limbs glinting in the midday sun. The movement triggered a response from her Tribe, as if they were suddenly reminded that the group would need to fight its way out. Valorous raised its swords, and the creatures snarled. Sinister smiles stretched over their faces, exposing razor-sharp fangs. An excitement for the impending carnage had been freed from within them.

Asha did not wait for the creatures to reach the bottom of the stairs. The beasts were roughly one hundred yards away when she let the first arrow fly.

Gold sliced through midnight black, and the beast crashed to the ground with a cracking snap. Asha's arrow was lodged through its eye.

The pack of demons paused, their convulsive heads twisting to stare down at the fallen creature. Slowly, the beasts turned back towards Valorous, their bodies erratically twitching.

And, as if the death of the beast beside them had unleashed their overwhelming thirst for blood, the pack took off down the stairs and barreled towards Valorous.

Asha had another arrow aimed in before they stepped onto the rocky ground. She felt the wind shift off the coastal edge of the cliff, and she adjusted her mark. The second arrow sailed moments after the beasts began their race across the open space, their long legs closing the distance in half the time.

She sent a prayer up to Ianoda as she pulled a final arrow from her quiver.

Fifty yards away, the creatures rapidly closing in, Asha let an iron arrow sail through the tense skies, finding its mark through the open, snarling mouth of the closest beast.

It collapsed to the ground, the remaining three fiends trampling over it without a second glance, as if the loss of their companion held no weight in their demonic minds. Their singular focus was fixated on blood and carnage.

Asha hooked *Windrunner* behind her back and pulled a long, Elysian blade from her side, courtesy of Anselem. He insisted she take it for the duration of the benchmark after overhearing Leadership's whispers in the colonnade.

The blade was lighter than she thought it would be, and she was surprised to see the simplicity of the craftsmanship.

Elysia was realm-renowned for their artistry and intricately designed blades, so when Anselem had handed her a sword with a plain, obsidian hilt and a single gold stone fixed atop the pommel, she was a bit... underwhelmed.

She gripped the sword tightly in her hand. The hilt felt worn but strong, as if the weapon held centuries of experience within its blade.

A gust of wind rushed across the cliffside, and, as if a whispering sigh had been carried along with the breeze, Asha heard a hushed voice mutter, *"Behind you."*

She whipped her gaze from the creatures before her, their shredding nails only yards away, and as she turned, she was met with a final creature silently skulking towards Valorous.

She had no idea from where the beast had come. She did not know if it snuck out from the portal above and crept around, unnoticed, to the backside of the gated area, or if it simply formed from thin air.

Asha did not take the time to contemplate the answer as she raised her sword and swung down hard, severing the beast's fidgeting head from its pale, black-veined neck.

Midnight-black blood poured from its body, and the burning reek of the creature singed her nostrils. She shoved down a gag as the stench saturated the air around her.

The clinging of metal rang out behind her, and she turned to see Jeremiah, Ronin, and Varrick all clashing with the remaining demons. Their swords crashed with the long, stygian nails the beasts were using to swipe at the men; the nails were sharp enough to sever flesh.

Varrick was closest to Asha, and she ran to his side, helping him battle against the thrashing demon. Snarls ripped from its throat as it sparred with the pair. The beast swiped, and the warriors dodged, returning the attack until the exchanging swings turned into a dance.

From across the field, Asha heard a hissing cry pierce through the air as Ronin shoved his blade through the neck of the beast he battled. Black blood poured down his sword, soaking his hands and the rocky stones at his feet.

Asha shifted to the side, dodging another swipe of the claws her and Varrick fought, and as she moved, she felt a whip of wind brush past her head as Varrick swung his sword down beside her, right into the skeletal face of the creature.

Black blood sprayed out, spattering across the warriors' faces. She did not waste time wiping it from her cheek as she whipped her eyes across the field.

Her heart dropped, and a curdling scream shot from her throat. But the warning was too late, and she watched the puncturing nails of the final beast pierce through Jeremiah's side.

Before she processed what she was doing, her legs were moving—sprinting across the field. Wicked ice rampaged through her veins. She sheathed the Elysian blade and lifted her palm towards the beast, barreling into the darkness inside her and pulling forth her power. Frozen shards hurled themselves into its chest, knocking the creature back against the rocky earth. The beast was still thrashing on the ground as she crashed to her knees beside Jeremiah.

She did not know if it was luck or if the prayers she had sent to Ianoda had been answered, but Asha released a tight-chested sigh when she confirmed there was no poison coursing through the gashes in Jeremiah's side.

Ronin and Varrick were right behind her, and Jeremiah gasped as they tried to move him. Crimson blood poured from his side and soaked the light rocks beneath him.

"We need to get him back. Now. He doesn't have much time."

Jeremiah moaned in pain as he lifted his arm and pointed behind Asha. She whipped her head around to see the beast slowly rising to its feet. She stuck out her hand again, summoning flames into her palm. She did not think the creature could feel, but in its dead eyes she saw fear take control.

It lunged for Valorous, but Asha did not falter as the beast was met with a wall of fire. The sound that escaped its mouth was not of this realm, or any like it, but a deep, sinister screech that rattled through the winds and into the earth. A sound that stretched into the depths of the Seven Hells.

Asha dropped the wall of engulfing flames, and all that was left of the beast was a pile of ash.

She turned back to her Tribe. Varrick and Ronin stood wide-eyed. Jeremiah's eyes flickered as he began to lose consciousness.

She cut her gaze to the other two men. "Later," she promised, her mind singularly focused on Jeremiah.

"Are you okay?" Ronin asked.

Asha's brows bunched together.

"You're bleeding," Varrick answered, pointing to her nose. She wiped her face to find bright crimson staining her fingers.

She nodded, wiping her hand on her shirt.

"Get him out," she ordered.

The two men bent down to hoist Jeremiah up, balancing his unconscious body between their shoulders. They took a step toward the suspended, arched passage and paused.

"Are you not coming?" Ronin questioned, concern filling his tone.

"I will be right behind you."

Varrick and Ronin stared at her long enough that she added, "I promise."

They glanced at one another and then to Jeremiah, knowing the decision had already been made. He did not have much time.

She waited for the trio to cross through the gate and disappear into the tree line before she turned towards the marble stairs. The shadowed portal was still, but the Hound still sat perched atop the landing, guarding the gate to whatever lay beyond.

Asha crossed the field, slowly making her way to the bottom of the stairs.

Three pairs of demonic eyes stared down at her, and another trickle of blood dripped from her nose. It smelled metallic and bitter. She wiped her face once more, and a smear of crimson mixed with the drying black blood of the beast Varrick had slain.

A menacing snarl escaped from each of the Hound's three mouths. Their teeth were barred, attention focused singularly on Asha. On the center neck of the Hound hung a silver-plated collar with a large gold pendant in the middle. An eye with three overlapping triangles had been carved into the center of the gold amulet.

Asha had been in this moment before, in this same instant of space and time.

Her heart raced, threatening to rip from her chest. But

this time, she did not turn to run.

She waited.

She knew he would come.

Asha plunged into the darkness of her mind, summoning the flames within her veins. She brought them to the surface, not yet unleashing them above her skin.

The Hound snarled once more and then, with the smallest ripple in the shadowed circle behind the dog, the man stepped out from the portal and onto the marble platform.

He carried the essence of undefinable beauty. His snow-white hair hung loose, falling in silky waves down to his shoulders, and contrasted against the fully black ensemble he donned. His alabaster-pale skin highlighted the sharp angles of his clean-cut face, and his obsidian eyes were spotted with so many crimson flecks that they looked nearly filled in with red.

A sinister sneer spread across his face as she looked up at him, and she returned it with a smirk of her own. She could feel a spirit of malignity boiling beneath the surface of his veins, but she did not balk. Instead, she raised her palms to face the top of the platform as she said with a contemptuous smile, "I've been waiting for you."

Her words dripped with venom, and the man's crimson eyes narrowed slowly as she twisted her wrists. Blue flames sparked into her hands.

A devious, tempter's smile broke across his face. "Tell me you want the Seven Kingdoms, and they shall be yours."

Asha could see the Darkness prowling in his eyes, hear the baleful promise hanging on his words.

No man had the power to promise such impossible things, but as she stared deeper into his ominous eyes, Asha knew with every part of her soul that the being standing before her was anything but human. A wolf in sheep's clothing, and within his eyes lingered an evilness that ran deeper than even the Seven Hells could hold.

Asha took a deep breath, her magic buzzing beneath her skin, and looked up at the man with a devilish smile of her own.

"I'd rather watch you burn."

His crimson eyes splayed wide as she dove deep into the darkness roaring inside her. And as her power flared, he stepped back into the shadows beyond the marbled archway, sealing the portal behind him. The flames poured from her hands, burning the three heads of the Hound to ash and scorching every piece of marbled stone beneath it.

"ONLY THE DOMINIONS MAY WIELD THE KEYS TO THE KINGDOM. AND AS THE STARS FALL FROM THE MOONLIT SKY, THEY SHALL SAVE THE LOST SOULS FROM THE DARKNESS. ETERNALLY CHOSEN TO DELIVER JUSTICE AND ORDER FOR THE LORD OF LIGHT."
—LEGENDS OF DARNELLA: AN EXTENSIVE COLLECTION OF THE FABLES OF OLD

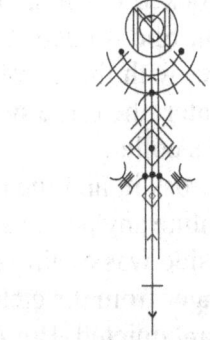

CHAPTER THIRTY-FOUR

Asha hated the East Wing.

Every time she was here, Anubis seemed to be patiently lurking outside the door, waiting for his moment to enter.

She sat quietly by Jeremiah's side, unwilling to move since Valorous had carried him into the room. In the silence, she replayed the events they had survived through her mind.

After she destroyed the Hound, Asha made her way up the stairs, staring at the pile of soot she had created on the landing.

Several pieces of ash picked up in the air on a passing breeze, flittering off with the wind. She sighed, letting out a held tenseness in her shoulders. As she turned to make her way back down the marble staircase, a bright gleam glinted in the center of the ashes. Reflecting the sun's rays was a round pendant, made of pure gold with emeralds circling the edges.

She bent over, brushing aside the residue, and picked up

the gold piece. It was roughly the size of Asha's palm, and fixed on the side was a locked clasp, as if something dangerous was hidden within. She flipped it over in her hand, revealing an engraved eye, with three overlapping triangles knotted together in the center; the same symbol she had seen dangling from the Hound's collar.

She ran her thumb across it, and the energy reverberating from the locket was unlike any power she had felt before, as if the magic trapped inside was calling out to be freed.

Asha removed her finger from the etching, and the energy pulsing from the pendant quieted. But Asha's own magic still felt a silent pull from the power within, as if the otherness locked inside recognized something within her and beckoned to be rejoined.

She tucked the amulet in her jacket pocket, ensuring it was safely secured, and turned down the staircase, running back to the rocky opening to meet her Divisionmates.

She managed to catch up to Ronin and Varrick, slowed down by dragging Jeremiah's unconscious body. She crossed the last stretch of space from the wood line to the boulder, reaching out her hand. She grabbed onto Varrick as Ronin touched the rock, and Valorous was instantly flickered back to Base.

The Tribe landed in the central courtyard outside the Academic Building. As the Division crashed into the grass, Asha sent a frantic warning down the Bond to Uriel, praying he could feel her plea to get Khalfani.

Moments later, a snow-white firebird landed in the courtyard, trailed by a gold-feathered phoenix. Khalfani let out a cry of pain and terror as Ronin and Varrick began dragging Jeremiah across the yard and into the East Wing.

Asha screamed across the courtyard to the running Rapha, commanding them to bring a vile.

The healers kept running, assuredly already having several small glass tubes in their pockets.

Asha reached out her bloodied hand as she approached the feathered beast. A Rapha placed an empty vial in her other hand, and she lifted the bottle to Khalfani's eyes. The firebird let out another screeching cry, and Asha spoke softly to the bird, trying to calm her.

"I will not let him die," she whispered, looking into the glowing eyes of the phoenix. She knew it was improper. That a warrior should never look directly into the eyes of another rider's phoenix, but as the pair locked their gazes, Khalfani calmed her frantic thrashes and leaned her head down, tilting it to the side.

Asha let the firebird read the promise in her gaze, the vow in her heart. She would not let Jeremiah die.

Khalfani's tears filled the vial Asha had pressed against her face.

She secured a top onto the bottle and took off running once more, following Ronin and Varrick into the East Wing.

Asha had poured the tears into the gashes on Jeremiah's side hours ago, and although the skin had closed and color began to return to his too-pale face, Jeremiah had not woken up.

A second Rapha came into the room at some point to check on Asha. With the dried, crusted blood still caked on her face and the burn marks on her clothes, Asha looked nearly as bad as Jeremiah. But as the healer approached, Asha waved him away, confident the only wounds she had were merely surface-level.

Hours passed, and the sun set; night flowed into the room. She never once let her face falter. She never once showed any sign of distress or panic. She would stay strong.

She would let Ronin and Varrick believe everything would be okay.

Everything had to be okay.

Asha, Ronin, and Varrick were all gathered around Jeremiah's bed when a single knock sounded on the door, and it softly swung open. His emerald eyes went straight to the warrior lying unconscious on the bed, before he instinctively moved them to Asha.

The unwavering, strong mask she had held for the last several hours began to unravel when his eyes met hers.

"Go down the hall and get looked at by the healers," he instructed Ronin and Varrick. "Then take a moment to go to your rooms and wash and change."

The Valorous men hesitated for a moment before realizing his words were not a suggestion. They silently stood and exited the space, turning down the hall towards the Rapha examination rooms.

Anselem shut the door, and once the hinges closed, tears streamed down Asha's face.

He crossed the small distance of the room, and she stood up. He wrapped his arms around her, and she let the tears silently fall from her eyes. Her body shook as soundless sobs escaped.

Once her cries had slowed, he pulled his face back, gently taking her chin between his fingers, and raised her sapphire eyes to meet his gaze.

"Tell me what happened," he said softly.

Asha told him about the benchmark—about the creatures and the Hound. She told him about the gated area and how it dampened her powers.

His eyes flared wide as she explained that she had forced her powers to break through the barrier, but he did not comment as she continued to tell him about the portal and the man who had emerged.

He only nodded when she finished giving him as many details as she could recall—about the man, the creatures, and her powers slicing through the magic-restricting air.

"What are they?" she asked, as images of the skeletal creatures and their reeking black blood flashed through her mind.

Anselem sucked in a deep breath.

"Eligos," he replied, his voice solemn.

Asha had never heard of the creature before, and her brow crinkled. But before she was able to ask where the beasts had come, a croaking voice broke through the room.

"What in the Seven Hells is an Eligos?"

Asha and Anselem both whipped their heads to the bed beside them, and two tawny eyes stared up at them.

Asha threw her arms around his neck, and Jeremiah let out a soft whimper.

She pulled back, careful not to hit his side again.

"Sorry," she said, refusing to let go of his hand as she released her embrace.

He gave her a warm smile. "Hi, Ash."

"Hi, Jer." She smiled, wiping the few tears that had pooled in her eyes.

"So... an Eligos?" he asked again.

Asha turned her gaze back to Anselem, and as if he could read the thoughts running through her head, he replied, "I'll go get Ronin and Varrick."

She nodded, and he slipped out of the room.

Jeremiah looked at Asha once more, taking in the sight of her blood-crusted face. "Are you okay?"

"I'm fine. No need to worry about me."

He gave her a look that told her to do the same for him.

She rolled her eyes, and he let out a small laugh, wincing as his side moved.

"I suppose I will have to save my humorous commentary until after you heal," she teased, giving him a wink.

He gave her a soft smile.

"I will let Khalfani know you are okay."

He nodded, still exhausted from losing so much blood.

A few quiet moments later, the door opened, and the three warriors filed into the room.

Anselem closed the door behind him, and Asha looked at him before she spoke. He nodded once, giving her the encouragement she needed to continue.

She took a deep breath, looked each of them in the eyes, and Asha told her Tribe everything.

CHAPTER THIRTY-FIVE

After the completion of their final benchmark, the Soturi cadets were given a one-week break before the graduation ceremony.

Valorous spent several days healing before they began preparing their equipment and firebirds to head to their assigned war camps after the Marking. Jeremiah, thanks to Khalfani's tears, fully recovered after a few days.

On the last evening before graduation, Anselem saw Asha leave the group celebrations with Valorous and head in the direction of the clock tower roof. He gave her a bit of time, unsure if she needed to be alone, before he gave in and followed her. He silently climbed the stairs, and as he opened the tower door, he saw her sitting on the edge, quietly watching the waves crashing on the horizon.

"You okay?" he asked, sinking into the open space beside her.

"No."

"Want to be alone?"

"No," she whispered.

He was quiet as she stared down at her scarred hands. He knew, most days, she still saw her dried blood caked onto them.

"I'm not sure I'll ever be okay again. I'm not sure I'll ever be me again. It's like I've lost myself and don't know how to get her back. Like he took a part of me in that room."

Anselem went to reach for her hand but paused. "May I?" He knew how it felt for one's body to not be their own. How it felt for it to be violated beyond recognition. And he knew the only thing he could offer her now was the choice in who touched her. She glanced down at his hand and nodded, and he took hers in his.

"Ash," he breathed, and her sapphire blue eyes dragged up to him. There was still a fire burning in them, but even he could see the flames were a little less bright.

"No matter how far you may go, or how distant you may feel from yourself, no matter how many moons and suns separate us, and no matter how many scars and wounds cover your heart, my soul will always recognize you. And I promise on the days you lose yourself, I will wade through the Darkness to come and find you. I will always come and find you, Asha."

She looked off in the distance, quiet. Anselem stared at her and his racing mind, for once, fell quiet. She had come to him like wildfire. Burning every idea and every purpose he had ever known. She had captured him in the labyrinth of her soul, and he knew he would be content to wander through its depths for the rest of his life.

"Anselem?" she said, turning to face him.

"Yes, Seven?"

She was quiet for another long moment, and he simply

stared back at her, taking in those consuming sapphire eyes.

"I just want you to know, you are the kindest thing that has ever happened to me, even if that is not how our tale will be told. On the days when the Darkness convinced me I was too broken to be saved, too far gone in the depths of the abyss, you saw the faintest of embers still fighting to stay lit. You found beauty in parts of me that no one ever stayed long enough to discover. You showed me how acceptance and understanding can turn even the darkest, coldest hearts into the brightest of homes." She squeezed his hand. "Thank you."

Silver lined his eyes, and he squeezed her hand in return. He swallowed the lump in his throat and nodded, knowing his voice would fail him if he spoke. She turned back to stare at the setting sun, and as he continued to look at her, it seemed as if a weight she had carried for far too long finally lifted from her shoulders.

CHAPTER THIRTY-SIX

Asha and the Soturi cadets stood in a half circle around the Stone. The bright morning light poured in through the arched windows, and the golden phoenixes sparkled above. The group waited in silence for the Leaders to join them.

As they waited, Asha could feel the pulsing magic radiating off the Stone of Gilgal, the same as the last time she stood in the room.

But she was not the same. She was different.

Changed.

The doors swung open, and the four Division Leaders sauntered in. No other Leadership was with them.

Anselem filed in last, and when he walked into the room, her heart beat differently. And she swore that when he looked over at her and smiled, for a moment, she forgot how to breathe.

"Good morning," he called to the gathered warriors. The voice of Lieutenant Eros was nowhere to be found. The

Commander was the one who addressed the group, with an air of gravity and pride in his words. "Today, each of you will join the hundreds of warriors who came before you. You will become part of a cause—a purpose—greater than yourself. You will become warriors. Not soldiers. Not cadets. Warriors."

He glanced around the room, his gaze landing on Asha as he continued. "You have fought and battled your way to a place only you could earn, only you could accomplish. Be proud of what you have done, where you have come from, and where you will go.

"The road to victory begins with one step, and today— here—you take that first step. And once you leave, and you find yourselves on the battlefield for the first time, make sure whatever army you face, forever remembers the day they fought against the Soturi."

Asha's heart swelled with pride.

Anselem instructed the cadets, one by one, to receive the Soturi Mark.

Valorous was last in the line of cadets, and Asha watched her Tribe, one after another, step up and place their hand upon the Stone of Gilgal.

First was Varrick.

Then Ronin.

And lastly Jeremiah.

The Mark was etched proudly onto each of their arms.

Finally, Asha stepped up, the very last to approach the Stone. She could feel the eyes of every warrior in the room on her as she placed her hand on the rock. Her power surged inside her as her fingers brushed the monolith, as if the magic pulsing through her veins recognized the Stone's energy and might. As if it knew they were formed from the same place long ago.

Her power hummed within her, and she concentrated on keeping it contained as the magic within the Stone began to wind its way to her hand, the eternal flame inside blazing brighter.

And just like that, after months of fighting, after years of pain and loss, Asha watched the ink weave its way up from the Stone, burning the sacred Mark onto her inner forearm.

A small tear of triumph escaped her eye as she watched the ink brand her. Eight lines of equal length branched out from a central point, containing runes at each end intended to connect the human realm to the divine. Two half-circles curled around the bottom of the relic, interrupted by vertical lines jetting all the way down to her wrist. More rune inscriptions were etched within the lines.

Protection for the protectors—a permanent reminder of who they were and who they would always be. A sacred gift from Ianoda intended to guide the warriors when they were lost. An enduring compass to find the way back home.

As the last of the ruins was etched into her skin, Asha stepped forward, joining the eleven warriors to her left.

Anselem went down the line, the Skeleton Key in hand, and unlocked each of the warrior's iron bands before returning to his place beside the other Leaders.

The Leaders all raised two fingers to their brows as they said in perfect unison, "May you always live on and burn well."

Twelve warriors, forever bonded by blood, sweat, and sacrifice, raised their hands to their brows in silent response.

Now, until the flames claim us, we are called Soturi.

Acknowledgments

My first thank you will always & forever be to my Lord and Savior Jesus Christ: Thank you for answered prayers, endless grace, and for being my true light in the darkness. Thank you for being the one to grab me by the hand and pull me out of the shadows. Thank you for being the first to show me sacrificial love, and for guiding my lost soul back home.

For my husband and the love of my life: This story would never have been possible without you, for so many reasons. Thank you for showing me the type of love that I only believed could be found in fairytales. Thank you for your endless support and for giving me the encouragement to pour my soul into the words and pages of a story that I'd held inside of me for so long. I love you, D, until we are nothing but ashes & embers. And even then, I promise to follow you, into every lifetime.

For my sister, Maddie: Thank you for being my person and my confidant. You are the brightest, kindest soul I have ever known, and even that is an understatement. I love you, moo, always. No matter where and no matter what.

For my mom: Thank you for always keeping me grounded. For having an endless love for your family and for teaching me to do the same. Thank you for showing me complete love, acceptance, and understanding throughout my entire life and to always have an open heart.

For my dad: There is no one else in life whose footsteps I would have wanted to follow. Thank you for teaching me what selfless love looks like and for always bringing laughter into the dark times of life. You made me believe in myself and gave me the confidence to know that I could do anything I put my mind to, thank you.

To Clayton: Thank you for being the brother I never knew I needed. Thank you for being the one to enjoy reading as much as I do, and for always nerding out about a new story with me. You helped revive in me a love for reading that had been quiet for a long time.

To Jamie and Malcolm: Thank you for being two of the truest, most loyal of friends. Thank you for the contributions each of you made towards this novel and its development, and for your help in making this dream of mine come to life. I could not ask for two better people to have in my Tribe.

To my Counter Sniper teammates: I'm not sure any of you will be caught dead reading a romance fantasy novel, but on the off chance you find yourself having waded through this journey with me, thank you. And thank you for the inspiration each of you helped weave into this world and its characters.

To all my family and friends: I wish I could list every one of you by name, but you know who you are. Thank you for shaping me and supporting me and loving me through the years. You have molded me into the person I am and each of you has left a mark on my heart that I will always hold close. Without you, this story would not have been possible.

And finally, to you, reader: Thank you for embarking on this journey with me. Your support means more than I could ever express through words on a page. I am so excited to continue this story with you and I can't wait for what is yet to come. But while we wait, live on and burn well.

Until the flames claim us,
Cam